LATE HAVE I LOVED THEE

ETHEL MANNIN

LATE HAVE I
LOVED THEE

'Late have I loved Thee,
O Beauty, so ancient and so new,
Late have I loved Thee.'

(Confessions of St. Augustine.
F. J. Sheed's translation.)

G. P. PUTNAM'S SONS
NEW YORK

Fifth printing

To

ISABEL FOYLE

in devoted friendship, and deep gratitude for introducing me to Fr. McGrath's Life of Father John Sullivan, S.J., *without which I should not have discovered that most human of saints, Augustine of Hippo, or been moved to write this novel—which, it if does no more than induce non-Catholics like myself to read Fr. McGrath's book, and the beautiful impassioned writings of St. Augustine, will have been worth doing.*

CONTENTS

ACKNOWLEDGEMENT

For patiently answering innumerable questions which arose in the writing of this book, and for valuable advice and criticism, I am indebted to Mr. Gilbert Turner, and for courteous assistance on matters concerning the Society of Jesus to Fr. Stephen Brown, S.J.

Part I

THE MOUNTAIN

'In the rash lustihood of my young powers
I shook the pillaring hours
And pulled my life upon me.'
(Francis Thompson.)

I

SOMETIMES, when two or three of the older generation are gathered together and the talk turns upon books and authors someone inquires, "What became of Francis Sable, I wonder? One never seems to hear of him nowadays. . . ." Then they fall to discussing what was his last book, and no one quite remembers, because all that was back in the reckless 'twenties and this is the frightful 'forties, and even the Walpurgis night of the 'thirties has dimmed. But it was somewhere in the early 'thirties that Francis Sable 'faded out', they all agree, and then someone asks, a little nervously, if he is dead or not—or perhaps just disappeared into Hollywood, as other authors have done, never to be heard of again, except for their names on the screen in all that rigmarole of producers, costumiers, script-writers, and so on before the film proper begins. No one seems to know whether he is alive or dead, and the younger generation, never having read him, are indifferent. They have heard of him, of course, just as they have heard of Henry James, and eventually they may, in their own Americanised idiom, 'get around' to reading him, along with the eminent Edwardian. Occasionally someone writes to him, care of his publishers, for permission to quote something from one of his books, or, it might be, include one of his poems in an anthology, and then his brother, Sir Steven Sable, replies, mentioning that Francis died in 1946; but this is very rare; to all intents and purposes Francis Sable is forgotten.

He died at the age of forty-seven. There was nothing about it in the English press. Nothing at all. If that seems incredible to those few who remember what he was it should be realised that when a man's life is fantastic his death is liable to be no less so.

For the benefit of those Young who are of their generation and take their literature in neat expressionist doses from the pages of the New That and the Modern This, with a strong flavouring of something called Dialectic Materialism, let it be stated quite simply at the outset, in the face of the snooty indifference of surrealists and social-realists alike, that Francis Sable was not merely a best-selling novelist and a very good minor poet of the 'twenties, but probably one of the most brilliant writers—in terms of style and wit—since Wilde. When the modern generation turns back to him, and it will, it will discover this and come howling into print with it as something new; they will make a cult of putting Francis Sable on the literary map. Not that it will matter; he belongs on a much bigger map than that.

2

He was born at Crag House in Cumberland in 1899. The Sables had been landed gentry for generations. Francis, as the second son, 'escaped'—it was his own word—the title. There never developed in him, as in his brother, the sense of landlordism. He regarded his father's, and later his brother's, attitude to the tenantry as purely feudal; he was impatient of it, and a little contemptuous. Sir John Sable prided himself on being a good landlord and a benevolent landowner. Had he not given a hilltop to the nation? Did he not open the grounds of Crag House to the public when the rhododendrons were in flower— banks of them, avenues of them, acres of them—regardless of the orange-peel, cigarette cartons, and greasy paper with which his kindness was annually rewarded? He regarded the private ownership of land as a sacred trust—like the imperialist ownership of backward countries—and flattered himself that he did not betray that trust; that, indeed, no Sable ever had, nor, he trusted, ever would. He counted himself fortunate that Francis was his second son and not his heir. Francis, he feared, took after his mother's people who had Liberal leanings. Steven, thank God, showed no such dangerous tendency. Francis's attitude completely baffled him; according to Sir John's reasoning, when he so magnanimously gave his hilltop to a grateful nation, that it might be freely enjoyed by them and their heirs forever—such of them, that is, as had the strength and fortitude to climb up to it over the privately owned scree and boulders—it might have been expected that Francis would approve, since he so strongly objected to the private ownership of land; instead of which Francis was as contemptuous as though the entire hill had been enclosed behind barbed wire entanglements. He refused to attend the ceremony when the slab, declaring the hilltop a gift to the nation, was set up. It was disgusting, he declared, Sir John Sable or anyone else 'giving'—he put the word in inverted commas—a hilltop, or a forest, or a lake, or anything else that was not morally his to give, to those to whom it by right belonged. That anyone should hold such perverted notions was disgusting to Sir John, and, he was extremely glad to say, to his heir.

When Sir John disposed so magnanimously of his hilltop Francis was in his first year at Oxford, and Shelley, the atheist and revolutionary, was his idol. Francis's atheism was as shocking to his mother as his rather vague socialism was to his father. Lady Sable was a deeply religious woman, and when her youngest child, Cathryn, was twelve years old—and Francis eighteen and Steven twenty—she was received into the Catholic Church, an event which greatly upset her husband and elder son, but the atheist Francis not at all. As he saw it, if you were going to be an orthodox Christian it was the Catholic Church or nothing; his father's strict, conventional Church of England brand of Christianity he considered so much humbug. His mother's devotion to the Church was something he could respect; for her Christianity was not a convention, but a way of life. What his father and brother contemptuously referred to as 'the mumbo-jumbo' of Catholic ritual had at least the virtue of aesthetic appeal. It was beautiful, and what was beautiful was good; but it was not for him. He found philosophy more interesting than religion; religion, he declared, was a refuge for the unhappy, for those who, having little or no joy in this life, fastened their hopes upon life after death. His mother, he knew, had never been happy in her marriage; she had never loved the man she married; she had been persuaded into it by an ambitious mother who dearly loved a title, and by the fact that she was already turned thirty and until then no one had wanted to marry her. She had five sisters, all of whom had married well—in the social sense—and Sir John Sable's offer rescued her both from the dreaded 'shelf' of old-maidhood and from a growing sense of inferiority. She had been in love at twenty-five, but the young man had not wanted to marry her; in fact he had wanted everything but that—and anything but that, and her humiliation had been deep. Sir John Sable was nearly twenty years her senior, but he did her the honour of wanting to make her Lady Sable, and her mother over-ruled her misgivings about not being in love with him. "Even if you were in love with him," her mother argued, "it wouldn't last for more than a year or so; it simply means you are beginning where you would be in about twelve months' time anyhow! Romantic love never lasts. It's not as if you were a young girl, in any case." That weighed with her; it was not as though she were a young girl; she had known romantic love once, and it had led nowhere, except into a morass of hurt and humiliation. If she didn't do the sensible thing and become Lady Sable she would probably never get another chance of marriage.

So she became Lady Sable, and of the deep personal humiliations of her loveless marriage she said nothing to anyone all her life; she suffered intensely, for she was a woman of deep feeling; she felt that she had sinned against her husband, and she knew that she had sinned against herself. John Sable had loved her, within the limitations of an unemotional nature, at the time of their marriage ; he had thought her charming and she had the important qualification of being a gentlewoman; and for him too it was becoming urgent that he should marry; he was already nearly fifty, and there was the need for an heir. . . . He never understood her; on the one hand, it seemed to him, she was crassly sentimental, always regretting a romanticism which never had and obviously never could enter into their marriage, and on the other hand shrinking from any manifestation of sensuality which, as he saw it, was a natural part of romantic passionate love. Their marriage would have worked well enough, he thought, but for the impossible emotional demands she made on it—of both herself and of him. She was self-confessedly not in love with him when she married him, and he considered that on the whole he brought more to the marriage than she did. Putting it at its lowest level, he felt she might at least have the *courtesy* not to suffer so obviously. . . . He hadn't, after all, compelled her to marry him!

That he might have wooed her, made an effort to win her over to him, emotionally, and through that win her physically, could never have occurred to him. He was completely unimaginative—Francis thought him, quite simply, a fool—and had no feeling for such emotional nuances. For a year or two he felt aggrieved, but as time went on he accepted the situation, and wished for no more than that she would. A discontented woman was a bore. He early decided that his wife was a bore. Fortunately they did not need to see a great deal of each other. Fortunately there were horses and fishing-rods and guns: and he was interested in the management of his estate. Dorothea, regrettably, did not shoot and was an indifferent horsewoman. Nevertheless she should have been able to interest herself sufficiently in the children, the house, her social relaxations and duties. She had all the money she wanted; she was free to go to London, Paris, Biarritz, the French Riviera; she ought to be happy enough. 'Ought' was a favourite word of his. People ought to want what was usual, obvious, and something he called 'normal'. A woman 'ought' to love her husband; given a fine home and plenty of money she 'ought' to be happy. Those who didn't want and think and feel what they 'ought' to want and think and feel were neurotics, fools, bores, and he, Sir John Sable, who prided himself on his normality, had no patience with them. Life was what you made it. A thing was right or wrong, good or bad, and anyone who jolly well didn't know what was right and what wrong, what was good and what was bad, had better be locked up. There was the Church of England; there was *The Times*; there was the Conservative Party (thank God); there was the British Empire; any right-minded person knew that all these and all they stood for were Good. Outside of this obvious Good there was a lot of dam' nonsense called free-thinking; a lot of criminal lunatics called socialists; there was, in fact, the rabble and all it stood for, all so obviously Bad that it wasn't worth discussing. You treated your tenants decently and they respected you and were grateful. The rabble didn't want half the things that people like Francis thought they wanted. The older women on the estate bobbed a curtsey to her ladyship, and people like Francis could call it feudalism if they liked, but it had significance; it showed that the people of England were sound at heart; it was a good thing; it was a jolly good thing. What was wanted was more curtseying and less cant.

Lady Sable had been bitterly disappointed that her second child was another son; she felt that she had done her duty in producing an heir for the baronetcy, and if she had to have another child she wanted a girl, for herself. She was resentful when after six years she found herself pregnant a third time, but when the child proved to be a girl she was filled with such joy, such gratitude to God, that she was a changed woman. All her discontent and apathy fell away from her. She could not give sufficient thanks or praise to God for this blessing. The deep religiousness of her girlhood, which had subsided when she fell in love and had not—contrary to the theories of the anti-religionists—been restored either by her disappointment in that romance, or by the unhappiness of the first six years of her marriage, was now revived in an overwhelming flood. Her soul which had slept for ten years rose up and magnified the Lord. She loved God as never before.

It took her twelve years to reach the Catholic Church, even so. She experienced no sudden conversion; it was a slow, gradual process of revelation, rather; of natural spiritual development. From the very beginning of that spiritual rebirth which began with the birth of her daughter the compass was set, and she followed it, patiently, steadfastly. The Church as she had always known it satisfied her less and less. It could not fulfil her spiritual needs. Under the guidance of a Catholic woman friend, Mrs. Lester, she began reading Catholic literature. Cardinal Newman's sermons made a deep impression on her. Even so it was another five years before she took the bold step of attending a retreat with her friend. Mrs. Lester helped her rather than actively influenced her. When she returned from the retreat many things were clearer in her mind, and she was ready for instruction.

Her husband and elder son were horrified—they were shocked, as she had known they would be. John had always been quite rabidly anti-Papist. She had feared a rationalist ridicule from Francis, but Francis said, simply, "Obviously one has to be

Catholic or nothing." His father said, coldly, "*Roman* Catholic,
I suppose you mean—we are all Catholics." Dorothea remained
silent. She had known beforehand what they would say; only
Francis had surprised her.

Steven said, bitterly, "My God, what a family! A Papist
mother and an atheist brother! Cathryn, I suppose, will become a
Methodist! Or a nun!"

"Give me the Holy Romans, every time!" Francis murmured.
"Those tin tabernacles are so depressing. Cathryn would make a
lovely nun. The angels would lean out of the gold bars of heaven
to take a squint at her."

The girl looked from Francis to her mother, troubled. She
loved her mother more than anyone except Francis, but Francis
was special and apart. With Francis she had climbed up into the
clouds that always rested on the highest hills; with Francis she
had seen an eagle in the air; with Francis she would one day
climb a white snow mountain . . . he had promised her. She
would do whatever Francis wanted her to do, be whatever
Francis wanted her to be. . . .

Francis saw the question in her eyes. He smiled at her and
swept it away.

"Did you get those fresh studs put in your climbing boots?"
he asked.

Lady Sable's eyes darkened with anxiety.

"It's too early for climbing yet. There's still ice on the rocks.
Francis, you mustn't think of taking her yet——"

"The ice makes it more like Switzerland," the girl said, eagerly.

"She's safe enough with me," Francis assured their mother.
He smiled at his sister again. "Let me see those boots. . . ."

They went out together followed by their mother's anxious
eyes. Francis was dear to her, as Steven, allied with his father,
could never be. But Cathryn was the child God had given her for
herself, and the child she hoped one day to give to the Church
. . . for since her conversion that was all her prayer. Francis
represented a double danger to this beloved child ; there was the
spiritual danger of his atheist influence on her, and the physical
danger of the passion for climbing he had inspired in her.

Steven had always been impatient of the little sister, and he
went away to school just at the age when she was beginning to be

aware of him; it could be said that they never really knew each other. But at six years old Cathryn adored Francis, and the boy loved the doll-like little girl with the long straight flaxen hair and the big dark eyes; he had the feeling of wanting to protect her. By the time she was twelve and he was eighteen he was aware of her beginning to 'catch up' with him as a person; he no longer wanted to protect her but to share things with her—he shared Oscar Wilde with her, his *Soul of Man* and his poetry; he shared Shelley with her ; and his passion for climbing. At twelve she was like a young colt with her long thin legs and her straight hair falling over her face. She would be a beauty presently, he thought. And Cathryn was convinced that she would never fall in love with anyone who did not look like Francis, and who was not altogether like Francis. Physically they were alike; both had their mother's thick fair hair, fine dark eyes, sensitive features and hands. With hands like that, Dorothea thought, Cathryn should be able to play the piano; she was always urging that Cathryn should take care of her hands. But Cathryn was impatient of such counsel; for her good hands meant hands light on a horse, hands that could grip the naked rock, hands that could make a paintbrush do what she wanted on canvas. She had known since she was about eight that she wanted to paint, just as Francis knew that he wanted to write. These talents they inherited from their mother, who had published before her marriage a small volume of mediocre verse, and who all her life painted mediocre watercolours. But Francis's verse was not mediocre, and from the beginning Cathryn's painting showed very emphatic promise; both had a vitality lacking in their mother, but they had inherited her sensitiveness and imaginativeness . . . as surely as Steven had inherited his father's matter-of-factness.

Living as they did in the very heart of the high hills it was natural that all the Sable children should climb from an early age, but whereas Steven climbed as naturally as he tramped over the fells, swam in the lake, rode, fished, shot, with Francis climbing was a passion, and everything he did on the great crags of Wasdale—the Needle, the Pillar, Scafell Pikes—he regarded merely as exercise climbs for more serious work in Switzerland. What has become known as World War I cut across his climbing plans, however, as it cut across his career at Oxford. In the year 1917, in which his mother was received into the Church he was called up for the Army. Steven had been in two years by that time.

Francis, with one pip up, was on the verge of being sent to France when the war ended, to his great relief, not because of any physical cowardice but because he regarded what he called 'the whole shooting-match' as a colossal bore and a shocking waste of time. Steven came out of the war a captain and with a decoration and a limp.

Steven had no wish to return to Oxford; he preferred to study estate management at home. At the back of his mind there was, unacknowledged, a dislike of the idea of being up with Francis. He had no taste for coming down with second-class honours whilst Francis romped away with a first. Which of course he did; he read classics and came down with a first in 'Mods' and 'Greats', and won the Newdigate with the poem that is still his best-known.

He made his first visit to Switzerland in 1920, soon after his twenty-first birthday, whilst he was still at Oxford. Cathryn pleaded passionately to be allowed to go with him, but for once Francis saw eye to eye with his mother in the matter of Cathryn and climbing.

"When you're older," Francis promised.

"We can't have little girls mucking about on the Matterhorn," Steven told her, "and big brothers don't always want their little sisters at the other end of the rope!"

She shook her rain-straight fair hair back from her face with a little angry gesture. At fifteen she was still a young colt.

"I'm as good as Francis!"

Francis smiled. "Not quite, darling."

Ah, but Francis could be cruel, too. Steven's sarcasm meant nothing to her, but the most minor disagreement or rebuff from Francis was a wound in the secret places of the heart—those places to which Francis alone had access.

Dorothea was determined that Cathryn should never go climbing anywhere out of England with her permission. When the girl was twenty-one she would no longer have authority over her, it is true, but by that time much might have happened; she might be married and absorbed in home, husband and children; or Francis might be married and Cathryn have ceased to identify herself with him; or Cathryn might lose her passion for climbing in a passion for painting.

Francis did his best to overcome his mother's phobia about accidents on mountains. He tried to convince her that the Alps were no more dangerous than Great Gable and Scafell. He pointed out that every year climbers fell off the local crags; that climbers were buried in the little churchyard at Wasdale no less than at Zermatt; that you could fall off a ledge on Great Gable as easily as off a ledge on the Matterhorn, but that there was no reason to suppose you were going to fall off either, any more than there was any reason to suppose that if you went on travelling in trains you would sooner or later be killed in a train-smash. But it was no use. Lady Sable fretted and worried when any of her children climbed in the local hills, particularly when Cathryn went, but despite that perpetual nagging anxiety she had not the same terror of the familiar hills as of the Alps. The thought of mountains in connection with Cathryn terrified her. It was torment enough that her beloved Francis should cross glaciers and nego-tiate crevasses, but it was more than her spirit could sustain that the one precious child she had born for the Catholic Church should imperil her life in such a fashion.

Cathryn was fiercely impatient of her mother's 'mountain mania', as she called it; she considered it neurotic. She was determined that as soon as she was of age she would go off to the Alps with Francis without her mother's consent if she could not go with it. She was convinced that once she had gone and safely returned her mother would be cured of her phobia.

Dorothea hoped that when she was seventeen Cathryn would study art at the Slade School, in London, but by that time Francis had gone to Paris, as so many young men of the rentier class and with literary leanings did in the 'twenties, and nothing would satisfy Cathryn but that she must study art in Paris—the Académie Moderne was anyhow better than the Slade, she insisted, and with her brother in Paris no one could say she was not properly chaperoned.

Lady Sable did not consider Francis anything like an adequate chaperon, but Mrs. Lester's daughter, Sue, who was the same age as Francis, was a fairly well-known painter, with a studio in Paris. It was a pity that Sue was not a Catholic like her mother

—Mrs. Lester had been converted late in life—but she was a responsible serious young woman, and was at least not anti-Catholic. Lady Sable knew her very well and had confidence that her precious Cathryn, her ewe lamb, would be safe with her in the big and wicked city. And at least in Paris there were no mountains or dangerous high hills—there was, in fact, she reflected with satisfaction, nothing climbable nearer than a night-journey away. Absorbed in painting and the new life Cathryn would have other, safer, things to think about. Francis, too, writing a book in Paris, would have no time for mountains. So that though it took the ewe lamb from her side Paris could be said to have compensations.

3

Paris in the 'twenties was full of earnest English and American boys and girls who had gone there ostensibly to study art or write books, but especially to Study Art. Montparnasse became the 'artists' quarter' in a revived *vie Bohème*. It was the era of the Grand Chaumière and the Café de la Rotonde. The Grand Chaumière by day and the Rotonde by night. At the school they chalked out their pitches on the floor and all industriously painted the same things in the same way; many of these daubs eventually found their way to the walls of the Rotonde. It was the done thing to gravitate between the Grand Chaumière and the Académie Moderne; Julien's was more serious, but it did not admit female students, so that the other two were more 'fun'. In the evening one went to Carlarossi's for *croquis*—quick sketching classes, the nude models, male and female, holding the pose for five minutes only. Negresses were much in the vogue as models at that time. Artistic young women adopted such pet-names as Fifi, Kiki, Bébé. And there was dancing upstairs in the evening at the Rotonde. It was fashionable to assert that in the evenings the Rotonde filled up with American tourists who had all gone to see the artists, who, it was alleged, were really all across the road at the Dôme, using the Rotonde only at midday; many of them did remove their genius to the Dôme, in the evenings, it is true—or to Baty's, on the opposite corner; Baty's disappeared in the 'thirties—but plenty of Grand Chaumière young people swarmed up and down the staircase at the Rotonde the moment the music began upstairs. There was always a concertina, and tangos were popular, and the female waist was somewhere round the hips. Clothes had never been uglier nor youth gayer. It was the era of tea-dances, dinner-dances, champagne-parties, tangos and Jazz. There was a lot of money about, and people were mad to spend. The students sat about interminably at the cafés and discussed the whiteness and blueness of coffee-cups, took themselves very, very seriously, and spelt art with a capital A.

It was all very young and naive and, in retrospect, looking back from the frightful 'forties, across the wasteland of the 'thirties, rather touching. Because at that time it was possible to believe that the war to end wars had been fought and won, despite the Treaty of Versailles, or because of it. The Kaiser was banished to Holland, to spend the rest of his days harmlessly contemplating the windmills and dykes of the dullest landscape in the world, and though a man called Adolf Hitler lived and moved and had his being, the world was still in the blessed condition of not having heard of him. German militarism—Prussianism, it was called then—was crushed, the French were on the Rhine, and all was well with the world . . . particularly if you viewed it through the rosy haze of *vin rouge* on the terrace of the Rotonde, or further down the boulevard at the Café des Lilas, or from the terrace of the Deux Magots or the Flore, if you preferred the Quarter. (You didn't go to Montmartre, of course, because it was full of tourists; it was not until the 'thirties, when Montparnasse became a congested area, that All the Really Serious Artists rediscovered Montmartre, though no one could say it was as convenient as the Quarter or Montparnasse; of course if you really couldn't bear Montmartre there was nothing for it but to go right out beyond the Observatoire to the Lion de Belfort.) There was the League of Nations, there was the Kellogg Pact, there were Disarmament Conferences . . . and Paris was the centre of European culture. You changed your dollars or pounds into francs and got value for your money. The gaiety had the naïveté of a children's party; there was none of that hectic eat-drink-and-be-merry-for-to-morrow-there'll-be-another-world-war atmosphere of the 'thirties.

Francis Sable took a furnished apartment at the top of a tall modern house near the Observatoire. There were plain cream-coloured walls and bookshelves, and low divans strewn with bright-coloured cushions. The apartment had a balcony from which you could look across the chestnuts of the Luxembourg Gardens to the white domes of the Sacré Cœur crowning the hill of Montmartre. In the bright, white, slightly clinical atmosphere of this apartment Francis Sable wrote his first three books; that is to say he lived there for the greater part of three years. Later on, though he kept the apartment on, he lived and worked in hotels and pensions and villas all over Europe. He spent three months in a dark little pension in the Via Sistina in Rome working on a collection of poems. He lived for six months in a villa beside a cobbled mule-track that wound up through the olive-groves of a hillside in Rapallo, and wrote what is perhaps his best book there. He visited Siena, Rimini, San Geminano, Assisi; he went to Venice and spent part of the summer on the Lido; he always followed periods of intense writing activity with a period of 'playing'. Sometimes he played in the fashionable playgrounds of the Lido, the plages of the French Riviera, or at Biarritz. At other times he went climbing at Zermatt or Chamonix. Cathryn still begged him to take her when he went climbing, but he always refused. She was not a good enough climber, for one thing—and he had an Oxford friend who was—and for another he had to some extent grown away from her since coming to Paris. He attracted women and was attracted by them, in an amused sort of fashion; he took none of them seriously and he never imagined himself in love.

In Paris he did all the fashionable things of the period—he drank in the Ritz bar, he went to all the smart night *boîtes* on both sides of the river; he went to concerts and the opera and the theatre and all the highbrow studio films, and to a great many parties, some in untidy Left Bank studios, others in elegant draw-ing-rooms in the Étoile district. He was generally considered charming and amusing, and a little aloof. One pretty and wealthy little American, who published and edited a quarterly devoted to literature and the arts, complained of him that you could have a love-affair with him and still not know him any better. The woman to whom she said it retorted bitterly that so far as she could see no one had ever had a love-affair with Francis Sable but only an *affaire*. They did not complain that he was cynical; on the contrary he was always, as the little American said, 'vurry sweet', but it was as though some part of himself always remained detached, denying mental and emotional intimacy.

He took Cathryn about with him a good deal in Paris, and it was the current ribald joke in Montparnasse and the Quarter that the two Sables were married to each other. Cathryn had numerous admirers but other than as friends she was indifferent to them. She was well aware that her beloved brother had grown away from her since the days when they climbed on Great Gable and Scafell together, and that it was only she who cherished the dream of their one day climbing together in the Alps. But she herself did not change, except in outward appearance. She lost her straggly coltishness and put on a gracefulness inherited from her mother; she plaited her fine straight, curiously childish, hair and wound it in a crown round her small beautiful head. Her intelligence put on knowledge like a dress, but emotionally she was still the young girl prepared to be whatever Francis wanted her to be, to do whatever he wanted her to do. Her happiest times were when he was in Paris and they did things together. When he was away she became absorbed in her painting, and waited for him to come back. She was fond of Sue Lester, but if she could not be with Francis she liked to be alone, and after a year with Sue she took a studio of her own in the student quarter off the Boulevard Raspail. She calmed her mother's alarm at the move by assuring her that the room was in a house full of students like herself, and that Sue was only just round the corner, which was true. She stayed in this house only six months. Her fellow-students were too rowdy. She had the feeling that for them painting was not a serious and difficult craft but a glorious lark, an excuse to get away from home and live what they believed to be *la vie Bohème*, which meant, so far as Cathryn could see, an endless series of alcoholic parties and promiscuous sex-affairs. The majority of the students when they were not in the schools turned their days and nights into an interminable students' rag. They were not really interested in painting, she felt; they merely liked the life—since with incomes behind them they hadn't to earn their livings at it. They put the paint on with palette-knives and deceived themselves they were incipient Van Goghs, overlooking the fact that Van Gogh had genius. The young men grew beards and went in for corduroy suits; the girls wore 'apache' scarves and affected eccentric make-ups, and they were all quite conscientiously immoral.

It was a bore, Cathryn thought; it was a shocking bore. Why didn't they either learn to paint, or go home, back to New York, Minnesota, London, Birmingham, Blackpool, or wherever they came from? They cluttered up the overcrowded art-schools, they cluttered up the cafés; they used primarily for rowdy parties the studios that serious painters needed for their work; they cluttered up the whole lovely city of Paris. . . .

She made these reflections one day sitting alone in the Select, next to the Rotonde, having gone there for her midday meal because she was as tired of the Rotonde as of the people who went there, and because at the Select the *plat du jour* was always good and cheap. At a table across from her a short, square, thickset middle-aged woman, who wore a shabby mannish suit and a bow-tie, made a crayon and charcoal drawing of her. Anna Kallinova was well known in Montparnasse and the Quarter. She knocked up a living making sketches of tourists as they sat on café terraces; she sold them, at two hundred francs a copy, unexpurgated editions of banned books; from time to time she got herself secretarial work typing manuscripts for authors and would-be authors. She had recently done some typing for Francis Sable, and she knew Cathryn by sight long before she had met her at a studio party given by Sue Lester. She had an aggressive manner; she always made a point of not being impressed by anyone, neither their looks, their fame, their breeding, nor anything else. It always gave her great pleasure to be introduced to a well-known person and pretend she had never heard of him or her; she specialised in that sort of thing; typically, as Cathryn was generally considered lovely she liked to refer to her as 'that odd-looking little sister of Frankie Sable'. Nevertheless, below the façade of all this was a rough good-nature, and she could draw. The quick, slick café-portraits were mere hackwork done for the sake of ten or twenty francs; the things she liked doing were etchings. In these she stood revealed as an imaginative artist and a fine craftsman. It was bad luck, she always said, that there was so little demand for the one thing she could do well.

If she got five hundred francs for an etching she considered herself in luck; she more commonly got only two hundred. Ten years later the same etchings changed hands for twenty guineas and more. But that didn't do Anna Kallinova any good, for she had died in a sanatorium at Vence years before. That she 'had a lung' was a secret she kept so well that none of the Paris crowd had any idea of it.

The sketch she did of Cathryn that day at the Select hangs today at Crag House, next to a remarkable painting Cathryn did of Francis early in 1928.

When she had finished the drawing Anna came over to Cathryn and pushed it in front of her.

"How's that for ten francs?" she demanded, in her brusque manner.

Cathryn smiled. "It's very good indeed, but I don't want a picture of myself!"

"Probably not. But I want ten francs so that I may eat. You can give it to your brother. He adores you, doesn't he?"

She called a waiter and ordered the *plat du jour* and a Bock. Cathryn pushed a ten-franc note across to her and Anna stuffed it into the breast pocket of her jacket without a word.

"What were you frowning so hard about?" she demanded.

"I was thinking what a lot of bogus people there are cluttering up Paris."

"There always were. What about it?"

"I can't live with them, that's all. I must find a place to live where I can be quiet and alone and work."

"I'll take you to it when we've eaten," Anna said. "It'll cost you two hundred francs a month. I imagine a Sable can afford that."

"I've been paying more than that a week."

"More fool you! But spoil the Egyptians, I say! And you rich English and Americans are a godsend to the thrifty French. *Vive la France!*"

She snatched the plate of food from the waiter before he could set it in front of her, and began to eat ravenously. When she had eaten, she swallowed the Bock in one long draught, then called for *l'addition*.

"On the principle of spoiling the Egyptians, let me pay," Cathryn suggested.

"I've money, thanks. Haven't I just sold a drawing?"

Anna flung the ten-franc note on the table and got up.

They left the Select, crossed the boulevard and turned up behind the Dôme.

"There's no water in the place I'm taking you to, at least only on the ground floor, and you're at the top. Also there's no heating. You can get an oil-stove for the winter. No one will come near you. There are too many stairs to climb and no comfort when you get there. It's an attic with a good skylight. I've got the one next to it. I used to have both—the room with the skylight to work in, the room behind it, which is really only a cupboard, to sleep in, but I can't afford both."

"Where do you work now?" Cathryn inquired.

"I don't. At least not that kind of work. I draw people in cafés, and I type obscure poetry and precious prose for people like Frankie Sable, and sometimes I address envelopes at so much a hundred. That is how the poor live. Your brother can put it into a story or a poem. It's amusing so long as you only read about it."

The attic to which Anna conducted Cathryn up four flights of dark narrow stairs had only one visible virtue—that it was light. But it had for Cathryn the virtue of being as solitary as a monk's cell. It contained an iron bedstead with thin-looking bedding, a plain deal chair, a bare table supporting a jug and basin.

"It's somewhere to sleep and you've room for an easel, and no one will disturb you. What more do you want?" Anna demanded.

"Nothing," Cathryn agreed. "I'll move in tomorrow."

"You can move in today, so far as I am concerned, but if you can let me have the two hundred francs not later than tomorrow it would help."

"You can have them now," said Cathryn, "and I'll move in today."

Anna gave a wry smile. "It seems we've done each other a good turn. I'll come with you to your place and help you bring your stuff. I'd like to see your work."

Cathryn flushed slightly. "You'll probably hate it. I paint in tempera."

Anna glared at her. "Why the hell should I hate it? The sooner we get back to tempera and craftsmanship and real painting the better! What started you using this medium? Your feeling for colour?"

"Partly. But also because I found it a more expressive medium for the sort of thing I wanted to say. You can be emotional in oils, but not in tempera. I liked the discipline of it!"

She smiled and added, "I hope that doesn't sound priggish, but it's a little difficult to put into words. I got so tired of all the splurges of paint in the schools. I had to find my own way."

"Every artist worth anything always does. It's about the only useful thing the schools ever teach us! So you left the schools and went back and had another look at Botticelli and Bellini—was that it?"

"More or less. I looked at the modern tempera painters too. Then I began to study Cennini's manual and to experiment a little on my own. I found egg-tempera gave me what I wanted and hadn't been able to get till then—some special quality of colour. For my purpose it was the perfect medium. Now I don't want to use anything else."

"And now you'll be able to work in peace without all the clutter and clatter of the arty-party crowd all round you."

"Yes." Cathryn looked affectionately round the white-distempered walls of the little room. "I'll be all right here. It's what I've been wanting."

"Good. Let's go and fetch your stuff."

4

Cathryn never changed her address in Paris after that. She lived and worked there for the best part of seven years. Sue came to see the attic and declared that she would die of cold there in the winter, and Francis was quite angry about it.

"There's no need to live like a Montparnasse bum!" he said, violently. "Art doesn't demand the mortification of the flesh!"

Cathryn said, "You remember that lovely Sunday when we went down to St. Cloud by steamer and walked about in the woods—they were covered with little white anemones with stalks like green threads. Windflowers they call them in England. You remember?"

"Of course I remember, but what has it got to do with your living and trying to work in this frightful room?"

"We had a serious talk. I reminded you that once you said I would make a lovely nun, and I wanted so terribly for you not to joke but to tell me what you really wanted me to be—I told you that and you said 'I want you to be yourself.' " She smiled. "This funny room is me being myself. Don't you see? I've already begun work here. I know I can work here as I want. Anna is a good critic. She helps me. She's already helped me more than anyone."

"More than Sue?"

"Sue isn't really a good painter, Francis."

"I suppose that's what Anna says?" He was a little nettled. He was fond of Sue, and if her work wasn't first-rate, at least it was vigorous, masculine—the highest compliment he could pay a woman painter.

It was Cathryn's turn to be nettled. "Anna does say it, but I thought it long before I knew what Anna thought about Sue Lester's work. She's what you say poetry should never be, Francis—derivative. Every picture of hers you look at you feel you've seen it all somewhere before. Whereas the smallest drawing of Anna's is different. It's all Anna, nothing but Anna."

"All the same Anna's work isn't known outside a small circle in Paris, whereas everyone interested in modern painting in London, Paris, New York, has heard of Sue Lester."

"That doesn't prove anything!"

"On the contrary, darling heart, it proves a devil of a lot! Let's go and lunch up in the Bois—the Cascade would be nice on a day like this."

He said no more about the room. He believed that she would tire of it when the winter set in, and as he did not intend being in Paris for the winter she could use his apartment then. He went South in the winter, but Cathryn did not use his apartment, that winter or any other. She felt that Anna would despise her forever if she did, and she was not sure she would not despise herself. She believed that Anna was right in her insistence that soft living softened an artist, whether it was painter or writer.

"It's a pity you have an income," Anna said. "If you had to earn your living you'd learn in the artist's best school—hardship."

Cathryn said, "You haven't an income and what happens? You're so busy trying to earn your day's food and the rent that you haven't time to be an artist! Look at all that typing, all that envelope-addressing!"

"That's because I haven't the courage to starve! If I had an income I'd probably be a good mediocre facile painter like Sue Lester. As it is, when I do manage to turn out anything it's good. I'm not in the position to spawn often, but when I do it's an event! Security is a great danger to any serious artist."

Cathryn protested, "Francis has security, but he manages to be first-rate! Even his first book had a tremendous *succès d'estime*, and I showed you his Newdigate poem—wouldn't you call that first-rate?"

"In its class. Like his novel. First-rate in that brilliant amusing superficial manner of Oscar Wilde before he went to prison and suffered. After that Wilde wrote *De Profundis*. There's as yet no profundity in Francis Sable. It's all been too easy for him—in every way, materially and spiritually. He hasn't suffered in any way. It's easy enough to be witty when you've nothing to worry you—when you're well-fed and comfortably housed and have money and to spare. If Francis Sable could have his heart torn up by the roots, then he might write a really great novel, a really great poem. The poem probably wouldn't win any prizes, and the novel wouldn't sell nearly so well as his brilliant three to date—or is it four? But such a poem or such a book would be remembered when the rest were forgotten. And it would be good for him—spiritually. The preservation of one's integrity—that's important. At present Francis Sable isn't preserving it. I'm not sure that he has any to preserve!"

"Anna!"

"Well, has he? Or don't I understand your English language? Integrity is honesty, isn't it? I don't mean the honesty of not thieving, but honesty of intellect and purpose. Would you say your brother had that? He writes for the sake of brilliance, doesn't he, to show off his classical knowledge, his erudition, his wit. Everything he writes is an entertaining intellectual exercise. If you suggested that in all great work there is depth and feeling he would think you were being embarrassingly sentimental. Isn't that so?"

"I don't know. I really don't know." Cathryn was troubled.

"Ask him if he thinks heart in a literary work is essential to greatness."

One evening when they were dining together in a small restaurant on the Quai Voltaire Cathryn did ask him, and he laughed.

"Darling, whoever could have put you up to asking such a blush-making question! Was it some ardent admirer of the alleged poetry of Ella Wheeler Wilcox, or the romances of Ethel M. Dell? Or have you been reading Laurence Hope—'We have had, we have loved, we have known'?"

With her child-like candour she answered, "It was Anna who told me to ask you."

"That frightful White Russian!"

"She's my best friend, Francis."

"Never mind, darling, you'll grow out of it—I hope!"

"There are times when you're not really very nice, Francis."

"I expect so, darling. But as I'm Oscar Wilde, Lord Byron, Percy B. Shelley, and all the amusing brilliant heartless people rolled into one, you ought not to expect me to be. Drink up your wine, sweetheart, then your big-hearted brother will take you to a lovely party where all the young men will make love to you and you'll be the belle of the ball!"

"I don't like parties, Francis. I'm going home."

"Darling, nobody really likes parties, but that's no reason for not going to them. You'll never get on if you spend your nights shivering under the eaves like poor Tom Chatterton. You know what dear Ella says, 'Laugh and the world laughs with you, Weep and you sleep alone'!"

She got up. "I don't intend to go home and weep. I've got some work to do."

"It's the same thing. Play and the world plays with you, work and you work alone."

He said, following her out on to the Quai Voltaire, "You won't become a prig, will you, Cathy?"

"Not if you don't become a cynic!"

He laughed and took her elbow and they crossed the road to the river and leaned on the parapet.

"You don't approve of me any more, do you?"

"I think you waste yourself. All these parties. And rubbishy people. They only hang round you and invite you to their drawing-rooms and studios because your work is so talked about, and because you come of what's called good family—every kind of snobbery comes into it. It's all so—trivial, Francis!"

"D'you think I don't know that as well as you, little funny? Of course it's trivial. It's all part of our trivial post-war age. Everyone has too much money, and everyone wants to be gay, after being so madly ungay for four years! One is of one's generation."

"One doesn't have to be. And it's not true that everyone has too much money. There are hundreds of thousands on the bread-line everywhere. Look at people like Anna Kallinova."

He stiffened again. "I'd rather not, if you don't mind."

"Once you'd have cared. Now you might as well be Steven."

"Except that Steven is a bore."

He straightened himself and looked round and she knew he was looking for a taxi. In a few moments he would be gone.

She said quickly, urgently, "Francis, don't be angry! It's because I care so much—about you as a writer, I mean. It's not enough, is it, to be all *Antic Hay* and *South Wind*. Not enough, I mean, to be just clever, even when it's a brilliant cleverness. Greatness is more than that. It's something deeply felt—the heart torn up by the roots. You'd agree with that, wouldn't you?"

"Yes, of course. But being human and liking my life very well as it is I intend to take every precaution against having my heart torn up by the roots!"

"Wouldn't you like to write a really great book?"

"Not on those terms! It gives me the willies even to think about it!"

She persisted, "You'd have to love someone terribly to suffer as much as that, wouldn't you? Perhaps you will one day, Francis."

He wanted to say, "I love you, little funny, as much as I'm ever likely to love anyone." But there are some things too difficult to say. For the English public-school and university man, anyhow.

He said, simply, "Perhaps. Who knows? But I must be getting along now. I must get a cab. I have to get to the Étoile."

Bitterness caught her again. "That bogus princess's?"

A taxi approached and he signalled to it. He ignored the question.

"Can I drop you anywhere?"

She shook her head. A dark tide of unhappiness was rising in her. 'Francis,' her heart cried, 'Francis, come back to me! Where have you gone?'

He climbed into the taxi, gave the driver the address, instructed her, "Take care of yourself!" and dropped back into the interior darkness of the cab.

She walked slowly in the direction of the Rue Bonaparte. They would never climb the white mountains together now. Nor even climb up again into the clouds on Scafell Pikes. Because the Francis with whom one could do those things had gone. He had been swallowed up in the gaieties of the post-war Paris; swallowed up in his literary success. Yet in some of his poems, even his recent ones, there were flashes of something beyond the intellect, flashes of recognition of eternal things, the authentic vision of Atlantis. He had to feel something deeply; he had to suffer. It was strange to want someone you loved to suffer; perhaps merely the sweet pain of loving would suffice—that pain which she seemed to have carried within herself since she was a child, and which, though she did not know it, gave that peculiar quality of lostness and other-worldness to her pictures. Be yourself, he had said to her, but to him her heart cried, out of its loving, 'Francis, *find* yourself. . . .'

5

As the taxi crossed the Pont Royale Francis sat frowning at his thoughts. Cathryn had irritated him, but she had also shaken him. So his writing was all *Antic Hay*, was it? Well, he freely—indeed gladly —acknowledged the fact that he was not emotional. That much at least he had of his father in him! He shuddered to think what would have become of his writing if he had inherited his mother's emotionalism—her over-emotionalism, really. But he was not cold; he wouldn't have it that he was cold. He felt a deep affection for his mother, at times a quite extraordinary tenderness, and he was very fond of Sue Lester. He found her attractive too, in her dark self-contained way with its suggestion of suppressed passion; they did not have an *affaire* because Sue had her own terms, and they included love; the man who possessed Sue would have to be in love with her—or need her very terribly. He loved her, but he was not in love with her as she understood it, and he did not need her at all, which she knew well enough. But what he felt for Cathryn with her soft questioning eyes and her crown of soft child's hair was something more deeply felt than anything else; there was a curious ache in it—a carry-over from the protective feeling he had had for her when he was a boy. What he felt for Cathryn was something special and apart, because she herself was special and apart. If he ever fell in love, he thought, it could only be with someone who looked like Cathryn, and was in herself like Cathryn, and that could not be because there are no identical twins in human souls. If anything happened to Cathryn his heart would be torn up by the roots all right, but he had the feeling it would not profit his writing, because he could no more imagine life without Cathryn in it than life without the sun in it. . . .

He felt that he was being morbid, and tried to switch off his thoughts. Anything might happen to anyone. He himself might well be run over by a Paris 'bus or a Florentine tram. The streets of Paris and Florence were far more dangerous than any of those crags and glaciers of which his mother was so terrified, poor dear. But ruling out accidents there was no reason why anything should happen to either of them; they were of healthy stock, and not foolhardy enough to drink the Paris water or brave the English winter.

But the conversation with Cathryn disturbed his complacency. For, he admitted, he had become complacent. He was twenty-seven and extremely successful, and it was not a cheap success; he had the kudos as well as the sales. He was not merely the famous writer; he was the distinguished writer. He did not write for shop-girls and typists and suburban housewives—though here and there some exceptionally intelligent and discriminating shop-girl or typist or suburban housewife might read him. He was conceited—there was no doubt of it. Intellectual-snobbish, too.

And social-snobbish. All of that. Anna Kallinova would say in her blunt way that he had been spoilt and she would be right. But so long as one could acknowledge that one was conceited, snobbish, spoilt, one was not beyond redemption. Cathryn had disturbed his complacency by asking him wouldn't he like to write a great book—the implication being that to date he hadn't. Which was true, of course. Wilde made his reputation with witty amusing trifles like *The Importance of Being Earnest*, and *Lady Windermere's Fan*. He had to suffer, as Anna had said to Cathryn, before he could write *De Profundis*. A play like *The Importance of Being Earnest* was brilliant, but it was not a great play. A great play was *The Cherry Orchard*. All the same, Wilde's brilliant trifles had lasted. The very antithesis of dispassionate writers like Francis Sable you had writers like D. H. Lawrence, spreading their emotions thick all over their books—positively stripping naked, body and soul, in public. People liked it; they lapped it up; they loved it; it shocked them and excited them—had in fact on them an effect the exact opposite of what Lawrence preached—gave them sex-in-the-head, self-consciously, instead of in the blood, 'dark and untellable', where he insisted—and with what tediousness he insisted!—it should be. To any admirer of the Lawrence school the writing of Francis Sable could only seem bloodless—like the writing of Henry James. Bloodless, sexless, cold; still, Henry James had lived, and without his emotions being ravaged he had contrived a considerable output. But had it greatness? Did it bear comparison with, say, *The Brothers Karamazov*, or *Madame Bovary*? Oh, but those soul-obsessed Russians, and those sex-obsessed French! The Russians wearied you with the introspectiveness of their characters, and the French with their lusts.

'No man ever attained supreme knowledge unless his heart had been torn up by the roots.' Francis Thompson had used the quotation as a text for his poem *A Holocaust*. But did a writer, or any artist for that matter, need supreme knowledge? Was the holocaust of self necessary—or even desirable? Integration was essential to a writer; could creativeness emerge from disintegration? He doubted it. He doubted it but he did not know. It seemed to him, when the searchlight was turned on the inner man, behind the façade of the brilliant successful Francis Sable, that he knew very little about anything that really mattered. He knew a good deal about literature, ancient and modern, and the Italian Renaissance. He had read a good deal of philosophy; but, it came to him, his world was cerebral; he had no real contacts with people, least of all with the women he embraced.

In common with so many of his generation and class he was having a good time all over Europe; the Rivieras—French and Italian—the Lido, were all equally their playground. You lived much the same life in Florence, Rome, Venice, Athens, Vienna, as you lived in Paris or New York; you met much the same people; you met many who were indeed the same people; you moved around together like a Cook's tour. When you went to St. Moritz for the winter sports and ran into people you had met in the summer during the Wagner Festival at Bayreuth, and those people you had but lately talked with and drank with and been bored by in Paris, you did not feel that it was a small world; there was a dreadful inevitability about it. It did not surprise you when you met in Munich the people you had last seen in Hamburg, and you felt fairly certain that if you went on to Vienna you would meet them again there; and in Paris again when you got back. You went South, but decided to cut out the 'obvious' places like Monte Carlo, Cannes, Mentone, and went instead to small fishing villages near Toulon . . . only to find that the rest of Montparnasse had had the same idea. When Villefranche looked like becoming the Montparnasse of the Midi you thought to lose yourself in a big noisy city like Nice—and you all met again there. Europe was too small for all the people using it as a playground and pretending to work in it. The saxophones at the Bal Négre, the Bal Tabarin, the Bal Bullier, the Bal This, That and the Other, demanded, 'Ain't we got fun?' Ain't we? Up to a point. But beyond that point lay satiation and ennui.

Could it be that already by the time he was twenty-seven Francis Sable was beginning to feel he had had enough?

"Wouldn't you like to write a great book, Francis?"

He didn't know. He was too busy being successful and having a good time. No one called him a socialist any longer. He no longer called himself one.

Only the thought of anyone owning a mountain or a moor or a lake or a forest still had power to make him angry. . . .

He smiled at the thought.

As the self-confessed arch-criminal Gilles de Rais said, 'Even I am redeemable!' Even I, Francis Sable, atheist and *bon vivant* . . . but why stay on here in this modern Babylon, wasting energy, wasting time, wasting life? Why do they call it being a *bon vivant* when it's such *bad* living? It's all such nonsense; all such rubbish, all so boring, all these good times. 'Good times are chronic nowadays.' By God, they are!

If he went back to England now all the rhododendrons would be in flower, great banks of wine and mauve, great drifts of soft flame under the beech-trees, clouds of coral against a background of firs and cedars. . . .

A deep nostalgia for the Cumberland fells and the high hills and the cool grey stone of Crag House swept him. In a few weeks' time it would be Cathryn's twenty-first birthday; they had talked of going home for that, but why wait, when the rhododendrons would not? He would call round for Cathryn in the morning and they would get the night-boat. Why stay upon the order of their going? What was to stop them? They were both free. He had a diary full of engagements, but what of that? Dates were made to be broken.

At the party the princess—she had an unpronounceable name that might have been Russian or Polish, but she claimed to be a princess by marriage, and as she was very rich nobody asked questions—splendid in black velvet and diamonds introduced him to an American girl called Merrilee Browne.

"Such a clever girl," gushed the princess, "and simply longing to meet you! She's just had her first novel published."

"Bad luck!" Francis murmured. The princess gave him a startled glance, decided that she had misheard, and tactfully went head without comment. She turned to the girl.

"Merrilee, darling, may I introduce Mr. Francis Sable, the very famous English author?"

The very famous English author bowed, stiffly, but Miss Browne smiled and held out a friendly hand.

"I'm very honoured to meet you, I'm sure," she said, in a soft American voice. "But will you tell me, please, why it's bad luck to have got one's first novel published?"

"It's simply that when everyone is writing novels it's so much

more distinguished not to have written or be writing one!"
Francis told her. "There's a distressing modern tendency to rush
into print on a wave of adolescent outpouring."

"If Keats hadn't we'd have lost a whole lot," Miss Browne
suggested, thoughtfully.

Francis knew that thoughtful tone. In a few minutes she'd
be asking him what he thought of Shakespeare, had he read
Voltaire, what did he mean by Happiness, what was he After,
what did he understand by God, what did he think of Life. . . .

"Unfortunately we're not all Keats," he said quickly, and
before she could comment on this fact of life added, "May I get
you a drink?"

"Please," said Miss Browne and smiled, very sweetly.

He struggled through the tail-coats and the bare backs to
the buffet table from which drinks were being dispensed, and
she followed him to make sure of him. She did not let him escape.
He was introduced to various other people, and Miss Browne
was introduced to other people, but somehow whenever there was
a moment's respite Miss Browne was at his elbow.

She was a tall good-looking girl with intelligent eyes and
attractive figure. She wore a long dress with sleeves, and the
fact that she was not half-naked like the other women added to
her interest. The dress was a green and silver brocade that reminded Francis of the sea—the English sea. She hadn't cut off her
hair like the majority of women at that period; it was long and
thick and dark and coiled low on the nape of her neck. After
several glasses of champagne Francis longed to remove the pins
and see it stream about her shoulders like a cloak. Before the
night was out he had told her so, and before the dawn broke she
had done it herself, in his apartment.

He wakened late, with a confused memory of her. The heavy
sweetness of her perfume still clung on the stale air. He leapt out
of bed and drew back the long red velvet curtains and opened the
windows. He had slept with them closed—horrible!

He went back into the room, pulled on a dressing-gown,
then stepped out on to the balcony, drawing in the clean air.
He had a hangover—a bad one. In fact—he realised—he felt
awful. He glanced at his wrist-watch—he had gone to bed with it
on. It was nearly midday; no wonder the sun was so bright. . . .

What was there he had been going to do today? Something to do with Cathryn? No, no. Something to do with the girl he had met last night; the girl with the great cloud of black hair and the dress like the English sea? What was her name? An odd sort of name. Merrilee. That was it. Good heavens, he had promised to meet her at the Café des Lilas at one o'clock and give her lunch at the Medici Grill—they were to walk down through the Luxembourg Gardens; she loved the Luxembourg Gardens, she said—and then they were to get a taxi and drive out to Versailles—or was it Fontainebleau? One of them, anyhow. Did he really want to carry out the program? He really didn't know. Perhaps when he had bathed and had some black coffee he would know. He felt terrible. She wouldn't be there, anyhow. She must be feeling pretty ill herself.

By the time he had bathed and dressed and taken his *café noir* it was nearly one. She wouldn't be there, of course, but a stroll down through the gardens would help his head. And with a hangover one always felt better after eating. It would be pleasant in this sunshine on the terrace of the Medici.

She was sitting outside the Café des Lilas, a glass of *Champagne natur* in front of her. She looked fresh and cool in a light blue suit with a crisp white blouse.

She smiled at him as he approached her.

"Good morning. Did you sleep well?"

He told her, brutally, "I slept like the besotted."

"I'm sorry. You'll feel better after a hair-of-the-dog, and when we've eaten. It's a lovely day for Versailles."

"It's Versailles, is it? Are you sure you feel equal to it?"

"Equal to it? I feel fine!"

They were lying side by side on the hot imported sand on the crowded plage of Juan-les-Pins a month later, when he suddenly started up.

"Good heavens, I've just remembered!"

Without stirring she murmured, "What have you forgotten, honey?"

"It's my sister's twenty-first birthday today! I meant to be back for it! I must send a wire. . . ."

She let the sand run through her fingers, her arms straight along her side.

"The night of the princess's party you told me you were going to spend your sister's birthday in England, at the ancestral home. The rhododendrons would be out, you said. Great banks of them. You got quite lyrical about them, I remember. . . . I guess maybe you forgot that time and the rhododendrons wait for no man."

Francis sank back into the sand. He said savagely, "You're right, sister. I guess maybe I forgot!"

He could get the night-train and be back in Paris the following day; but what was the good of that? Why in hell hadn't he remembered yesterday? What was the matter with him, for God's sake? What was he doing, wasting his time here with all this riff-raff of lounge-lizards, *rentiers, nouveaux riches*, parasites? What was this girl who called him 'honey' to do with him? Or he with her? What's Hecuba to me or me to Hecuba? They both called themselves writers, then why in hell didn't they *write*? He knew the answer she would make. 'You can't be writing all the time, honey. You gotta live.' You gotta live, all right, but was this living—or merely the dreary round of a good time? 'Wouldn't you like to write a really great book, Francis?' . . . and, 'They're all so rubbishy, Francis. It's all so trivial.' Oh, of course, you little funny, don't you think I don't know it? 'Then why do you do it, Francis?' How do I know, Cathy, how do I know? Perhaps because I haven't yet found myself. Or perhaps because this *is* myself. . . .

He sat up. "I'm going to get dressed and go and send that wire, and tomorrow I'm going back to Paris."

"You've said that every week since we've been here."

"I happen to mean it this time."

"Sure, honey, you've meant it every time you've said it."

He got up and picked his way between the sweating all but naked pink and brown bodies, male and female, young and old, frying—under their coatings of oil—in the sweltering sun.

He sent the telegram, and next day found him in a train all right, but the train wasn't going to Paris; it was heading for Italy. And Merrilee Browne, cool as a shell, in pink linen, and feeling 'fine' in spite of a 'thick' night, was by his side.

6

It was a great disappointment to Lady Sable that Cathryn did
not want to spend her twenty-first birthday in England. She could
have borrowed a very nice house in London and given a proper
coming-out party for her, and with her birthday coming so con-
veniently in June she could have been launched on the London
season and returned to France, fashionably, at the end of August.
But Cathryn, tiresomely—and so stupidly—wrote that she did not
want any of that; she hated the thought of the 'season', just as
she had hated and resisted the idea of being presented at Court.
She was sorry, but that was how she felt about it. Sir John, when
he read the letter passed to him by his wife, felt that socialism
was once again rearing its ugly head in the family. Still, Francis
seemed to have got over his Oxford attack, so perhaps the girl
would come through all right, though all this *vie Bohème* stuff
in Paris didn't help. She should never have been allowed to go.
He had always said so. Still, no use crying over spilt milk. Got to
look on the bright side of things. Her mother had better go over
and give a party for her in Paris. He couldn't be expected to make
the journey himself. He was an old man now, nearing eighty, and
not as robust as he was, since a heart-attack at the beginning of the
year. Dorothea, therefore, wrote and suggested a Paris party.
Cathryn replied that she would be happy to see her mother in
Paris, but that the only party that would give her any pleasure
would include '*only your darling self and the only two friends who mean
anything to me here—Sue, and the Russian woman artist I have told you
about, and who has helped me so much. Francis, unfortunately, is still in
the South. I would like us just to have a little dinner in a small restaurant
Francis and I have been to a lot, on the Quai Voltaire. They specialise in
duck, which they do in a special way, very deliciously, and they have a very
good vin à l'oignon that goes excellently with it. It is an unpretentious
little place. Or there is that nice little place on the Boul' Mich' I took
you to last time, if you remember, and we sat on the terrace and saw the
sunset and Notre Dame looking so lovely in the evening light.*'
        Dorothea sighed over this letter. These various nice little
unpretentious restaurants were not her idea of a celebration for her
adored Cathryn's coming-of-age party. She had visualised a

stately London house, the staircase flanked with hydrangeas, and a ballroom with massed red roses everywhere and a great glittering chandelier. And Cathryn, in white satin with gloves up to her elbows, dancing with eligible young men of good families. And a champagne-supper, and a nice paragraph about it all in the Court Circular. Something similar could have been arranged in Paris, if Cathryn was set against London. Or there could have been a good party at Crag House. One wouldn't have been able to have assembled such a good list of people together, of course, but still, there could have been some quite presentable county names. But all this hole-and-corner Paris Left-bank nonsense. . . . How did she expect to get a husband like that? Or did she, dreadful thought, contemplate marrying some Bohemian artist person? It was all very upsetting and worrying. John was quite right, of course; she should never have been allowed to study art in Paris. But then she hadn't dreamed that Francis would go off and leave her so much alone, or that Sue would allow her to move into a place on her own. She had seen Cathryn's attic last time she had been over and had felt like crying. It seemed to her completely in-explicable that a girl of Cathryn's class and education should choose to live in such a place—in such a slum. For what else could you call it? Cathryn had insisted that she was quite com-fortable there; that the frightful oil-stove thing warmed it quite adequately in winter; that it was no trouble to her to carry the water up all those flights of stairs; that she could get a hot bath whenever she wanted it at Francis's place when he was in town, and at Sue's when he wasn't. That it was above all a good place to work in. Cathryn had positively pleaded all this. And still Lady Sable felt like crying. She begged Cathryn to move—'for my sake'. And then Cathryn had been a little angry and said that that was an unfair appeal, and that she was sorry, but she wasn't moving for anyone's sake, and please she would prefer not to talk any more about it.

Lady Sable had appealed to Sue. But Sue had merely pointed out that as the place suited Cathryn there was no more to be said about it. Some people had no feeling for comfort; Cathryn was evidently one of them. And she had certainly got a good deal of very good work done there.

So she had been defeated and had resigned herself to the

thought of her daughter living in 'squalor'. Just as she had resigned herself to Francis's atheism. And Steven's anti-Catholicism. And the unhappiness of her marriage. And now she must resign herself to these ridiculous birthday plans. One's children could be very disappointing. But still there was the hope that eventually Cathryn would turn to the Church. She was at least not against it, which was something, nor was she an atheist.

Cathryn had half expected that Francis would return from the South in time for her birthday, and before opening his wire she was confident that it would be to say he was returning. But it was merely a greetings telegram, and as it was not sent till midday it did not reach her till the late afternoon. She tried not to feel hurt and disappointed, but it was no good; she was hurt, and bitterly disappointed.

Her mother had arrived in Paris the previous day, and was staying with Sue. They spent the morning of Cathryn's birthday together shopping and lunched together in the Bois; in the afternoon Lady Sable rested until the evening; then they met in the restaurant on the Quai Voltaire. Cathryn went there alone, Anna having declined the invitation.

"I wouldn't fit in," she declared. "I don't belong to your world. Your mother would be horrified. Sue Lester belongs. It's much better there should just be the three of you. You can stand me a dinner some evening when your mother's gone back. I've brought you a present." She flung a small paper packet down on the table.

Cathryn picked it up wonderingly. When the wrapping was removed she held a topaz in a setting of beautifully wrought silver in her hand.

"Anna, how beautiful! Where did you find it?"

"I didn't buy it, if that's what you're wondering. Nor did I steal it. It belonged to my great-great-grandmother and is the last of the few bits of jewellery I brought from Russia. The rest went long ago—it was all worth more than this, but not as beautiful, apart from the sentimental value. I couldn't bring myself to sell this, even when I hadn't a *sou*, but I didn't know I was keeping it for you all these years! Don't ask me how I can bear to part with it—it gives me pleasure to give it to you."

Cathryn hugged her. "I'll value it always, and I'll always wear it."

"You can't wear it with the pearl necklace your parents have given you," Anna objected. "It's too much. And you must wear the necklace tonight or your mother will be hurt."

"I can wear it in my beret," Cathryn said.

"You can't wear a beret if you're going to dress up."

"But I'm not going to dress up. I'm going as I am."

"Isn't that disrespectful to your lady-mother?"

"I don't mean it so and can only hope she won't think so."

Lady Sable was disappointed when Cathryn arrived wearing a rather shiny navy blue coat and skirt and a scarlet beret, and Sue frowned. Really, Cathryn might have taken a little trouble to please her mother on this one occasion, having so deeply disappointed her by refusing to have a coming-out party. She herself was elegant in very *chic* black with a chinchilla wrap, and she wore a spray of orchids.

Cathryn greeted her, "You're looking very grand, Sue!"

"I thought I'd honour the occasion."

"I only wish Cathryn had felt constrained to do so," Dorothea said, eyeing the girl disapprovingly. She was wearing the clothes she had worn all day. She might at least have changed into a dress.

"But mother darling, I'm very grand! I'm wearing this wonderful pearl necklace you and Daddy so sweetly gave me, and this magnificent topaz from Anna"—she indicated her beret—"and I've washed behind the ears!"

"It's a wonder you're able to attend to your toilet even that much living in the squalor you do!"

Cathryn suppressed her irritation. "That subject is taboo, had you forgotten? These lovely roses are from you, of course." She bent forward and inhaled the scent from one of the massed dark red roses of an elaborate centre-piece. She pulled out a rose and tucked it into the buttonhole of her shabby jacket.

"Since you wouldn't have a proper party it was the best I could do. There should have been a ballroom with hundreds of them!"

There was bitterness in her voice again, and Sue, aware of it, changed the subject by handing Cathryn a small tissue-paper-wrapped parcel she had had beside her plate.

"I can't compete with pearl necklaces and topaz brooches," she said, "but it has a certain antique value."

Sue's gift was a silver trinket box of Adam design, and Cathryn was delighted.

"I'll keep the pearls and the topaz in it," she declared.

Steven had commissioned Lady Sable to buy a pigskin dressing-case for Cathryn in Paris. Cathryn had no use for anything so luxurious, but nothing would stop her mother carrying out the commission. Cathryn kept thinking of all the more satisfactory ways of spending the money—of all the books it would buy, and the painting materials, and the flowers; and how you could go to Switzerland and back for less than half of it. . . . Why did people insist on giving one expensive presents for which one had no use? Besides, the real value of a present was in the loving care and thought the donor had expended on the selection of it; the cost was nothing in comparison with that; and an expensive present from someone with plenty of money meant so much less than a single rose from someone to whom a few francs or a few pence meant the difference between having a meal and going without.

She would have given the pearl necklace and the Adam box for a single rose from Francis. But the loveliest gift he could have brought her was his presence at that table that evening. She had a fantasy in which the door suddenly opened and he walked in, having travelled up by day-train, or come by 'plane. . . . But deep down in herself she knew it would not happen.

"Did you hear from Francis?" her mother asked. It was very wrong of Francis not to be there, but she had given up expecting anything of her children. Sue was very disgusted that Francis had not returned to Paris for the occasion, but Francis for all his charm was a very unsatisfactory person, and why she loved him as she did, she told herself angrily, she really could not imagine. She was forever trying to root him out of her heart, but somehow never succeeded, though she recited his faults to herself frequently like a litany. *Le cœur a ses raisons*. . . . Yes, indeed; but at twenty-seven one ought to know better; one wasn't a schoolgirl to be romantic and sentimental against all reason. She knew very well that Francis was fond of her, that he liked her as a person, and was attracted to her as a woman. She knew that he would like nothing better than an *affaire* with her. That she could be with him at that moment in the South or in Italy instead of the American girl—that he would have preferred her, had he been given the choice. But she also knew that he did not love her as she understood the term; she was not prepared to be one of the women Francis Sable had had an *affaire* with. It wasn't good enough. She wanted marriage or nothing. Marriage was a vote of confidence. Though if he had been in love with her but opposed to marriage, as part of his modernist non-religious outlook, she supposed she would have dispensed with the legal ceremony. But if he had been in love with her he would have wanted to please her, presumably, so that didn't come into it. . . .

All this ran through her head whilst Cathryn was showing Francis's telegram and Lady Sable was declaring that it was too bad that he hadn't come back and that his present hadn't arrived on the day. Francis was really very thoughtless. But Francis wouldn't have thought to send a present, she thought, and the same thought came to Sue. They drank champagne first to Cathryn, and then to Francis—'Wherever he might be.'

At approximately the same time Francis, in a fishing village on the Italian Riviera, poured out Chianti from its straw-covered flask, and leaning across the red-checked tablecloth of a small restaurant on the harbour, drank to Cathryn.

"I hope she got the roses," he said.

Merrilee started. "Oh, gee, honey, you'll never forgive me, but I clean forgot to send the wire to the florist's!"

Francis stared at her. What he said to her is not printable.

She flared at him. "You should have done it yourself when you sent the greetings wire! It was only an afterthought, anyway!"

"Afterthought or not, I had it, didn't I? And you offered to send off the wire to the florist's as you were going to the post-office. The florist's is just round the corner from where she lives— she'd have had them this afternoon. . . . You didn't want to do it, that's the truth of it! You had the unconscious wish to forget!"

He was white with rage.

"Oh, cut out the Freud," Merrilee said, and drained her glass.

Francis got up. "I'm going," he said.

"Where?" Her tone was bored. She poured out another glass of wine.

"I don't know. But anywhere out of here."

She smiled. "O.K., sweetheart. See you at the hotel later."

"You'll do nothing of the kind."

For once she misjudged him. When she got back to the hotel an hour or so later he had gone. They told her he had caught the night-train for Rome.

7

During the next three years several things of importance happened in the Sable family, the first of them being the death of Sir John from a recurrence of his heart trouble in 1927. He had never been the same after his illness the previous year, and his second attack was followed by a stroke. His end was then only a matter of a few weeks.

Cathryn and Francis came home, Cathryn from Paris, Francis from the island of Ibiza, in the Balearics, which had suddenly become fashionable with the literary and artistic set who regarded Paris as 'empty' in August, and therefore intolerable. They returned from a sense of duty towards their mother. Cathryn felt that she had never really known her father. She could only remember him as an old man. By the time she was ten years old he was already seventy. She knew that she had disappointed him, as she had her mother, by not doing the right social things, but he had been on the whole, she thought, remarkably kind and patient and tolerant of what he could only regard as her eccentricities, and she felt a certain sadness in the thought that he had not been spared long enough to have the chance of seeing her successful in the life she had chosen for herself. She planned an exhibition of her pictures in Paris the following spring and if she had no more than a *succès d'estime* she would have liked him to have had at least that much satisfaction in his errant only daughter.

Francis could not feel grief of any kind at his father's death. He was frankly glad that 'the old bore' would not be about any more. He could not see that any single person had cause to mourn him. Not even Steven, he thought cynically, since he would now reign in his stead. He came back for the funeral solely because he believed it would grieve his mother if he stayed away. He could not understand why she should be as stricken as she apparently was. He had never been aware of any great devotion between his parents; on the contrary he had always suspected that the marriage was not a happy one. Why, then, the tears?

Cathryn said, "Don't you see, it's just *because* their marriage wasn't really happy—she has no happy memories to comfort her; she has nothing but regrets."

Francis said, impatiently, "It's all the sheerest sentimentality! She didn't love him, so what is she mourning? I've a good mind to ask her! People need to be jolted out of their unconscious insincerities! She feels she *ought* to mourn him, so she weeps and wraps herself in black and mourns! I shall tell her so!"

"You mustn't, Francis. As a writer you ought to have more imagination! How do we know what she mourns? What their married life might have been, perhaps——"

"What it never could have been! Of all the futile human emotions remorse is the worst! What has she got to be remorseful about, anyhow? She was what is called a good wife, wasn't she? She ran the house efficiently, did the necessary amount of entertaining with the necessary amount of charm, and was faithful——"

It was Cathryn's turn to be impatient. "You know all that's quite superficial! A man wants more than a good housekeeper and hostess in his wife. Perhaps she feels she cheated him in some way—cheated him emotionally. Perhaps she feels she ought to have made more effort in their personal relation——"

Cathryn's guess was right. Now that he was gone from her in the flesh Dorothea could remember John Sable as he was when she married him, a handsome, vigorous, charming middle-aged man, a gentleman in the real sense—though Francis and Cathryn, she thought sadly, would probably sneer at the word; Francis, anyhow—and he had restored her *amour propre*, so sorely hurt by her first and last romantic love, by paying her the compliment of wanting her to marry him. If he had not been romantically in love with her at least he had been sincerely fond of her and prepared to be a loving and devoted husband, and she had repaid his kindness with the ingratitude of her discontent. She had in her own estimation sinned grievously and far more against him than against herself. It is true that since the birth of her daughter she had tried to make up for these first ten years of her married life. In those mellower years he had teased her, telling her that it was demonstrably true that in married life the first ten years were the worst. . . . But by then she was a middle-aged woman and he had turned sixty; she had, she felt, wasted the best years of their life together, and it was this that filled her widowhood with pain—that aching, intolerable pain of remorse, at which Francis sneered. She knew nothing of his conversation with Cathryn but she felt that he thought her grief all nonsense and humbug; he could not conceal the fact from her. He didn't understand, of course; how should he? Nor did she want him to have this understanding, since he could only come to it through the personal experience of pain.

She knew that Steven sincerely mourned his father, but that did not bring them together. She and Steven would never come close, she thought; they were different kinds of people. He was the son and heir she had borne for John, and he had been John's child all along, just as Cathryn had been hers. Francis had his moments of sweetness—he had been unexpectedly sweet about her joining the Church; she would always be grateful to him for that—but once he had gone to Oxford she seemed to lose him; during the vacations he was so often away climbing, and when he had finished with Oxford he had started spending most of his time abroad. Very often for weeks at a time she had no idea where he was. Cathryn, on the other hand, in spite of her persistence in living in Paris long after she had ceased to be an art student, never lost touch; she came home fairly frequently, and she, Dorothea, could go to her in Paris occasionally. And Cathryn now, it seemed to her, understood her grief at John's death. Cathryn had her own private sorrow, because she had disappointed him as a daughter.

"I wish he had lived to have seen my exhibition," she said more than once. "He might have felt better then about my choosing that kind of life instead of being Sir John Sable's daughter."

Her mother pressed her hand. "He will know about it," she said, in a low voice. "He will know about it and understand and be glad."

Cathryn said, fervently, "Oh, but I wish I could believe! I wish it so terribly!"

"Perhaps God will give you the grace. I've prayed for it since you were born."

Lady Sable's voice was no less fervent.

Cathryn admitted to her for the first time—and it was the first time she had admitted it to anyone—"I've prayed too. I know what you want for me, and something in me, deep down, tells me you're right. Sometimes I seem to come so near. Once I was in Notre Dame when Mass was being said. I knelt down and wanted to be part of what was going on. I couldn't follow the Mass and I had a queer feeling of unhappiness, of being shut out. . . . It was like wanting to pray and not knowing how to. Then a verse of a poem Francis loves came into my head."

She pressed her fingers against her eyes for a moment, swept by emotion. Then she looked up, resolutely. "He told me once he thought it was probably the most beautiful poem ever written —it's the famous one by Joseph Plunkett, '*I see His Blood upon the Rose.*'"

Her mother looked at her, bewildered.

"Francis loves that poem? But he makes a boast of being what he calls a free-thinker, and he never loses an opportunity to write or say something against the Church——"

"He would say that for him it's just a very beautiful poem, but its beauty is in its religious intensity. You remember the last verse—'All pathways by His feet are worn——'?"

Lady Sable finished the verse, softly, her voice a little unsteady:

> 'His strong heart stirs the ever-beating sea,
> His crown of thorns is twined with every thorn,
> His cross is every tree.'

"No one could love that in a purely literary or aesthetic sense," Cathryn declared. "Francis deceives himself. Something in him responds to it, something higher than intellect, though he can't bring himself to acknowledge it."

Lady Sable said quickly, "You believe in something higher than intellect?"

"Of course!" There was surprise in Cathryn's voice.

"Do you give it a name?"

"It could be called faith, I suppose."

Lady Sable closed her eyes for a moment. The faith that precedes reason. . . . Was it happening, then, at last, the ewe lamb coming at last into the fold?

"Certainly what happened to me that day in Notre Dame had nothing to do with intellect," Cathryn went on. "Nor was it emotion. The poem came to me like an answer to a prayer—a prayer for comfort, not to be shut out. And then, too, it was like a prayer—it was as though I prayed it. Then I had the feeling that though something was going on that I had no part in and that I didn't understand, one day I would understand, and have a part in it."

"Please God," Lady Sable said, and that too was a prayer. She offered no comment on what Cathryn had told her, out of her heart; instinctively she felt that Cathryn had to find her own way; a pattern had to be worked out, but it could only be evolved from within herself. She could do no more now, she felt, than she had always done—pray.

Cathryn had been very unhappy that day in Notre Dame. It was the day after her twenty-first birthday. She had been deeply hurt by Francis's neglect. She wanted to pray that she and Francis might be close again, as in the old days. The conversation they had had a month ago, the night of the princess's party, had stayed with her. She wanted to pray that Francis might stop wasting himself and give his genius a chance. Passionately she wanted him to be again the shining one with whom she had climbed up into the clouds and seen an eagle in the air, the lordly one for whom she was prepared to be anything, do anything, because she believed in him. You could not believe in the Francis who wanted only to be successful and famous, and who went off with Merrilee Browne. . . . Holy mysteries were happening at the altar and she wanted desperately to pray. She buried her face in her hands, trying to press back the image of Francis, and then the poem had come to her, and Francis was saying, "Listen to this, Cathy. Sometimes I think it's the most beautiful poem ever written—'I see His Blood upon the rose' . . ."

During the general discussion of family plans Steven revealed that but for Sir John's sudden death his engagement to Miss Honor Dawsett, whom he had met at a shooting-party in Scotland last year, would have been officially announced. He proposed now that it should be officially announced at Christmas and that the wedding should take place in the spring. Dorothea was greatly relieved; she had no wish to go on living at Crag House; she would like, she said, to have an apartment in Paris in the Étoile district, or perhaps a smallish house; she would then be near Cathryn and hope to see something of Francis in his comings and goings between Paris and the rest of Europe. It was unanimously agreed that this was a good plan. Steven made a well-intentioned but pompous little speech hoping that they would all nevertheless continue to regard Crag House as their home. Lady Sable and Cathryn thanked him, half embarrassed, half touched, and assured him they would. Francis gave him an amused smile, and murmured, "Spiritual or temporal?"

"Both!" Steven snapped. Really, Francis became more insufferable as the years went on.

Both Cathryn and Lady Sable had hoped that Francis would spend a few weeks in England, the rest of the summer, at least; Cathryn had cherished a hope that they might 'scramble' on Great Gable and Scafell again. "For old times' sake," she said, a little wistfully. If he waited a little the weather might clear; it couldn't rain forever! Must he really go back immediately?

"I must, Cathy. Steven gets on my nerves, and Cain and Abel aren't in it the moment we're in the same room!"

"But you're not going tomorrow?"

"The day after."

"Then if it's fine tomorrow why don't we spend the day on the hills—we could get out early and get back late; you could have supper in your room—you needn't see Steven!"

"Darling (a) it isn't going to be fine tomorrow, and (b) this is Steven's house now, and we can't use it as an hotel and just order meals in our rooms when we feel like it! I'd hate to do it, anyway."

"All right, we'll get back in time for dinner, all correctly."

"No, darling. I'm going to London tomorrow, and flying to Paris the day after. Come and have dinner with me in London and see me off. We'll stay at Claridge's and do the thing in style!"

She shook her head. "Mummy would be hurt. I couldn't go off like that. Besides, I haven't the clothes for that sort of thing any more." She hesitated a moment, then said, "Francis, when are we going climbing in Switzerland together?"

"You can't spend a night in London because it would hurt mother, yet you calmly propose we should do the one thing that would throw her into a panic! You're an odd one!"

"She needn't know. At least not till it was safely all over! Couldn't we go in the spring?"

"We might."

"You won't commit yourself, will you?"

"How can I? How do we either of us know where we'll be or what we'll be doing in the spring? You might be married—or anything."

"No, Francis, I'm not the marrying kind. You said I'd make a beautiful nun—don't you remember? Don't look so startled— I'm not contemplating entering a convent, but I can imagine it more easily than I can marrying! I'm not likely to be married, but you might be involved in another love-affair!"

"I notice you assume that I also am not the marrying kind— though for a different reason!"

"I wish you would marry. Why don't you marry Sue? She loves you."

"Is that what she told you?"

"She doesn't talk about you. But it's obvious. Why don't you? You're fond of her, aren't you?"

"Since when was being fond of a person sufficient reason for marrying them? Why should you want me to marry, anyhow— when you're apparently resolved not to yourself?"

The colour came into her face. "I choose to live celibately. It's different, isn't it?"

"I see. St. Paul's 'It's better to marry than to burn.' But I don't happen to be a disciple of St. Paul's."

She said, despairingly, "Oh, Francis, isn't it awful—we never used to be like this! I mean we always seem to quarrel when we meet nowadays, whether it's in Paris or at home! What is the matter with us?"

"The matter is that you've turned into such a damned little prig! Either I'm not being a serious enough writer, or else it's my morals!"

Her eyes filled with tears. "I'm sorry," she said, helplessly.

She wanted to cry, "Oh, can't you see? It's because I care about you so much!" But she couldn't say it; once it would have been possible; but in recent years he had got too far away from her.

He saw the tears in her eyes and because he couldn't bear them but couldn't say so, he said, irritably, "If you didn't try to mother me so much we'd get on better! Get a mac and let's go for a walk in this damned rain—it's no use waiting for it to stop!"

Her face lit up immediately. When he held the door open for her he suddenly bent and kissed her forehead.

"You're a little funny," he said.

8

Cathryn's exhibition of paintings in tempera the following spring attracted a good deal of attention; columns were written about her as the promising young pioneer in the revival of a neglected medium. Her painting had a curious quality of purity, Francis thought, standing in the middle of the gallery and taking a preliminary general survey; a quality of coolness without coldness; it was not merely purity of colour—clear brilliant blues, the bold use of vermilion, and the delicate use of gold leaf—and the strong, clear light—but of spirituality in the conception. It was the luminous quality of her own personality, he reflected; a quality of chastity utterly remote from frigidity—a passionate chastity. Technically there was in her work all that attention to detail of the Italian Primitives—the meticulous tracing of a gold thread in a brocade, the careful and loving delineation of each separate sepal in the calyx of a rose. Yet there was nothing of the finicking and photographic, but a quality of imaginativeness and illumination.

"She has genius, the little one," Francis murmured to Sue, as they passed from a tiny picture of a side chapel in St. Sulpice, exquisitely painted and full of feeling, to a large portrait of Lady Sable, her distinguished grey head against a perspective of an avenue in the gardens of the Luxembourg, flowing in a few inches into a sunlit eternity. Sue bent forward to examine closely the painting of a whorl of crimson and gold gauze spun out round the sitter's bare shoulders.

"That use of gold leaf," she said. "Where did the child learn it? Certainly she didn't get that from Anna Kallinova, whatever else she got from her!" There was a hint of jealousy in her voice; she did not like Anna personally, and she knew that Cathryn had learned a good deal from her, and nothing at all from the well-known Sue Lester.

"She got it," Francis told her, "by spending her nights studying Cennini's handbook by the light of a candle in her attic. Cennini never had a more conscientious pupil, I assure you! Here's her portrait of you—I hadn't seen it before. She's made you look like a Leonardo Madonna——" He turned and regarded Sue, critically. "Now I come to think of it you do, rather."

She laughed embarrassed. "She tends to spiritualise all her sitters. Look at this of you! She's made you look more like your namesake of Assisi than I should have thought possible!"

"Why—wouldn't you say I had a spiritual face?"

"No."

"Really?" He was amused. "And I thought I had such a sensitive face!"

"It's sensitive, but not spiritual. It's a worldly face. If I painted you I'd see you quite differently from how Cathryn's painted you. She's idealised you—painted you either out of illusion, or what she would like you to be. I'd paint you as you are."

"Do you really know me so well?"

"Not all that well, but better than Cathryn does. I've seen you as she hasn't. I've seen you tight, and I saw you when you were telling Merrilee Browne you'd like to see her hair loosed about her like a cloak."

He laughed, but he was no longer amused.

"Perhaps Cathryn sees me as you never have—at the other end of a rope on a stiff rock-climb, for instance, and listening to Bach's St. Matthew Passion. One has, after all, other moments than in American bars and the arms of the Merrilee Brownes!"

So he was vulnerable, she thought. She was astonished at the strength of her desire to hurt him; she fought back the impulse of retort and instead smiled at him.

"I'm sorry," she said, but already he was not listening. He was bending forward and closely examining a small picture.

"Look at this," he said, and something in his tone made her look first at his face. He was obviously startled, but it was more than that; there was almost a look of awe in his rapt gaze.

She turned to the picture. It was the head and shoulders of a man at an open window. The casement opened on to a sunlit formalised landscape, with a white-peaked mountain in the distance of the long, curiously dream-like perspective. In the foreground a pigeon took bread from the man's hands—very fine beautiful hands—and a red rose, painted with exquisite formal precision, lay on the window-sill by the grey bird. The man looked out of the window, so that his face was in profile, but it was unmistakably Francis's profile. The picture was full of a golden translucency, and of a quiet strong conviction.

"I didn't know she'd done that one," Francis murmured. "I remember she did a profile sketch of me one day when we sat at the Dôme. I didn't know it was a note for anything."

They both referred to their catalogues. The title of the picture was simply 'Saint Francis'.

There were voices speaking in French, and Cathryn came into the gallery with the proprietor. The exhibition was not yet opened to the public; Francis and Sue were there merely as friends of the artist.

"Here she comes," Sue said. "We can ask her why she's canonised you."

Francis said sharply. "No—d'you mind? Not now, or ever."

He went forward to meet Cathryn. He took both her hands.

"My dear," he said, "may I congratulate you, very sincerely? It's a wonderful exhibition!"

She was startled by the warmth of his tone.

The proprietor beamed. He was a fat oily little man in a striped suit. He spoke in English.

"Miss Sable paints very attractively," he said, and bowed to her. "Already we have sold several paintings and drawings. It is an interesting medium, this tempera. We come now to put the red stars on the pictures sold. Tomorrow Lady Sable will open the pre-view for us, and the day after we are ready for *tout le monde*. But tomorrow is an important day, when the critics are there. I think we shall get a very good press and sell very many more pictures." He turned to Sue. "Perhaps one day we may have the honour of an exhibition of your own work in these galleries, Miss Lester?"

Francis moved away. At thirty-three and a third per cent, he thought. Why must an artist deal with such tradespeople? He paused before the picture of a shell, cavernous and strange, and in a moment Cathryn came up to him.

He smiled down at her. "Who taught you to paint perspectives like Giorgione, Leonardo, and God-knows-who all rolled into one?"

"Perhaps it's just that I've looked at so much work by people who could and did. Are you going home for Steven's wedding?"

"Good God, no! Are you?"

"I must. Mother would be so hurt if I didn't."

"Steven is such a bore. He's father all over again, but more pompous. The old boy had a sense of humour, at least. Who is this Honor person he's marrying?"

"She's well-connected——"

"I'm sure she is. I'm equally sure she's boring. No one but a bore could bear to marry Steven."

"Steven's not such a bad old stick, really, Francis!"

"That exactly describes him—not such a bad old stick! What *could* be more boring! His fiancée's probably the female counterpart—a perfect dear!"

Cathryn laughed. "You're naughty, Francis. She's really quite nice."

"I knew it. 'Really quite nice.' Damned with faint praise. Darling, you *can't* go to their frightful nuptials!"

"Of course I'm going. And if you wanted to be nice you'd come, too."

"But I don't want to be nice. It's the last thing in the world I want—ever! I don't in the least mind if people say, 'That frightful swine, Francis Sable.' What I couldn't *bear* would be if anyone should say, 'That perfect dear, Francis Sable'!"

"I don't think you need worry that anyone is likely to, Francis darling!" Sue had come up behind them, having shaken off the proprietor.

He bowed to her. "Thank you, Sue. Now why don't we all go and drink champagne up at Fouquet's to the success of the exhibition?"

"Couldn't we just go across to the Dôme?" Cathryn suggested. "I'm not dressed for the Champs-Élysées."

"Darling, you never are, and you never will be, which is very foolish of you—don't you agree with me, Sue? But of course you do. But with your pearl necklace and your distinguished profile no one will mistake you for anything but a lady, and you can't drink champagne on the Dôme terrace—it would be so vulgar. . . ."

They came out into the sunshine of the Boulevard Raspail and Francis hailed a taxi. The city was beautiful in the late afternoon sunlight, with the boulevard trees still fresh with spring. In the Champs-Élysées the chestnuts were coming into flower. When they crossed the Place de la Concorde and turned into the Avenue de Champs-Élysées Cathryn half closed her eyes to get the perspective of the long sweep up to the Arc de Triomphe, and wondered why she had never painted it, and in that clear yet mellow light. She felt an immense happiness; it pervaded her as the clear soft light pervaded the boulevard; she was flooded with it; it was a happiness both exultant and serene. Francis had thought her work good—the work that represented nearly seven years in Paris. He talked nonsense and said outrageous things, but it didn't matter; she had seen his eyes when he had taken both her hands, and all the time he talked nonsense his eyes still held that light; it didn't matter what people said; what counted was the tone of the voice, the look in the eyes—the perspective that opened up in the dream-landscape of the soul. . . . She smiled out at the fresh green of the trees and began humming a little air.

She was an odd-looking little thing, Sue thought, in her shabby blue coat and skirt, with the red beret pulled down at one side, the topaz shining in it, and the soft fair crown of her hair catching the sunlight; odd because of the contrast of her delicate sensitive face and the *gamin* suggestion of her clothes; and the contradiction in the suggestion of childishness in the softness of her features and the mature wisdom of her eyes.

Francis looked at her, half-smiling. He, too, was aware of the contrasts she presented, but her childishness filled him with tenderness. She was lovely, but it was a beauty that was more than delicate features and soft gold and white, but had almost everything to do with her own curious quality of inner radiance. There was vitality in the warmth of the brown eyes, and in the grace

and quickness of her movements, in every line of her young lithe
body, but there was serenity, too, the rare quality of stillness.
It came to him, in a flash of realisation, that she was like the
Filippino Lippi *Virgin* in the Uffizi Gallery—there was the same
tender childishness, the same suggestion of spirituality.

He suddenly realised that the little tune she was humming
was the last aria from the St. Matthew Passion, 'Lie softly . . .'

He smiled at her. They had gone to London specially to hear
it on Passion Sunday that year and made a pact that wherever either
of them were they would always go back for that. 'All our lives,
until death do us part', had been their laughing pact. He hummed
the air with her.

Sue looked at them both. How alike they were, the brother
and sister! Suddenly she saw in Francis's rapt face what Cathryn
had seen when she painted 'Saint Francis', and was filled with
humility. She had the feeling that the girl of twenty-three knew
more than she would ever know; she would have liked to have
painted them both as she saw them now, 'But I couldn't do it,' she
thought, sadly. 'It's not merely that I'm not a good enough
painter—I'm not a good enough person. . . .' That, it came to her,
was the basis of Cathryn's genius, her goodness, her essential
purity of spirit, with its inspired vision. . . . Had Francis genius?
Brilliance he had, but was it genius? She didn't think so. Francis
was of the world and genius is of higher inspiration, fashioned
of finer material. If he had latent genius it would take Cathryn
to bring it out; the need was to bring to his soul the look she
could in rare moments bring to his face. . . . But Francis, she
supposed, would deny the existence of a soul, though he loved one
of the most beautiful religious poems ever written, and what was
perhaps the loveliest of all the sacred music ever composed.

9

At Christmas that year Francis took Cathryn with him to
Austria, for winter sports. In the 'twenties small new off-the-
beaten-track places became the vogue. The Intelligentsia, and
those who fancied themselves as such, and Society—and Fringes-
of-Society—Bright Young Things then made a beaten track of

their own to these obscure places. They endured every kind of discomfort and inconvenience for the sake of being somewhere different; the winter sports facilities were a great deal better in the places which catered for this trade, but St. Moritz? My dear, so terribly hackneyed! So *nouveau riche*! Now there's a little place near Salzburg—or Vienna—or Munich. . . . (In the summer it was, Cannes? My dear, so *vulgar*! Now there's a little place near Toulon—or in the Balearics—or the Estoril . . .) In a short time, of course, news of the little place got round, and then 'everyone' flocked there, and up went the prices, and the little place began to give itself airs, and if you had discovered it late and referred to its charms you were met with, My dear, you can't go *there*! All Bloomsbury, Montparnasse, and Greenwich Village are there! If you really want to get away from the old familiar faces you want a place like St. Moritz (or, in the summer, Cannes, or Mentone, or Monte Carlo) . . . so deliciously *Victorian*, you know. By the end of that ginned-up decade the Montparnassians were turning their attention to Corsica and Sardinia, having exhausted the rest of Europe—that is to say their limited conception of it—though the Mayfair playboys and playgirls were more conservative—as befitted their class—and showed a tendency to cling to their old-fashioned Riviera plages, with their imported sand, their casinos, Ritz bars, 'Jimmy's', and 'Sunflower Sam's'. . . .

The little Austrian place which Francis Sable had set his heart on for the Christmas of 1928 was the mountain village of Drindel, in the Tyrol, in the shadow of the Drindelhorn. He had been there in the summer and had been enchanted by it, and it had had for him what was the great virtue of not yet having been discovered by the English and Americans, neither the Montparnassians nor the general run of tourists. Later on, of course, it got out that it was 'Francis Sable's place', and then it filled up with the clientèle of the Café Royal and the Dôme.

Francis was not much inclined to take Cathryn on his climbing expeditions. His Oxford friend was a fine climber, and when he could go with John Framley it would have been absurd to have gone with anyone else—certainly anyone as inexperienced as Cathryn. Admittedly the only way anyone could get experience was by practice, but being himself beyond practice-climbs he was not disposed to 'climb down', literally, to Cathryn's level of proficiency. Cathryn, for one thing, had no experience on ice. But winter sports were another matter. Cathryn had no experience of skis, it was true, but her ski-ing lessons would not in the least interfere with his own expert activities. Ski-ing was not something you did 'with' someone; it didn't call for companionship, like climbing; and Cathryn would be easy, and therefore restful, to be with when they weren't ski-ing.

He was so mentally tired that winter, in fact, that he felt that Cathryn would not merely be restful, but was really the only person he could bear to be with, because with her one could be silent, need make no effort. And all the summer he had been making efforts, being oh so bright and amusing, both as a person and as an author. He felt a strong need to go somewhere quiet and obscure—not one of the fashionable quiet obscure little places, but somewhere which, for the time being at least, really was. It would be fatal, he knew, to go anywhere recommended to him by any of his own circle, no matter how unspoiled it was alleged to be. Bloomsbury, after all, was unknown to Manchester and Surbiton; for most people from such places it would be off-the-beaten-track all right; most of the 'little places' in Europe were unknown to the ordinary tourist, but they were full of all the usual faces for someone from Montparnasse. But the only people to be found on the snow-slopes in Francis's Tyrolean village were the people who lived in it or in the neighbourhood. There was no hotel; there was only a small *Gasthaus* which didn't reckon to open in the winter, except for the *Keller*. It opened for Francis and Cathryn because they had driven out from Schultzburg, twelve miles further up the lake, and sent the taxi away, and it was dark and cold, and they were anyhow such a very pleasant young couple, and so obviously prepared to accept just whatever was offered them, both as to food and accommodation. They were also so very obviously brother and sister and not an illicit pair of lovers, which was also a point in their favour.

The village was a mere straggle of wooden houses with deep eaves and ornately carved balconies, clustered round a church with a wooden spire and a blue clock-face. Behind the village the Drindelhorn rose white and massive; a little below it lay the lake, already frozen hard at its still, shallow, reedy end, and the rest of it filmed with ice. The *Gasthaus* faced down the cobbled street of shops and houses, and the church spire rose up behind it, bright against its low-huddled darkness. The ground-floor rooms, the café, and the *Speisezimmer*, were dark and hung with small dusty antlers and fading photographs of mountains, but on the first floor all was blue-washed and bright. There was a small crucifix at the top of the stairs, and a tiny lamp glowed red under a medallion of the Sacred Heart. In every room there was a cheap colour-print of a holy picture. The place was warmed by tall tiled stoves which were periodically stuffed with wood. At times the heating was intense, and the double windows were hermetically sealed till the spring. The heat brought out the heavy smell of the wood; it was not a good smell, but one got used to it.

Cathryn loved even the rank winter smell of the unaired wooden house. She was so happy that she felt her happiness round her like a light. She felt she knew for the first time the meaning of the words 'entranced' and 'radiant'. She had at times the feeling that other people must see a light round her—the radiance of her happiness. There was after all, outside of fairy-tale, such a thing as being enchanted. This was enchantment. The Drindelhorn was the white mountain of her dreams. It was the formalised mountain of a child's imagination. It was the mountain she had painted in her picture, without ever having seen it. It was the mountain she would one day climb with Francis. She felt that she could never look at it enough. Its white beauty held her spellbound—and that was another word, it seemed to her, she understood for the first time, spellbound.

She was fascinated by the way in which the mountains came right down to the lake, so that water and mountains and sky formed a unity. In the summer the cattle graze on the lower slopes of the mountains, which are dotted with hay-huts fashioned of huge logs piled one upon another. There are orchards, and an occasional small restaurant where you may sit on a wooden veranda and let the beauty of mountain and lake and orchard and pasture-land seep into you, whilst you drink beer cold in stone mugs and eat white radishes as big as young turnips cut so that they are like wood-shavings, falling in thin salted spirals from the hand. In winter there are no footpaths and no cattle, and all that was green is become white. It was a white world as Cathryn saw it that first time, the mountain-sides striped and criss-crossed with the marks of skis, the hay-huts half buried in the snow, and towering over all the white massiveness of the Drindelhorn, its glacier ice glistening green where the sun caught it. Was there anything in the world more satisfyingly beautiful than white mountains against a clear blue sky, Cathryn wondered, whenever she looked across the valley, pausing to take in that beauty anew, which she did innumerable times a day.

"Is it a difficult mountain to climb?" she asked Francis, a little wistfully one sunny morning, as they toiled together up a snow-slope. They both stopped and leaned on their ski-sticks and looked across the valley.

"The Drindelhorn? It depends which side you tackle it, I believe. This side, by way of the east ridge, it's fairly easy, by all accounts. According to the guide-book there is a spot near the summit which is 'a little nasty', whatever that may mean!"

"It's a 'little nasty' making the hand-traverse on the *mauvais pas*, but I hung on . . ."

"This would be something a bit different. The Pillar and the Needle are stiff, but they're straightforward—they keep to the rules! You can either go up them like a fly up a wall, or you can't go up at all. You haven't got ice and snow to cope with, or the sort of wind you get on a high peak. The weather is such an enormous factor on a high mountain, and it's apt to wash out the rules."

"I'm sure I could manage it, all the same. I've got to begin somewhere. Couldn't I begin with the Drindelhorn next spring or summer?"

He laughed. "You do persist, don't you, darling? I don't promise. We neither of us know what we'll be doing next spring or summer—need we have all that over again?"

"I'm sorry, Francis. It's naughty of me. It's so lovely being here now that it's ungrateful of me to be thinking about any time but the present. I'm not really ungrateful. It was lovely of you to bring me here. I don't care about Switzerland any more, if I can come back here."

"You don't need me for the Drindelhorn, you know. There are always guides."

"What a dreary idea, to go climbing with a guide!"

"John and I often have a guide."

"But that's different, isn't it? You've got each other. But just oneself and a guide would be—well, *triste*!"

He smiled. "I suppose so." There were times when she was such a little girl, he thought, instead of the now much-discussed young tempera painter, Miss Cathryn Sable, who was to have an exhibition of her pictures in London in the spring, following on her Paris success.

"I would never climb without you," Cathryn declared, and there was such finality in the statement that there was no more to be said on the subject.

She could have climbed on Great Gable and Scafell many times during the past few years with Steven. When she had been at Crag House soon after his wedding she had watched him and Honor set out, Steven with the rope over his shoulder, for a day on the rocks. They had invited her to come with them, but she had refused. If you had had great happiness in doing one particular thing with one particular person, she thought, you could never get any pleasure from doing it with anyone else. She couldn't imagine herself climbing with anyone but Francis, and since he had begun going to Switzerland with John Framley he hadn't wanted her. Perhaps, she thought sadly, she would never stand on the Great Gable traverse again, never again scramble up into the 'Dress Circle' and watch the roped parties going up the Needle like flies up a wall—or be one of the flies herself; never again negotiate the difficult rock face of Scafell Pinnacle, or make the hand-traverse over the *mauvais pas* on the Pillar Rock; never again battle with winds so fierce that at times you had to crouch low and hold on to the rocks; never again stand above great white seas of cloud, thick waves folding and refolding, forming and dissolving and reshaping, the green and brown earth completely shut off, invisible, even the stones underfoot become part of this ethereal world of sun and wind and changing cloud. She could have it all again by going with someone else, or by going alone, but she did not want it, except with Francis. If she did not climb the Drindelhorn with him she would not climb it at all, however many times she might come back to the Tyrol. Now she did not ask for anything ambitious—for the Matterhorn or Jungfrau or Mont Blanc, or any Alp; the Drindelhorn had no Alpine grandeur, but it was the mountain she had painted into her picture of 'Saint Francis', and for that there was no explanation on any material plane, but there was in her a slow unfolding of belief in a knowledge transcending reason. Since the talk with her mother at the time of her father's death she had given no hint of this to anyone, nor discussed it any further with her mother, but it escaped into her painting; it was the essence of the quality of spirituality in her work.

The elderly Frau and Herr Amanshauser who owned the *Gasthaus* took a great liking to their young English guests. They had four grown-up children, all away from home, and it was good to have young people in the house again; in the summer, of course, they had many, but then they were too busy to heed them, with visitors coming for meals all the time, as well as those staying in the house. Now they could be all one family together, and it was like having Johann and Lotte at home again. Johann and Lotte were the two unmarried ones, they explained. Lotte was about the same age as Miss Sable; Franz came between her and Johann, but Franz was married, as was Heide, the youngest. The two unmarried ones lived and worked away from home, Lotte in Vienna, Johann in Salzburg, but both were coming home for Christmas. Then they would really be a family! Mr. Francis and Miss Cathryn would take the place of Franz and Heide and they would have a happy Christmas, all one family together. . . .

They had no idea that Mr. Francis was a well-known and highly successful English author, or that Miss Cathryn had already caused a stir as a painter, but they gathered from Francis —who spoke bad German, but spoke it fluently—that he was interested in books and that his sister 'painted a little'. The Amanshausers were delighted with this information; Johann worked in a bookshop, so he and Mr. Francis should get on well together; also Johann spoke good English, so would be able to converse with Miss Cathryn, who had no German. Lotte had no English, but she spoke good French—though it really would not matter what language Lotte spoke, they assured him, for she laughed and sang so much, was altogether so gay, that her conversation hardly counted.

Francis listened to all this with grave misgivings. The girl, he thought, sounded frightful—all that laughing and singing and gaiety! She probably giggled and yodelled and coquetted at one and the same time; Johann was probably merely a pious bore. The Austrians were lighter on the hand than the Germans, of course, but even so . . .

"Must we be roped in for this ghastly family party on Christmas Eve?" he inquired of Cathryn. "Couldn't we go off out for the day and spend the night in Zell-am-See, or go on to Salzburg?"

"I don't see why you should assume it'll be ghastly," Cathryn protested, "but even if it is it won't hurt us to be amiable for the one evening. You can see how much it means to the Amanshausers, and they've been sweet to us."

Francis sighed. "All this Christian charity! But another thing, you know, these people are Catholics—Christmas isn't the bank-holiday guzzle for them it is for us! Frau Amanshauser's making a Crib—I got a glimpse of it when I went into the kitchen this morning for the sandwiches. That sort of thing isn't up our street! We're bound to say or do the wrong thing—I am, anyhow!"

"Ordinary good manners should see us through, surely?"

"You don't suppose they'll want to drag us off to Mass on Christmas morning?"

"Of course not. Why should they? Did mother ever try to drag us off, as you call it, when we were at home? What are you so frightened of?"

"An orgy of sentimentality! It's as bad in its own way as the English guzzle. In fact I'm not sure that it's not worse—the sins of the spirit are always worse than the sins of the flesh Isn't that good Catholic doctrine? The flesh is weak and bound to sin, but the spirit ought to know better—isn't that the argument? Whether it is or not it's my own firm belief. The carnal sins don't touch one's inner self—one's integrity. But the sins of the spirit —things like humbug and hypocrisy, all the forms of insincerity and self-deception, strike at the very roots of it! And sentimentality is one of the deadlier sins!"

"I should have thought it one of the least important! After all if people like to wallow it doesn't do any real harm!"

"Oh, but it does, it does! It's degrading, it's besmirching! It's all so bogus—so false! It makes people false in relation to each other and false to themselves. In families it's a smothering, destroying, *awful* thing—like drowning in a sea of treacle!"

Cathryn laughed. "Mr. Francis Sable makes it abundantly clear that he strongly disapproves of the nauseating sin of sentimentality! But really, Francis darling, I don't see why you should assume that the Amanshausers intend celebrating Christmas Eve with an orgy of sentimentality. There'll be a Christmas tree, and lighted candles, and I suppose we shall drink mulled wine—it'll just be simple and homely, I imagine!"

"And darling Johann will be there, and laughing Lotte, and that sweet Miss Cathryn taking the place of darling Heide, and the nice Mr. Francis deputising for our beloved Franz—and how sweet that our two names are really the same! Oh, my dear, can't you just *see* how sweet and cosy and gooey and awful it's going to be? If I have to be there I shall get drunk, and then I shall probably take laughing Lotte out into the snow and rape her!"

"If you behave badly I shall never forgive you—never, never, never! Promise you'll be good, Francis!"

"You know I never make promises. You don't suppose they'll sing carols, do you? *Stille Nacht, heilige Nacht*, and all that?"

"Probably. What's wrong with that? We'll give them the old Catholic *Adeste Fideles* in return! Don't be such a heathen, Francis!"

"Darling, I'm going to Salzburg for Christmas! I can't *bear* family Christmases! You shall stay here and play Christmas trees and carols and happy-families with Poppa and Momma Amanshauser, and Lotte and Johann, but your big brother has remembered a very dear cousin in Salzburg who would be dreadfully hurt and lonely if the nice Mr. Francis didn't go and spend Christmas with him—or shall I make it her?"

Cathryn was not listening. Whilst Francis had been running on there had been the sound of a car driven up to the front door of the house, and Cathryn—a little bored with Francis's tirade——had got up and gone over to the window. The young woman who stepped out was very strikingly dressed. She wore a full-skirted coat of wine-coloured velvet, with fur at the hem, neck, and wrists. On her dark head she wore a round fur hat. A most dashing-looking young woman, Cathryn thought, and called out to Francis, ignoring his question:

"Look! A Russian princess! Straight out of the fair scene in *Petrouchka*!"

Francis came and peered over her shoulder. The young woman looked up to the upper windows of the house as if expecting to see someone she knew. She had warm colouring and wide dark eyes. She looked happy and excited. She was smiling.

Francis murmured:

> 'He said, "She has a lovely face,
>   God in His mercy give her grace . . ."'

He blew her a kiss.

"Francis!" Cathryn exclaimed, and tried to pull him away from the window. But she was too late. The young woman had seen him and his gesture—and she kissed her hand to him in return, with the most charming smile and the utmost grace. Then she swung round whilst the front door opened and both the Amanshausers ran out and Frau Amanshauser swept her into her arms and pressed her against her large bosom, kissing her on both cheeks and crying to her, excitedly.

"Well I'm damned!" said Francis. "Laughing Lotte!" He smiled at Cathryn. "I think perhaps that cousin in Salzburg will survive Christmas without me after all. . . ."

10

Lotte Amanshauser did not rouse any very strong emotion in Francis, but he liked her gaiety and good-nature, and he thought her extremely attractive, in a flashing, vivid Viennese fashion. He found her a great deal more entertaining than he ever had the self-consciously intellectual and literary Merrilee Browne. Lotte had no pretensions to intellectuality, though she was not stupid. She was buyer to the dress department of a big Viennese stores, and her work took her a good deal to Paris. She loved clothes, and brought real artistry to the selection of them, whether for herself or for her firm. She was surprised to learn that Cathryn was an artist and yet—apparently—took so little interest in clothes.

"Does she not want to express beauty in herself as well as in her pictures?" she demanded. "What she has is in good taste, yes, but it is not clever or amusing, it has no *chic*."

"A woman who is naturally lovely does not need to be *chic*," Francis suggested. "You would be just as lovely whatever you wore—and loveliest of all with nothing on at all!"

She flushed slightly. "That is something you should not say to me, Monsieur."

"I am sorry. But I thought the truth was always acceptable to a woman when it was complimentary."

"Not when it is offensive to her modesty, Monsieur."

That, he thought, was charming. Coming from Cathryn it would have had no special value—though Cathryn, of course, had an artist's natural acceptance of the beauty of the nude—but coming from this sophisticated, worldly creature gave it a curious piquancy. He suspected that her sophistication was purely superficial and that actually she was every whit as much a 'good girl' as Sue Lester, or Cathryn. Ah, but Cathryn was more than that; Cathryn had a deep fundamental goodness. Cathryn was something apart. Sue had no real moral scruples, he thought; what passed as her virtue was really nothing but her pride. The middle-class morality of not making oneself 'cheap'. His heart hardened a little with the thought of her. She was kind and generous in so many ways, but mean with herself. Did he judge her too harshly? Perhaps. But of her pride there was no doubt. And if one greatly loved had one such pride? She would say that never having greatly loved he was not in a position to know. That he greatly loved Cathryn would not count with her. But for him love was one thing, sex was another. He had never yet known the fusion of the two. He might have, he reflected, a little bitterly, with Sue, if she had given him the chance. Lotte was more honest, he thought; she was virtuous out of moral and religious conviction; you could not affront Sue's modesty; you could only hurt her pride. Poor Sue! Why didn't she make up her mind? You had either to be a good Christian or a good Pagan; there was no half-way house. At least there was, if you insisted, but it was a very draughty and uncomfortable place, inhabited only by uncomfortable people who didn't know whether they were going or coming . . . like Sue herself.

But why think of Sue when the sun was brilliant on the crisp dry snow, and Lotte Amanshauser went flying past you like a streak of scarlet, graceful as a bird on the wing? How much more sensible to speed after her and collide with her, so that you both tumbled in the deep snow at the bottom of the run, which gave you an excuse for kissing her. . . . She would pretend, of course, that it was no excuse, but she would laugh, with a flash of most wonderful teeth. And, blessedly, she would not take you seriously. Oh, that terrible deadly seriousness of intellectual women! Even when they were frankly Hedonist, like Merrilee Browne; it might be only temporary, but for the time being you belonged to them, body and soul, and they insisted on 'belonging' to you. They wanted to be all cosy and intimate—just because they bedded down with you. It was frightful. Lotte, he thought, would never be possessive; she wouldn't presume. He chuckled at the thought of how all the feminists would rise in a monstrous regiment of emancipated women at such an expression of male sexual vanity. Lotte wasn't a feminist, however; she was content to be feminine. Her charm lay in that, and when she fell in love it would be her glory. She did not coquette; that the male found her attractive she had known since adolescence, and if the amiable young Englishman had been indifferent to her she would have run to the mirror to see what was wrong with her complexion, her hat, her dress. Male compliments and amorousness sometimes went a little too far and had to be rebuked, but even that she could do gracefully. She was unashamedly something which all the emancipated post-war women professed to despise, a man's woman. . . . So was Sue, he thought, if only she would allow herself to be—but for her damned pride. It was odd, he thought, how his thoughts kept coming back to her, always a little angrily. Something in him resented her.

Johann Amanshauser was as taken with Cathryn as Francis was with Lotte, but from a somewhat different angle. He was a serious young man, but he was not solemn, as Francis had imagined him. He had the same deep natural religiousness as Cathryn. It was a quality which he quickly recognised in her. She was for him, quite simply, the most intelligent girl he had ever talked with.

He had young men friends with whom he discussed matters closest to his heart, but no young woman friend. . . . But here was a girl, not herself a Catholic, yet who was acquainted with the lives of a number of saints, who felt herself close to the Church, yet awaited the grace of conversion. This to him was tremendously exciting—a much more intense excitement than Francis derived from his laughing kisses with Lotte in the snow.

Cathryn liked Johann more than she had thought it possible to like anyone who was not Francis. Had he not been preoccupied with saving her soul for God he could very easily have tipped the scales over just that very little which was all that was needed to make her in love with him. She knew that what she felt for Johann was quite different from what she felt for Francis, and she had never felt anything in the least like it for anyone else. He was quite different from Francis in every way; he was as dark as Francis was fair; his face was as expressive as Francis's was withdrawn; it was a finely drawn face, with deep-set eyes and a mobile mouth. It was an essentially serious face, yet it smiled readily; physically there was the same suggestion of vitality in Johann's masculinity as in Lotte's femininity, but whereas Lotte's vitality expressed itself in physical exuberance, in her gaiety, in dancing and singing, in ski-ing and skating, in general high spirits, Johann's was expressed in his quick lively mind. He was greatly drawn to the Jesuits. He saw them as the intellectuals of the Church, the philosophers. He was a tremendous admirer of the German-Jesuit philosopher, Father Przywara, and of the philosopher-saint, Augustine. He had liked Latin when he was at school and had continued his study of it afterwards, and when he discovered St. Augustine he believed that it had been God's will working in him that he should make these studies, that he might read such inspired and inspiring works as *De Civitate Dei* and the *Confessions* in the original noble Latin.

He told Cathryn all this and very much more with the eagerness which was part of his charm. He talked to her of St. Augustine when they rested on their ski-sticks on the snow-slopes, and when they trudged up the snow-slopes; he talked to her of St. Augustine when they sat in the sunshine on the wooden terrace of a *Hütte* which supplied refreshments to the ski-ers. Cathryn felt the bright strong mountain sun reflected from the snow pour burning on her face and bared arms, and the faith that precedes reason and surpasses it burning in the soul of Johann Amanshauser and reflected like sunlight off snow into her own soul. This was the revelation for which she had waited; here was the ultimate perspective whose end was Eternity and whose light was the radiance of that Supreme Good which is God. But in all directions new perspectives opened up in this radiance. It was as though she, the artist, so dependent upon vision, was seeing for the first time; now her vision was limitless because it reached to God, to that Truth which is absolute and immutable.

A dark fire glowed in Johann's eyes as he unfolded for her the endless avenues of Augustinian metaphysics. From faith to understanding; from understanding to faith—and God had sent him to her to guide her, but given him only a few days in which to accomplish the task; then she must go away, and perhaps they would never meet again on this earth, but if she had found her way—and he was sure she would, for the desire was in her—they would meet in the life everlasting.

"But we shall meet again here, among these mountains." Cathryn insisted. "I know it! I must go back to Paris after Christmas, but I can come back, and I will!"

He shook his head. "Surrender yourself to God's will. It may be that you will return and it may be not. You will write to me, perhaps, and I shall answer."

She cried, eagerly, "I shall write to you! No one has ever helped me as you have. Isn't it strange that when at last Francis and I go to the mountains together we should come here? It was always Switzerland we talked about and that I dreamed of, and then suddenly he decided on this place!"

He smiled. "That you find it strange shows that you have still some way to go. As St. Augustine said, to guide to the way is one thing, to guide in it another. I am perhaps the lamp through which the light is reflected; I am not the light. But you will find the way, for your feet have long been set in it. For you the night of the heart is ending, for you have seen the Dayspring from on high. . . ."

His eyes were on the white mountain as he said it, and there seemed to her a light in his face. She wanted to paint it in all its transparent luminousness—the light of the illumined spirit, the light on the white mountain, the light dissolving the long night of the heart. . . .

Francis and Lotte came along the crowded veranda of the *Hütte* where the ski-ers sat at little tables, drinking coffee, talking, laughing, many of the men stripped to the waist, browning their bodies in the sun. Lotte wore her scarlet ski-suit; Francis wore a bright blue sweater with his dark trousers; they made a decorative pair; Lotte was holding his arm and they talked and laughed animatedly as they came along the terrace.

"Let's all go down to the village and drink mulled wine," Francis suggested. "It is, after all, Christmas Eve!"

"We'll ski down," Lotte said, "and whoever falls first will pay for the wine."

"Poor Cathryn," Francis murmured.

But as it turned out it wasn't Cathryn after all, but Francis himself, because he was, as Cathryn was quick to point out to him, 'showing off'.

But Johann, who was an expert, knew that Francis bungled his Christiania deliberately. . . .

II

Christmas Eve was not at all the orgy of sentimentality Francis had dreaded. Frau Amanshauser stood lighted candles in every window of the house, and the candle-lit tree in the window of the café. A number of people came in during the evening, driving up in sleighs, or arriving on skis, and drank mulled wine, admired the Christmas tree and the Crib and sat round smoking and talking. Lotte played the piano, and the entire company—it numbered about a dozen at that time—sang *Stille Nacht*. They sang it so well and with such obvious deep feeling that Francis could not find it in his heart to be impatient. Lotte sang a few carols solo; she had a thin sweet voice, and she sang without self-consciousness or affectation. Frau Amanshauser, her large person clothed in purple silk, with a good deal of old-fashioned lace cascading over her bosom, and her hair, which had been in curlers all the morning, most impressively arranged, dispensed small sweet cakes and slices from a large spiced cake. Herr Amanshauser sat

in a high-backed chair with a large tankard of beer beside him—
he considered mulled wine effeminate—and smoked a long pipe,
on the lidded china bowl of which was painted a picture of the
Schloss at Salzburg. When Lotte had finished with carols she
delighted Francis by playing Mozart's *Rondo in A Minor* very
charmingly. Cathryn sat under the light with a sketch-book and
make sketches of various people, but of Johann she made a
number. Johann sat watching her, and his heart ached with love
for her, and he longed to take her in his arms; it was a strange and
bewildering sensation, for he had never felt like that about any
woman before and it troubled him. It could not be sin to love
with such passionate tenderness, and yet he had schooled himself
since he was seventeen to the idea that for him love must mean
love of God, love of his neighbour. He had formed a certain
habit of mind out of this self-discipline, and it was so strong in
him that though he was immediately alive to Cathryn's white and
gold, Fillipino Lippi Virgin loveliness, he was still more strongly
aware of the emanations of her spirit. What he was quite unaware
of was how little it would take from him—the touch of his hand
on her arm in a gesture of intimacy—to break down her own
reserves, against which breakdown his own defences would have
been utterly inadequate. Without any such gesture from him she
would never overcome her own habit of mind and acknowledge
that what she felt for him was more than love as she had always
understood it, but what she had never expected to feel, which is
in-loveness. When he smiled at her, with deep tenderness, she
had the sensation of her blood melting, and of her heart pausing
and listening, waiting . . . for a sign. But he did not give the sign.
For him, self-trained in the Augustinian school, love must water
not the old deep-rooted carnal desires, buried out of sight, but
the seeds of the spirit, that the garden of Cathryn Sable's soul
might blossom as the rose . . . to the glory of God.

Francis, also watching her, thought, She is on the verge of
being in love with Johann, but it is St. Augustine who will win
her . . . for the Church. He found, to his surprise, that he was no
longer opposed to the idea. It would make their mother happy,
and if it was what Cathryn wanted, well, people had to fulfil
themselves in the way most natural to them. She had been more
than half-way to the Church for some time. But to him, too, it

seemed strange that by his sudden decision to come to this obscure little place in the Salzkammergut he had brought her straight to the one person who could quicken her steps along the rest of the way.

It did not surprise him that after the music Cathryn accompanied the Amanshausers to midnight Mass.

He asked her on Christmas morning, "Has Johann disposed of the last of your doubts?"

"Through St. Augustine—yes."

"Shall you receive instruction when we get back to Paris?"

"I shall go to England. There is an Irish Jesuit priest in London I specially want to consult. Johann told me about him and recommended that I should approach him."

"Then you will stay on and arrange your exhibition, and Montparnasse will know you no more for a time?"

"I probably won't ever go back. Mother and I could perhaps take a small house in London and furnish it from Crag House— she only has that furnished apartment in Paris and she would like her own things about her again—she was saying so only recently. She only went to Paris for my sake. She would much sooner be in England."

"But London! How could you bear it after Paris?"

"There's that terrible *fin de siècle* feeling about Paris now."

"D'you think you won't feel it in London too? Don't tell me you're going to live in Chelsea in a poky little converted working-class house with the front door conscientiously painted blue?"

"Preferably in a tall narrow house with a crinoline balcony and a vine, and a view of the river. Will you come and stay sometimes?"

"Perhaps. Will the place be strewn with Jesuits?"

"Oh, of course, darling, *strewn* with them! And you shall come and feed the gulls from the balcony and play at being St. Francis. . . ."

He looked at her sharply. "You're fond of that theme, aren't you? Are you trying to auto-suggest me into piety, or what?"

"You wouldn't be a good subject for auto-suggestion, Francis darling!"

"Then why cast me for the rôle?"

"It made a good picture, Francis, and the mountain came true!"

It was their first reference to the painting.

He said, almost angrily, "It was a good picture, Cathryn, but it has no more to do with me than the mountain has to do with you! Now stop talking nonsense and get your boots on and let's get up on to the snow!"

12

The Amanshausers parted with the Sables with reluctance, and many injunctions to come again soon; there would always be room for them, they declared, and if they came in the spring before the tourist season began they would have some fine picnics in the mountains.

"It is beautiful here when all the apple-blossom is out," Johann told Cathryn.

"If you could come at Easter," Frau Amanshauser coaxed, "Johann and Lotte will be here."

Francis translated this into English for Cathryn, who turned to Johann, smiling. "That would be lovely!"

He returned her smile. "If you could come at Easter it would be very fine. Perhaps by then you will have been received into the Church and make your Easter Communion here. It is the most beautiful time of all in the Church. But you cannot promise to be ready by then, and no one knows what may happen."

"It's what I am always telling her," Francis said. "But she will never accept it!"

"I wish life weren't so uncertain—so unpredictable! I like to be able to say 'Next spring I will do this,' and 'Next summer I will do that,' and feel confident that I will."

Aware that Lotte was being shut out, Francis dropped into French. "Personally," he declared, "I enjoy the uncertainty of life—I like the adventure of living on those terms!"

"But it means so many disappointments," Cathryn protested.

"But surprises too!" He turned to Lotte. "Do you like to be certain of everything in advance, Mademoiselle?"

She laughed. "Oh, but no, Monsieur! I, too, like surprises! I cannot agree with Mademoiselle that uncertainties mean many disappointments; it is surely planning this and that which brings them. For myself, I make no plans, but I am being constantly pleasantly surprised. Such as by the visit of yourself and your sister here this Christmas, Monsieur!"

He smiled and bowed. "Perhaps one day I will surprise you by turning up in Vienna and taking you to dinner. Would you like that?"

"If it happens you will see. And if it doesn't happen, Monsieur, it is still a very sweet thought."

"Then, *Aufwiedersehen*, Lotte."

"*Aufwiedersehen*—Francis."

She gave him her hand and he raised it to his lips. They smiled at each other.

Cathryn and Johann shook hands, simply. They said *Aufwiedersehen* but they did not smile, and they turned from each other abruptly.

Frau Amanshauser kissed Cathryn on both cheeks. Cathryn did not need to understand German to know that she was repeating her injunctions that they should both return in the spring—*im Frühling*.

Cathryn was pensive for the greater part of the journey back to Paris. Francis wondered whether she was brooding on Johann —or St. Augustine. Actually her thoughts were a fusion of both, since she could not contemplate the endless perspectives of Augustinian philosophy without thinking of the man who had opened them up for her in all those mountain mornings of sun and snow. She speculated, too, upon the Irish Jesuit, Father Connor, whom Johann had recommended as an authority on St. Augustine. It seemed to her that not merely were new avenues of thought opening up but a whole new material world, for she was resolved upon leaving Paris. She had reached, she felt, the end of a phase.

Francis was also aware that Cathryn had reached the end of a phase. He envied her that, but Paris was too lovely a city, and too congenial a city, for him to wish to live anywhere else in Europe; if you were going to be attached to a city, he thought, Paris was the obvious one to attach yourself to; it was the most civilised of cities—with Vienna as a good second. But France was the fountainhead of European culture, and in Paris you felt yourself part of that great free-flowing fountain. All that was most interesting in music, painting, literature, and the ballet—which embraced so many of the arts—was coming from Paris. He found it difficult to understand why any artist—using the term in its broadest sense—who was free to live in Paris should choose to live anywhere else. And apart from its physical beauty Paris was a good city to live in—good to work in and good to play in . . . despite the American occupation! But Cathryn had to follow her own daemon, and the following, apparently, led to London, and an Irish Jesuit priest, and all hull-down in the wake of St. Augustine.

He himself returned to Paris rested but restless. He no longer had the feeling of mental and physical exhaustion with which he had left the city, but he was aware of an inner weariness.

He said to Sue, "At times I feel like the girl in the Peter Arno drawing—the one who says to the 'sugar-daddy', 'You're so good to me and I'm so tired of it all!'"

"Who would you say was your 'sugar-daddy'?" she inquired. "Paris? Or the great British and American publics who read your books?"

"Everything. The life I've made for myself. What is called my success."

"You'll hardly deny it is success?"

"In material terms, of course."

"You've got the kudos as well as the cash," she pointed out. "What more do you want?"

He groaned. "Oh Lord, this conversation's getting like one of those frightful conversations that earnest Americans involve one in—you know, that awful moment when the creature leans forward and asks you very solemnly, in the best Wellsian fashion, 'What do you want from life? What are you up to? What do you need for happiness?'"

"Why don't you go to America? You could do a lecture-tour and have an enormous success with all the literary societies and women's clubs. You'd probably sell some film rights too, and end up in Hollywood!"

"I'd been thinking of it. Everyone tells me that New York under prohibition is madly gay—cocktails out of soup-bowls and all that. One might get a satirical novel out of it. Have another, by the way?"

'Another' was a champagne-cocktail. They were sitting on the terrace of the Dôme, glass-screened off from the cold winds and heated by braziers. It was one of the virtues of Paris, Francis always thought, that you could 'sit out' in all weathers. The French were civilised; not a doubt of it.

Over the second cocktail he told her, "I have acquired a secretary, by the way. He attached himself to me. He's American and very serious and a terrific fan of mine. His name is John B. Puckhurst, but he says everyone calls him Junnie, so I call him that too, though with an English accent. I don't know yet whether he's an asset or a liability."

She laughed. "I know Johnnie. His family stopped his allowance because they said he wasn't doing any good. He was supposed to be working at the Sorbonne, but they got wind of the fact that he was just fooling around the Quarter, so they said come home or we cut you off. He let them cut him off, and he's been pestering everyone for a job for weeks. He asked me for an introduction to you, but I headed it off."

"That was comradely of you! But he dispensed with the introduction and came up to me one day at the Lilas. I stood him a few drinks and we got mellow together, and the next I knew he was opening my mail and banging on my typewriter. Oh and bringing me coffee in bed and turning on the bath and answering the 'phone and telling everyone I was still in Austria—only he did that once too often, for Cathryn rang up and she said 'So am I', and came round. He certainly relieves me of a lot of the fan-mail, for what he doesn't approve of he just quietly does away with. He won't have me worried. Isn't it sweet?"

"He'll land you in trouble one of these days."

"The most disastrous thing about him is that he has no humour and is apt to take one quite literally. There is a frightful woman-fan who keeps pestering me with her quite incredible verses. I told Johnnie that whenever she sent anything he was to write quite politely and say Mr. Francis Sable asks me to say he is very sorry but has no time to read your revolting verses and that you know what to do with them. Of course I meant him to put it in more parliamentary language, but I saw the carbon-copy and he had said precisely that. Signed yours very truly John B. Puckhurst, Sec. I haven't heard from her since, though—unless of course Johnnie just destroyed it—so perhaps it's all for the best. But my publishers were frightfully annoyed when their legal adviser wanted some alterations I wasn't prepared to make, and I told Johnnie to tell them that their solicitor could go hang himself—only hang wasn't the word I used. Anyhow it wasn't what Johnnie wrote to them. They wrote very frigidly and said they had passed 'a modified version' of my secretary's remarks on to their solicitor. . . . Well, that's Junnie. Maybe he'll shape all right when I get him trained. Would you care for the loan of him when I go to America?"

"What on earth would I do with him?"

"Paint him, draw him, let him bring you coffee and answer the 'phone. He's not at all shy. He went round the schools posing in the nude to earn the honest franc before he decided to make me his bread-and-butter. He's also been photographed for hair-lotion advertisements, also toothpastes—he has the usual American excessively good teeth, if you remember."

"I don't, but anyhow I don't want him, and I'm sure he's a mistake in your life, Francis."

"He's wonderful copy. He fascinates me. I find him quite unfathomable."

"You'll probably write a cruel, brilliant book about him."

"Probably. Whatever one wrote about him would be cruel, unavoidably."

"Not if you had a little heart, Francis—if you could see him as he really is, a rather pathetic little creature——"

Francis gave her an amused look.

"I didn't know champagne could affect one like that, Sue darling—I thought only gin made one maudlin. Let's go back and see what the pathetic little creature has arranged for supper. I told him our guest would be Miss Sue Lester, the famous artist. He loves celebrities. I ought to warn you he calls me Mr. Francis, Sir. I suggested that as between old collegians he could cut all that out and just call me Francis, but he said it wouldn't be right. For his sake, now, I'm sorry I didn't inherit the title, but it means a lot to him that he can write home to his folks—he always calls them that—and tell them he is working for Mr. Francis Sable, the famous English author, younger son of the late Sir John Sable, Bart."

Johnnie was very happy indeed to be working for Mr. Francis Sable, the famous English author. He had an unbounded admiration for the works of Mr. Sable. Mr. Francis Sable, Mr. Aldous Huxley, Mr. D. H. Lawrence, these were his gods, and in that order. It would have been worthwhile to have come to Europe if only to have met Francis Sable; and now here he was living in his apartment, privileged to serve him—to relieve him of the burden of his mail, and to make his valuable life as easy and comfortable as possible. Everything he did for his employer he did out of his admiration for him as a writer; he had dedicated himself to the cause of sparing the great Francis Sable all the tedium and irritation of mundane matters, in order that he might be free to write further masterpieces. No task was therefore too menial for him to perform. When he declared that he felt himself honoured to be allowed to serve Francis Sable he meant it, quite simply. He hoped that in time Mr. Sable would recognise his devotion, make him his literary executor and his official biographer.

Francis was quite well aware of all this, but whereas it seemed to Sue rather touching, it merely amused him. Cathryn had warned him, "You'll never get rid of him, you know. If you ever sacked him it would break his heart." He had laughed. "Hearts don't break so easily," he had said. "All that would happen would be that he would decide that my works were over-rated, that he had grown out of them, and then attach himself to another of his literary idols. I'm not a person to him; I'm merely an intellect."

But that is where he was wrong. Johnnie admired Francis as a person. 'Fine' was the word he used about him. He loved him as much as one man may love another without being homosexual —and Johnnie was not that. He was attracted to girls, but unfortunately the ones whom he thought attractive found him boring, because of his deadly, humourless seriousness, and the girls who were attracted to him because he was their idea of an intellectual he considered stupid; so that it was difficult for him, particularly as he was of an emotional disposition. No girl could command John B. Puckhurst's love unless she was a one-hundred per cent admirer of Francis Sable, and as Francis Sable was a man's writer rather than a woman's that further complicated

matters. He was inclined to think that without being a homosexual he was by way of becoming a misogynist. He had an idea,
too, that this was in the best Sable tradition, since though it was
true Mr. Sable had affairs with women it was apparent that he
did not fall in love with them. At least, he was nearly thirty and
had not so far done so. He hoped he would not become emotionally involved with Miss Lester; he had heard her criticising Mr.
Sable as a writer; besides, she was such a mediocre painter. . . .

The evening Sue came to supper he had taken a great deal of
trouble. Although he did not approve of Miss Lester, he would
always take trouble for any guest of Mr. Sable's. He bought some
pink roses for the table—only half a dozen; he would not wish to
be extravagant with Mr. Sable's money—put out the best lace
mats, and cleaned the silver—regretting that it was not better,
but then of course Mr. Sable had only taken the place furnished;
there was no doubt the most beautiful Georgian silver in Mr.
Sable's ancestral home. He knew nothing about cooking before
he came to work for Mr. Sable, but when he found that his
employer liked sometimes to eat at home he bought a selection
of cookery books, and after studying them decided that cooking
was Nothing Much. He attempted only simple things and because
everything he did was a labour of love he did those few things
carefully and well. It was quite simple, he found, to roast a
chicken and serve it up with bread-sauce and a thin gravy—
the chip potatoes you bought in packets and merely heated up in
the oven. No one ever guessed, and guests almost invariably
exclaimed, 'What marvellous chip-potatoes! How clever!'
So far no one had asked him how they were done. . . . Sweets he
never attempted; Mr. Sable's guests had to content themselves
with dessert and an assortment of cheeses, but as he always
produced a good assortment of both the guests were very well
satisfied. Mr. Sable looked after the wines himself, of course, but
Johnnie always watched what was served so that in time he would
know about wines too. He was always invited to eat with Mr.
Sable and his guests, but he never did. He felt that they would
prefer to be alone; also he usually had matters to attend to in
what he always referred to as 'my kitchen'. He always joined the
party for coffee. "But you *will* always tell me, won't you, Mr.
Francis, sir," he pleaded, "when you want to be alone with any-

one? I mean a *tête-à-tête* with a lady or anything like that—I can always busy myself in the study. There are always letters awaiting attention."

Gravely Francis had promised him that he would tell him should he ever wish a *tête-à-tête* with a lady, or, he could not resist adding, 'anything like that'. The phrase was, he thought, so deliciously ambiguous, and, as Peter Arno would say, 'fraught with interest'. He felt he understood for the first time the expression, 'a pregnant phrase'. In some moods he found Johnnie 'a great joy'.

He was in such a mood the night Sue came to supper, baiting him, very subtly, so that Johnnie did not know he was being baited, and leading him on, in a fashion which Sue regarded as completely damnable. When Johnnie was out of the room, making the coffee, she said in a low voice, "You're being beastly to that boy, Francis. Can't you see that he takes everything you say terribly seriously, and that he adores you?"

"I can't resist the one and I can't bear the other! The combination of the two is too much for me."

"Then you should get rid of him. You'll go too far one day and he'll realise what you're up to. He might kill himself—or anything!"

"Really, Sue! You do strike the high note at times, don't you? He would do nothing so interesting, I assure you. He has the soul of a butler! An English butler, at that!"

She said, angrily, "Why should butlers be assumed to have inferior souls?"

"Because, Sue darling, they couldn't bear to be butlers if they hadn't! Junnie has been to what he calls kulledge, and he fancies himself as literary, and he calls himself my secretary, but he's really nothing but a manservant. Watch him when he comes into the room—so unobtrusive; the perfect butler!"

"You're a beast at times, Francis."

"It's better than being a sentimentalist, anyhow. I'm not a Shavian, but I quite agree with Tanner—it was Tanner, wasn't it?—when he said, 'I don't mind a cynical devil, but I really cannot stand a sentimental one.' "

There was a discreet knock, and then Johnnie entered with the coffee tray. He set it down on a low table beside Sue.

"Do join us, won't you?" Francis said.

"Thank you very much—if I'm not intruding."

Francis said shortly, "If you're invited you're obviously not intruding. Will you pour, Sue?" He turned to Johnnie again.

"Would you say that you had a soul?"

Johnnie assumed a thoughtful expression.

"It would rather depend on one's definition of soul, wouldn't you say?"

"Defining as soul all the non-physical part of oneself."

"Then one has mind and emotion," Johnnie said, eagerly. He loved intellectual discussion. "On the other hand the soul is generally assumed to be immortal, whereas mind and intellect obviously are not——"

"So that you would say that you have no soul, Johnnie—nothing to speak of, that is to say?" He turned to Sue. "I was right, you see."

Sue smiled at Johnnie. "Mr. Sable talks an awful lot of nonsense, don't you think?" Why had Francis to be such a swine? It was horrible to see the boy taking the bait, swallowing it, floundering, and Francis sitting on the bank, watching, waiting, with his amused, ironic smile.

Johnnie looked shocked. "I'd hardly say that, Miss Lester," he said, coldly.

Deliberately Sue upset her coffee. "Oh dear! Now look what I've done! I'm so sorry—do forgive me——"

Johnnie rushed away to fetch a cloth and she turned furiously to Francis.

"If you don't stop it I'm walking out—here and now!"

"Don't be silly, Sue. He loves it!"

Johnnie came back with a cloth and cleaned up the mess, then he said, "If you'll pardon me, Mr. Francis, sir, I think I should go and straighten up my kitchen now."

He would never forgive Miss Lester her insult to Mr. Sable, never! Spoiling everything, just as they were getting a really intellectual conversation going. Women were a curse. They had no intellect. It was women like Miss Lester who made men misogynists. He clattered the dishes into the sink. He hated Miss Lester.

13

In the spring Francis went to New York, leaving Johnnie in charge—like a faithful watch-dog, Sue thought, a little bitterly. Johnnie would attend to the letters that arrived in his employer's absence, type the manuscript of a new novel, and count the days until the great man returned. Then he would fill the apartment with roses, and every leaf on the chestnut trees in the Boulevard de l'Observatoire would burst out singing. Whenever he saw Sue Lester, which was quite often, at the shops or the cafés, he thought all over again how much he disliked her, and of her lack of appreciation of Francis Sable. Ah, but Miss Cathryn knew better; she had painted her brother as a saint. He was sorry Miss Cathryn had left Paris; with Mr. Francis away it would have been nice to have had some good long talks with her, some really intellectual conversations about art and literature, and the existence or otherwise of the soul—he could hear himself asking her, "What do you mean by mind, Miss Cathryn?" He loved conversations that bordered on the metaphysical—and on the inner and ultimate meaning of the writings of Mr. Francis Sable, with particular reference to his poetry, the alleged obscurity of which Mr. John B. Puckhurst strongly denied. Mr. Sable did not, after all, write for the masses, and all significant art was necessarily esoteric. 'Ultimate', 'esoteric' and 'significant' were words which figured largely in Mr. Puckhurst's vocabulary.

In London Cathryn and Lady Sable settled into a terrace house in South Kensington. It was a part of London they both loved; it had, as Cathryn said, both architecture and trees, and it could be somewhere on the Right bank of Paris. The house was small and pleasantly old-fashioned, with steps up to a pillared porch, and a small front garden with lilac bushes and a laburnum tree. At the back there were steps down to a walled and paved garden with a plane tree, and a few more lilac bushes, some box borders, tubbed bay-trees, and an ornamental though quite useless—in so shady a garden—sundial. The rooms of the house were high-ceilinged and well-proportioned, and when they were filled with furniture imported from Crag House they had that air of good taste which Lady Sable had missed in her *apartement meuble* in Paris. She felt that she had at last a real home of her own again.

In this house she was happier than she had ever been before, for against this background of material contentment, the satisfaction of her new home, and of having Cathryn with her, she had the profound happiness of the fact that Cathryn was regularly visiting Father Connor, receiving instruction. God had answered her dearest prayer; she had borne a child for the Church, and that child her ewe lamb. All the joy she had known at her daughter's birth returned to her, and she knew again the exultation of the soul that magnifies the Lord, its cup running over. When she eventually met Father Connor she found him *simpatico*. He was a distinguished-looking man of about fifty, with white hair, deep-set eyes of a startling blueness, a lean, brooding face, and considerable personal charm. Lady Sable found his air of distinction very gratifying, for in all matters, spiritual or temporal, she was convinced that it was always an advantage to deal with a 'gentleman'. She was a little wounded when Cathryn, to whom she made this comment on the Jesuit, accused her of snobbery. She protested that she was not a snob; she merely liked good manners and charm; it helped, she insisted; there were so many uncouth and graceless people with whom one had to deal. . . .

Cathryn thought of the brusque, ungracious Anna Kallinova, and what she supposed her mother would regard as the lack of polish in manner and manners of Johann Amanshauser, and was not convinced. It happened that Father Connor had a fine head—satisfactory to draw—and a kindly gracious manner, but it did not seem to her important; you could learn as readily from people who were brusque and curt, like Anna, or shy and tentative like Johann. Father Connor could have been bald and ordinary-looking, so far as she was concerned; given the same wisdom and sincerity and kindly patience she would still have liked and respected him. She felt drawn to him not by his distinguished appearance and charm of manner but the feeling of goodness in him—that fundamental goodness she also felt in Johann. She felt that she gained greatly by every visit to him, and not merely in the understanding of Catholic doctrine; she was convinced that even if he had never studied philosophy and theology he would still have had a deep understanding of human nature—of its inherent weaknesses and its spiritual needs. If only Francis would meet him for just one hour, she would think, surely then he would re-assess his present materialist values. . . . She talked of him sometimes to Father Connor.

"He has it in him to be so fine—both as a person and as a writer," she insisted, "but he has this purely materialist outlook— it's as though he wilfully blinds himself——"

The priest reminded her of St. Augustine's assertion, 'We need despair of no man so long as he lives', and added, "We will pray that he may be given the grace to see truth."

Cathryn was not ready to be received into the Church by Easter. Her conversion was complete before she left Austria; Johann had helped her to the faith that is essential to understanding, but with her lively inquiring mind, and her scrupulousness, understanding could not be for her other than a lengthy and painstaking process.

She wrote to Johann, sadly, that she feared she would not that year see the valley break into its foam of apple-blossom, nor hear Mass at Easter with him in the little church. She had made a vow that in spite of her longing to see him she would not go again to Mass as an outsider. "It is not that my faith wavers," she wrote him, "but that there is so much to understand. Perhaps I have too questioning a mind?" He replied to her, "St. Augustine answers your question—'It is . . . necessary that everything which is believed should be believed after thought has led the way; although belief itself is nothing, other than to think with assent. . . . Everyone who believes, thinks—both thinks in believing, and believes in thinking.' St. Augustine has further said, 'God forbid that we should believe there to be no need to accept or to seek a reason for what we believe, since it would not be possible to believe if we had not rational souls.' See also St. Peter on the subject of reason and belief, and the Prophet Isaiah. For the rest, whether you return to us with the apple-blossom or the wild flowers of June, or the winter snows, you will find here those who love you and pray for you, holding you always in their most loving thoughts."

His words both encouraged her and comforted her. And in the further reading of St. Augustine she found that which comforted her on the one hand and saddened her on the other, for she found these words, '. . . it often comes to pass that he that is far distant from thee in body is united to thee, because he loves that which thou lovest. And oft-times it comes to pass that one standing beside thee is far away from thee, because he loves the world, while thou lovest God.'

The one who stood beside her was Francis back from America, and spending a little time in the Kensington house—but he was intent on returning to Paris before the white candles of the chestnuts vanished from the gardens of the Luxembourg and the wooded avenues of the Champs-Élysées.

"Can you bear not to be in Paris in the spring?" he asked her. They were walking in Kensington Gardens.

"If I were anywhere but here I would be in our mountain place in the Tyrol."

"Why don't you go? You'd be in time for the apple-blossom! And the Amanshausers would receive you with open arms, literally. What is keeping you? Mother isn't lonely in London, and it would hardly delay your entry into the Church! You're as good as in it already, anyhow!"

She smiled, sadly. How far he was from her, in truth! And it was in truth that he was far from her, he who was so dear to her.

"Would you say that to be within sight of a meal for which you hunger was as good as having the meal?"

"Is it so great a hunger?" He was puzzled. He too recognised, with sadness, how far apart they were now; they moved in quite different worlds, it seemed to him.

"Yes, the most terrible longing." She added, as though half to herself, " 'What the parched soul longs for lies hidden in a secret place.' " She looked at him, her eyes dark with pain. "Oh, Francis——" She broke off and he did not press her to continue, for the very reason for which she broke off—that they no longer spoke the same language.

They walked together through the springtime world, those two who loved each other so dearly, but both were filled with sadness. For a time they walked in silence, and came down to the Serpentine, where the willows trailed long strings of green beads to the water.

"London is beautiful in the spring, too," Cathryn said at

last. "Kensington Gardens are as lovely as the gardens of the Luxembourg, and lovelier than the Bois——"

"And Richmond is lovelier than St. Cloud. I know. But there's that—*je ne sais quoi*—What is it? In London even on a spring day the air feels somehow stale and used up. And there's always that suggestion of stewed tea and stale buns, and the stale smell of beer in unaired pubs. No feeling of lightness and gaiety. On a day like this, for instance, one wants to sit in the sun and drink a glass of *champagne natur*, or a champagne cocktail, but London doesn't permit of such harmless gaieties. In these gardens there's an open-air tea-place, as we know, but however good the weather it will not open until Easter, and all you can drink at it is tea or those so-called mineral waters, and no one could possibly call either of those beverages gay. Give me the Luxembourg and its little pond and the Capoulade across the road, and you can keep your Serpentine—and this horrible bit of middle-class whimsy-whamsy, Peter Pan. You can't, surely, want to paint in London? Have you done anything since you've been over?"

"No. But I don't think that's anything to do with London. I've made a drawing of Father Connor."

He made no comment, and they turned their backs on Peter Pan and walked on in silence.

14

In a smaller room of the West End gallery in which Cathryn had her exhibition of tempera paintings there was a collection of etchings by Anna Kallinova. It had been Cathryn's idea, and the proprietors of the gallery agreed to the joint exhibition. Cathryn persuaded Anna to bring the etchings to London herself, and to stay in the South Kensington house. They would have the place to themselves, Cathryn urged; her mother wanted to make a visit to Crag House, and all the dates fitted in very well, if Anna would agree to them. Anna finally agreed. It was her first visit to England.

Cathryn met her at Victoria. She stood with the small crowd of other waiting people at the end of the arrival platform, and everyone, it seemed to her, found the person they had come to meet before she did; everyone had someone to greet and kiss.

She was beginning to be anxious when she saw Anna's square, thick-set figure stumping along with a large portfolio of the precious etchings under one arm, and a battered-looking Gladstone bag in her other hand. She was exactly as Cathryn had last seen her in Montparnasse, hatless, aggressive-jawed, bow-tied, wearing the same old black shabby suit, thick stockings, heavy down-at-heel shoes. The same, yet somehow different. Shabbier; older; a little lost. Cathryn felt her heart contract. Dear Anna! She went forward to meet her.

Anna's face lit up at the sight of her. She dumped the Gladstone bag, leaned the portfolio against her side, and took Cathryn's hands and kissed her on both cheeks.

"It's good to see you, my dear!"

"I'm glad you're here, Anna."

Cathryn seized the Gladstone bag and looked round for a taxi.

In the taxi, Cathryn said, eagerly, "Tell me about Paris! Did you see Francis?"

"I saw him just before I left. He was down at the Flore with Johnnie—people have taken to going to the Flore lately— Old Ford Maddox Ford gives it a certain *cachet*, I suppose. Anyhow it stands in relation to the Magots as the Dôme does to the Rotonde! Your brother sent you the usual messages—love, and best wishes for the exhibition. He said you were joining the Catholic Church . . ." She looked at Cathryn inquiringly.

"Does that disappoint you in me very much, Anna?"

"It's not a question of disappointment. Human beings are complex. I could never even contemplate it myself. Too materialist a mind, I suppose. I never know how people get past little difficulties like Transubstantiation and the Immaculate Conception. The usual anti-Catholic objections, I suppose. Don't try to explain to me. I've had people try before and it's no good."

Cathryn smiled. "No, it's no good. Without faith there's no understanding. You have to *see*. I've realised for the first time what that expression we use so casually really means, 'I see.' "

"I don't see! Though I'd seen it coming in you for some time, and if it all makes you happy, and provided it doesn't have a bad effect on the work——"

"You'll see the work," Cathryn said.

Anna approved of her first glimpses of Kensington, and agreed that it was faintly reminiscent of Paris—but only faintly, she insisted, for Paris was *sui generis*.

Cathryn showed her over the house, and Anna behaved rather as though she were in a museum, carefully examining any and everything of interest, a Dresden chandelier, a Venetian mirror, a Chippendale side-table, the Adam fireplace in the drawing-room, a Sickert drawing. . . . When the tour was finished she observed, drily, "There are some nice things. But I wouldn't want any of it. There's nothing like being able to put everything you possess into a bag you can carry yourself and walk off with it to the next place. It leaves you free. And the older I get the more I feel that freedom is everything."

"Supposing you make a lot of money from the exhibition?"

"I won't. But if I did I would go to the South and take a room with a view and only draw when I felt like it. Not to be touting round the cafés would mean a lot. To be free to do the things one wanted to do. I'd buy freedom with any money I had, not carpets and furniture and the rest of it. I had a house once, full of things—lovely things. In a place that used to be called St. Petersburg."

Cathryn suppressed the questions that leapt to her mind. There were some things one did not ask. It was enough that Anna had once had possessions and now had nothing, and was glad. She desperately wanted to help Anna as repayment in some small part of the debt she felt she owed her, and which, in fact, could never fully be paid off. It was not merely that Anna had found her a place to live in Paris—a place in which she could work, or even that she had taught her so much, far more than she had ever learned in the art-schools; Anna's criticism had been of immense value to her, but more important to Cathryn than anything else had been Anna's own personal integrity expressed through her work and her criticism. She had no affectations, no pretences, above all no self-deceptions. She had courage, vigour, and complete honesty. She had taken some gruelling criticism from Anna, and through it had finally expunged every trace of falsity from her work. Anna had ranted and roared on occasion; had accused Cathryn of every artistic sin; accused her of sentimentality, falsity, insincerity, humbug, affectation, pretentiousness, derivativeness. She had reduced Cathryn to tears; she had infuriated her; she had alienated her. But always in the end, when the storm had abated, Cathryn's own fundamental integrity had had to admit that Anna, ranting, raging, roaring old Anna, was right. After the Paris exhibition Anna had offered no more criticisms; her pupil had graduated; or, as Anna had said, in her brusque fashion, "You'll do." The highest praise she had given Cathryn was simply, "It comes off." 'Marvellous', 'wonderful', 'brilliant', were words she never used; what more could an artist ask, whether it was a painting, or a poem, or any other created thing, than that it came off—was what the creator of it had intended it should be, fully and freely, said what it was intended to say, and that effectively? It was the triumph of all great works of art, that they came off, and when that was said everything was said; they might or might not be beautiful; what did people mean by beauty, anyhow? The English poet, Anna declared, had given the answer when he declared that beauty was truth, truth beauty, and that was all we knew or needed to know. Some people took longer to learn that fact, that was all; and some people never learned it at all. People like Sue Lester, for example, painting away year after year, being hung in the Salon and the Royal Academy, having exhibitions and getting good notices, and it none of it mattered; it was none of it worth doing; it had all been said before and said more effectively. Because Sue Lester was in herself an ineffective person; she was good-natured, kind, generous, sincere—but it was easy enough to be sincere when you had nothing much to say; it didn't make a great demand of you. It was for people like Francis Sable that it was difficult, because he was a highly complex person, and an artist with great gifts, who could exploit them in various directions. It was not easy for people like Cathryn, in spite of a fundamental integrity, because she had first to find herself; there was the Cathryn willing to be anything, to do anything, that her adored brother wanted her to be or to do; there was the Cathryn avid for any life that could be shared with Francis; and the Cathryn thrown back on herself because Francis had grown away from her, and who, detached from him, could see his faults and want differently for him, and for herself; the Cathryn who spiritualised what could not be materialised, whose passion—using the word in its broadest sense—was directed into spiritual channels because it was frustrated in material ones; sublimated, the Freudians called it, didn't they, in their frightful jargon? The Catholic Church was right for Cathryn because she felt that it was; because it was the logical conclusion of a long slow process of spiritual evolution. It was queer, that Cathryn should have thought it might come as a shock to her, and a disappointment, that she shouldn't have realised that anyone close to her had seen it coming for a long time; as to disappointment, how be disappointed in something natural and inevitable? It meant that Cathryn had found herself, and that was important to her as an artist, all else apart. In Anna's opinion some of the new work for the London exhibition surpassed the best of what had been shown in Paris. It was first-rate. It came off—magnificently.

As to her own part in the exhibition, if she could sell a few things, enough to enable her to leave Paris and stay for about six months in some high place in the South, such as Vence, she would be satisfied. At her age she couldn't last much longer on one lung; but a Montparnasse garret was no place to be ill in; and Montparnasse wasn't a good place in which to keep one's health a secret. She'd managed it for years, but only by creeping away, out of sight, into hospital, when she got ill, and then giving out that she'd been away in the South; and as she always looked better when she came out of hospital people believed it. She had only to let people like Francis Sable or Sue Lester know that she was ill, of course, and the nature of her illness, for them to come round helping her right and left; but she didn't want it; she didn't want their blasted charity; besides, they'd shove her away into a sanatorium, where she would spend the rest of her days among 'the spit-and-cough chaps', as an English girl she had met in the hospital last time called those of their fraternity, admiring the scenery and waiting to die. They'd told her at the hospital she might live a long time, years, if she would be 'sensible', look after herself, leave the city, go into a sanatorium. It never occurred to them she might not want life on those terms. It wasn't as though she were young; she was in the middle fifties; she had lived a lot of life, and she was tired—desperately tired. But one didn't die of hunger if one could help it; and one had still a few things left to say. It was why one went on touting round the cafés of Montparnasse and the Quarter, to keep off the bread-line, to raise the hundred francs a month rent for the garret—not on the principle of life-at-all-costs, just for the sake of dragging one's sick carcase about, but because one had still a few ideas left in one's head, and the itch to translate them into line. During the October Revolution, after Anton and Nikolai had been murdered as 'whites', and she had escaped with a few others, she had asked herself to what purpose had she been at such trouble to preserve her own life when everyone she cared about, parents, husband, son, were dead? But there was that perpetual reassertion of the creative urge, giving meaning and purpose to life. If anyone asked what old Anna Kallinova, trapesing round the cafés, had got to live for, the answer was that she had still something left to say and the artist's urge to say it.

Cathryn was always insisting on her indebtedness, but she, Anna Kallinova, was indebted to Cathryn Sable. But for her she would never have made the effort to arrange an exhibition; of her own work, the things she wanted to do, she did what she could when she could, and then did nothing more about it; she made no organised effort to sell anything; she had had a few small semi-private shows of her work from time to time in other and more successful artists' studios; occasionally an American bought something of hers because someone had told him that she was an artist who might have value later on. She had completely no commercial instinct, and once she had done what she wanted she lost interest in it. People weren't much interested in etchings, anyhow; they were too 'difficult' to look at; people liked colour, and something that didn't make too much demand of them—most people, that is. But Cathryn had pressed this idea that she should share the London gallery with her, urging that she would certainly sell a few of her things, and that in London she could ask high prices, and she had allowed herself to be persuaded. It might mean a precious few months' freedom at Vence or some such place, where her soul could breathe properly as well as her one over-strained lung. A few more months of life, even. . . .

What was important, however, was not that Anna Kallinova should sell enough etchings to give her a few months of freedom, but that Cathryn Sable's genius should be recognised and acclaimed. Cathryn would go on, of course, whether it was or

not, but what she had to say was of importance not merely as
adding to the sum of truth and beauty in the world, and as such
should not be kept hidden, but it was of importance to contemporary art. There was so much bad painting going on, so many
pernicious influences contributing to the destroying of painting
as a craft, and to all that Cathryn Sable's fine craftsmanship, and the
impetus her work would give to the revival of tempera painting,
was a counterblast. Hers was the dual mission of adding to
the *illumination* of life—as very few contemporary artists did—and
of educating her fellow-artists. Though, of course, Cathryn
painted as she did for the same unself-conscious reason that a
bird sings as it does—because it was her nature to express herself in that way. With her capacity for painstakingness, and her
passion for pure colour, tempera was her natural medium; just
as with her sense of line and clear-cut design acid and metal were
the natural media for Anna Kallinova. Had not her own life
been etched in acid? There were not in her, as in Cathryn Sable,
deep pure pools of light and colour.

Cathryn's success in London was a repetition of her Paris
début; she sold a number of her pictures and received good
notices. 'Promising' was the word most of the critics used about
her, and it exasperated Anna. What fools they were! Just because
she was young! Cathryn's work was not promise; it was fulfilment. She had been full of promise when she first came to
Paris at seventeen; at twenty-four, after seven years' hard work,
she had magnificently fulfilled that promise. She was disgusted
when one of the papers referred to her as the sister of Francis
Sable, the writer. What did it matter whose sister she was? One
fool actually declared, 'The brilliance which is reflected in the
prose and poetry alike of Mr. Francis Sable's work is a feature of
the remarkable collection of paintings and drawings of his sister,
the twenty-four-year-old Miss Cathryn Sable now showing at the
Piccadilly Gallery . . .' It was quite possible for there to be the
same quality of light and feeling in a painting as in a poem, but
there was no similarity between the quality of Cathryn's painting
and Francis's writing. Her work had none of that diamond
quality of brilliance which characterised his; it was like trying to
compare Botticelli's *Primavera* with Aldous Huxley's *Antic*

Hay. If she was to be likened to anyone, she who was so essentially herself, let it be with the artist who was the master of tempera painting, Botticelli himself!

Cathryn was a little amused by Anna's exasperation.

"Anna darling, what does it *matter* what they say? The only critic who can ever really matter to one is another artist whose work one respects. What you say matters—it matters enormously! Francis always says about book-reviewers, those who can write, do; those who can't, review. It's the same in our trade—those who can paint, do; the others turn critic, and as they don't know anything what they say is of no importance."

It pleased Anna that Cathryn referred to painting as a trade; she had none of that sickening high-falutin' My work, My Art, stuff of the Montparnassians. Ah, she was a good girl; she was good stuff; she was an *artist*. If only the fools had said that about her; just that and nothing more! But they didn't because they didn't know the meaning of the word.

She was quite indifferent to her own notices. It really did not matter what anyone thought. It hadn't mattered all these years and it couldn't matter now. A charming old peer who told the proprietor of the gallery that Miss Sable's work was not up his street—'Too Botticelli, y'know, and I never could stand 'im'—bought two of Anna's etchings—one of the flower-market under the trees behind Notre-Dame, one of a *can-can* number at the Folies Bergères—'all those flounced drawers, y'know, charmin'!'—for fifteen guineas each and thought them cheap at the price. Sir Steven Sable, at his sister's suggestion, commissioned her to buy in his name anything she thought he might like—'something simple', he requested; so she chose for him the thing Anna liked least because she considered it 'obvious'—a string of barges on the Seine, below the Pont Neuf. A few other smaller things were sold, and Anna cleared about fifty pounds after the galleries had taken their commission, and considered she had done well. Fifty pounds was more money than she had had at one time since she left Russia. For fifty pounds you could live for six months in a place like Vence, if you knew how—and she did. Six months of freedom, of life—as opposed to Montparnassian existence.

Anna returned to Paris before the exhibition was over, in spite of Cathryn pressing her to stay; but Anna had not been feeling well; she knew the symptoms, and was terrified of being taken ill away from the privacy which was hers in Paris. She made various excuses to Cathryn about the need to get back, and since she seemed set on going Cathryn saw her off at Victoria at the end of a fortnight.

"I'll never be able to thank you adequately, so I won't try," Anna said, leaning from the window of the boat-train. What she meant was that she had been happy for the first time since 1917. She pressed Anna's hands. "Bless you," she said. "I'll send you a postcard from Vence. If we don't meet again this side of the Styx keep in touch, won't you?"

"Of course," Cathryn promised. "But of course we'll meet again. Why shouldn't we?"

"There's no of course about it," Anna said, drily. "If you're not coming back to Paris, and as I'm not likely to be in London again——"

"I shall ask you," Cathryn said, firmly.

Anna smiled. "Good-bye, my dear."

"*Au revoir*," Cathryn said. "Thank you for everything."

"Nonsense. Just keep going, that's all."

Cathryn waved until Anna's smooth-cropped head was no longer distinguishable at the window, then walked away, feeling sad. In spite of her vehement *au revoir* she had the feeling that they never would meet again. 'Just keep going.' It was all you could do, whether you were inching your way up a smooth rock-slab, or groping your way along the various artistic precipices, or up the seemingly unclimbable peak of spiritual salvation. You had somehow to keep going.

15

In the summer Francis had all his arrangements made to go climbing at Zermatt with his friend when Framley was suddenly seized with a septic appendix and rushed off to hospital. Francis, who had lent his apartment for a month to a couple of Americans he had met in the South—their occupation would be 'super-vised' by the faithful Johnnie, of course—found himself suddenly not merely at a loose end, but homeless. It was bad luck on poor old Framley, of course, but it was also a dam' nuisance. It was not merely the practical side of the situation which bothered him; he had arranged his mind as well as his papers, and told everyone he would be out of Paris. He had already gone from Paris in all but the flesh. It would be all too difficult to rearrange things now; he would have to go somewhere, even if he didn't keep to the Zermatt arrangements. It crossed his mind that he could take Cathryn; then, decided against it; it would be maddening to be in Zermatt and not do the climbs he and Framley had planned, and obviously they were beyond Cathryn. He could go alone and climb with a guide, of course; he turned the idea over in his mind, then rejected it; to climb with a guide and no one else would be, as Cathryn had said, *triste*. The guides were good fellows, but they climbed professionally, not adventurously. Then it came to him, Why not go again to Drindel and let Cathryn realise her dream of climbing the Drindelhorn? She had her heart set on it; all these years, since she was a kid, she had been dreaming of 'the real mountain' they would one day climb together. This seemed to be the opportunity. They needn't say anything about climbing to their mother; they could tell her, simply, that they were going to have a holiday together in the Tyrol—which was true. If she asked about mountains they could say that there was nothing much to climb there, which again was true; the Drindelhorn was nothing much by all accounts; probably he and Cathryn had done far stiffer rock-climbs on Scafell and Great Gable. . . . There was the glacier, of course, but it wouldn't take her long, with her natural aptitude, to get used to ice. With a month at their disposal there would be plenty of time for test-climbs before they tackled the summit. If he was ever going to take Cathryn on a mountain holiday everything pointed to doing it now. He went to London specially to discuss it with her.

Cathryn, of course, was tremendously excited by the proposition—and Lady Sable was immediately anxious. She had hoped that Cathryn had got over her mountain mania, since she had said nothing about it in recent years.

She said at once, "The Tyrol—that means you'll be climbing mountains, I suppose?"

"My dear mother," Francis said, "there are no real mountains in the Tyrol!"

But Lady Sable was not all that ignorant.

"What are you talking about?" she demanded. "There's the Grossglockner, and the Kitzsteinhorn——"

"We're not going anywhere near the Grossglockner and the Kitzsteinhorn. At Drindel there's nothing but the Drindelhorn, and anyone who has been up and down the Pillar Rock and the Napes Needle as often as Cathryn could skip up and down the Drindelhorn blindfold!" There was after all, he told himself, a deal of difference between a lie and a hyperbole. His intention, he assured his conscience, was not to deceive, but to set her mind at rest. (But, insisted conscience, how can you do that except by wilful deception?)

"Isn't there a glacier on the Drindelhorn?" Lady Sable persisted, fearfully.

"A glacier is nothing like so difficult or dangerous as a stiff rock-climb." (The Drindelhorn glacier was not reckoned to be difficult, he told his conscience.)

"People have lost their lives on them, all the same!"

"My darling mother, people have lost their lives as a result of riding in trains and 'buses or merely climbing ladders to pick apples! A glacier with a guide who has been doing it for twenty or thirty years is nothing. When people come to grief on mountains it is either from carelessness or over-ambition. There's nothing even ambitious, let alone over-ambitious, in going up the Drindelhorn, and I've no intention of being careless. I am, after all, not without experience by now, you know. You don't really suppose I would let Cathryn take any risks, do you?"

Lady Sable could only say, helplessly, "Accidents happen even with experienced climbers. One sees reports in the papers every week during the summer months——"

Cathryn said, "Accidents can always happen to anyone anywhere. If nothing happened to me on the difficult climbs at Wasdale why should anything happen to me on an easy Austrian climb? You surely didn't live among climbing people all those years without learning that height has nothing to do with it— that a ten-thousand-foot Alp can be a lot safer than two thousand feet of sheer rock in the Cuillins!"

Lady Sable felt herself defeated in argument and tried to be what her son and daughter urged her to be—'sensible'!

John had always said that she was 'neurotic' about this climbing business. But it hadn't upset her when he and the boys had gone climbing on Great Gable or Scafell; or even greatly worried her when Steven and Francis had taken to going farther afield to Ben Nevis, for practice on snow and ice, preparatory to Switzerland. She had always felt a little anxious, of course, but it was only when they took Cathryn with her on any of their climbs that she had felt really agitated, so that she was incapable of peace of mind until they were all safely home again. It was wrong, of course, since God's will would be done in any case, and she tried hard to overcome it, but deep down in her the nagging dread persisted. She was so very precious, her ewe lamb, and even more precious now that she was about to be received into the Church. But as Francis said, why *should* anything happen to her, guided by an experienced climber like Francis, and on a mountain that was not even difficult? It was only that one was over-anxious when something or someone very precious was involved. And it would be true to say that Cathryn was dearer to her than life itself, for she was an old woman and must soon finish with this life, whereas Cathryn was young and had genius and was the fulfilment of her dearest dream; Cathryn's life had importance and value; her own none.

Francis was inclined to be impatient of his mother's anxiety; Cathryn was distressed by it. It seemed to her important that she should succeed in reassuring her mother before she went off on this most wonderful of holidays. She could not imagine herself not going now that Francis had asked her. She was going to climb, at last, the 'white mountain' of her dreams, and with the only person with whom she could climb it. She acknowledged to herself, too, that the possibility of meeting Johann again was involved in her excitement. It only wanted her mother's blessing on the great adventure to complete her happiness; unless she had that it was spoiled, since it was very difficult to be happy even doing what you most passionately wanted to do, and had dreamed for years of doing, if in the doing of it you made someone very dear to you unhappy. Her mother's peace of mind over the adventure was essential to her happiness. Which meant, she reflected ruefully, that her wanting to secure her mother's happiness was purely selfish. 'If I were unselfish,' she thought, 'knowing that all this that I have wanted so much, and for which I have waited so long, and despaired of ever coming true, distresses my mother I would give it all up. But I can't, I can't!' It would have been hard enough before, but now there was added to it the hunger to see Johann again. She admitted that deep longing to herself, but to no one else. But not even to herself did she acknowledge that she was in love with him.

After a great deal of prayer and struggle Dorothea reached the point at which she could at least pretend to her children that she was no longer fearful of the Austrian holiday. She went out and bought Cathryn a new sweater at Lillywhite's, and a woollen hood, the long ends of which could also serve as a scarf.

"You'll need warm things when you get above the tree-line," she said, bravely.

"Mother seems to have got quite interested in the expedition at last," Francis said.

"I think we've convinced her there's nothing to worry about," Cathryn agreed. "It's a great relief."

Determined that they should go off without worrying as to whether she was happy about their going, Dorothea, resolutely, went to see them off. It was at her suggestion that they opened a bottle of champagne before they left for Victoria. They caught the train with only ten minutes in hand—this was Lady Sable's doing; she had deliberately cut things as fine as she dared, determined that there should be no prolonged farewells on the platform.

As they were going straight through, doing the night-journey, Francis and Cathryn both wore the ski-ing kit they preferred for climbing. They were a splendid-looking young couple, their mother thought, proudly, so good-looking, their figures so straight and slim and athletic. They had such a shining look about them, she thought, as they leaned from the carriage window, their fair heads together; they were so animated and gay; they were like a pair of excited children . . . ah, but what else were they but that? *Her* children, the beloved Francis, and the precious ewe lamb. . . . Her heart contracted, but she smiled, and frantically waved.

"Good-bye, darlings," she called, and blew kisses after them, "Have a lovely time! Good-bye, Good-bye. . . ."

For a long time after she left Victoria she continued to see their laughing faces, their waving hands, and hear the long whistle of the train echoing that most forlorn of all words, 'Good-bye'. Good-bye. God be with you. How many people remembered that it meant that? Good-bye, my darlings. *Good-bye.*

They had agreed to spend the next night in Vienna, and Francis had booked rooms for them in a little dark *Kaiserlich* hotel, in a narrow side street off the Stefansplatz, at which he had stayed a good deal himself. The rooms were dark, facing either into the narrow street, or into a well courtyard, and the furnishings were heavy and the wallpapers dark. There were tall tiled stoves in each room, and the floors were bare wood, highly polished, the curtains heavy and dark and fusty. The entrance-hall was oppressive with antlers and stuffed stags' heads. The whole place was altogether heavy and dark and old-fashioned, and Cathryn loved it, and the aristocratic names on each door, the Graf this and the Baron that, and an absurd delightful rough-cast 'grotto' at the top of the stairs, with a charming little blue and white and gold Madonna in the niche above.

When they had washed and changed into town clothes they went out, because Cathryn was far too excited at being in what Francis called 'the second loveliest city in Europe' for the first time to feel any need for rest after the night-journey—and Francis never wanted to rest when the sun shone and there was wine to drink and baroque architecture to look at. Cathryn was so enchanted by the baroque that she was not sure that Vienna was not more beautiful than Paris. When they sat on the Mozart-platz drinking coffee with a thick foam of cream on the top, and eating small exquisite marzipan cakes, and contemplating the lovely fountain, she felt quite sure that it was the first of all European cities . . . but if you loved baroque, said Francis, there was Munich to consider, and Würzburg, and Salzburg, and they would spend a little time in Salzburg on the way back, because apart from the baroque—and the lovely intimate squares of the *Innere Stadt*, and the rushing torrent of a river, and the chestnut trees—there was the whole of the Untersberg range just behind. . . .

In the evening they sat among the red plush, gilt, and mirrors of Sacher's Bar, and dined in the Drei Husaren, a small *chic* restaurant off the Kärntnerstrasse, to the gipsy music of an Hungarian orchestra.

Francis admitted, "I always tell myself that I loathe all this *tzigane* stuff, and yet it always stirs me in some queer sort of way. It's all such sentimental, romantic nonsense, really, but if one were in love I imagine it would be almost unbearable!"

Cathryn was in love, and it *was* almost unbearable, and yet at the same time she felt that she never wanted it to stop. It was so wild and passionate, and happy and hopeless . . . like loving Johann.

"I shall bring Lotte here sometimes," Francis said. "She'd love it!"

They had called at the stores for which Lotte was clothes-buyer during the afternoon, but as is so often the way on such occasions she was away in Paris. 'And whenever she is in Paris I shall almost certainly be out of it,' he thought, 'and so we shall never meet. But perhaps it's as well.'

After they had dined, feeling gay from the Tokay, they climbed into an open carriage and drove right round the Ringstrasse. Cathryn felt as though she wanted to bow to everyone, right and left. Francis declared that he felt like 'the last of the Hapsburgs'.

When they had finished the circuit of the Ring they drove down to the Stadt Park and drank champagne to the insidious melodies of Strauss waltz music.

"It seems to be an evening for bad music—in this city of good music," Francis observed.

"But it's perfect!" Cathryn cried, adding, shamelessly, "I love it! I'd like them to play everything—the *Blue Danube*, the *Barcarolle*, the waltz from *Der Rosenkavalier*—everything sad and haunting and sentimental!"

Francis laughed. He was feeling a little like that himself.

"I shouldn't worry! If we sit here long enough they probably will!"

He was right; they did. They both loved it . . . even Francis. He could not remember when he had last felt as light and happy and unaffectedly gay as this. So much that passed for gaiety was so madly ungay; one had to be ginned up for it. He and Cathryn, it is true, were full of Tokay and champagne, but their gaiety had begun with nothing more than coffee on the Mozartplatz. Perhaps the last time he had felt as gay was when he had been rushing down the snow-slopes with Lotte Amanshauser at Christmas.

It was a soft warm night, and there was a drenching sweetness of lilac and syringa on the air, and it seemed as though it would never get dark. It was past ten o'clock, but children still played under the trees, raced round the flower-beds, got in the way of grown-ups on the paths; people were continually arriving at the café, and the orchestra's repertoire of heart-melting music seemed as endless as the summer night.

Cathryn wanted it all to go on for ever—the long light night, the music, the happy cries of the children, the clatter of cups and saucers as the waiters flung them down on the tables, the movement of people, coming and going at the café, promenading the walks, and the stream of traffic along the boulevard bounding the park, and the throb of it like the pulse of the city's blood along the arteries of its streets. She wanted it all to go on forever, timeless in eternity, because she and Francis were close again, their thoughts and moods and reactions flowing together as it were in one blood-stream, one flow of the spirit, so that they talked and laughed and fell silent, and there was the sense of mindless communion and the superfluousness of words. And it was all timeless in space, all something happening in a dream from which they would one day wake—but not yet. This was the long midsummer night of a dream in which anything might happen, so long as the light held and the music rose and fell, and people came and went in a dark murmurous tide. In this dream Johann came striding across the grass to where they sat, and he held out both hands to her and pulled her to her feet. "They're dancing over there under the trees," he said. "Come." They went hand in hand across the grass, between the white and purple lilac and the waxen whiteness of the syringas, past the rose-beds, to where the trees were strung with small coloured lights. Then she was in his arms and held against his heart, and they moved together to the music, limb to limb, their cheeks sometimes brushing, and there was no time, only the rhythmic movement of their bodies and their blood flowing together, in the endless light, to the endless music.

Francis said, "Why don't we dance?" and they tilted their chairs up against the table and crossed the grass to the wooden dancing floor under the trees. They moved coolly and feather-light together, so that it was as though each danced alone, and then a sturdy young man stepped out of the watching crowd when the music paused a moment and smiled at her and said something which she did not understand to Francis, who smiled and nodded and answered him and turned away; and then she was clamped to the strong thick body of the stranger and reality broke through the dream and her spirit panicked away from it. The young man periodically tightened his hold on her and smiled at her and asked her questions, but she did not know what he said, and he had no language but his own, and she wanted only release from him. Francis passed her smiling down at a girl he had picked at random from the crowd; she was plump and swayed her hips, and Francis held her stiffly, a little away from him. When the tune finished he and Cathryn came to each other again with a sense of rescue, then moved feather-light together through a waltz, and the dream closed in again . . . Francis, her heart cried, how did we ever get so far apart?

They went back to their table and finished the champagne and presently the music ended and the light began to go. They became part of the dark tide flowing towards the gates. As they strolled back under the trees of the boulevard Cathryn murmured, "We're not really drunk, would you say, Francis darling? Or at least only a very little. . . ."

"But enough," Francis said, "to justify another cab."

There were a string of open carriages in the middle of the boulevard, the horses standing with drooping heads.

In the carriage Cathryn leaned her head against her brother's shoulder.

"Let us drive all night," she murmured drowsily, and fell asleep.

16

They decided to walk the twelve miles out from Schultzburg; it was only a matter of four hours' walking, or perhaps a little more as they were walking with heavy packs, but even if they took as long as five hours to do it they would arrive at Drindel in the early evening.

"And we need to start getting into training," said Francis.

The route ran all the way beside the lake, but they had no need to touch the road at all; a narrow path twisted away over the lower slopes of the mountains, winding through orchards, pasture-land, woods of beech and larch and pine, past hay-huts, and an occasional squat wooden farmhouse. At times the path climbed a little and the white dusty road below dropped out of sight. There was the occasional huddle of a village along the lake —a straggle of wooden houses, a toy-like church tower, a land-ing stage thrusting out into the water, rushes growing up round its wooden supports. A child's toy of a paddle-steamer fanned out a white wake on the lightly rippled blueness of the lake. They could make out the small dark figures of passengers awaiting it as it turned in towards a pier. There was the tinkle of bells on the cattle grazing on the sunny slopes, and the chug of the steamer carried clearly in the stillness across the water. Clouds gathered and melted and regathered round the tops of the mountains. At the far end of the valley, at the head of the lake, above Drindel, the white peak of the Drindelhorn thrust up dramatically against the blue of the sky. The mountains at the other side of the valley looked huge until you looked at the Drindelhorn, Cathryn thought, and then they seemed only high hills. In the winter, when they and the valley were all one under the snow, they had all seemed equal, but now they appeared to reach only shoulder-high to the Drindelhorn, for all they had snow on their summits. She had seen the valley clothed in its summer gold and green so often in her mind that coming to it then she had the feeling not of seeing it like that for the first time, but of it being how she had remembered it.

When it had been all settled that they were to go together Francis had written to the Amanshausers to inquire if they would have rooms for them for three weeks in June, when, presumably, they would be busy with the holiday season. Frau Amanshauser had written by return that even if they were full from cellar to attic there would still be room for Mr. Francis and Miss Cathryn. But they were not full; they had with them only a nice quiet elderly couple from Vienna who did no climbing but only pottered about on the lower slopes, and two young Germans who used the place only as a base and went off up into the mountains for days at a time. She was sure that Mr. Francis would be glad to know that his fellow-countrymen had not yet discovered Drindel, despite his forebodings. Mr. Francis was, indeed, extremely glad of that piece of information; but he was also glad to know that the inn was not swarming with enthusiastic German and Austrian youth all anxious to rope him and Cathryn in—literally—for expeditions. Johann, Frau Amanshauser had added, was hoping to be able to arrange his summer holiday so that he would be there for two out of the three weeks of their stay. "That would be nice," Cathryn had said, when Francis told her, which, with the colour that beat up into her face as she said it, he considered a pretty piece of understatement. . . .

As they trudged along the narrow path on the lower slopes of the mountains that sunny afternoon they had no idea whether Johann would be there when they arrived or not. But it was Friday, Cathryn recollected; even if he hadn't been able to arrange his holiday when they were there perhaps he would come for the week-end . . . if he loved her enough. She caught herself out on the thought. He did love her; but not in that way. Something in her unashamedly wept—side by side with the something which equally unashamedly exulted in the thought that whatever way he loved her she would see him again, hear his voice, know the touch of his hands, sit at the same table with him, climb the same mountain paths.

The track dipped down into a small pine wood and climbed up to a clearing; there was the tremendous resinous smell of the newly cut timber added to the strong sweet smell of warm pines. They emerged from the dappled shade of the woods into the meadow brightness of treeless grass-slopes, where the grass stood full of flowers—tall white daisies, wild canterbury bells and lupins, yellow toadflax—and ready for hay. With the mellowing of the afternoon sunshine the whole valley seemed to have become a great bowl brimming with gold light, and the bottom of the bowl was blue glass. They sat for a while with their backs against a hay-hut watching the clouds smoking over the peak of the Drindelhorn. At the opposite side of the lake the flanking mountains were growing sombre near their summits as the sunlight retreated from them; the rock faces began to look dark and cold as the desolation of evening crept down on them out of the sky. On the Drindel side of the valley the sunshine lay in a warm golden flood.

"It looks terribly lonely up there now that the sun's off it," Cathryn remarked, gazing at the *massif* opposite. "It would be frightening to be lost up there, with the darkness closing in."

"There's hours of light yet," Francis said, carelessly. "But all the same we'd better push on."

They scrambled to their feet and went on, Francis leading along the narrow track; above them the grasslands went up to the rim of the bowl; the mountains behind were out of sight; below them the slopes flowed down in sections of hayfields, pasture, and orchard, to the hidden road. Cathryn's remark about the loneliness of the mountains stirred something in Francis's mind. The mountains were not lonely; the loneliness was in the human beings who looked at their immensity and became aware in that moment of their own smallness; the mountains, in their immutability, filled one with the realisation of human futility and insignificance. The centuries were added to each other like milestones along an unending road, every century with its wars and revolutions and its 'progress', and the mountains stood there with the winds and clouds going over as they had always stood; they had always been; they always would be; they were the same today, yesterday, and forever. At this moment of time children and dogs were leaping and playing round the pond in Kensington Gardens, and the gardens of the Luxembourg; in London, Paris, Berlin, Vienna, people were going in and out of restaurants, cafés, cinemas, shops, pushing their way in and out of 'buses; the cities were teeming with life, the factories humming with machinery. It was all going on at this moment, the eating and drinking, the buying and selling, the pleasure-hunt, the treasure-hunt, the pushing and jostling, the hating and loving, people eating ice-creams, banging typewriters, having afternoon tea, book-keeping, writing books, fornicating, buying evening papers—as though being part of it all were not enough and they were avid of still more buying and selling, lying, cheating, a still wider range of murders, fornications, pleasures, and the lies they called politics. There was all that, and much more; and there was this—the peak of the Drindelhorn thrusting up into the sky, changeless, timeless; 'before beginning and without an end, only Thy laws endure'. Day after day, night after night, week after week, month after month, year after year, generation after generation, century after century, whatever happened, earthquake, pestilence, tidal waves, world-wars, the Hundred Years' War, the French Revolution, the Russian Revolution. Whilst they hanged a man, whilst a child ate an ice-cream on a street-corner, whilst the red 'buses swirled round Piccadilly and the crowds surged along the Boulevard des Italiens. Whilst all the swirling, surging, pushing, jostling, was going on. When you were part of it all again yourself; long after you were dead, and all your generation. . . . A cold wind shivered through the empty wastes of what you were pleased to call your soul, a terrible loneliness—the awful ultimate loneliness of each and every human being, only acknowledged in moments of revelation, when the sun was withdrawn and an evening coldness crept down out of the sky. But then you drew the curtains, switched on the light, and it was the *apéritif* hour and you had 'appointments', and there was night, with Neon signs and the Jockey Club, the Bœuf sur le Toit, the Embassy, Ciro's . . . all the things you did to keep on living, to light and warm and fill the empty spaces in your soul . . . and to hell with immutable things and the eternal verities.

When you came to the mountains you wondered why you ever went away, why you ever went back to the swirling and pushing and jostling. . . . He spoke his thought aloud almost before he had realised it. "Why do we, Cathryn?" he demanded.

"I suppose because we couldn't work here," she answered him.

"But couldn't we? Couldn't you paint here? Couldn't I write?"

"For a time. But only for a time."

"Other people live out their lives here."

"They are born and bred here. Their lives are here. Ours aren't. For good or ill we're that something we call 'civilised'. We need the thing we call culture. The culture of cities. If you'd been born and bred here, or come here when you left Oxford, you wouldn't have written one of your books. You couldn't have. You wouldn't have had the material. I might have painted but not the pictures I have painted. I might not have painted at all—if it's true that all art is neurosis. I wouldn't have had the neurosis! Besides, I'd have been too busy milking the cows and getting in the hay!"

"We might have been happier."

"That's another thing. We might have been. The point is we can't go back. We——" She broke off suddenly and caught at Francis's arm. "Francis—look! It's Johann coming up the path!"

The track had begun dropping down; they were nearly at the outskirts of Drindel. They stood still and Johann came up the path to meet them. He wore *Lederhosen* and the usual green Tyrolean hat, with a pheasant's feather. He was very brown. Cathryn's heart plunged wildly.

He smiled as he approached them.

"*Grüss Gott!*" he greeted them, and they shook hands.

"I have arrived myself only an hour ago," he explained. "We thought perhaps in such fine weather you would be walking out. I am sorry I did not get farther along the way to meet you."

"How did you know we wouldn't be coming by the road?" Cathryn demanded.

He smiled. "I did not think you would be the kind of people who would walk on a dusty road when they could walk along a hillside. Let me take your rucksack, please. It must be heavy by now."

He helped her off with it and settled it on his own strong back, and they went on down into the valley, walking in single file on the narrow path, Johann leading, Cathryn in the middle. When he had asked them about their journey she spoke the question uppermost in her mind.

"How long are you staying this time?"

"I have the two weeks," he told her. "It is my holiday. I have arranged it so."

He turned suddenly and smiled at her.

"If they had not given it to me I should have left them," he said, simply.

She thought he must hear the wild happy plunging of her heart. Certainly he must see the colour beat up in her face.

He did see it, and was glad. There was a wild singing in his own heart. He no longer offered any resistance to the idea which had grown steadily in him since he had known she was coming back—the realisation that he more than loved her; that he was, in fact, in love with her.

The Sables had their supper alone. It was early yet for *Abendessen* Frau Amanshauser explained, but they would want something after their journey and their long walk, and Hans and Willi, the German boys, were not expected back till late, if at all that night, and Herr and Frau Knoedl never came in until about nine these light evenings. She gave them a small table to themselves in the window, from which they could look down the entire length of the street. The balconies of the wooden houses were gay now with hanging baskets of pink and scarlet geraniums, and window-boxes of pink and white and purple petunias, and there were baskets of petunias hanging from the lamp standards in the middle of the street. The *Gasthaus* Amanshauser was similarly beflowered, as Frau Amanshauser said, beaming, 'for the summer season'.

When they had eaten Francis said, "What do you feel like doing, Cathy? Are you too tired for a stroll round the village, or shall we just sit in the café and have a few drinks and talk to the Amanshausers?"

She confessed to him, "More than anything I should like to walk and talk with Johann—alone!"

She was glad that he was lighting a cigarette at that moment, and not looking at her, and then the smoke wreathed up between them, a thin pungent veil. Francis always smoked Turkish. He smiled a small smile and waved away the smoke.

"It's not so very long ago that you assured me that you were not the marrying kind—don't you remember? You conveyed that I also wasn't, but for less commendable reasons!"

"Oh, Francis, I was a terrible little prig! You were quite right!"

"Darling, you were sweet. You were twenty-two and had never been attracted by anyone, so you had come to the premature conclusion that you never would! But do tell me—would you marry Johann Amanshauser, if he wanted that?"

"I don't know, Francis. How can I? I haven't thought about it. I've only realised for about five minutes that he is in love with me! I've got to get used to that idea first. It's all so bewildering ____"

She moved restlessly, and her eyes were troubled.

That was clumsy of me, he thought. 'Tread softly lest you tread on my dreams.' I should have known. It's all so tentative and delicate and unrealised as yet. They're caught in a holy miracle and blinded by it. 'O happy, happy love!'

He said, gently, "Let's go into the café, and if Johann is there or comes in I'll talk to Poppa and Momma and you can go into a huddle with him, or go for a walk, or whatever you decide between you."

In the café they found Herr Amanshauser sitting by the window reading a paper, holding it to catch the fading light and peering closely at it. Johann was behind the bar, leaning on it and talking to two sun-browned, grimed, mountainy looking young men—the two Germans who had just returned. All three had stone mugs of beer in front of them.

Francis sat down beside Herr Amanshauser, who immediately laid aside his paper. Cathryn hesitated a moment, then sat down beside Francis. There was obviously nothing else she could do, she told herself; there was only one possible move and it was for Johann to make it.

He made it, unhesitatingly. She had barely seated herself when he finished off his beer, excused himself to the two Germans, and came over to her. He said the thing she wanted him to say. It was as though she had willed him to say it.

"Are you too tired to come for a walk?"

She smiled up at him. "I am not tired at all."

Francis smiled at her and continued his conversation with Herr Amanshauser.

"Come this way," Johann said, quickly, when she headed for the exit into the street, and with a hand on her shoulder turned her in the direction of a small door beside the bar. He opened it for her and she found herself in a passage in the kitchen regions. He opened another door and they came out into a lane between the inn and the church.

"We go can through the churchyard and on to the hillside," Johann said.

The grass grew long and full of wildflowers between the

graves. A low stone wall divided the graveyard from the surrounding countryside; she was reminded of the churchyard at Wasdale.

They came out on to the slope she and Francis had descended earlier.

"We might go up as far as the hay-hut and get the last of the sun," Johann suggested

They walked in silence, side by side, the westering sun in their faces. When they had walked for a little their hands came together naturally but they did not speak. As they neared the hut he said, "I was sad that you didn't come at Easter."

"I wasn't ready."

"You could have come all the same."

"I wanted to, but I thought you would be disappointed if I came back without being able to take part in the Easter Sunday Mass."

"You could have taken part in it."

"I wanted to be really a part."

"But you've come back after all before you are received into the Church! What is the difference?"

"Francis wanted me to come. He suggested we should climb the Drindelhorn together. Ever since I was fifteen I have been wanting to climb a mountain with Francis, but he has always gone off without me before. He was going to Zermatt but the friend he was going with got ill."

"Why didn't he take you there?"

"He thought it would be too difficult for me—and that I'd like to come back here."

"Would you rather have gone to Zermatt?"

"I wanted to come here. It seemed too good to be true when Francis suggested it."

"It seemed too good to be true when I heard you were coming!"

They walked on in silence again and in a few minutes came up to the hay-hut. They stood looking down into the valley. It was empty of light now, but for a faint flush from the glow in the west. The lake looked cold and grey.

Johann turned from contemplation of the valley to the girl at his side. He stood looking down at her, wonderingly.

"It's wonderful that you're here again," he said. "I didn't know it could mean so much. I thought when you were here before that all I cared about was your joining the Church. . . . Yet even then——"

He broke off and looked away from her. "It's been very difficult for me. I should explain——" He looked at her again, helplessly. "I loved you from the beginning, you see, but I did not want to be in love with you—you understand? I was not given the vocation to become a priest, but through St. Augustine, I believed it was His will that I should try to live like one."

Cathryn sat down and leaned back against the hay-hut and he dropped down beside her.

She said, gently, "Since it was not God's will that you should be a priest why should you believe He wished you to live like one?"

"It seemed so to me. I did not fall in love with anyone. I did not feel attracted to anyone. I was attracted to you in the first place because I found I could talk to you. I liked you, and then I began to feel that I loved you, and on Christmas Eve I suddenly realised that you were beautiful, and I wanted to put my arms round you. I wanted to kiss you when we said Good-bye."

She said, softly, "I wanted you to, too. Why didn't you, Johann?"

He stared across at the darkening mountains; his face was troubled.

"I had been reading St. Augustine for ten years and I had formed a certain habit of mind. There is a word for it, nowadays, is there not—what is it in English? Inhibition! I had formed an inhibition. 'Love, but take heed what you love', said St. Augustine. And 'you cannot become spiritual without you cease being carnal'. I had trained myself in that Augustinian discipline."

She said, in a low voice, "St. Augustine also said that 'because a thing is hard it is not therefore right'."

He turned to her, smiling, all his tension relaxed. "In *De Civitate Dei*. Can you quote the whole passage?"

"Only imperfectly. I remember the context. About people losing their humanity by remaining outside of human affections."

" 'If some are so strangely vain and inhuman as to take pride in being absolutely callous to everything and in being left un- moved and uninfluenced by any affection, they lose their whole humanity rather than find true tranquillity of mind.' " He took her hand that lay beside him in the grass. "I was in danger of losing my humanity until I met you, Cathryn." He raised her hand to his lips.

Then he looked at her. "Does it seem strange to you that I have never even kissed a girl's hand before?"

She said, her voice unsteady, "Does it seem strange to you that I also have never been in love before and never kissed anyone? I believed just as you did that all this wasn't for me. Only this evening my brother reminded me."

"Was it difficult for you, too?" He kept her hand, holding it in both of his own.

"Not in the way it was for you. I was only afraid you would never love me in the way I wanted."

"I didn't know until this afternoon that you wanted me to, and even now I keep wondering if I am not mistaken—believing what I want to believe——"

She smiled, but her eyes were soft.

"No, Johann, you aren't mistaken."

He turned to her then, and his arms went round her.

"Cathryn! *Liebchen! Mein Herzliebchen* . . ."

It was dark when they came down the hill together. They walked in silence until suddenly Johann said, softly, "We shall be married—when?"

She answered, dreamily, "When the apple-blossom comes again."

"Not until then? It is almost a year."

"When the snow comes, then."

"That is a promise?"

"It is a promise, Johann. We will be married at Christmas."

"We shall be quite poor."

"I lived in a garret in Paris."

He stopped suddenly in the path and put his arms round her and kissed her.

"We shall be so happy!" he cried. "Let us go quickly now and tell everyone!"

They ran down the rest of the hill, then skirted the churchyard and went soberly into the *Gasthaus* by the front door. Still holding hands they came into the café. It was now full of smoke and people. Through the haze she saw Francis leaning against the bar and Frau Amanshauser behind it.

"*Wir heiraten!*" Johann cried, and his voice had a ring in it. Everyone looked at the two at the door—the dark broad-shouldered young man in *Lederhosen*, the slim childish-looking girl in ski-ing clothes, her almost flaxen hair twisted in plaits round her small head.

They advanced into the room and went over to the bar, and Herr Amanshauser emerged from a corner, and Frau Amanshauser came from round the bar, and other people crowded round, all talking at once; there were congratulations and calls for drinks. The Amanshausers knew everyone in the café—apart from the two German boys and Herr and Frau Knoedl they were all local people. Frau Amanshauser and Herr Amanshauser in turn embraced Cathryn, and though she did not know what they said it was evident that the news gave them pleasure.

When he could get near her, Francis said, "Is this serious, Cathryn? You haven't known each other five minutes!"

"We've been waiting for each other all our lives!"

He smiled. "Quite. That is in the best romantic tradition. But a love-affair is one thing and marriage is another, sweetheart. You are an English girl of what is called good family, marrying an obscure Austrian book-seller's assistant, the son of a Tyrolean inn-keeper! You are also the distinguished young tempera painter, Miss Cathryn Sable, but you are going to become Frau Amanshauser . . . and incidentally you don't speak a word of German!"

She laughed. "I soon shall now!"

She turned as someone put a glass of wine in her hand, and smiled into Johann's glowing eyes. He touched her glass with his and raised his own to his lips.

"To the future," he said.

"To the future," she repeated, then looked at Francis.

"I don't believe a word of it," he said. "But here's hoping!"

When she was finally able to escape to her room Cathryn took off her clothes, pulled on a nightgown, washed in cold water, took the pins out of her plaits and loosened them, then got in between the cool clean sheets and lay flat and still, her arms along her sides, relaxed. She had this ability to relax when she

was tired. The beginning of the day seemed part of another life—
had she and Francis really breakfasted in Vienna, in the dark little
hotel, admitting to each other that they had just a little—just a
very little—of a hangover? Had they really got into a train and
gone to a place called Schultzburg in the mountains, and then
walked the twelve miles to Drindel? All that seemed far away and
long ago. But what had happened since was near and real. The
walk up to the hay-hut, and the talk there, and the bewildering
miracle of being in love, and then the promise to marry—she
who had declared that she could not imagine herself marrying,
or falling in love with anyone who did not look like Francis and
who was not altogether like Francis. She would marry Johann
and they would live in a room at the top of an old house in Salzburg, and the river would rush past under their windows. She
would be Frau Amanshauser. She had given him her promise.
She had told Francis that they had been waiting for each other
all their lives, and that was true. She had drunk to the future, to
her future with Johann, that meant, and everyone else had drunk
to it, but still it was not real. It was real for Johann, but not for
her. When the snow came . . . it was all so far away. She had first
to climb up into the snow with Francis. That is what she had come
there for. One day, oh a long, long time ahead . . . so long
that you could not think so far . . . she might become Frau
Amanshauser . . . but not yet . . . not for a long time yet. . . .

She sank into deep white drifts of snow . . . of cool sheets
like snow . . . deep snowdrifts of sleep.

17

Francis said at breakfast, "Don't you think you were a little
hasty last night in promising to marry Johann? I lay awake half
the night thinking about it!"

She smiled. "We want each other," she said simply.

"You don't have to marry each other, dammit!"

"Johann is a good Catholic, and I hope to become one."

"There will be children—a lot of children if you are good
Catholics. What is to become of your painting?"

She stirred her coffee, thoughtfully. "I have painted a lot of pictures, why shouldn't I now create in another direction and have a lot of children?"

"You're marrying out of your own world, is what I'm trying to say. I'm not concerned with class—plenty of one's own class are not of one's own world, God knows!"

She smiled. "What is my world, Francis darling?"

"You know quite well what I mean—writers—painters——"

"I've only known one painter intimately, Anna Kallinova, and only one writer—Francis Sable."

He tried again. "If Johann were an artist of some kind——"

"He's something more important for me—he's a Catholic. But if it helps you to feel better about it, without being either a writer or a painter he knows a good deal about both literature and painting. . . . Also he loves me. Also I love him! May I give you some more coffee?"

He passed his cup and she filled it.

"What are we going to do today?" she inquired.

"If you can tear yourself away from your betrothed we are going up to the glacier to give you some practice with step-cutting."

"It's a good day to go—Johann has gone to Vienna to buy me an engagement ring."

"What do you suppose mother is going to say about all this—with her feeling for class?"

"The fact that he is a Catholic will compensate for all the rest."

"Even your living in Austria?"

"Mother's dearest wish was that I should be received into the Catholic Church. Once that is safely achieved nothing else I can do can upset her very seriously. Why do you worry so much about me, Francis?"

"For the same reason that you worry about me, I suppose, funny one. Come on, if you've finished, let's go."

They went out into the bright sunshine and walked through the little town, lively with its Saturday busyness, and up on to the grassy, flowery pastures of the Drindelhorn. They took only one rucksack, which Francis carried; since they were going no farther than the lower slopes of the glacier the only 'stores' they would need would be their lunches.

"If we were conscientious," he told Cathryn, "we'd each carry a rucksack weighted with stones, by way of practice, and before we do the big climb you should have some practice with the weight you intend to carry then."

He had borrowed an ice-axe for Cathryn from the Amanshausers; there seemed no point in buying one, he said—"Unless after this you become a confirmed mountaineer," he added.

Which means, Cathryn thought, that so far as he is concerned this is my first and last climb. In future she would be able to climb with Johann. Did she want to? She didn't know. First there was this thing she had to do with Francis. She would certainly never do the Wasdale climbs with anyone else, not even with Johann. It startled her when, as they walked on up over the grassy slopes, Francis suggested that when they did the big climb they should take Johann with them.

She said immediately, "Oh, but that would spoil it!"

He turned to look at her. "What *do* you mean? I thought you were so madly in love with him that you would stop at nothing— not even marriage!"

"I mean that climbing this mountain together is something private between you and me. Something we talked of as children, and when we were adolescent. I've always dreamed that one day we would do it together—just we two. I can't suddenly take someone else into the dream! Don't you *see*?"

"I'm afraid I don't see. Three is better than two for a climb of that kind, with a novice."

"So that I can be all cosy in the middle of the rope, you mean? But I'm not such a beginner as all that, you know! I thought I could be said to have served my novitiate on Scafell and Great Gable!"

"It's years since you've climbed anything."

"It's like riding and swimming—once you can do it you never forget how."

"The point is I haven't climbed the Drindelhorn—I don't know what problems it may have in store for us."

"You mean you think we need a guide?"

"I'd like to discuss it with Johann, anyhow."

Now that they were actually there, the mountain looming up before them, he had a feeling of responsibility he had not expected to feel. Cathryn had been all right on rocks when they had climbed together, but that was years ago; she was out of training; and he had no idea what were the particular problems of this particular climb. And Cathryn had no experience on steep, hard snow-slopes and on ice. If she had had even a little training on Ben Nevis it would have been useful. Still, she was good on rocks, and that was important; she wasn't, as she herself said, such a beginner as all that. Plenty of people had gone straight from rock-climbing to snow and ice work. Well, anyhow, he told himself, as they plodded on, they would see how she got on . . . and what Johann recommended.

Cathryn had no such misgivings. She had complete self-confidence, and was supremely happy. The sun shone, and she was on a mountain at last with Francis. The thing she had wanted to happen was going to happen, was in process of happening. But it must be kept between the two of them; this was something which belonged to Francis and herself and no one else. The dream could only be realised in the terms in which it had been dreamed; in this dream of the white mountain Johann had no part; what was between her and Johann was quite another dream.

They moved onwards and upwards through the sunlight. Through the pinewoods with their strong sweet smell; across the steep grass slopes; across the torrent below a waterfall; on through the rough grass of wasteland, to the edge of the scree; on over the desolation of the scree into a wilderness of boulders, and on up to the great rock cliffs that flanked the glacier, and up, slowly, doggedly, and the sun moving over, and the hours, timelessly. And inside oneself the deep quiet satisfaction.

They ate their lunch at the foot of the glacier. It was steep, a rough, frozen torrent, caught between rocks of ice. They studied it whilst they ate.

"We could get a good way up it by keeping to the snow at the sides," Francis said, "but for practice we'll go up over the ice. When you're ready. . . ."

She got up. "I've been ready for the last eight years or so," she told him.

When they came down off the ice the sun was sinking.

"We must get a move on," Francis said. "We don't want to

find ourselves in that wilderness of boulders with the light going."

She was all right, he thought; she hadn't forgotten her rock-climbing; she was sure-footed, her sense of balance was perfect, and she kept her head; and she had that most invaluable of assets to a climber, a capacity for endurance, for going on when dog-tired.

"We'll get an early start tomorrow," he told her. "We'll start out before it's light and get right up to the hut below the peak—at least we'll see how far we can get."

"Tomorrow's Sunday."

"So I believe. What about it?"

"One doesn't climb on Sundays."

He stopped in his track and stared at her.

"Why on earth not?"

"One goes to church." She smiled at him, but he frowned.

"If you'd told me this earlier we might have stayed over in Vienna for the week-end! There was no point in coming here to waste a day. What do you propose we do all tomorrow—mooch about in our best clothes like the villageois?"

"I propose to hear Mass in the morning and Rosary and Benediction in the evening. In between we might go for walks."

"So you do intend we shall mooch about in our best clothes! And will you tell me, please, why it is all right to walk about on the flat on a Sunday and all wrong to do that more strenuous moving about we call climbing?"

"For one thing the Amanshausers would be very shocked if we treated Sunday like any other day and went off climbing. It would hurt them. For another thing to go climbing tomorrow would"—she smiled—"interfere with my devotions!" Then, as he turned away, she caught at his arm. "Francis—don't be angry. There are things we'll never agree about, aren't there?"

"Unfortunately! But if you intend to keep the Sabbath holy I shall go on up the glacier alone tomorrow and reconnoitre. I suppose Johann wouldn't come too?"

"No." It seemed strange to her that he should have asked.

They went on down the track, in single file, silent, estranged.

When they were off the scree and on to the grass they walked abreast again. She said in a small voice, "Franci-is," dragging out the final syllable questioningly.

He smiled and repeated her own name similarly. It was how they had approached each other in the old days when about to ask favours of each other.

She slipped an arm through his.

"Well—what is it?"

"You're not cross with me, are you? I mean—I may be silly about Sundays, but I was all right on the ice, wasn't I?"

He laughed. "I won't be got round."

"But I was all right?" she persisted.

"You'll get by."

"And Monday we'll start out early and go right up to the hut?"

"We'll get an early start, but how far we'll get depends on what Miss Cathryn Sable is like on really hard ice. I have an idea it's not so easy above that glacier. I'd like to discuss it with Johann."

They sat together in the café after supper and Hans and Willi, who spoke English, joined them. The Germans declared that the Drindelhorn climbed from this side was not difficult, but it was hard work, and unrewarding—not worth the effort. Francis explained that the Fräulein had no experience on snow and ice. They regarded her with interest. Ah, so. In that case it was a good practice climb.

Johann said sharply, "It is more than that! There is an ice-couloir. And the spur below the peak. Such things are not for beginners!"

Cathryn looked at him. "One has to begin sometime with the difficult things!"

"One does not begin with the Drindelhorn!"

Cathryn appealed to the Germans. "But I am not beginning with the Drindelhorn. In England I have done difficult rock-climbs. Would you say I could go up the Drindelhorn?"

"And down it," Johann muttered.

Hans smiled. "If you can handle an ice-axe, Fräulein, and if you go with two climbers of some experience."

Willi supported his friend, eagerly. "Come with us, Fräulein—we would get you up and bring you down safely!"

"You are kind, but my brother and I must do this thing together—the two of us, only. No one else. It was arranged long ago."

Hans shook his head. "No, Fräulein. With a beginner there should be two experienced climbers on the rope. It is better so."

"I have told her that," Francis said. "I think Johann should come with us."

Johann said, stubbornly, "Cathryn must not climb the Drindelhorn yet. She is not ready. It would be madness. I have climbed that mountain since I was a boy. Herr Francis has not climbed it at all."

Francis said quickly, "I propose to do so before I take my sister."

"Even so, once is not enough. The weather changes. You climb perhaps on Monday and it is easy going; the weather is good. You take your sister Tuesday and the conditions are quite different."

"In that case I shall never climb it at all!" Cathryn cried, despairingly.

Johann said, quietly, "If you love me you will not climb it at all!"

"But that is absurd, Johann!" Francis protested. "That is sheer emotional blackmail. Because you love Cathryn and are afraid for her—no, Johann, I cannot accept that! You, an experienced mountaineer to make such an appeal—it is unworthy!"

"Yes, I love Cathryn and I am afraid for her."

Hans shrugged. "There is no more to be said." He got up and motioned to his friend.

Cathryn looked after them despairingly as they turned to leave the table.

"You both say I can do it?"

"With two experienced climbers with you," Hans repeated. His friend insisted, smiling. "With us you could do it, Fräulein."

When the Germans had gone Francis smiled at Cathryn. "Well?"

"We shall climb it together, you and I," she declared, resolutely.

"Unless Johann will join us?"

"I refuse to consider it. There is no more to be said, because if Cathryn loves me she will not attempt it."

"I do love you, Johann, but I refuse to be blackmailed!"

He looked at her, puzzled. "What is this word you use? Blackmailed?"

"It is an unfair appeal to the emotions," Francis explained. "To ask Cathryn not to do something she wants to do because she loves you."

"I cannot see that it is unfair."

"It looks to me as though you two had better fight it out between you." Francis rose. "I'll leave you to it."

Johann said quickly, "We will go. We can talk better away from here. Will you come, Cathryn?"

She shook her head, impatiently. "There is nothing more to say. I came here to climb the Drindelhorn with my brother and I intend to climb it with my brother, and no one else, and nothing and no one is going to stop me. Not even you, Johann."

"Cathryn—please."

Francis said, "Why don't we adjourn this committee until I have made my reconnaissance and reported back? If I make the ascent myself and consider it too difficult I shall refuse to take you, Cathy, and that will be that! Can't we leave it at that for the time being?"

Cathryn rose. "Yes, we'll leave it at that."

"*Aufwiedersehen*, then." Francis left them.

Cathryn turned to Johann :

"Don't let's discuss it any more, please," she said quickly, and led the way out.

They walked all the way to the hay-hut in an oppressive silence. When they reached the hut she flung herself down.

"I'm tired. It was my first day on the ice and we got half-way up the glacier. I'm not such a novice!"

He sat down beside her. "I got this for you in Vienna today."

He put a small case into her hand. She smiled at him, melting to him again.

"Did you find what you wanted?"

"What I wanted costs more money than I am ever likely to have, but this I found in an antique shop."

She opened the case. The ring was a sapphire in an old-fashioned setting of seed-pearls, and she exclaimed, delightedly, "How did you know I love this sort of thing?"

"I noticed that you wear always an old-fashioned topaz brooch."

She slipped the ring on to her finger.

"The size is right?" he asked anxiously.

"It is perfect!"

She put an arm round him and kissed him.

"You are sweet, Johann, and I love you!"

He held her. "*Liebchen*, you are very precious to me. It is why I say no to the mountain. But if you must do it let me come with you, as your brother suggests."

"No, Johann. There was a thing Francis and I said we would do years ago when I was a child. We called it climbing a white mountain together. I did a painting of Francis two years ago with a mountain in the background. I didn't know it at the time, but it was this mountain. It is a thing we must do together, Johann, the two of us and no one else. Oh, but it will be all right! Why do you worry so? Francis is a very experienced climber. He has climbed the really big things—Matterhorn faces, Monte Rosa, Mont Blanc, the Eigerwand—all the more difficult peaks. I shall be quite safe with him. And you know that the Drindelhorn is not difficult climbed from this side—you have done it yourself, so you know."

He buried his face in her shoulder.

"I love you so much, and it means so much to me to love you —more than you can possibly understand. It makes me afraid."

She held him to her as though he were a child.

"It will be all right," she said, softly. "I will do just this one thing with Francis and then I will be content. But this one thing I have to do, and perhaps that is something you can never understand. But in time we shall understand each other, my darling. In time. . . ."

"You defeat me in all directions, don't you, *Herzliebchen*?"

"Is that how it seems to you?"

"One has no defences any more. . . ."

"After this," she promised him, "I will never worry you again. We will live happily ever after."

He raised an arm and drew her down to him.

"I love you," he said, despairingly. "I love you—too much."

18

The discussion was resumed the following evening. Francis spent the day on the Drindelhorn with the two German boys—they had no scruples about climbing on Sundays. He left them at the *Hütte*; they intended going on next day. When he got back to the inn in the evening Cathryn greeted him, eagerly.

"How was it?"

"Boring, rather. No special difficulties on the glacier, a pretty steep pull up to the cornice above the ice-fall, then a cat-walk of a snow-ridge to the base of the Schwartzkogel. I had a good close-up of the peak through the binoculars. It's hard going, but climbable."

Johann said impatiently, "Of course it's climbable! Your English rocks are climbable but people quite often break their necks on them, I believe!"

"They quite often don't!" Francis was beginning to find the discussion boring. After all Cathryn was not altogether a novice; she was a good rock-climber and had acquitted herself admirably on her first day on the ice yesterday. And they weren't going to attempt the peak tomorrow or the next day or the next. She would get in plenty of practice before they made the final assault on the citadel. Cathryn was born and bred among the high hills; climbing was in her blood. She had come to the mountains at long last to climb—really, Francis finally demanded of Johann, what was all the fuss about? Did he seriously propose that Cathryn Sable should content herself pottering about on the lower slopes? It was too ridiculous.

Johann said, stubbornly, "I too was born and bred among the mountains—not high hills, but mountains! Climbing is in my blood, also. But I say that one does not begin with the Drindelhorn!"

Irritated, Francis asked, "What does one begin with, then—the ascent of the Schmittenhöhe by funicular?"

"The Schmittenhöhe is not a mountain," Johann replied.

Humourless fool, Francis thought.

"Really? What, then? A nice easy walk up the Geisberg with beer and *Würstchen* at the Zeppezauerhaus? Or isn't that a mountain either?"

"The Riesenalp from Glocken is a good mountain to begin with," Johann said.

Francis stared at him. "What on earth do you mean? It's a far more difficult glacier—you have to climb the ice-fall, and there's some stiff work on the summit——"

"You do not have the cliffs and precipices on the Riesenalp peak which you have before you reach the summit of the Drindelhorn."

"Personally I thought the Riesenalp peak was hell. And at this time of the year there will be swarms of *Wandervögel* being hearty at the Glockendorf *Hütte*——"

"You lose them before you reach the Pitz *Hütte*, and it is there one stays the night."

Cathryn was beginning to feel as bored and irritated by the discussion as Francis. She turned to Johann.

"I'll climb the Riesenalp with you, if Francis will come——"

"Oh, leave me out of it!" Francis put in, quickly.

"All right. I'll climb the Riesenalp with you, Johann, and if I don't have any difficulty with that it's agreed that there shall be no more argument about my doing the Drindelhorn with Francis. Is that agreed?"

"It is a good practice climb," Johann conceded.

"Is it agreed or isn't it?" Cathryn persisted.

Johann sighed. "It is agreed. I still say——"

Cathryn cut across him. "You don't still say anything, any more! It is agreed. Very well then, when do we go to Glocken?"

They left the following day, taking rucksacks and climbing kit and following the path above the lake. The sun shone and the air was warm and still and full of the smell of hay and byres and pines. The lake was a Midi blue. The immensity of the mountains was intensified by the clear air. London, Paris, Vienna, were merely names, places on a map, the crowds and the swirl of traffic something in a dream dreamed long ago. To be walking on a hillside with Johann, this too was happiness. It wasn't the deep, rooted kind of happiness that happened with Francis, and could only happen with him, but it was joy, light and golden as the air, and you wanted it all to flow on timelessly for ever.

The *Gasthof* to which they came at the mountain village of Glocken late in the afternoon was wooden, its gables and balconies ornately carved, its windows gay with boxes brimming with petunias. There was a field full of flowers in front of the house, and beyond the field the lake. Behind, the grassy lower slopes of the mountain went up steeply to the base of the great cliffs of bare rock and the desolation of boulders and scree. A hut was visible, very small, on a terrace some way up the mountain; it was the Glockendorf *Hütte*, Johann told her; the Pitz *Hütte* was a great deal farther on, below the summit; unless you knew where to look it was difficult to pick it out without binoculars.

There were a number of holiday-makers at the *Gasthof*, including some English visitors, but there was accommodation. Johann had a small room at the back, facing the mountain; Cathryn a small room overlooking the lake. She leaned out of the window, the velvet softness of petunia petals brushing her chin, and she tried to think of Montparnasse, the Dôme, the Rotonde, Anna Kallinova; of South Kensington, the museums, the park, Knightsbridge, the fashionable shops, the big red 'buses, her mother, but none of it seemed real. Even Father Connor was shadowy. Even Francis farther up the lake. All that was real was herself and Johann in this village under the mountains, the scent and feel of petunias, the clouds going over the Riesenalp.

When they walked together hand in hand through the long twilight after supper they talked of the next day's climb, but of the Drindelhorn not at all. They would spend the next night at the Pitz *Hütte*, climb the peak the day after, and be back in Glocken by the evening. The following day they would return to Drindel. That would be Thursday, Cathryn reflected; perhaps she and Francis could go up the Drindelhorn on the Friday, returning on the Saturday; it was either that or leaving it over till the Monday, to avoid Sunday climbing, and the sooner it was safely achieved the sooner Johann would be relieved of his anxiety. There was a thing to do, and the sooner it was done the better. It had waited years too long already. . . .

There was the steep zigzag course up to the weather-beaten old Glockendorf *Hütte*, over grass slopes, through pinewoods, across streams, up over the higher pastures, the grass growing rougher, and boulder-strewn, with the thick low scrubby bushes

of *Alpenrosen* and *Preiselbeeren*. Then, because there were too many
people at the *Hütte*, on again, to eat their lunch among the
boulders, then on and up through a wilderness of rock and stone,
and into the thin mist of a cloud, and the bright sunlit valley and
the flowery pastures dotted with hay-huts far down below, a part
of another world. Even the great white peak was out of sight
now. There was nothing but this desolation of rocks and scree
and boulders, misted and cold. They walked in silence, talk and
laughter falling away from them with the sunshine and the green-
ness. Then there was the hut, low and squat, built solidly of
stone, crouched at the base of the summit, which was a mountain
in itself, Cathryn thought.

Inside the hut there were people studying maps, people
playing cards, people eating sandwiches and drinking hot coffee
from thermos flasks; there was a clutter of rucksacks, ropes, ice-
axes. There was a long bare table, benches, an oil-lamp suspended
from the ceiling. There were wiry-looking, red-faced Englishmen
in shorts; sturdy, sun-tanned *Wandervögel* in *Lederhosen*; hardy-
looking females in breeches and ski-ing trousers worn with open
shirts; a general atmosphere of untidiness, *camaraderie*, toughness,
Bergfreundschaft. There were guides with battered green hats,
puttee-bound legs, weather-beaten faces. There were steaming
bowls of *Erbsensuppe*, and mulled wine drunk out of tin mugs;
there was talk in two languages of rock-faces, scree, snow-slopes,
cornices, ridges, couloirs, glaciers; of holds, crampons, pitons, and
the weather. The mist drove past the window of the hut like a
thin grey smoke. Presently a wind got up. It was intensely cold.
A guide brought in an armful of wood and kindled a fire. One of
the *Wandervögel* produced a mouth-organ. The hut filled with
warmth and smoke and singing. People kept going to the door
of the hut to look at the weather.

Cathryn leaned her head against Johann's shoulder; she was
sleepy from the warmth and smoke and the wine, after the day in
the open air.

"Is it going to be bad weather tomorrow?" she asked, drowsily.
"Everyone seems anxious."

"The guides seem to think it might snow, and going up to
the peak in new snow is a little difficult."

"I shall manage," Cathryn murmured. "Whatever it does,

wind, hail or snow, I shall manage. What are the sleeping
arrangements?"

"Just bunks. One room for the men, another for the women.
There are a few small rooms for married couples."

"It would be nice if we were a married couple. . . ."

"Next time we are on a mountain together we shall be, please
God!" She saw the glow in his dark eyes.

She rested her arms on the table and her head on her arms and
smiled at him, sleepily.

"Then we are going to climb more mountains together?"

"*Natürlich!* With me you are safe, always."

Her mind said, "Francis is just as good a climber—perhaps
better!" But there was that in his eyes and voice which stilled
all argument. 'What so wild as words are!' She was aware of the
warmth of his skin as he leaned close to her. She loved him.

Of the ten people, including Cathryn and Johann, at the
hut, two parties of three set off for the peak with a guide to each
party, leaving shortly before Cathryn and Johann, and two went
down. It was dark when they all left the hut; the mists had
cleared and the stars were bright; there had been no *Neuschnee*. It
would be light by the time they reached the glacier, Johann said.

As they were leaving the hut he put an arm round her
shoulder, turning her to him, and kissed her lips. Her hands
went up to his neck, instinctively, and for a long moment they
clung together.

"Did you sleep well?" he asked, when the kiss was spent.

"Like the dead," she told him. "All that very fresh air! All
that mulled wine! And you?"

"I haven't slept properly since I knew you were coming to
Drindel, and that I was in love with you! I think I shall never
sleep properly again till we sleep together. Must we really wait
till Christmas, *Liebchen?*"

She smiled, dreamily. "Ask me again when I get back from
the Drindelhorn. . . ."

Then they were moving, single file, through the starlight,
through the sharp coldness, over the icy shale, and in the distance
the small moving lights of electric torches carried by the parties
ahead of them. The great wind of the night had dropped.

The glacier in the dim light between dark and dawn was like a rough sea that had frozen, Cathryn thought. They stopped and roped-up. The other two parties were out of sight. For a long time the glacier was an undulating, gently ascending river of ice, criss-crossed with crevasses. You went slowly on and up, picking your way, occasionally jumping a crevasse, and the daylight strengthened. The summit was out of sight. You did not look for it. You saw only the next few feet of the glacier. You went slowly, cautiously, concentrating. Slowly on and up. Once Johann looked back at her.

"All right?"

She smiled. "Fine!"

They went on, their eyes on the ground, Johann pausing here and there to probe with his axe. Here and there they made a détour; sometimes they retraced their steps, Johann muttering, *"Es geht nicht."*

Then the glacier rose more steeply, and the flanking rocks became towering cliffs. They paused at the base of what looked to Cathryn like the Niagara Falls frozen.

Johann stood contemplating the ice-fall. The rock walls which enclosed it were holdless, unclimbable.

"It's not as difficult as it looks," he told Cathryn. "But I think we put on the crampons."

They clamped the steel spikes to their boots and began to climb. Up through the spurs and stalactites and seracs, over the humps and rocks of ice, and between the pinnacles, then a glassy slope that called for some step-cutting, and they were in the midde of the ice-fall. There was no more walking after that; they climbed steadily. The sun came up and the ice became dazzling and they put on their goggles.

They climbed slowly, steeply, doggedly, and time passed, timelessly, a succession of careful movements and the slow onward and upward slither of the rope.

They came off the ice at last on an almost vertical snow-slope, with a cornice thrusting far out like a roof. The steps which those ahead of them had kicked and scraped into the hard surface were visible.

"See, we have a staircase made ready for us!" Johann cried. They went up; even with the staircase ready made they were a long time going up, and when they were just under the rim of the sky-line Cathryn, who had not slipped on the ice, missed a foothold and slipped. For a few moments she clutched wildly at the icy surface of the snow-slope, then she had kicked a hold into the snow with the toe of one boot and was holding on to the rope, steadying herself. Johann, with the rope belayed round his ice-axe driven into the snow a few feet beyond the rim of the slope, looked down at her, smiling.

"For that," he said severely, "you will lose a good mark!"

"Sorry," she said. "So long as I'm not disqualified!"

She came up the remaining few feet and sat beside him in the snow. It was their first rest since they had left the hut.

They stopped only a few minutes. They had climbed up into the wind. They were on a narrow ridge that wound round to the base of the peak; on one side the steep snow-slopes fell away down to the glacier; on the other there were a series of precipices dropping thousands of feet into the valley. Clouds poured down into the valley from the peak. The rocks of the ridge were icy and treacherous, thin snow concealing the ice. They went on hands and knees across the ridge; the wind tried to blow them off, and the clouds to blind them, but they went on.

They went on, poised on a knife-edge in space, interminably it seemed to Cathryn. Several times they stopped, clinging to the rocks with hands and feet and knees, unable to move because of the velocity of the wind. They crawled on, mindlessly, and came out at last on to a terrace below the summit.

"From here it is all, what do you call it—plain sailing."

"I'm glad to hear it," Cathryn said. She thought, 'This is the mountain that is easier than the Drindelhorn. . . .'

The plain sailing included a narrow icy ledge with sheer rock slabs at one side and space at the other, inching up the icy slabs when the ledge gave out, holding on, it seemed to Cathryn, by one's finger-nails and knees, an encounter with a hurricane on some exposed rocks, hacking a way up a wall of frozen snow . . . and when we have done it all, it suddenly came to her, we have to do it all again in reverse. . . .

They met the other two parties coming down.

"*Sieg heil!*" they called.

"*Sieg heil!*" they gave them.

They have the ridge ahead of them, Cathryn thought, and the snow-slopes and the cornice, and the ice-fall, and the glacier . . . but they also have the *Hütte*, with steaming bowls of *Erbsensuppe*, and a fire, and no wind lashing you, and a bunk in which you can lie flat. But flat. . . .

This was a good climb for beginners, Johann said; very well then, it was a good climb for beginners. Keep going. It was what Anna had said about work. It was all you could do. Keep going.

Several times it seemed to her that they must be at the summit. She could see nothing above, and the ground seemed level. But Johann said No. The wind lashed them and the clouds went over. There was a wilderness of rock and snow; there were more rocks to climb, another ledge to edge along. And it was intensely cold. She stumbled once or twice from weariness. Her eyelashes froze. When Johann turned round she saw that his eyebrows were white with frost, and his eyelashes rimmed like her own. There was some more scrambling up over icy rocks. Through a hole in the clouds she had a sudden glimpse of the valley, sunlit, thousands of feet below. So the sun was shining down there; people would be walking about, smell grass and flowers and byres; and there would be hot coffee for breakfast. . . . And down there there would be, blessedly, no wind. . . .

She pulled herself up over yet another icy boulder and stood beside Johann on a small snowy plateau. He turned to her smiling and held out his hand.

"Congratulations on your first peak! It was not so difficult, was it?"

"No," she said. "It wasn't so bad!" She thought of the ridge and the ice-fall, but still, there they were. . . .

"It is a pity we have no view today," Johann said.

The clouds were thick below them now, in a white sea. The wind tore at their clothing and snatched their breath. Why did one climb mountains? It was an unpleasant and exhausting business doing it, and the summit was a desolation—what more desolate and beginning-of-the-world than the top of Scafell Pikes, with the wind whipping up the snow like a dust-storm, and tearing at you with invisible frenzied hands?—What was there rewarding in the achievement? As often as not there was no view, because of the clouds. You climbed because of some curious compulsion in your self. Some *je ne sais quoi*. You either had it in you or you hadn't, and if you hadn't nothing could make you understand. 'Why do it?' people who hadn't asked, puzzled, impatient. And you couldn't tell them. Because you didn't know. All you knew was the compulsion. But the compulsion was not for this mountain, if you were Cathryn Sable. This mountain you climbed merely to prove that you could climb a mountain—to satisfy Johann. It was the apprenticeship you served for the mountain you would climb with Francis. . . .

"We must be going down," Johann said. "We don't want to find ourself on the ice at midday, with the sun shining."

They began the descent. Scramble down the boulders, drop down on to icy ledges; edge along, holding on to the wall of rock with your finger-nails; down the snow-slopes, slow, slow, well away from the cornice; crawl along the knife-edge of the ridge with the clouds trying to blind you and the wind trying to tear you off, and every now and then a glimpse of the sunlit valley, just to let you see how far you had to fall, if you did . . . keep your eyes on the rock, your hands on it, your knees, the toes of your boots; keep your mind on it; keep your eyes on Johann's behind; keep going. . . .

Down the snow-slopes to the ice-fall, the cornice over you like a roof. Down the ice slower than ever you came up it, because now the sun is touching it and it is running with water, and every now and then a piece comes away in your hand or cracks under your feet.

"You are safe with me," Johann had said. Very well, you are safe with him. You keep going.

Through the cracks between the humps and boulders and stalactites, down on to the glacier itself, and now the snow has gone and there are more crevasses. And you are tired of ice and snow and crevasses . . . but you are going down into the sunlight, into the green world where people drink hot drinks and lie flat and perfectly still, and there is no longer any need to keep moving. . . .

When they came off the glacier and paused to take off their crampons and goggles and to unrope, Johann smiled at her.

"Tired?"

"I'm fine."

"You have been splendid!"

"But this is only a beginners' climb, so it doesn't count!"

"This is not a beginners' climb, *Liebchen*. The route you are going up the Drindelhorn is much easier!"

She stared at him.

"I thought this was to be training for the Drindelhorn?"

"I had to satisfy myself you could climb!"

"So you give me the difficult climb first! Weren't you rather taking a chance?"

He smiled, contentedly.

"With me you are safe, always."

"Then you won't worry now about the Drindelhorn?"

"Not now." He took her face between his hands and kissed her, held her a moment, then, "We must be going," he said.

19

Francis entirely agreed that the sooner he and Cathryn climbed the Drindelhorn and got it over the better. It had for him none of the sentimental importance, the psychological significance, it had for Cathryn. She had this *idée fixe* that she had to climb a mountain with him, and part of the *idée fixe* was that it had to be the Drindelhorn, because it was like the mountain she had painted as the background of his portrait. For her, he knew, it had a mystical importance. For him it was something he would do to please her. And the sooner they got on with it the better, because whilst she and Johann had been away at Glocken the two young Germans had returned from their Drindelhorn expedition and had been discussing an ascent of the Kitzsteinhorn that was new to him; they had suggested he join them, and he had told them that if they could wait till the following week he would be delighted; he would start out with them on the Sunday. They would wait until then, they said, but they did not want to wait beyond that, as they had climbed everything worth climbing in the district, but to have an experienced third person with them they would wait till then. It suited Francis very well, therefore, that Cathryn was set on climbing the Drindelhorn on the Friday, the day after her return from Glocken.

"Friday," said Frau Amanshauser, "is not a good day to do anything important—like getting married, starting a new job, moving into a new house, or climbing a mountain for the first time."

They assured her, laughing, that they were not superstitious. They appealed to Johann. There was only one day on which he would not climb, he said, but that had nothing to do with superstition.

Francis resisted the temptation to ask what religion was but that, and it was agreed they would start out in the morning. They would get back on the Saturday, and on the Sunday he was going off for a few days with Hans and Willi.

"So!" was all the comment Johann offered. He would have Cathryn to himself. Cathryn could not think ahead. She and Francis were about to climb the white mountain.

"After the Riesenalp it will be easy for you," Johann told her. "For one thing you have not to go over the glacier in the dark, and you have not to climb the ice-fall. There are some very steep snow-slopes, and there is what Francis calls the cat-walk, but it is not like the Windy Ridge on the Riesenalp. But all the way to the summit you are exposed to the wind. Those are the bad things, but you come to the summit after a night's rest—you do not have to face it after already climbing for hours, and that is something."

She smiled at him. "The only thing which is really important in all this is that you are no longer worried about my doing it! What will you do when I am away?"

"Pray for you."

"But you cannot pray for me all day and all night and most of the following day!"

"I shall spend many hours praying for you, day and night, and when I am not praying for you I shall read St. Augustine."

"Will that help?"

"It will help."

She pressed his hand.

"And when you come back we will arrange to be married—soon."

"I didn't promise that! I said you could ask me."

"But you want it, too?"

There was the dark urgent glow of his eyes.

Her smile was tender.

"Yes, Johann, I want it too. . . ."

They had walked up to the hay-hut together after *Abendessen*. They would not see each other again for two days, and they were agreed that it was a very long time.

"Poor Johann! You take your holiday when I come so that we can be together, and then I go off for days on end!"

"But soon we shall be together for always, *Herzliebchen*."

"Francis would say that that was the terrifying part of marriage."

"Francis has never been in love."

She looked down into the valley; it was slowly filling with a sad grey light that seeped into it out of the fields, out of the mountains, out of the sky.

She said, in a low voice, thinking aloud, rather than addressing Johann.

"He could be right," and quoted, softly—

> 'What pleasure have we
>   Of our changeless bliss?
> Nay, if love lasted
>   There were joy in this . . .'

"Why shouldn't love last?" he demanded, almost angrily.

"Because," she said—

> 'Life's way is the wind's way;
>   All these things
> Are but brief voices
>   Breathed on shifting strings.'

"If you believe that why are you going to marry me?"

"Francis would say because of the biological urge of Nature! I would say because I love you, and love is not reasonable."

"Perhaps we don't mean the same thing by love. Love is reasonable just as faith is reasonable. Faith is immutable or it is not faith. Love is immutable or it is not love."

"The person or the thing you love might change."

"Shakespeare has given you the answer to that." He smiled. "I can quote too—'Love is not love which alters when it alteration finds. . . . Oh no, it is an ever-fixèd mark . . .' If you changed I should love you for what you had been, for my memory of you, and for what remained unchanged—because no one changes utterly."

"Conversion is an utter change," she suggested.

"No. St. Augustine could not have become a saint unless he already had it in him to be a saint. His passion was carnal; it became spiritual. The intensity of love was the same. It was re-directed from the drain, where it was wasted, into the garden, where it served to make beauty spring. It is thus he himself describes it." He took her hand.

"We shall neither of us change, *Liebchen*. We do not love lightly. We shall love each other always."

"Always is for ever, and forever is eternity."

"Yes, forever is eternity. It is to the grave's edge—and beyond."

He put an arm round her shoulder and drew her close to him.

"Tomorrow you will realise the dream you have had since you were a young girl. It is important to you; it means very much to you. Then you will come back to me, and there is our own dream, the dream we have made together. We are dreaming it together now, and we shall never wake. . . ."

It was just getting light when Cathryn and Francis left in the morning. Johann had insisted on getting up to make them coffee and see them off. He stood at the door of the *Gasthaus* and waved to them till they were out of sight down the empty street. He looked like a monk, Cathryn thought, in his long brown dressing-gown with the knotted cord. . . . The knotted cord of chastity, poverty, and obedience. The knot of the climbing rope round your waist; the knot of safety in the cord that was a life-line. . . .

They went on up through the pastures, through the woods of pine and larch, through the wasteland, to the glacier, desolate in the grey light, a corrugated mass of ice and fissures. They went on up through the hard snow at the sides, under the walls of rock; there was no need of ropes or crampons. They climbed, steadily, silently, and the sun climbed and somehow it was broad day-light. Above the glacier the snow-slopes were sheer up to a jagged cornice, they roped up, they kicked and hacked steps, and climbed up slowly into the wind. At the top of the ridge the wind was a howling fury. It was a blinding wind; a wind that strangled the breath. They buried their chins and mouths in the collars of their leather wind-jackets and struggled on.

The mountain resented you, Cathryn thought; it resisted you with all its force; you had to fight it; it fought you back, with rock and ice and roaring, bitter wind. But you struggled on; you kept going. These were what Johann called the bad things: the good thing, the supreme thing, was that you were fighting this fight with Francis; it was something you had to do; and it had to be this mountain, with the white, conical, formalised peak of a child's dream. The steep, icy snow-slope above the glacier seemed endless. Waiting whilst Francis kicked or hacked a step you took your eyes off the blinding whiteness and looked at the ridges beyond. They were scribbled against the sky like a child's drawing. Only the scribbling was solid rock, and every tiny wavy line of the scribble was intricately composed of terraces and ledges and vertical crags which had somehow to be edged along, crawled along, inched up, hanging on by your finger-nails and the toes of your boots. And all the time the wind hurling itself at you, blinding you, roaring at you, suffocating you. But you were doing what you had wanted to do for more than seven years, and you kept going. Your legs and feet, and the minutes and the hours, kept passing each other; slowly, but they passed.

You came out on to the cat-walk that connected the snow-slopes with the rock *massif* of the Schwarzkogel. You wondered how many hours it would take to traverse that jagged granite mass; what the ridge that connected it with the summit was like. . . . Then you were crawling on all fours along the cat-walk, very slowly, your head down like an animal sniffing a trail. The sun was up and the glare was blinding. You drove your ice-axe deep into the snow and fumbled for your goggles. The wind tried to tear them out of your hands, but somehow you got them on. Clouds poured down from the peak like smoke vomited from the mouth of a volcano; clouds churned as though they were boiling in the cauldron that was the valley some ten thousand feet below. You could not see or hear or think. You were merely an automaton, that blindly, mindlessly, kept going . . . in an inferno of wind that lashed and raged and roared at you. You crept along behind Francis, and the rope crept between you, a life-line. Once, driving his axe into the ridge a few feet ahead of him, the snow cracked and crumbled and a small avalanche went sliding away down the slope. He drove his axe in again, beyond, and it held. They crawled on.

Then at last they were on a terrace at the foot of the Schwarz-kogel, their backs against the rock, not out of the wind but at least not attacked by it on all sides.

Francis smiled down at her.

"All right?"

She nodded. "Fine."

"This little lot"—he jerked his head at the labyrinth of crags, spurs, promontories, precipices, behind them—"isn't as bad as it looks. The terrace goes a good part of the way, then a couloir brings us out almost on to the top. The ridge to the summit isn't too bad—at least one doesn't have to crawl. Shall we go on?"

They went on over the terrace, the wind lashing up at them from below, hurtling down on them from above. The peak was out of sight now. There was only the narrow snowy terrace, with the wall of granite slabs at one side, and space on the other. The terrace narrowed and terminated in a great bastion of jagged rock.

"This is easy," Francis said.

It was the easiest going they had had yet; there were hand-holds and footholds. If only it weren't for the snow, Cathryn thought; it dislodged itself from upper ledges as you reached up, or thrust up an ice-axe to find a hold, and came down into your face, pouring over your head and shoulders; if only it weren't for the wind whipping at you all the time, stinging the balls of your eyes, exhausting you . . . only of course exhaustion was merely something in your brain; your body, your legs and feet, and arms and hands and shoulders, kept going, automatically.

You reached the top of the bastion and worked a way down the other side, into a recess; then you toiled up the other side; it was the same struggle all over again. You froze; you sweated;

you ached; you slipped; you scrambled; you groped for foot-holds and handholds; you hung on by your nails. Francis was always above you; the rope moved up, like a snake moving over the rocks; you went up after the rope, and Francis was on a ledge above. He looked down once.

"You see what I mean about this being a boring mountain?"

You saw what he meant. In your aching bones you felt what he meant; but this was the mountain you had set yourself to climb, that you had waited years to climb, and now you were climbing it, so you went on and up, mindlessly, timelessly, and at last you reached the couloir. For a good part of the way it was a steep ascent of frozen snow, and you hacked a way up; then it narrowed into a chimney, and the rocks dripped in places, making holds slippery and difficult. Occasionally it was narrow enough to straddle, so you inched your way up, and when you couldn't straddle it you hung on by friction . . . or so it seemed, your back against the wall behind you, your knees and feet pressing at the wall facing you. A huge smooth boulder near the top shut out the sky; it looked completely unclimbable, but Francis was swarming up over it, and where Francis went you could go. You held on where there was nothing to hold on to; there was the pressure of your belly against the stone, there was the desperate straining physical effort, the tremendous effort of will, and then somehow you had made it. . . . You were on top.

"Good girl. Another twenty feet and we're there."

You went on again; up to the next pitch, and at last you reached the scribbled skyline, the crest of the ridge, were no longer in a chimney but out in the open, with the wind shrieking at you from all directions at once, and the powder-snow whipped up into a snow-storm about you. You went on over a slope that seemed almost flat, and down into a hollow that was relatively out of the wind and to leeward of the white dust-storm. Francis slipped his pack and flung himself down.

Cathryn slipped her own pack and sat down beside him.

Francis pushed back the mitten from his left wrist and looked at his watch.

"Two o'clock. That's not bad going. We should be at the hut soon after four. Let's have some coffee."

Cathryn removed her mittens, fumbled with the straps of her rucksack, pulled out a thermos flask.

She said, pouring coffee, "If we reach the hut by four why don't we go on up to the peak?"

"I know the feeling—get it over with! We'd get up it all right before dark, but we couldn't get back to the hut before dark. And there are some tricky bits. Much better to do it in a good light, and when we're fresh. You'll have had enough by the time you get to the hut."

Another snow-slope, another ridge, then they were in under the great white mountain of the peak itself, corrugated with terraces, jagged with spurs and promontories, cleft by deep couloirs, its summit visible only momentarily when the wind moved aside the folding and refolding curtain of cloud.

The hut was the merest shelter; there were bunks, a table, a couple of benches. There were some ashes and charred wood in the fireplace, and a new-looking cigarette carton. There were a few sticks in one corner of the hut, but as they had no means of supplying further fuel, there was, as Francis said, no point in lighting a fire; such wood as there was would burn for only a few minutes.

"But we're out of that infernal wind—that's something."

"It's almost everything," Cathryn said.

They unpacked, set out the Primus stove and various packages and tins. They finished the coffee in one flask and saved the other for later. They ate bread and *Würstschen* and saved the cheese. The tinned soup they would save till they came down from the peak next day.

When they had eaten and rested they went out and looked at the peak through the binoculars. They brought its ledges and crags and couloirs and precipices close to them. It was beautiful, Cathryn thought, and terrifying. Beauty and terror—but the elements of Greek tragedy demanded pity and terror, and the mountain was pitiless. You were an intrusion, and with all its elemental forces it ejected you. But it was made only of rock and stone, and snow and ice; it pitted its strength against you, but you pitted your will; in the end it was your will which was the magnet which held you to the almost holdless slabs, your will which glued you to the cat-walk ridges, beyond the power of the wind to dislodge. The mountain could win only if you weakened. It was the triumph of the spirit over the material.

They returned to the hut and crawled into the bunks, wrapping their blankets about them. They lay listening to the wind, talking desultorily, letting tiredness dissolve in their limbs in a blessed relaxation, softly, softly. . . . The last aria of the St. Matthew Passion ran through Cathryn's mind, drowsily . . .

'Lie Thou softly, lie Thou softly, softly here.'

In the soft flow of relaxation, the soft flow of the music, she fell asleep.

Francis did not sleep so easily, in spite of their early start following on a short night, and the day-long battle with the wind, and the drowsy reaction of mental and physical relaxation.

He thought, When I have finished with this mountain and restored Cathryn safely to the arms of Johann, I shall climb other mountains with Hans and Willi; so many more peaks added to one's collection. I shall go back to Paris and correct the proofs of a book; I shall write another book; I shall go to more parties, and there will be another Merrilee Browne . . . because Sue will not be added to the collection. . . . You made love to the Merrilees because the Sues were not available, except on their own terms— and you did not accept their terms. And the Sues went on being interesting because of their inaccessibility, which was clever of them, but profited them nothing in the end. Very well, then— you would make love to more women, only it wasn't love, and you would drink more drinks and have more fun, only it wasn't fun, and you would pack more bags and do more journeys because there was a devil of restlessness in yourself, and you had to keep moving. . . . Then you became mentally and nervously exhausted and you had to get away, and you climbed more mountains, froze on more ridges, sweated on more rock-faces, and you were refreshed mentally and physically . . . and went back to Paris and wrote more books, went to more parties, made love to more women . . . and that was your life. Well, what about it? Thousands would envy you. It was a comparatively easy life. Your books didn't take much out of you because you wrote from something called your intellect, not that mushy mess

of emotions called the heart. You had success; you made money—
a lot of it, and fairly easily; you had an amusing time; you were
free, you had no responsibilities because you didn't permit them.
There was a time when you had fancied yourself a socialist, a
Shelleyesque revolutionary, when you had uncomfortable things
called principles and ideals . . . well, you had grown out of them.
If you thought about it—which you very seldom did—you found
that the principles still held. You still maintained that no one
should own a mountain or a lake or a moor or a forest; you were
still aware of the inequalities and injustices of the existing
social system, but you could not concede that Soviet Russia was
the solution, not because it was communist but because it wasn't.
If you analysed your political idealism you found you believed in
an old-fashioned thing called democracy; you wanted a socialist
democracy. But you did very little analysing. The fact was you
didn't care enough. You did not, fundamentally, like the human
race. In the mass it was smelly and stupid and brutish. What was
it Wilde had said about democracy—that it was a bludgeoning of
the people, by the people, for the people. But it needn't be. The
real thing wasn't. Not that you cared. You were entirely sympathetic to the Aldous Huxley character who said, 'Dam' the
poor, drat the poor, blast the working-classes!' Social revolution
was a social need, all right, but it was their business, not yours.

There you were, then, Francis Sable, aged thirty, ten thousand
feet up on the Drindelhorn, and that was your political philosophy,
and for the rest you were an Epicurean. Yours was the carnal
life which Augustine of Hippo, philosopher, scholar, mathematician, lived for thirty-three years before he abandoned
Manicheeism for Christianity, replacing the glorification of the
flesh with its mortification. If you believed in the life-everlasting
you could afford to do that; if you believed that you had only
one life and this was it you couldn't afford to. And Francis Sable
couldn't afford to. So you gathered your roses—your women,
your mountains, and anything else that was going—whilst you
may. And you had fun. You enjoyed life. "Give me my moments!
You may keep your years!" That was it. Life as the gay stroll
through the fair. Only by the time you were thirty there was this
sense of repetition. You'd had it all, done it all, known it all, and
somehow when it was all added up it came to astonishingly little.

You were being cheated somewhere. There had been moments. The day when you had battled up on to Scafell Pikes with Cathryn and into a sunset for which there were completely no words, and had the feeling of standing on the roof of the world. (Well, anyhow, as Cathryn had said—she had been a long-legged colt of twelve, then—they were higher than anyone else in England. It had seemed, then, so immensely satisfactory.) And the range upon range of great hills spread out before them, all held in that tremendous light, all crimson and gold, and the snow flushed with a soft diffused rose, and the two of them glissading down through it with a feeling of having grown wings. . . . And the exhilaration of small triumphs on Pillar and Needle that meant so much. There had been moments. And other times. The first time you heard Bach's *St. Matthew Passion*; the first time you read *The Hound of Heaven*; the first time you stood in front of El Greco's *Agony in the Garden*. The first time you stood in the Piazza San Marco and saw the lines and colours of that dream in mosaic they called a church. There were adventures and excitements of mind and spirit as of the body. At Oxford it had been all you asked. You were fond of quoting Wilde—'Life is a series of bad quarters of an hour with some exquisite moments.' You still thought it true, but it was no longer good enough. You felt you were being cheated somewhere; life ought to be more than that. What was it for Cathryn? A dream, he thought, an endless dream from which she never woke; from which she had no desire to wake. She painted the landscape of a dream, she flowed on a dreaming tide of mysticism towards the Catholic Church, and in a dream she would marry Johann Amanshauser. Even this mountain, with all its rigours, was part of the dream . . . and so instead of lying restless in her bunk ten thousand feet up the mountain tormenting herself with questions to which there were no answers she lay sleeping peacefully. He envied her . . . which, he told himself, a little angrily, pulling the blankets up closer round him, was ridiculous. He closed his eyes, resolutely, but he did not sleep. The wind howled and the sky darkened, and it was evening.

He got up and lit the candles they had brought with them, got the Primus stove going, opened the soup and poured it into the small camp saucepan. His movements and the light, and the humming of the Primus, wakened Cathryn. She lay for a moment, confused, staring at the shadows on the walls and ceiling.

"It's night," she said, wondering.

"It's the night between nights," he told her.

She raised herself on an elbow in the bunk and looked at him.

"When did you read St. Augustine?"

"Is that Augustine? I thought it was Francis Sable. I'm sorry it's been said before."

She swung her legs over the side of the bunk.

"It's all been said before—everything."

He stirred the soup. "That's a disheartening thing to say to a writer," he observed. "But if you want to be helpful you can lay the table. Whilst the soup is heating I'll carve the *caneton*."

"But there's no orange salad."

"Really? And no Pommard, I suppose?"

"I'm afraid not."

"In that case we'll just have cheese. This is a very inferior *Gasthof*. We won't come here again. The soup is out of a tin, I wouldn't wonder."

He poured the soup into tin mugs.

"*Diner est servi, Madame.*"

He glanced at his watch.

"They'll be serving *Abendessen* downstairs."

Johann, her heart cried suddenly, tomorrow I'll be back with you! We'll walk up to the hay-hut together, and I will marry you, Johann, soon, soon . . .

They slept badly. The cold was intense. As soon as it was light they got up, heated coffee, having first washed out the soup saucepan and tin mugs with snow. They clasped the mugs of hot coffee in both hands, thawing their fingers. They ate bread and sausage, and clasped the tin mugs until there was no more warmth left in them. They repacked their rucksacks, leaving the remaining provisions, and the Primus stove and cooking and eating utensils, to await their return to the hut; they refilled their flasks with hot coffee, and put chocolate and raisins into their pockets.

"We'll travel light this time," Francis said, "and we should be back here not later than one o'clock."

The wind tore at them the moment they set foot out of the hut, and the clouds swept up from the base of the Schwarzkogel like an intercepting army between themselves and the peak. They went a short distance through hard snow along the terrace from the hut and began to climb. The peak appeared to be composed mainly of a series of steep buttresses of jagged rock; there were plenty of holds, but the going was slow because of the snow; every hold had to be groped for with hands or ice-axe; the edges were precipitous and icy, and in one place undercut, which meant crawling under the shelving rock. But it was the snow which made everything, simple in itself, difficult, Cathryn thought, and a line from *Alice* came into her head—

'If this were only cleared away,' they said,
'It would be grand.'

And if only someone would close a gigantic door in the heavens and keep out that infernal draught they called a wind. . . .

They went on and up. The sky imperceptibly lightened and then long coils of cloud lay across a crimson backcloth. Peaks thrust up above a sea of cloud, jagged rocks islanded in a thick churning sea; their mountain bases ten thousand and more feet down in a wooded and pastured valley had no reality. The floor of the world was this dense mass of cloud; the peaks were mountains in themselves, unrelated to scree-slopes, snow-slopes, glaciers.

The snow hardened and became ice; they stopped on a narrow glazed parapet which ended at the base of a tall spire of rough rock and put on crampons. The crampons gripped the ice and they moved forward to the spire. At the other side of the spire, Francis knew, the parapet went on again. You could not go over the spire; you could only go round it. With your left arm you got a grip of the rock above your head where the parapet ended, drove in the toe of your left boot, then reached out with your right arm for a handhold round the bulge of the rock, then stretched out with your right leg and groped with your right foot for the parapet you knew was there. You gripped, you stretched, you groped, and with a concerted effort of body and will you were there. You belayed the rope on a jutting crag and waited for Cathryn. And Cathryn, steeling herself, gripped and stretched and groped and made it without knowing how. When she stood beside him on the parapet she was sweating.

He smiled at her, though his own body was wet with sweat, not from his own concentration of effort, of body and will, but on her account.

"That's the bit the guide-books call 'rather nasty'," he told her. "The final few hundred feet are no more than the Dress Circle on Great Gable, except that they're icy."

Except that they were icy, Cathryn thought, and except for the wind that seemed to make its own concentrated effort on that last lap. You did not quite know how you swarmed up those final icy slabs, but somehow you did, and somehow there were no more—no more slabs, no more spires, crags, promontories, buttresses, no more ledges, no more ridges; no more skyline.

No more skyline because you were on top.

You were at the top of the cone. You were at the summit of the white mountain, with Francis. There was nothing higher except the sky. The wind flung itself at you in a frenzy, and you crouched and gripped the rock; you could not speak to each other without shouting, so you were silent; but you looked at each other and smiled.

It had come true. 'There was a thing to do, and it is done now.' You were exultant; you were fulfilled. It was not merely a mountain peak. It was a peak of living. Your soul magnified the Lord. You crouched in the snow and said a prayer; your soul knelt down and chanted the *Magnificat*.

Then they began the descent. They slithered and dropped down the icy slabs; they sweated round the spire, moved cautiously along the icy parapet, removed the crampons, groped for holds on the buttresses, made a stomach traverse of the undercut ledge, groped for holds again, went on, laboriously, down, and the hours passed each other, and presently they were on the terrace to the hut . . . back in the hut.

"How does it compare, as a climb, with the Riesenalp?" Francis asked, as they heated soup on the Primus.

"The Riesenalp is more difficult."

"And more interesting!"

"I suppose so. But getting to the top didn't mean anything much. Just the usual feeling of satisfaction. This was different. But I knew it would be." She looked away from him suddenly. "I can't talk about it, Francis. Only—thank you for taking me."

He stirred the soup. "You're an old funny."

They drank the soup out of the tin mugs, ate the bread and sausage and cheese. "We've still got the chocolate and raisins," Francis reminded her.

"They'll do for tea," she said.

"Where do we have that?"

"Above the ice-fall."

They washed the mugs and the saucepan in the snow, re-packed the rucksacks, and set out across the snow-slope towards the crags of the Schwarzkogel scribbled against the sky. At the base of the *massif* they saw a party of three coming down. They sat in the hollow where they had rested before and waited for them.

There were two men and a woman. They greeted Francis and Cathryn in German and asked if they had been to the top, and how was it. Francis talked to them for a few minutes. They were Austrians, from Vienna. They inquired a little anxiously about the spire on the peak. Francis explained it to them; the woman decided that she would remain at the hut. Had the *Fräulein* been to the summit? *Fabelhaft!* They regarded Cathryn admiringly. They shook hands and parted.

Francis and Cathryn went on up the Schwarzkogel, and began the long slow descent of the couloir.

Cathryn found the chimney even harder going than coming up it. She slipped at the outset, in negotiating the chockstone, and it unnerved her. She slipped again half-way down. The first time she saved herself, wedging her body in a cleft between the chockstone and the granite wall. The second time she clutched and clawed frantically, swinging loose on the rope, before the tips of her fingers found holds and by a desperate effort she pulled herself in to the wall and found a foothold on a three-inch projection from the rock. Francis on the rope above her called down to her, "Take it easy. There's plenty of time." She was tired, he thought; this was her fourth day's climbing; but for this idiotic business about not climbing on a Sunday she could have had a day's rest in between. The buffeting on the peak, too, was more exhausting than one realised at the time; they should rest a few minutes before going on over the crags.

When they finally came down out of the couloir she leaned back against a wall of rock and smiled at him, wanly.

"That wasn't so good, was it? I'm sorry."

"It's always trickier coming down a chimney—coming down anything, in fact. We can rest a few minutes."

"We're due for tea at the glacier," she reminded him.

He smiled. She was game. She always had been, he remembered, from the Wasdale climbs. "All right. Let's push on then."

They went on over the Schwarzkogel, monotonously up and down, across snow-filled gulleys, along snowy ledges, over icy rocks. Cathryn found herself stumbling here and there. Yes, I'm tired, she thought, but there's nothing for it but to keep going. . . .

They were off the *massif* at last and strapping the crampons to their boots for the glassy frozen snow of the terrace leading to the ridge. They felt the impact of the wind as soon as they came out on to the terrace. Clouds were driving over the ridge. You didn't feel at all like going over that tight-rope-walk poised in space, you hadn't felt like it yesterday, and you felt even less like it today; because you were tired; because you had had enough of being slashed by the wind; but as Francis had said once to her when she was in difficulties on Great Gable, you either had to do it or stop up there all night, so you got on with it. . . . You became an automaton again, crawling along a cat-walk, holding on with hands and feet and the strength of concentrated will-power. Your whole being became concentrated into the supreme effort to hold on. You held on and kept going.

The ridge ran out to the crest of the steep snow-slopes, and you could stand up again. The steps which the Austrian party had hacked and kicked scarred the sheer whiteness in a twisting staircase.

"We'll use their steps and take it facing outward," Francis said.

Mechanically her mind registered, Take it facing outward. Keep going. You had a weak desire to sit down when you had been going for some time, but you cannot sit on a sloping wall. You can drive your ice-axe in and your heels in and brake yourself for a minute or two, but the wind rushes up at you from the glacier and hurls itself down at you from all the gorges, gulleys, funnels, of the peak; there is no peace, so you keep going. But when you get to the glacier you will sit on a boulder and let your arms and legs hang loose and the tiredness drain out of them. You will eat raisins and chocolate and when you go on again everything will be what Johann calls plain sailing. . . .

Francis was also going on mechanically. He was not particularly tired, but the wind and the monotony of the descent numbed the mind. Then suddenly there was a jerk on the rope and a jerk on his mind. Cathryn had slipped; he drove his ice-axe into the snow, leaned back, ground in his heels, felt the rope go taut, waited for the arresting plunge of Cathryn's own ice-axe, and in the split second in which he realised that she was still falling his own ice-axe hurtled from its hold. His hands clutched at the steps above his head for a hold, but the impetus of the falling weight at the end of the rope was too great and he went hurtling down the two hundred feet of snow-slope after her. He clawed at the snow as he fell but it was ice-hard, and the steps were a greyish twisting snake out of his reach.

The speed of his fall slackened; his hands dug into the white wall and held; he drove in the toes of his boots; there was no longer a drag on the rope. He hung on and looked down, and saw the boulder which had broken Cathryn's fall at the head of the ice-fall.

He climbed down.

She was lying in a curious position, her limbs unnaturally sprawled, and her neck curiously twisted. He thought at first the dark patch by her head was the rock exposed under the snow. Then as he came down to her he saw that it was blood. She had cracked her head against the rock.

Her eyes were open.

"Cathryn," he said. Then, still aloud, "She's unconscious."

Her rucksack had gone, her hood had gone. He pulled off his scarf and folded it and put it under her head. Then he knelt looking at her. After a moment he said aloud, "I don't know what to do."

If there was some hot coffee left, if there was some brandy. But there was no coffee left, and they had brought no brandy. All they had was some raisins and chocolate. It came to him that this was where they would have eaten them. He didn't know what to do.

He looked round, wildly. There were three people up there at the hut. Back up the snow-slopes, back along the ridge, up the couloir. . . . Supposing he went back to them. They could help him carry her down the glacier. But if she recovered consciousness and he was not there she would wonder what had happened. He couldn't leave her. But also he couldn't carry her down the glacier; they wouldn't be able to go down the easy way they had come up; the sun had melted the snow at the sides; they would have to go out into the middle of the glacier, thread a way between a network of crevasses from which the snowbridges had now gone. Accidents on mountains were the devil. But accidents on mountains happened. And it was said they more often than not happened on the easy places like this, because you got careless, particularly when you were tired. No use thinking of all that. Think what to do. If she recovered consciousness she might be able to walk down. Or would she be too weak? Or perhaps she had concussion. If she had concussion she mightn't recover consciousness for days. He looked at her. The dark patch in the snow by her head was broadening. He must stop the bleeding. He pulled out his handkerchief and lifted her head, turned it. Then he went sick. He fought with himself, half choking, but it was no good. Something came up in him, a black wave of nausea, hot and dark, uncontrollable. He retched.

She will bleed to death, something in him said. She will bleed to death. He went back to her. Her eyes stared at him, fixedly. Her mouth was open. It came to him that she was dead. She wasn't unconscious; she hadn't got concussion; she had cracked her skull wide open against the rock, and she was dead.

His brain told him that, but it could not make it real for him. He still didn't know what to do. You could go up the mountain for help, or you could go down it. Part of his mind worked very clearly. By the time he got back to the *Hütte* and had returned with help it would be too late to go down the glacier. By the time he had got down to Drindel and back again up the glacier it would still be too late to take her down. He couldn't leave her there all night. *Are you going to stop up there all night?* You never stopped up there all night, whatever your difficulties; you found a way down. There was a way now. You could not climb in the dark . . . except when you had to. People had climbed in the dark, and would again. Going alone he could go faster. He could be back at the *Hütte* in a few hours; he could get back to the glacier with one of the Austrians whilst it was still light; even carrying Cathryn they could get down off the ice before it was quite dark. He couldn't go back to Drindel without her. They had started out together; they must go back together. Perhaps it wouldn't be necessary to go all the way to the hut. Perhaps he could rouse the Austrians before then, if he shouted. Sound carried in the mountains. He cupped his mouth in his hands and gave a long yodelling call. It rose and fell in the deep silence. Then he listened. He thought he heard a faint answering call, but that of course was absurd. His call couldn't have reached the hut from that distance. He would call again when he was back at the top of the snow-slope. Better get going. . . .

As he climbed slowly up the ready-cut staircase it came to him that he no longer had an axe. And that there had been no scream when Cathryn slipped. She had gone without a sound. She would be expecting any moment to brake herself. She would have kept her head . . . until she crashed against the rock; then she would black out. That was the end, blackness, stillness, silence. Not knowing anything any more. Everything finished. Nothingness. He went on and up, into the wind. He stood on the terrace and cupped his hands and called again. And again he thought he heard an answering call. It was absurd, of course, an echo. That was what it was, an echo. Listen again. He called and listened, and there was the echo . . . or whatever it was . . . unmistakably.

He still had his rucksack; he slipped it from his shoulders, fumbled with the straps, fished out his binoculars. He swept them across the cat-walk, above the *massif* of the Schwarzkogel, to the terrace below the peak. Cloud drove across, misting the sight. He waited till there was a break in the continuously folding and refolding mist, then tried again. He could see nothing. But whilst he stood there he heard a call, rising and falling, a long-drawn-out yodelling cry. His heart pounded. He dropped the binoculars, cupped his mouth with his hands, and roared into the wind. He knew this time that the answering cry was no echo.

If he had a tent, he thought, he could have squatted in the snow and waited, but he had no tent, and he could not sit in the snow and freeze. Besides, whoever was coming might prefer not to climb alone. He went on back across the cat-walk. . . .

At the bottom of the couloir he called again. There was no answer. In a panic he got out his binoculars again and let them sweep the walls of the chimney. It took him some time before he made out the tiny figure clamped with its back against one wall and its knees against the other. . . . Thank God for that! He replaced his binoculars in the rucksack and waited.

The figure which finally scrunched down through the sweep of icy snow at the bottom of the couloir was the younger of the two Austrians. He said quickly, speaking in German, "We were watching you through the glasses. We saw what happened." He hesitated, then added, "Is the Fräulein badly hurt?"

"She is dead," Francis told him. He turned away, abruptly, and picked up his pack. He said in English, "Let's go——"

The Austrian said, helplessly, "I'm sorry."

They roped up and went back across the ridge, heads down to the icy snow, like animals trailing a scent. When they came out on the parapet of the cornice Francis said, "I should have thanked you for coming."

The young man made an embarrassed dismissing gesture. They went on down the snow-slope in silence . . . to the great boulder, to the brown patch in the snow, to the incongruously twisted dark heap that was Cathryn.

PART II

NIGHT BETWEEN NIGHTS

'Yea, faileth now even dream
The dreamer, and lute the lutanist.'
(FRANCIS THOMPSON.)

THERE was the long, slow difficult journey down the glacier in the fading light, but for Francis it had no reality. Ever since they had got back to the boulder his brain had been numb. The young Austrian took charge. He did what Francis had been unable to do: he tied his handkerchief round Cathryn's head, and his scarf round her face; he took Francis's handkerchief and tied her hands together on her breast. At his suggestion they took off their coats and tied the sleeves together and improvised a stretcher. Whatever the Austrian suggested Francis did. When the Austrian suggested that he, Francis, should take the lead across the glacier, because he was better acquainted with it, he took the lead; he kept his eyes on the ice and his mind worked automatically, so that he felt his way, made détours, zigzagged, with just that one part of his mind functioning. Afterwards he had only a blurred memory of the journey, and he had no recollection at all of the boulder-strewn wasteland below the glacier, or of the trees beginning, or of descending the pastures; or of coming into the little town, in the dusk, and people staring. Or of arriving at the *Gasthaus* and what happened there. Only one thing he remembered all his life—Johann coming into the dark little hall as they entered; Johann's eyes on the improvised stretcher, Johann lifting his face and looking at them . . . looking at them.

There was a cry, a savage frenzied shout.

"For God's sake!"

But it wasn't Johann who cried out; it was Francis. For God's sake stop staring. . . .

There was a doctor, there were police officials; there were questions, but what they were or what he answered he hardly knew. It was the doctor who released him from the nightmare. Herr Sable must go to bed, he said; he must be given a sleeping draught.

He slept his drugged sleep, and in the morning wakened exhausted and confused. He lay staring at the ceiling till the mists cleared. Something was wrong. Something terrible had happened. It came back to him, and with it the numbness—the self-protective numbness. He got up, washed in cold water, dressed. A telegram had to be sent. Decisions had to be taken. How did you word a telegram to a mother, to your own mother, to tell her that what she had always dreaded had happened, and her ewe lamb was dead? How did you ask her what was to be done—whether after the inquest the ewe lamb was to be brought home, or buried under the mountain on which she had died? How did you do these things, for God's sake? You couldn't do it; you couldn't humanly do it. Not possibly. But you had to do something. You did the cowardly thing; the only thing you could do; you wired Sue Lester in Paris. *Serious accident Cathryn on mountain please bring mother out by 'plane immediately prepare her for the worst wire time arriving.* He could have 'phoned Sue in Paris, but it was easier to send the telegram. An answer came in the afternoon. *Going London by midday 'plane will bring your mother Vienna first morning 'plane please meet.* He did not get the message till the following day, because when the telegram came he was lying unconscious on his bed, an empty brandy bottle in one corner of the room, where it had rolled when he had finally drained the last drop and it had slipped out of his fingers.

The Amanshausers opened the telegram. It was Johann who handed it to Francis in the morning.

"We will go to Vienna together," he said.

"I can't go," Francis told him.

"But your mother—how can you not go?"

"The point is how can I go?" Francis's voice had an edge to it. "I persuaded my mother that something she had always dreaded would not happen. It has happened. Cathryn meant more than life to my mother. It meant everything to her that Cathryn should be received into the Church. You know that?"

"Yes," Johann said. "I knew that."

"My mother called her her 'ewe lamb'. Does your English run to that?"

"It's in the Bible. I know what it means."

"Very well, then. You will understand why I am not meeting my mother, now or ever."

"But she is coming here! And the other lady—how can you not meet them?"

"Because, my dear simple God-fearing Johann, I shall be drunk—dead drunk! By the grace of God I shall be unconscious."

"Not by the grace of God, Herr Francis."

"Ah, go to hell!"

Francis got up from the bed and moved over to the washstand. He had not shaved yesterday and he did not intend to shave today, and yesterday, coming from the mountain, he already had two days' growth of beard.

Johann stood watching him whilst he threw water on his face, then took a towel.

"Do you suppose I am not already in hell?" he asked, violently.

Francis took his coat from the back of the chair.

"Doesn't Mother Church comfort you in your hour of need?" he demanded, derisively.

Johann decided to ignore the taunt.

"It is terrible for all of us," he said, smothering his anger. "For you, for me, for your mother. We should try to help each other."

"We're each in our separate hells, eh? Very well. Only I happen to know a way out of mine. Take a tip from me, *mon vieux*, and if Mother Church lets you down try brandy!"

He attempted to brush past, but Johann caught at his arm.

"Stay here and rest. I will bring you *Frühstück* here. Coffee will do you good. . . . You will feel better; then we will discuss what is best to do."

"You mean coffee is good for a hangover, but I don't happen to have a hangover, and the kind of thirst I've got isn't settled by anything except more brandy."

Johann made a final effort.

"Your mother will be here by midday. If you have any feeling for her——"

Francis blazed at him.

"Good God, man, do you think I haven't? Haven't you imagination enough to understand that I feel for her so much that I can't bear it?"

"You make it worse for her by behaving in this way . . ."

"Nothing can make it worse for her! The worst thing that could possibly happen to her has happened."

Johann moved away and let Francis pass.

"You make it hard for Cathryn, too."

"Cathryn's dead."

"Her soul needs your prayers. Perhaps it is you who have no imagination, Herr Francis."

"I happen to be a rationalist. For me the dead are dead. Very dead. The thing we call a soul dies with the body."

"There is the life everlasting."

"It's no use telling that to a rationalist, *mon vieux*!"

Francis went out. He ran down the stairs and out into the street. It was no use trying to drink at the *Gasthaus*. The Amanshausers wouldn't serve him; at least they wouldn't serve him as much as he needed. And he had only a few hours in which to achieve the necessary blackout. In a few hours his mother and Sue would be here. At all costs he must not see the look in his mother's eyes, hear her stricken words. But for the inquest he could disappear; but he had to stay for that . . . or they would think he had murdered his sister on the mountain. Murdered her? Well, hadn't he? O God!

Johann went to meet Dorothea and Sue. He had no difficulty in identifying them because they were the only two women on the 'plane, but in any case he felt that he would know Cathryn's mother, intuitively. He introduced himself; Francis had sent him, he said, because he himself was too prostrate with grief. . . .

Lady Sable looked at him, the dark thick-set young man in the rough country clothes, twisting a battered green hat with a cord round it in his hands; she saw the strain in his eyes, and she said what she had to say, resolutely.

"You mean that my daughter is dead?"

He answered her simply, "*Ja, gnädige Frau.*"

Lady Sable closed her eyes and crossed herself, then they all three went out to the waiting car.

"When did it happen?" Sue asked, when they were in the car.

He told her. So that Cathryn had been dead when Francis had sent the wire. Francis could have telephoned to her studio. He hadn't done it for the same reason that he had her break the news to his mother—and for the same reason that he had sent this young man to meet them.

The young man was saying, still twisting the hat in his brown hands, "We were going to be married."

They both looked at him.

"She hadn't told me," Lady Sable said, faintly.

"She hadn't time, *gnädige Frau*. It was not until she came here this time that we knew we loved each other. But we knew it immediately, and the next day I went to Vienna and bought her a ring. When she came down from the Drindelhorn she was to tell me when we should be married."

He looked out of the window at the traffic streaming along the road from the airport.

There was a long silence. Lady Sable said at last, "You are a Catholic, I suppose?"

"*Natürlich, gnädige Frau.*"

There was silence again, and when he next glanced at her he saw that she had her eyes and mouth covered with a gloved hand and that she was crying, quietly.

He pressed his own hands together on the brim of his hat.

"It was God's will," he said, desperately.

She opened the handbag lying in her lap and brought out a small handkerchief and dabbed at her eyes and nose.

She said in an almost inaudible voice, "Sometimes it is hard for us poor sinners to acknowledge God's will. Fortunately Our Lady understands. She was a Mother and knew what it was to lose . . ."

She covered her face with her hand again, and for the rest of the journey did not speak.

Sue thought, bitterly, It would have helped her if Francis had come. She did not believe that Francis had sent Johann. She had a pretty good idea why Francis had not come. . . .

When they reached the *Gasthaus*, whilst Frau Amanshauser was showing Lady Sable to her room Johann seized the opportunity to speak to Sue.

"*Gnädiges Fräulein*, there is something I should say to you. It is about Herr Francis. He feels himself responsible for Cathryn's death. Her mother did not want her to climb a high mountain. I did not want it also. This Herr Francis knew. Finally I took her myself up the Riesenalp, which is more difficult than the Drindelhorn, but I did it because I knew that with me she would be safe, and I had to be sure. I believed that if she had no difficulties on the Riesenalp she would have none on the Drindelhorn. I was wrong, as we know. But she was tired, *gnädiges Fräulein*. She should not have done two big climbs in succession like that. She was impatient to do it, but if Herr Francis had asked her she would have waited a few days; she would have waited till Monday, since one does not climb on a Sunday. But that she should wish to climb on the Friday and Saturday suited Herr Francis, because he had other plans for Monday. That is why he cannot face his mother, *gnädiges Fräulein*. He has a bad conscience. He tries to drown it in brandy. It would not be good for Lady Sable to see him. He has not shaved for days, and that together with too much drinking makes him look—how do you say it?"

"I know. But what do you suggest?"

"I suggest that you should see him when he recovers from the drink——"

"When will that be?"

"Not till tomorrow morning, I am afraid——"

"Then you think I should try and settle his conscience! But that's not very easy, Herr Amanshauser. Remorse is a torture of the damned——"

"Yes, it is that, *gnädiges Fräulein*, and Herr Francis is tortured, but he is not damned. He has committed no mortal sin. At present he is trying to escape his remorse by drinking until he is unconscious and by refusing to meet his mother. But like that he cannot escape—never. This you must try to make him understand. I have tried, but with me he is impatient. With you, perhaps it might be different. Tomorrow, too, he must be sober because it is the inquest and he is the chief witness."

"Who else is there?"

"There is a young man, an Austrian, who helped after the accident. He was climbing with his sister and her husband and they saw the accident through their binoculars, from the *Hütte*. He was already on his way down when Herr Francis called for help."

"Where is Francis now, do you suppose?"

"He is either at a café in the town, or he is in his room, drinking. But even if he is in the house I do not think you should try to speak with him now, *gnädiges Fräulein*." His tone was anxious.

"But Lady Sable will want to see him."

"I will tell her that the doctor has given him a drug to make him sleep, and that it is best he should be undisturbed till the morning. Then if Lady Sable keeps to her room until tomorrow . . ."

There was no difficulty in confining Dorothea to her room; she had no wish to see anyone, and she accepted Johann's story about Francis and the sleeping-draught.

In the morning Johann went to Francis's room. He found him lying on the bed fully clothed. He had a raging thirst and he felt extremely ill. He felt that if he did not have another drink immediately he would go mad; he was trying to raise the strength to get up from the bed and go down to the café again when Johann entered. He had brought coffee and rolls, and a jug of hot water.

"If you've brought some nice strong black coffee you can take it away," Francis told him, angrily.

Johann set the tray down on a chair beside the bed, and carried the hot water over to the washstand.

"This morning is the inquest. We must be there by twelve o'clock. Your mother and Miss Lester are here and will expect you to go with them. I have brought you some hot water, so that you may shave."

"The devil you have! Service, eh? But there's one thing you forgot—the brandy!"

Johann said, quickly, "If you will begin to shave I will fetch you a brandy."

"*A* brandy? I need a bottle of brandy, and I need it at once. If I don't get it here I'll get it elsewhere, but if I have to go out for it there'll be no shaving done!"

"I will go and get you the brandy."

Johann went out, and Francis raised himself on to an elbow. God, I feel awful, he thought. He swung his legs over the side of the bed and got up slowly; he lurched over to the washstand and looked in the mirror above it. He stared at himself, fascinated. Curious how much difference a beard could make to a face. Only even without the reddish stubble the face that looked back at him didn't look like his own, he thought. The two days' heavy drinking had given him a puffy look about the cheeks. I look repulsive, he thought, and this morning I've to meet my lady-mother, and the virtuous Miss Lester. . . .

He poured some water from the jug into the basin and groped amongst the things on the washstand for his shaving-brush. When Johann came back with the glass of brandy he had removed the worst of the beard.

Johann had brought a large glass of brandy—a small one, he knew very well, would be of no use. Francis snatched it from the tray on which Johann, meticulously, brought it, and swallowed it at a gulp. It was liquid fire; it burnt his throat, but when it was down he felt it spreading in him with a warm glow. It was that much help that it would give him the strength to finish shaving and dressing, and get down to the café and fill up before he had to meet his mother and Sue.

When he had finished shaving he decided that he looked ill rather than repulsive. He changed from his climbing clothes into the elegant sports' clothes he had worn in Vienna with Cathryn. A bath would have been a good thing—a cold bath—he thought, but there was this urgency about filling up. . . .

Johann had gone out after handing Francis the brandy. He had gone in search of Sue.

When Francis came downstairs into the dark little hall he saw Sue standing gazing at the barometer. At the sound of his step she turned and her heart quickened. He still managed to look distinguished, she thought, though with the bags under his eyes and the slight puffiness round his cheek-bones he had lost that fine-drawn look which was a big part of his physical attractive-ness; he was a coarsened Francis, but he was still Francis Sable, with his distinction and charm.

He smiled at her and held out a hand.

"It was good of you to come," he said. "How is my mother?" Then, before she could answer, "but don't let's talk here. Let's go down to the café and have some drinks—we needn't leave here for nearly an hour yet, and there's so much I want to discuss with you."

It was better she should go with him than leave him to go off and drink alone, she thought. Perhaps he was over the drinking bout? His manner seemed perfectly normal. . . . She began to wonder whether perhaps Johann had exaggerated.

They left the *Gasthaus* and walked down the road in the sunshine. It was a lovely little town, she thought, with its wooden houses with their deep eaves, ornately carved, the balconies gay with petunias and geraniums, and the snow-topped mountains looking as though they were painted on a backcloth dropped at the end of the street.

They turned in at the Café Goldener Hirsch, on a corner; its terrace was flanked with flower-boxes where it met the pavement, and there was a red and white striped awning. The terrace was almost empty. Francis led the way to a table at the back. When the waiter came he ordered a large cognac for himself, and a champagne cocktail for Sue. "Don't tell me you're not in the mood for champagne," he said. "It's when one's not in the mood that one needs it most."

She had not known what to expect of him, but she had certainly not expected that he would behave exactly as though they had met by chance on the Boulevard Montparnasse on a bright morning. There was an inquest and a funeral in the offing, but he insisted on her having a champagne cocktail, and he himself sat there in his elegant wine-coloured jacket, with the Paisley silk scarf from the Rue St. Honoré tied with a characteristic careful negligence—he sat there turning the glass of cognac in his long fingers, the lapis-lazuli in his signet ring bright in the sunlight, a handsome, distinguished-looking, well-groomed man with dissipated eyes. . . . He swung the cognac round in the glass and sat looking at it, his head bent. He had a fine head, she thought all over again, and the sun had bleached his hair almost flaxen. He asked, almost casually, "How did my mother take the news?"

"She collapsed. The maid and I brought her round with sal

volatile. I wanted to get a doctor, but she insisted she was all right. After that she was very calm. But she said, 'Why did Francis send you?' "

"What did you say?" He drained his glass, then sat twisting its stem, gazing at it, intently.

"I said you were probably in a state of collapse yourself."

"I couldn't face her. I still can't." He motioned to the waiter and repeated the order, though Sue protested that she wanted no more.

"Forgive me a moment whilst the waiter's fetching the drinks, will you?" he said. "I've got to 'phone Heinz—the Austrian who is giving evidence. I should have done before I left the *Gasthaus*."

He went inside the café. The waiter brought the drinks. Sue sat sipping hers and smoking a cigarette. Francis was away about fifteen minutes.

When he reseated himself beside her he was a little flushed and his eyes seemed unnaturally bright.

"I'm sorry to have been so long," he said. "Trying to 'phone anywhere in these parts is the devil."

He picked up his glass and swallowed the contents and beckoned to the waiter.

"The same for you?" he asked her.

"I haven't finished this, and I don't want another, thanks— neither do you, Francis!"

"What *do* you mean?"

"You had some when you went to telephone, didn't you?"

Anger flared in him.

"Do you usually cross-examine your friends as to the number of their drinks?"

She answered, coolly, "Not usually. But you and I are due at an inquest in half an hour, and you are the chief witness."

He swallowed the drink and motioned the waiter again.

"I always go to inquests drunk, didn't you know?"

"You're being disgusting," she told him.

"And you are behaving like an hysterical female."

He took out his cigarette-case and she was aware of the un-steadiness of his hands. The whole business of opening the case, extracting the cigarette, igniting the lighter, was laborious for him. In the half hour since they had left the *Gasthaus* he had managed to get drunk.

The waiter came to the table and set the drink down before him. Before Francis could touch it Sue had snatched it and thrown it on the ground.

"You'll get the bill and we'll go," she said, furiously.

She stood up. Francis continued sitting. He smiled at her.

"You are behaving very foolishly," he said, and his words were a little blurred. "You will go and I shall come when I am ready."

He turned to the waiter again. Sue also turned to the waiter.

"The gentleman has had enough," she said, firmly.

The waiter shrugged. "I am sorry, *gnädiges Fräulein*. I cannot refuse to serve a customer without reason!"

"But there is a reason, don't you see?"

Francis smiled and addressed the waiter in German.

"The *Fräulein* is inclined to be hysterical, *Herr Ober*. Bring me a large cognac, and the bill."

When the waiter had gone Sue said sharply, "Pull yourself together, Francis, and let's go."

"You are making a scene," he told her, quietly. "People are staring at you. Either sit down and finish your drink or go."

She went . . . to Francis's relief. He sat there letting the cognac fumes rise in him, rise to his brain, misting it, numbing it, numbing everything, so that nothing mattered any more, and he could face anyone and anything.

The waiter who had served Francis knew all about the accident, and that the inquest was being held that day; he called a taxi five minutes before the court was due to assemble and helped Francis into it and gave the driver the address. He felt great sympathy for the poor Herr Sable. Had he been in his position he also would have had a few drinks beforehand; not a whole half bottle and all the others as well, perhaps, but then he could not take so much and still stand up, but certainly a few. He thought the young lady lacking in understanding. But then, he had often observed, many English ladies were like that in this matter of *Herren* and their alcoholic needs. . . .

As the court was a little late in assembling Francis got there in time. He caused a slight stir as he came in because an official at the door insisted on his throwing away his cigarette before going into the court-room, and Francis said that in that case the court could wait till he'd damned well finished the cigarette. . . . As the altercation was conducted in German neither Lady Sable nor Sue understood what it was all about, though it was obvious that Francis was being obstreperous . . . and that he was drunk. When he finally entered the court-room he sank down on to the nearest bench and sat with his face buried in his hands till he was called upon. Then he rose and walked only a very little unsteadily into the middle of the court and answered all the questions in a clear voice, his words a little blurred only to Sue, who knew how drink affected his intonation. For Francis the proceedings were like the walk down the glacier with Heinz, carrying Cathryn between them on the improvised stretcher; it was all something happening in the landscape of a dream. He answered the questions, he told the story. There was a blur of faces seated at a table, and when he turned there was a blur of faces sitting on benches, and at the end of a bench a figure in black with a gloved hand hiding her face—his mother; and next her Sue, in a black and white silk dress; next her sat Johann in his rough clothes; he sat leaning forward, staring down at his hands clasped between his knees. Next him sat the young Austrian, in *Lederhosen*, looking nervous. Their faces were all blurred to Francis, yet he was aware of each one individually, and he was aware of what Heinz said, and it bored him; after all he had told them the whole story; there was no more to tell; what did this Heinz young man know about it, anyhow? He had seen what happened only at a distance. There was only one person who knew what had really happened, but she was lying on a slab in the mortuary. Why did they have to keep chewing the cud like this? Outside the sun shone, and at the Café Zum Goldener Hirsch there was cognac and a sympathetic waiter called Franz, who knew that there were times when a man must drink, and drink hard. . . .

Then somehow it was all over; the court was satisfied; the court expressed its sympathy. There were officials who wanted to discuss arrangements; there was his mother's face emerging from the haze; his mother taking his hands and saying helplessly, "Francis, oh, Francis!" and leaning against him, her head against his shoulder. There was no reproach in her voice; only a bottom-less grief. He stood rigid whilst she wept against his shoulder; he had nothing to say; what was there to say? "Don't cry," or "I'm sorry." At least he could spare her—and himself—banality. Sue looked at him and her eyes were hard; they demanded, "Haven't you anything to say to her?" He moved away, and Sue put an arm round Lady Sable, and Francis escaped.

Now as on the glacier part of his mind worked very clearly. On the glacier there had been a thing to do, one supreme thing—you had to get down it and off it without falling into a crevasse. Now there was a thing to do, one supreme thing—to get away, before anyone overtook you; before they all got back from the court-house. Franz would help him. Franz understood.

He walked blindly down the sunny flowery street and turned in at the Goldener Hirsch. The terrace was crowded now with people taking their pre-luncheon *apéritifs*, and in the café an orchestra was playing a Strauss waltz. Just as Cathryn would like it, he thought; Cathryn, who loved Bach, in her *Blue Danube* mood, and why the hell not? It was only prigs and bores like Sue Lester and Johann Amanshauser who were all of one piece, all so damned logical and consistent. . . .

There was no room on the terrace and he went inside and found a seat near the bar. The waiter who had served him earlier was rushing about with laden trays. He caught sight of Francis and nodded to him. In a few moments he came back to him and put a large cognac down in front of him; Francis snatched it and swallowed it at a gulp.

"I've got to get away, Franz. What time is there a train for Vienna?"

"There is a train in half an hour," the waiter told him.

"All right; get me a taxi—and wrap a bottle of cognac up for me for the journey. And if anyone comes in asking for me you haven't seen me. I've got to get away, you understand?" He stuffed a wad of notes into the waiter's hand. "And bring me another drink while we are waiting for the taxi."

Franz telephoned for the taxi, brought the drink, saw Francis into the taxi, told the driver where to go . . . and ten minutes later was assuring Johann Amanshauser, and the dark English lady who had been with Herr Sable earlier, that he had not seen him, that he had not been back since he left to go to the court-house. . . .

2

He went back to Paris. He came off the night-train and after a few drinks at the station café got a taxi up to the Observatoire. He could not get into his apartment because Johnny was still in bed and had the door locked. Francis banged furiously and there were sounds inside the apartment; then the door opened, cautiously, a few inches on the chain, and the boy's scared face was visible in the small space. He gave a cry when he saw Francis.

"Mr. Francis, sir!"

He slid the chain and stepped back. He was in his dressing-gown; it was one which Francis had given him; it had been his own, but Johnny had admired it so extravagantly that Francis had felt he had better have it. The boy had nearly wept with joy. It was too big for him, but he never wore any other. He clutched it round him now, self-conscious because Mr. Francis had caught him *en déshabillé*—had he known Francis was coming had it been five in the morning he would have been up and bathed and shaved and dressed.

"I never got your wire," he said.

"I didn't send any. I left Austria suddenly. Johnny, I feel frightful. Is there any drink in the place?"

"Only some of that '75 brandy."

"Get it for me, and turn on a bath."

He went into his bedroom and flung himself down on the bed.

Johnny followed him a moment later with the brandy and a glass on a tray.

"Shall I get you some coffee, Mr. Francis?"

He put the tray down on the night-table. Francis raised himself on an elbow and reached for the bottle. '75 brandy and you were going to hog it as though it were the cheapest café cognac. . . . But O God, it did things to you.

He leaned back on the pillow.

"You can bring coffee and croissants when I've bathed, Johnny—I've not eaten for days."

"It must have been terrible for you, Mr. Francis, sir. I saw about it in the papers. I wanted to write to you, but I didn't know what to say."

"What are you talking about? Oh, I see. The accident. Oh, yes. I mean if you had written I wouldn't have seen it. I've been drunk for days. At present I feel as though I shall never want to be sober again. But you mustn't let me do it on '75 brandy, Johnny. There are certain forms of blasphemy that even I won't stand for. The sin against the Holy Ghost, you know. Or don't you know?"

"Yes, Mr. Francis," eagerly. "Mr. Aldous Huxley——"

"Dam' Mr. Aldous Huxley. Go and turn on the bath . . ."

Johnny trotted off, happily. It didn't matter how irritable Mr. Francis might be, or how unreasonable, it was wonderful to have him back. He had been through hell. You could see that. A man like Francis Sable didn't drink for days on end without a good reason. But if only he had known he was coming back! He would have had the apartment full of roses, and everything in shining readiness.

He wanted to sing for sheer happiness as he stood by the bath as the hot water ran in and threw in handfuls of expensive-scented bath salts and hung a large blue and a smaller pink bath towel over the hot-rail, only of course it wouldn't be right to sing when Mr. Francis looked so sick, and had this terrible tragedy. But he would get washed and shaved and dressed whilst Mr. Francis was bathing, then whilst he was having his coffee and croissants he would slip out and buy flowers, and a chicken, and some of that dry Rhine wine Mr. Francis so enjoyed. Then when Mr. Francis was more rested he would give him the manuscript he had typed for him—every comma of it a labour of love, but of course Mr. Francis wouldn't know that; though he couldn't help seeing how neatly it was typed—and tell him about the galley-proofs of the new book that had just come in, and which he was half-way through correcting; and there were various things in the mail that would need his attention. Oh, but it was wonderful to have him back—no one would ever know; it was the private glory of John B. Puckhurst, that most privileged of mortals—privileged to read the works of Mr. Francis Sable before they appeared in print, privileged to turn on his bath, to clean his shoes, to put him to bed when he was drunk, and to bring him prairie-oysters in the morning for his hangovers. . . .

It did not all quite work out as Johnny had planned, because the Francis Sable who came back unexpectedly from Vienna was not quite the same as the Francis Sable who had set out from London ten days ago. The Francis Sable who came back was not interested in manuscripts or proofs, and he dropped the entire batch of mail which Johnny had conscientiously acknowledged and set aside for his attention into the waste-paper basket.

"Why pester me with the manuscript?" he demanded, when Johnny brought it to him. "Don't you think I have enough with writing the dam' thing without having to go over it when it's typed?"

"You usually like to make corrections before it goes to the publishers," Johnny defended himself, hurt.

"Corrections be damned! Who cares whether Francis Sable takes out an 'and' and substitutes a semi-colon? What does it matter? What does anything matter except getting so dam' drunk you can't remember fair hair matted with blood, and a brown patch in the snow? That's what matters. Getting so blind you can't see *That* any more! I never realised before why they call it getting blind. You have to blind yourself to the things you can't bear to see—that you feel you'll go mad if you go on seeing. That's something you wouldn't know about, isn't it, Junny? You don't know a single dam' thing, do you, really, except a lot of hooey—that's good American, isn't it, Junny? A lot of hooey, I say, written in books by intellectual authors. You don't know anything about anything that tears your guts, do you? The heart torn up by the roots, Cathryn called it. You don't know anything about that, either, do you? But Francis Thompson did; he used it for a text for a poem called *The Holocaust*. You know all about that, of course, you know everything literary, don't you, you blasted little intellectual snob!"

Johnny turned away with a tight feeling in his throat. Of course Mr. Francis wasn't quite sober, but all the same he did say some terribly hurtful things at times. You had to make allowances, of course. Mr. Francis had had a dreadful experience. It was the most frightful tragedy. Resolutely Johnny made allowances. . . .

But it wasn't easy, and it got worse. Mr. Francis was not interested in anything except drinking. He ate almost nothing, though Johnny tried to tempt him with everything that he used to like; the most he ever took was a little coffee and a croissant sometimes in the mornings, though he always had to have a drink first, because he always felt 'like death', he said. But it wasn't just that Mr. Francis wasn't working, or attending to his literary affairs; it wasn't even that he was rarely more than half-sober, and that only in the mornings when he felt ill and morose, but that drunk or half-sober he was so unkind, said such horrible things. Of course he had always been rather sarcastic; you had to get used to that, and he had got used to it, but he had never said the sort of things he said now. Things that made you feel choked. Unfair, cruel things. Beastly things. You almost began to understand what was meant by that expression in the Bible about someone being possessed of a devil. Mr. Francis was possessed of a devil these days. A devil of unhappiness. That was it. Only being rational about it didn't prevent you from being hurt. And then nothing you did was right any more, and all the small things you did, like putting flowers around, and putting bath salts in the bath, and the towels to warm, and putting out his clothes ready for him to put on, he would just sneer at. "You ought to have been a butler, Johnny. Or a valet, or a lady's maid, or a wet-nurse, or a governess." You didn't want thanks; you only wanted to be allowed to help, to serve. You didn't ask for his friendship or affection; you had no right; he was the famous Francis Sable, whereas you were merely John B. Puckhurst; but you were entitled to respect, because you served faithfully, and you did your best—hell, you did your damnedest; you deserved something more than to be despised . . . for that's what it came to; you did your damnedest and he despised you for it. . . . You told yourself you'd give up trying; you told yourself you'd give up the job; but you couldn't, somehow; you had built up something in your mind about Francis Sable; he was one of the Lordly Ones; you fingered the row of his books along the chest of drawers in your bedroom and you forgave him; he had written those books; nothing could alter that. . . . Those books were your Bible, and the man who had written them was your God. Like Mr. Francis you were a rationalist, a free-thinker, so there was nothing blasphemous in that. The blasphemy was Francis Sable trying to kill Francis Sable the writer; because that's what it amounted to. He was sick; he was desperately sick, and you were merely Johnny and didn't know what to do, and it made you miserable; it made you so goddam miserable there were days when you felt you'd die of it. . . .

It was on one of those days that Sue Lester turned up at the apartment.

She was shocked by the boy's appearance when he opened the door to her. He looked ill; he looked damned ill.

"Hello, Johnny. Is Mr. Francis in?"

"He's in, Miss Lester, but he won't see you. He's sick."

She looked at him as he closed the front door.

"You mean he's dead drunk, Johnny. He's never been sober since he's been back, has he?"

"He's sick, Miss Lester." He followed her into the sitting-room. "He was devoted to Miss Cathryn. It was a terrible tragedy."

"Of course it was a terrible tragedy, but don't you think it was a tragedy for other people too—for Lady Sable, for example? She worshipped Cathryn this side idolatry! And there was a nice young Austrian who was going to marry Cathryn. Does Francis think he's the only one who's suffering?"

Johnny said, miserably, "It's worse for him. He feels he was responsible. I guess remorse is a pretty goddam awful thing, Miss Lester!"

Sue sat down. "Something's got to be done about Francis, Johnny. But I wish I knew what."

Johnny pulled forward a rose that had slipped in a vase.

"He'll get over it in time, I guess."

"In the meantime you're going to have a nervous breakdown if you don't watch out! Hasn't anyone told you you look damned ill?"

"I never see anyone, except the shopkeepers. We haven't been entertaining lately."

"Can't you see for yourself in the mirror?"

"I had a touch of the grippe—it pulls me down."

"You're loyal, my dear, but it's all wasted. You might as well go home—take a vacation, and come back when Francis is himself again, if he ever is!"

A rose petal fell on to the highly polished side-table. He had polished it that morning; he went on polishing things, caring for things. . . . He stood pulling the petal to pieces.

He stood staring down through his broad horn-rimmed glasses and pulling the petal to pieces, and he said in a choked voice, "I can't leave him. If it goes on forever I can't leave him; he needs me more than ever now." He forced himself to look at her, with what he believed would pass for a smile, but which, she thought, was like the twitch of a child's mouth before it starts to cry.

"We've got to remember what he was, and what we hope he'll be again."

She got up. "I didn't come to see Francis, Johnny. I knew it would be no good. I've seen him several times at the Dôme, but he wouldn't remember. I came to see you. Several people have told me how you looked. I know what Francis can be like. I came to tell you not to be a little fool, but clear out for a bit."

He dropped the last brown crumpled fragment of the rose petal into his coat pocket.

"You mean well, Miss Lester, and I appreciate it. But this is my job, and I'm not laying down on it!"

When he had shown her out Johnny leaned with his back against the door and buried his face in his hands. Oh dam' her, dam' her; why did she want to come here? Pitying him. Calling him a little fool. A punk painter like her pitying him, John B. Puckhurst, Francis Sable's confidential secretary . . . Francis Sable's butler, valet, general dogsbody . . . O God, it was bad enough without her coming here to rub it all in!

He heard Francis shouting for him and went in.

Francis was sitting on the edge of the bed, holding his head between his hands, his elbows on his knees. He had not shaved for days, nor changed his clothes, and his face was blotched and puffy.

"So you remember what I was and what I might be again, do you, Johnny? You thought I'd passed out, didn't you? But I heard your cosy little chat. It's the best of communicating doors, Johnny—so communicative! And you think I need you more than ever now, do you, you blasted little prig?"

Johnny said, resolutely, "I know you're unhappy, and I want to help."

"There's only one thing you can do for me, Johnny, and that's get to hell out of it! You heard what our lady missionary said, didn't you? Take a vacation till Mr. Francis is himelf again. That means take a vacation till Mr. Francis is dead—or you are! Don't you think I'm sick of the sight of you pansying about the place? Drunk or sober, half-drunk or half-sober, you bore me stiff! Is that clear? If there's one thing I can't stomach it's a prig. A blasted why-can't-you-be-good-like-me missionising prig! I'm going out now, and when I get back don't let me see you around. You can take a month's salary, six months' salary, a year's salary, only scram—that's good plain American, isn't it?"

Johnny stared at him, his face white.

"You don't mean it, Mr. Francis, sir? I mean I haven't done anything wrong! I've done my best. Honest to God, I've done my best! All along the line!"

Suddenly, shamefully, helplessly, he was weeping. There was the feeling of something collapsing in him, some kind of a dam that had kept everything back; now it slithered into a heap and the whole torrent of misery and despair came flooding over and everything was swept away. Everything he had built up, the citadel in which he lived and had his being; the citadel of his pride, his intellectuality, his conscientiousness.

He tugged a very clean white handkerchief out of his pocket and snatched off his glasses, dabbing his eyes, but something in him was broken, and now that he was doing at last what he had been wanting to do for weeks it felt as though it would go on forever.

He stood there sobbing and dabbing at his eyes and wiping his glasses.

"I'm sorry," he gasped. "I—seem to have gone to pieces——"

Disgust rose in Francis. Disgust and contempt.

"For God's sake! Get out! Do you hear me? Get out!"

Johnny turned and stumbled out. Without his glasses he was almost blind. He blundered out of Francis's room and into the little hall, caught his hip against a marble-topped side-table, groped for the handle of the door of his room.

Francis heard the slam of the door with satisfaction.

"Blasted blubbering little prig!" he said aloud, savagely.

He got up from the bed, stood a moment, swaying a little,

then went over to the wash-basin and threw cold water on to his face. God, he thought, I feel awful. He looked in the mirror. I look awful. I need a drink. I need people. I need taking out of myself. Why don't I ring up the princess? Clean up a bit and go up to Sandra's. Always good drink and plenty of it and amusing people at her place.

He looked at himself in the mirror again. You look the worse for wear, Francis, old boy, but you'll be all right when you've cleaned up. Francis Sable, the handsome and distinguished. Always so well-groomed. Let's go, then. Get shaved. No, ring the princess first. First things first. Where the hell's the 'phone book? Hell, make him do it. What's the good of keeping a dog and barking yourself? He shouted. "Johnny!" There was no answer. Furious, Francis crossed to the door and this time he roared. "Johnny! Are you deaf as well as dumb?"

He waited for Johnny's door to open; he stood listening. There was a sound of muffled sobbing.

"Blasted little blubberer!" Francis swayed along the passage and into the sitting-room. A smell of perfume. Good perfume. *Numero cinque.* That would be Sue. She had good taste. He groped for the indexed list of telephone numbers lying with the address-book and velvet-covered blotter neatly arranged on the writing-table. He sat down and found the number, then pulled the white enamelled telephone towards him. He gave the number, waited. God, I could do with a drink, he thought.

Then he was connected. "Oh, hullo, Sandra. This is Francis Sable. How are you, my dear? . . . Thank you. Yes, it's been ghastly. I need taking out of myself, as they say. Could I come along this evening? A party? Of course I don't mind a party. It's what I need. Does one dress? Not at all. I'd do more than that for a lovely lady! I ought to warn you, though, I look awful. . . . That's very sweet of you. I'll be along about nine then. *A bientôt.*"

He rang off. Nine; that gave one time to bath and shave and clamber into tails, and stoke up with a few drinks before going along. . . . No use asking Johnny to turn on the bath and lay out clothes. Johnny was sacked, anyhow. In good American fired. About time, too. Owl-faced little prig.

To bath and shave and struggle into a boiled shirt and tie a white tie was a tremendous effort—particularly with no Johnny to turn on the bath and put out things, hand you studs, cuff-links, shoe-horn. . . . But you made the effort, and when you came out of the bath you felt slightly less awful, and when you had finally tied the white tie you looked in the mirror again with something like your old confidence. One's hair at least didn't get the worse for drink—that was something. Damned good hair, the Sables'; thick and fair, with enough of a wave to give it interest; the kind of hair women fell for . . . but Cathryn's had been straight; straight as rain; Cathryn's hair. . . . O God! Well, get a move on; the sooner you got out the sooner you could get a drink; several drinks; buckets of drink, oceans of it, enough to drown yourself in. . . .

There was no sound as he passed Johnny's door. He called out, "See you're gone when I get back! You're fired! The nice kind missionary lady will probably put you up for the night!"

It was about two in the morning when he got back. He placed his silk hat and white silk scarf on the hall-table and groped a way into his room and flung himself down on the bed. He was drowning in dark waves; they went over and over him, endlessly, and that was all he knew, the dark waves going over. . . .

The room was full of sunlight when he opened his eyes. The curtains had not been drawn for the night. He lay still, trying to remember. He realised that he was wearing evening clothes. And that he felt awful. He needed a gin-and-tonic to pull him together. He needed a bath. Where the hell was Johnny? Then he remembered. He had sacked Johnny. He mightn't have gone, though. All that loyalty Sue had thought so touching. He got up off the bed, sat a moment on the edge holding his throbbing head in his hands, then went out and along the passage to Johnny's room. He opened the door. The room was empty; the bed had not been slept in. Unless, it occurred to him, Johnny had got up hours ago and made it. He was perhaps only out shopping.

He went into the bathroom and turned on the bath. Whilst he was lying back in the hot water there was a knock at the door, very loud and imperious. If that was Johnny gone out without his key he could go to hell. If it was anyone else they could also go to hell. The knocking went on for a long time and Francis lay back in the water with a feeling of triumph. Whoever it was could bang till they were blue in the face for all he cared. Besides, once you had not answered a knock you had to go on not answering; you couldn't suddenly give in. . . .

Whilst he was dressing the telephone bell rang. Busy morning, he thought, sardonically. He wondered whether he should answer. Disgusting instrument the telephone, really. No privacy. You could be in your bath, in the toilet, making love—anything. He decided to answer. He needed company. It might be one of the people he had met at the party last night asking him to something amusing. . . . He wrapped the bathrobe round him, thrust his feet into slippers, and padded into the sitting-room and sat down at the writing-table. He picked up the receiver.

Sue's voice, very angry, said, "Why the devil can't you answer the door? I've been banging for about a quarter of an hour. I'm in the concierge's office now, and I'm coming up. I've got to see you. Something has happened."

She rang off before he could answer. Hysterical female, he thought. He went into his room and put on pyjamas and dressing-gown and combed his hair; then there was the knocking at the door. He lit a cigarette before answering. With his unsteady fingers he was not inclined to light one with Sue looking on. . . .

He let her in. "I was in my bath when you were knocking hell out of the door," he told her. "I'm sorry."

She walked into his sitting-room, pulling off her furs. He took them from her; he held them against his face a moment before laying them down; silky and soft, and they smelled nice.

"I've come about Johnny," she said, brusquely, seating herself and taking a cigarette-case out of her bag. He took the lighter out of his dressing-gown pocket and ignited it and held it out to her. She took it from him, but made no comment on his hands.

"Did he go to you after all last night?"

"Go to me? Why should he?"

"I sacked him—I couldn't stand his solemn owl-face and his ghastly loyalty any longer! I told him to clear out—that you'd probably put him up for the night if he had nowhere else to go!"

"You told him that?"

"I hope you didn't mind, but you seemed to take an interest in him. He got on my nerves. I couldn't stand him a minute longer."

"He didn't come to me." She blew out a spiral of cigarette smoke, and it wreathed up between them. "He did something much more drastic than that. You'd better brace yourself for a shock."

He said quickly, "You don't mean he did himself in?"

"He tried to. He threw himself off the Pont Neuf about midnight. He was fished out by the river-police and taken to hospital."

"Good God! What will happen to him now? Will the police prosecute?"

"In this country, apparently, they don't. The French are more civilised than we are in these matters. But the doctor who looked after him is being a little sticky. He rang me up and asked if I would come and see him at the hospital. It seems that Johnny told them that he had been working for me and fallen in love with me and it was no good, and that he couldn't stand it any longer!"

He stared at her, bewildered.

"Why on earth should he tell them that?"

"What you call his ghastly loyalty still operating! Don't you see? The doctor asked him questions and he had to say something, and he was determined not to involve you. The doctor was very *simpatico*, and most anxious that I should try to comfort Johnny and get him into a better frame of mind before he left hospital. At his suggestion I had a talk with Johnny, alone. I asked him what it was all about and he said he couldn't go on. Those were the words he used, 'I couldn't go on.' I asked him why he had said it was on account of me, and he said he told the doctor the first thing that came into his head, because all he could think of was that he couldn't drag Mr. Francis into it. Then he began to cry."

Francis pressed out the end of his cigarette in an ash-tray. There was a little silence between them, then he asked, without looking at her, "Where is he now?"

"I brought him back to my place. He'll stay there until we can make arrangements for him to go back home."

"Is that what he wants?"

"Yes. In his own words he's through with Europe. For the time being he's through with everything, poor kid."

He thought, Why did she have to add that? He asked, after a

moment, "Would it help at all, do you think, if I came to see him?"

"I'm afraid not. I asked him that, and he became hysterical immediately. I should say it's extremely important that he shouldn't see you."

Francis pressed his hands to his face.

"O God!" he said.

Then he looked at her. "What can I do?"

She saw the pleading in his eyes and the hardness and anger in her collapsed. She had come to reproach him and denounce him. Now she could only pity him.

She said, gently, "I don't think there's anything you could do."

"That's my punishment!"

He got up and stood leaning against the window, his head on his arm. The balcony was bright with Johnny's window-boxes, full of pink geraniums and white daisies and a blue edging of lobelias. There was a clematis in a tub which he had been training up the wall. Solemn, conscientious, humourless Johnny, with his fanatic loyalty, jumping into the darkness from the Pont Neuf. . . .

"To go all your life with the knowledge that you took your sister to her death on a mountain, and drove a boy to suicide. . . ."

She sought for something to say that was not banal, but there seemed nothing, and he went on, "Remorse—the most futile of all human emotions. I said that once to Cathryn when my mother was being miserable about my father after his death."

She said, her throat aching, "You didn't have to feel remorse about Cathryn—it's what I wanted to tell you at Drindel, but you didn't make it possible."

"I took Cathryn with me to Drindel because I'd been let down by Framley and didn't want to go away alone. I could have taken her on some other kind of holiday, but I wanted to go climbing, and I knew she would jump at the suggestion of a climbing holiday. I took her knowing that my mother had a phobia about her climbing mountains. I knew that it would worry her and make her unhappy, but I did it. When I got Cathryn there I took her up the Drindelhorn immediately after she'd done another strenuous climb, instead of letting her have a day or two's rest. I did that because it fitted in with my own plans. She fell because she was tired. Then you tell me I need have no remorse. . . ."

She was silent.

"After all of which," he went on, relentlessly, "I turn myself into such a swine that I drive a wretched boy into jumping into the Seine!"

"Francis, don't! This is just—masochism; self-flagellation."

"And futile, like remorse, eh? Then what must I do to be saved?"

The old cynicism was back in his voice.

"If you could get back to work." Then, as he made an impatient exclamation, "Oh, don't sneer, Francis! You know it's possible to lose oneself in work! That sometimes it's all that's left to people like us—creative people! You've tried to escape through drinking too much, but you know that's no good. It's like plunging into a dark tunnel—you've always got to come out the other side eventually, and then it's all the same, nothing is changed. You can't turn life into a series of tunnels! You can't keep on running away. I'm sorry if it all sounds very lady-missionary, but it's true."

He turned suddenly and went over to her, taking her hands and pulling her to her feet, holding her against him.

"You can help me, Sue. I need someone. Someone close to me. Someone on my side." He smiled, a little wrily. "*Are* you on my side?"

"I love you. You know that. Oh, Francis, why do you make everything so difficult?"

He put his arms round her and kissed her mouth. There was hunger in the kiss, and despair. A cry went echoing through 'all the lonely purgatories of the mind'—Come close to me; love me; be on my side! She felt the hunger, of flesh and spirit, and heard the cry, and her blood answered it, and her mind, and her lips.

She said, when they sat together on the settee, "You shouldn't stay here alone. It's bad for you."

"Perhaps. What then? Come and stay here with me. Or shall we take a place together outside of Paris—at St. Cloud, or Fontainebleau, perhaps?" He smiled. "It would be in the best artistic tradition to go and live out at Fontainebleau!"

"No, Francis. I'm not living with you."

"No?"

"No."

"You mean you're not what is called living-in-sin with me, is that it?"

"Put it like that, if you like. I'm not going to be an *affaire*. It wouldn't be any good to either of us."

"I see. It's marriage or nothing, is it, like any little suburban bourgeoise who trades her body for a lawful husband, security, the social and economic and moral kudos of the married status?"

He got up, angrily, and went over to a cocktail cabinet.

The colour beat up in her face. "You know perfectly well that security and conventional respectability don't come into it! You're being really rather insulting, Francis!"

"Really? What does come into it, then, and what will you drink?"

"I don't want anything to drink, and I'm going."

"Don't be silly, of course you want a drink, and you're not going."

He poured out gin and tonic-water and came back to her with the drinks. She took hers from him and put it on a small table beside the settee. She was furiously angry.

He took a deep pull at his own drink, then repeated:

"What does come into it?"

"What is the use of discussing it?"

"To try and understand each other," he suggested. "You said you wanted to help me. I've told you how you can—by coming close to me, letting me love you. I need someone—I need you. I've needed you for a long time."

"I'm not stopping you loving me. The trouble is you don't! You need a mistress, and I attract you because I've always been the one woman who's been difficult for you! I haven't fallen flat for your looks and charm and brilliance and all the rest of it like the others!"

He drained his glass and got up to refill it.

"You're bitter, aren't you?"

"Yes, I'm bitter."

He came back to her with the drink.

"You're starting that again!" she said.

"One has to do something. I should be better occupied making love to you, but you don't allow it!"

She got up. "I'm going."

She crossed the room and picked up her furs.

"If you get lonely you can ring me. I don't go out much these days."

He went over to her and stood beside her, touching her furs.

"What would be the use of ringing you? You're with me now, and I'm more lonely than if I were alone! I'd do better to go to Sandra's where one gets lost in the crowd."

"And in the drink!"

"Yes—and in the drink."

She turned away and he followed her into the hall.

"You might ask Johnny to let you have the key before he leaves Paris—he had one, and I expect he had it in his pocket when he left here. If he still has it get it from him—and keep it."

"Keep it?"

"I like to think you might one day use it!"

"If I get it from him I shall post it back to you."

"Don't do that, anyhow. I'd much sooner you dropped it down the nearest drain. Much less hurtful, for at least then I could go on hoping!"

He took her hand and kissed her fingers.

She smiled, wanly.

"Now you're just being gallant!"

"O God!"

Her eyes filled with tears. There was nothing to say. Only this ache in the throat, and the swim and blur of tears that must not be shed. She walked away and down the stairs and out into the bright morning.

Francis watched her for a moment, then closed the door softly and went back into the sitting-room. He picked up his drink and finished it, then noticed hers, untouched. He sat down and took the glass into his hand.

"*You're starting that again.*"

Well, what else? Work, Sue said. Sit down and write. But what? Create something; make people come to life; breathe the breath of life into creatures of the imagination. That's what you're there for. That's your natural function. Write something deeply felt. *Wouldn't you like to write a really great book? It's not enough to be just clever.* The heart torn up by the roots.

The holocaust of self. Disintegration. A writer needed to be whole. Remorse was not merely the most futile of all human emotions but the most destroying. Johnny, you little fool, why did you have to do that? Francis Sable isn't worth all that expense of spirit in a waste of emotion! He swallowed Sue's drink, and then as it spread warmly in him, mounting to his brain, he thought, But it could have been worse; you haven't got Johnny's death on your conscience. Thank God for that! Or rather thank the Paris river-police! Why had Sue come and told him about Johnny? She could have spared him that, since there was nothing he could do. She probably thought it would shock me into what is called pulling myself together, he reflected. Poor Sue. She means well, and now I'm making her miserable, too . . .

He poured himself out another drink and took it with him into the bedroom. He began pulling out drawers, opening cupboards. What did the well-groomed Mr. Francis Sable wear today? Are we double-breasted and man-about-town, or are we a little negligent, the man-of-letters? O God, what did it matter? He took the first thing that came to hand, which was a brown corduroy velvet suit. It didn't matter, but all the same he carefully selected a cream silk shirt and a flowing brown silk tie, and tucked a cream silk handkerchief into the breast pocket. A boy tries to drown himself because of you at midnight, and a woman breaks her heart because of you at midday, but so long as you remained alive on the face of the earth your aesthetic instinct—and therefore your sartorial taste—would remain unimpaired. Francis Sable might be drinking himself to death, but at least it should be recorded that he did it with a little elegance. . . .

3

In the hall it occurred to him that there was now no Johnny to attend to the mail. He took a large batch of letters from the wire basket on the back of the door and glanced through them. They were mostly sent care of his publishers, which meant fan-mail—or abuse; either way he wasn't interested. Of the others he recognised several handwritings and postmarks and decided that he couldn't be bothered. There was one letter with a Wien post-mark. That might be from Johann. He stuffed it into his pocket and went out.

He went first to the Café des Lilas, because it was the nearest. He felt that he needed a pick-me-up, and ordered a champagne cocktail and a cognac; he poured the cognac into the champagne and drank it, then strolled down through the gardens of the Luxembourg, telling himself that the air would do his head good. He sat for a little while under a small twisted hawthorn tree on the terrace that overlooks the pond, and then suddenly he remembered the letter in his pocket. He tore open the envelope and stared for a moment at the flowery German script. '*Mein lieber Francis.*' He had always been Herr Francis to Johann. He turned to the back page and saw the signature, and his interest quickened. It was from Lotte.

She was going to be in Paris on the sixteenth; she would like very much to see him, if he also would like it. She had not written to him about the tragic happenings because at such times there is nothing to say; one knows that those who love one feel for one. '*Und ich liebe Dich, Francis.*' If he would like them to meet would he ring her up? She gave an address and telephone number in the Rue St. Honoré. Lotte. Well, it would be pleasant to see her. She was nice to look at and easy to be with. She would be sweet to make love to. Up to a point you could make love to her, but only up to a point. But the difference between Lotte and Sue was that Lotte would not want you to make love to her seriously, not even, as the matrimonial advertisements put it, 'with a view to marriage'. Lotte did not want you to take her seriously, whereas Sue, God help her, did. She wanted you to take her so dam' seriously that she wanted you to marry her. And if you went with a promise of marriage you could go to her tonight and she would not send you away. No moral code was involved with Sue; it was merely her damned pride. . . .

He folded Lotte's letter and replaced it in the envelope and went on thinking about Sue. Why didn't you marry her and have done with it? A civil marriage was the merest legal formality. If it didn't work another legal formality would get you out of it —if you felt a need of that legal extrication. Why didn't you marry Sue? You knew that the answer was because some tattered shred of decency left in you told you that it wouldn't be fair to her; you were fond of her and attracted by her, but you knew dam' well you weren't in love with her—not, at least, as she understood it. You knew it and she knew it. You could only make her unhappy.

He got up and left the gardens and crossed the road into the Medici Grill. Better eat something. Besides, to have a meal passed the time. Passed the time until—when? You had nothing whatever to do. He ordered a meal and the waiter gave him a paper to read whilst he waited. He noticed that the date was the seventeenth. That meant he could go and see Lotte after lunch. It would be something to do. . . .

But by the time he had lunched and had several cognacs, some *vin à l'oignon* and some more cognac, he did not feel like doing anything except going back to his apartment and sleeping. He would ring Lotte in the evening, or the next day; there was no hurry.

He did not ring her that evening, or the next day. At noon the next day she called. He was lying on his bed in the lounge-clothes in which he had come in late the previous night, and he was thinking the two thoughts he always thought in the mornings since he had returned from Austria—that he felt awful, and that he must have a drink. When the knock came his first reaction was to let the knocker knock it out; then it occurred to him that it might be Sue, too proud to use the key. He got up and went to the door.

He had a confused impression of Lotte standing there vivid and lovely in a red hat and dress, and of saying something to her, and then the floor came up to meet him and he clutched at the hall-table to save himself. Lotte caught at him and he somehow stumbled into the sitting-room and collapsed on to the settee. He sat with his head between his hands for a few moments, then looked up. The girl was kneeling on the floor in front of him, looking at him, anxiously.

"Are you all right? What can I get you? Have you some brandy in the house?"

Had he some brandy! There was a little left in a bottle in the bedroom, but whether the bottle was on the bed or under it or rolled to a corner of the room he had no idea. Presently he would go and get it, wherever it was; for the moment he wanted only to sit still. He took one of Lotte's hands and held it to his throbbing forehead.

"You are ill, Francis. And you are here all alone?"

He looked ill, she thought; desperately ill; there were sacs under his eyes, and his eyes had a dulled look, like an old person; the flesh above his cheek-bones was puffy, and his hands trembled. That he had been drinking heavily was quite obvious to her, but it was more than that, she thought, he was really ill. She had no doubt that if, as it seemed, he had been drinking too much, it was because he was unhappy. She was completely without criticism.

She knelt between his knees and pressed her hands to his forehead.

"If you would like to go to your bed," she said, "I would go into your kitchen and make you something—perhaps you are feeling faint because you have not eaten."

He took her face between his hands. Darling little Lotte! What should she know of the lonely purgatories of the mind?

"You are quite right! I have been eating too little and drinking too much! You shall go and make me some coffee and I will get cleaned up, and we will go and have lunch. Then we will do whatever you would like! We will drive in the Bois, or go on a steamer to St. Cloud—anything you like . . ."

He kissed her forehead and got up, pulling her to her feet. He swayed a little, and she stood a moment, holding his arms, searching his face, anxiously.

"Are you sure you should not lie down for a little?"

"You go and make that coffee, my little one, and then I shall be fine!"

He kissed her forehead, and then with an arm round her shoulder guided her to the kitchen.

He left her there and went into his bedroom and closed the door. The bottle had rolled away into a corner of the room. He rescued it and there was still some left in it. He put the bottle to his lips and drained it. Then, with a tremendous effort of will, began his toilet. He washed, shaved, changed his clothes, selecting the wine-coloured jacket from the wardrobe, a grey silk shirt from a drawer, a wine-coloured tie from the long row of ties dangling from the back of the wardrobe door. He felt faint and his head throbbed, and he had a raging thirst . . . but no one should say that Francis Sable could not exercise will-power . . . on occasion.

When he went into the sitting-room Lotte was already there with the coffee; she had unearthed some croissants—they were stale, she said, but with butter they might not be so bad, and he should eat something. . . .

He drank several cups of the black coffee and forced himself to eat a croissant. Johnny had always urged him to take black coffee, to eat something, and it had always infuriated him. Because there had always been the it'll-do-you-good implication of criticism. There had been times when he would have taken the black coffee, gratefully, but for that. There was Johnny's loyalty and devotion, and Sue's love, but they were neither of them, for all that, really on the side of the sinner; they disapproved. Lotte was completely devoid of disapproval, she did not ask him why, she did not moralise, she did not talk about tunnels, or escape, or work, or urge that he should make an effort, and pull himself together, and the rest of it; she merely wanted that he should feel better; she was distressed that he felt and looked ill; she was on his side simply and instinctively. Psychology was not a word in her vocabulary; she loved him and her love was all tenderness and compassion.

They would lunch up in the Bois, he thought, under the trees. He felt a need for air.

They picked up a taxi in the boulevard and drove across Paris. Lotte sat with an ungloved hand in his and looked out of the window, exclaiming delightedly about this and that, and Francis smiled absently. They crossed the Pont Neuf and he gazed at it, fascinatedly, thinking of Johnny clambering up on to it in the dark, and he wondered where Johnny was, and why Sue hadn't been near; they crossed the Place de la Concorde and went on up the Champs-Élysées, and he thought of Cathryn on a golden evening in May, and the light in the sky, and the pervading happiness. They came up into the Bois and reached the restaurant in the thin wood, its terrace overhung by chestnut trees. He ordered cognac and two champagne cocktails to be brought immediately, then studied the wine-list. They must drink champagne, he thought . . . he felt as though he could drink a river of it,

but today he was going to remain sober; today he did not need to
escape. They discussed the menu together and decided on
madrilene en gelée, breast of chicken in aspic, with truffles, and
heart of lettuce, cold asparagus, *fraises des bois*, with *crême à la
Fontainebleau*. They drank a Cordon Rouge, 1911. The tables
with their sun-umbrellas under the trees, the women in their
flowery summery dresses, the stippled effect of sun and shadow,
looked like a painting by Pisarro, he thought. He felt better;
not a doubt of it, he felt much better. . . .

Between the *fraises des bois* and the coffee and liqueurs he took
her hand and kissed her finger-tips.

"Darling Lotte, you do me good!"

She laughed. "*Monsieur est galant!* But is he sure it's the lady
and not the champagne?"

"Without the lady," he told her, "I should merely be fading
into a fuddled dream by now; as it is I am escaping into reality
for the first time for weeks—a lovely reality that looks like a
Pisarro painting, with Lotte pure Renoir in the foreground!"

After lunch they climbed into an open taxi and drove round the
lake. Then they dismissed the taxi and walked until they found a
willow tree dipping its branches to the water. They sat on the
grassy slope under the willow, and it was like being in a little
room, Lotte said, with the long green hair of the tree enclosing
them. They watched boats on the water, the skiffs, and the punts,
they watched the ducks, they watched the water slipping by,
flecked with sunshine, dappled with shade, and were happy.
Presently Francis lay with his head in her lap; she stroked his
forehead, and sometimes he took her hands and kissed them, and
peace flowed in him. . . . Sue, he thought, instead of moralising
like a lady-missionary, a missionary lady, why didn't you think
of our sitting under a willow tree with my head in your lap. . . ?
'Tis a sweet thought, the Prince of Denmark said. But you would
not play Ophelia to my Hamlet. . . . Soothed by Lotte's hands
and the softness of the water he fell asleep. The people passing
along the path behind them would take them for lovers, Lotte
reflected. She smiled down at him, a little sadly, and brushed the
hair back from his forehead. I wish we were, her heart cried, I
wish we were. . . .

They drank their evening *apéritifs* at Fouquet's, and dined at Prunier's, then they taxied down to the Tuileries and sat on the terrace of a small café opposite the Théatre-Français and watched the fountain and the movement of the plane trees, and the lights come out in the clustered lamps. The lights came out and the stars came out, and it was time to take Lotte to her hotel. He sighed, and she took his hand.

"Why do you sigh, Francis? It's been such a happy day."

"Because it's been such a happy day, and now it's over. You are going back to Vienna tomorrow, and I am going back—to whatever it is lost people go back to after their days out!"

"Why don't you come to Vienna? Then we could spend Saturdays and Sundays up in the Wienerwald, or go out to Grinzing and sit under the trees and drink wine!"

"What would I do while you were at the stores all day?"

"You would do your own work."

"If I could do my own work there'd be no need to go to Vienna!"

She turned to him. "Francis——" she hesitated, then went on, flushing a little, "Isn't there someone? I mean who loves you and could help you? Someone in love with you, I mean."

"Yes. There is someone."

"Why don't you marry her? To have someone close to you always—that would help, wouldn't it?"

"If I loved her enough, but I don't, unfortunately."

She pressed his hand. "I'm sorry."

"I'm sorry, too. Let's have another drink!"

Lotte shook her head. There was already a pile of saucers in front of them.

"For me, no. But you have what you want."

Sue, he thought, would have said, 'And you've had enough too!' Perhaps that was why you couldn't be in love with Sue—she was too much the wife!

He ordered another cognac for himself, then turned to Lotte. He said recklessly, "Why don't you marry me, Lotte?"

She smiled, sadly. "Because you are not in love with me, either!"

"I love you very much, and—I want you very much!"

"It's not the same. But even if you were in love with me—you're not a Catholic. It wouldn't be a good thing."

"There are marriages between Catholics and non-Catholics."

"I know, and sometimes it's all right. But—I couldn't marry anyone who wasn't a Catholic. Any more than Johann could have."

There was silence between them, and then he said, "Tell me something. I've wanted to know, but I've never had the courage to ask anyone else. Where was Cathryn buried?"

"In England. Your brother sent a telegram that she was to be brought home. She was to be buried at a place called—I don't know how you pronounce it." She spelt it. "W—as—dale. It was a great grief to your mother that because she had not been received into the Church she could not have a Catholic burial. But Johann arranged with the priest at Drindel to say a Mass for her, for the repose of her soul. That comforted your mother. It was said before they all left, Johann said, your mother, and Miss Lester—and Cathryn."

"I see." He was silent a moment, then he asked, "Did Johann and your parents—everyone—did they all think it was very terrible that I ran away immediately after the inquest?"

"Johann said Miss Lester was angry, but that your mother said she understood. And Johann did. I think we all did. Only Miss Lester thought it made it harder for your mother. She said you were selfish."

"She was quite right. Selfish and cowardly—two of the meaner human failings, you see!"

"We're all selfish, one way and another, and we all get afraid at times." She smiled at him. "You're being morbid, Francis. Finish your drink, and then take me somewhere gay— somewhere where we can dance! Who said it was time to take me home?"

He laughed, happily. "That was just another of my morbid ideas! I thought you'd have had enough of me! We'll get a taxi and go up to the Bœuf sur le Toit."

Lotte's face ached with tiredness and she longed for her bed, but she had had a sudden vision of the desolation of Francis's return to the empty apartment. At least tonight, she thought, he would get into his bed sober, and waken in the morning not feeling like death . . . But she was resolved that something must and should be done; he couldn't be allowed to go on like that, escaping into drink. He was much too good a person to be so wasted.

Francis took Lotte to her hotel behind the Opera at four in the morning. He said, as he kissed her, "Thank you for every-thing, Lotte darling. You can't possibly know how much this day has meant for me. I shall always remember it and treasure it —and you!"

"It's been lovely for me, too, Francis. We will have other days like it. I will be in Paris again. You will come to Vienna. In the meantime I shall pray for you. Johann is praying for you all the time. He has a special devotion to St. Augustine, and he asks his help for you."

Francis smiled. "Between the two of you, not to mention St. Augustine, I ought to manage!"

"It will be all right, Francis."

He kissed her again, and they parted. He walked back down the empty Avenue de l'Opéra, and across the Rue de Rivoli, with its shadowy arcades, and through the gardens of the Tuileries. He crossed the Pont St. Michel and up the Boul' Mich'. Here and there were the lights of a *bistro* or all-night café; soon all the other cafés would start opening up; the sky was already lightening. It crossed his mind that he could stop somewhere for a drink, but he dismissed the idea; he didn't really want it; he didn't want to dim the memory of the sunny day, the starry night, of lying under the willow tree with his head in Lotte's lap, of dancing with her, light as a feather, light as Cathryn . . . of all her sweetness and uncritical lovingness. She was like a sweet and gentle mother, he thought, not in the least blind to her son's faults, but loving too much for any condemnation. His own mother had not condemned his selfish-ness and moral cowardliness; she had understood. . . . Ah, if you had only told me that, Sue, instead of reproaching me! Perhaps that was what a man was always seeking in the woman who loved him—the eternally forgiving mother! Perhaps that was what he fundamentally needed in the woman he loved.

He walked along the railings of the Luxembourg, crossed the deserted Montparnasse, and came into the short leafy Avenue de l'Observatoire. There was the clang of the iron gates behind him and the sleepy answering voice of the concierge as he gave his name, then climbed up to his apartment.

When he let himself in he saw that there was a light in his sitting-room. His heart quickened. Perhaps Johnny had come back. . . . He went into the room and saw Sue asleep on the settee, the table-lamp beside her picking her out with a stage spotlight effect. He turned on switches by the door and candles came to life in the pale green panelling of the walls, and Sue started up.

"What time did you get here?" he asked.

"Sometime before midnight. I got the key from Johnny this afternoon. He's sailing on Saturday. I thought I'd come and tell you."

"At midnight?"

She flushed slightly. "I was dining out beyond the Lion de Belfort and the taxi passed the door. I had a sudden impulse."

"I see."

He went over to the cocktail cabinet.

"Gin-and-tonic?"

"A small one, then."

He filled the glasses and brought them over to the table by which she sat.

"I also thought I might help you get to bed if you came in— under the weather. But I see you don't need help."

He laughed. "You sound quite disappointed!"

"On the contrary, I'm delighted. What have you been up to, might one ask, to come home at this hour so unnaturally sober?"

For the life of her she couldn't keep the edge off her voice. Why did he have to be so damned casual? Didn't he realise that for her to use the key like that was a big thing to have done?

He stood leaning against the table, fingering his glass. He looked happy again, she thought, and young. . . . Francis Sable himself again.

"Johann Amanshauser's sister called on me this morning when I had the world's worst hangover, but instead of lecturing me on work and escapism she made me coffee and was very sweet and sympathetic, with the result that we lunched together in the Bois, and after that we sat beside the lake and she very sweetly played Ophelia to my Hamlet. After that we dined, and later on we danced." He stood looking down at his glass, smiling . . . smiling at his memories, she thought, bitterly.

"You seem to have enjoyed yourselves. But I would have done all that with you yesterday—only you didn't ask me!"

"You didn't make it possible for me to ask you." He looked at her, still smiling. He added : "Would you have done all that —even to my head in your lap beside a public footpath?"

"That—no! I'm not a shop-girl!"

"Ah, that's just it, you see. Lotte Amanshauser most adorably is!"

"Why don't you marry your adorable shop-girl?"

"She's a good Catholic and doesn't believe in mixed marriages. Also she's not convinced that I love her enough."

"Otherwise you might?"

"I might. She's so beautifully uncritical, you see."

"And that suits your male vanity, doesn't it? You want a woman to think you're wonderful—above criticism?"

He went on looking at his drink, but he was no longer smiling.

"I want a woman who will have no illusions about me, but still love me."

"A woman called Sue Lester has done that for a long time."

"The woman called Sue Lester looks at me angrily and speaks to me in a hard voice."

She pressed her hands to her face for a moment.

"I'm sorry, Francis. But you're not easy. I did want to help you. I thought when you knew about Johnny it would . . ." she groped for words.

"Sober me up?" he suggested, with his old ironic smile.

"Yes."

"You seriously thought that as I was drinking too much because of one lot of remorse another lot piled on top of it would help me not to do it?"

He swallowed his drink.

"You didn't want to help me, Sue. You were angry with me and disgusted with me, and you wanted me to know it! I don't in the least blame you, but I'd sooner you were honest about it!"

She got up. "All right, I was angry with you and disgusted with you—over Johnny, and over the way you ran away from Drindel, without even waiting to see what the funeral arrangements were! But it's not true that when I got here and saw you were suffering that I didn't want to help you. I loved you, and I went away damned miserable. I didn't sleep all last night, and I thought about you all today. It's why when I passed the house in the taxi tonight I had an impulse to get out. I came prepared to be—anything you wanted me to be—anything you needed. . . . But now I see you don't need me, so I'll go."

He put his hands on her shoulders, smiling again.

"Not at this time of the morning, Sue. It's almost light. Almost time for breakfast! I never knew such a woman for *going*!" He pushed her gently down on to the settee again, then went over to the window and pulled back the heavy curtains.

"You see, it's daylight!" He opened the windows, and the first twitterings of birds in the chestnut trees of the boulevard came in on the cold grey air.

She persisted, "I think we should both try to get some sleep. I'm dropping with tiredness." She yawned, then added, "I might as well take Johnny's things while I'm here—if you'll help me get them together. . . ."

"After we've had coffee. Then I'll help you pack everything and get you a taxi."

"He doesn't want any of your books. I gather he's going to start a crusade against you when he gets back to the States. He considers you the supreme evil influence on your generation. That's what you've done to him! I warned you long ago, if you remember. I suppose you'll say it's all unimportant?"

"It is, relatively. Put your feet up and rest. I'll go and make coffee."

He went out and she stretched herself on the settee and tried to relax. But it was no good. Her nerves were taut. She had let herself into the apartment with a sense of having broken at last through her own defences; she had surrendered her pride . . . but there hadn't been any need, because the moment had come and gone in which she could come to him as she had then been ready to come. It hadn't worked out. I'm no good to him, she thought, bleakly; I never was, and now I never will be. . . .

When he came back with the coffee she asked him, "What are you going to do today?"

"Try to work, I suppose. I haven't touched anything, mail or proofs, or anything else, for weeks . . ."

"You think you'll be able to work now?"

"Sue darling, how do I know? How can I possibly know?"

Already, it seemed to him, he felt the grey wind of desolation sweeping round him again, despair creeping in on him. You could forget for a little while, whether by drugging yourself with alcohol, or lying relaxed under a tree with your head in a girl's lap, but the time came when the effects of the alcohol wore off, and when you must get up from the girl's lap, and what you had tried to escape from, what you had temporarily succeeded in forgetting, was still there, unchanged, and you were still there and unchanged; you closed your eyes and saw again the red-brown patch in the snow; and a darkness into which the pain and despair in yourself had driven a wretched youth who had faithfully loved and served you. You were still yourself, with your ultimately inescapable burden of remorse.

Sue urged work as escape, but when your work was creative how could you create with nothing to create from—when inside yourself was greyness, deadness, sterility—a hollowness?

He continued to drink more than of old, because to sit at a café and drink was something to do, and because after a few drinks he was less depressed, and then he had to go on drinking in order to slip back into that deep black well, but after the day with Lotte he did not again deliberately set out to drink himself blind.

Lotte returned to Vienna on a Tuesday, and Francis saw no more of Sue that week; but on the Saturday he had an unexpected visitor in the person of Johann.

He arrived at the apartment in the evening, just as Francis was going out for his evening round of the cafés—the Lilas, then up the boulevard to the Dôme, look in at the American bar of the Coupole, then down to the Boulevard St. Germain and the Magots and Floreur; if you wanted any dinner after that you had it at some small place in the vicinity of the Rue Jacob, or along the boulevard, or took a taxi across the river. . . .

"I didn't let you know I was coming," Johann said, "because I was afraid if I did you might make an excuse not to see me."

"You thought I might run away, in fact?"

"Yes."

"I've given up trying to run away. Where are you staying?"

"I came straight from the station——"

"You can stay here if you care to. There's a spare room."

"I'd like that. I have to return to Salzburg tomorrow night—
I must be at the shop first thing Monday morning."

"You came to Paris for twenty-four hours?"

"Lotte asked me to come. She told me to tell you that."

Johann twisted his green felt hat between his fingers. He
said, awkwardly, "She begged me to come. She is worried about
you. She said I would be able to help you—that none of your
Paris friends seemed able to. But you must forgive me, Herr
Francis, if I say that I came only to satisfy my sister, because
I do not think I can help you. I do not think people can help
each other. I think we have to work out our own salvation, each
in his own way."

Francis smiled. "The fact that you think that helps in itself!
Let me show you the spare room, then we'll go and drink."

4

The effect of Cathryn's death on Johann had been to plunge
him back into the conviction that God intended that his life
should be dedicated to a priestly continence. For a very little
while, a mere handful of days, he had been allowed to glimpse the
joys of carnal love, to know the bewildering, heady joy of another
human body clasped against his own, to know the tumult of the
blood, and the urgency of desire; he had believed that he was to
be allowed to know the consummation of this fierce sweet
hunger of the flesh—that he would not love God the less because
he loved the body as well as the soul of Cathryn Sable, for St.
Augustine himself had said that there was no estrangement from
God in loving a bodily form to the praise of the Creator, and it
was true that in loving Cathryn in her white and gold garment
of the flesh he praised God for the creation of so much loveliness,
grace, and purity. Love, but take heed what you love, St.

Augustine said, and he had taken heed. Behind the dark tumult of the blood was a shining wonder, a white radiance of reverence and awe in the presence of a miracle. 'God made the body good, since He is good', and there could be no corruption in loving that which is good—no corruption and no estrangement from God, and no soul-destroying imprisonment in the flesh. All this was true; God had vouchsafed him this understanding, but it was not God's will that either he or Cathryn should experience this sweetness. God of His infinite wisdom had called her early to Himself, and he, Johann Amanshauser, could only pray with St. Augustine, 'Because it is Thou who hast made me, let it be not Thy will to destroy me utterly. Scourge me so that I may be made better, not so that I cease to be; beat me so that I may be given a better shape, not so as to crush me to bits.' He had prayed, night and day, ever since he had looked into Cathryn's dead face, in an agony of the spirit that consumed him like a fever—'Thy will be done.' Over and over again he repeated, in passionate aspiration of belief, 'Sacred Heart of Jesus, I believe you love me *now*.' And over and over again, 'Our Father . . . Thy will be done.'

It had been as great a grief to him as to Lady Sable that Cathryn, on the threshold of the Church, could not be given a Catholic burial; one of the last things Cathryn's mother did before she took her ewe lamb back to England was to kneel with him before the Blessed Virgin in the lady-chapel of the little church, seeking the comfort of her compassionate love. They prayed together that God's will might be done in them; and they prayed for Francis, that in the love of God he might find peace out of pain. . . .

Lotte wrote to Johann when she got back to Vienna begging him to go and see Francis in Paris.

He is terribly unhappy [she wrote]. *I am not clever enough to do more than take him out of himself for a day, and I think he must sink back into himself when he is alone again. I can only pray for him. You could help him because you and Cathryn were close. You could give him Cathryn again; no one else could. I beseech you to go to him. Even if you think it no good, please go. I am sure he can reach Cathryn through you, and that he needs this, and that he can only achieve it through you.*

Johann had not been convinced, but he had felt that he could not refuse to go, both because Lotte so strongly besought him, and because even if the chances of being able to help Francis were remote, as he felt them to be, nevertheless if there was even an infinitesimal chance it was his duty to try.

Francis was greatly relieved that Johann did not think he could help him. He had been afraid that he had come to offer him the solace of the Church. When would the well-intentioned learn that you did not help the sinner by moralising about his sins? That nothing was more heart-hardening—more calculated, he thought, grimly, to drive one to drink? As a missionary, Sue, you missed your opportunities! Lotte was more effective in her simplicity. . . .

They sat on the terrace of the Lilas and Johann was apologetic.

"I do not want to intrude on you, Herr Francis. God sends us a cross and we have to find our own way of bearing it. We have to discover it for ourselves."

"Did you?"

"Yes, but then for me, as a Catholic, it is much easier. For you I do not know how it could be. That you should wish to escape I can understand."

"But there is no escape," Francis said. "I found that out. The only escape from life is into death—and I'm not suicidal. I don't know why one goes on living when one no longer has joy in life—pure habit, I suppose. And probably some sort of instinct that if one holds on long enough things will somehow get better, even though reason says they can't."

"One either dies of a wound, or recovers from it," Johann suggested.

"One might be left permanently crippled," Francis countered. "What I would call the damage to one's psyche. What you would call the soul, I suppose."

Johann was silent, and Francis tried to explain.

"You see, it's not merely a simple question of bereavement—of loss. In time, I suppose, one readjusts oneself to that. It isn't just that Cathryn is no longer in the world, but the feeling of guilt—of responsibility."

"I took her up a much more difficult mountain than you did.

It was just bad luck that she should have had the accident on a not-so-difficult mountain, and on an easy part at that."

"But as a climber you know that the accidents happen more often than not in the easy places, because it's at those places that one becomes careless. Cathryn slipped on the snow-slope because she was tired, and she was tired because I wanted to get the Drindelhorn climb over. I wanted to get away with Willi and Hans on the Monday, and I knew Cathryn wouldn't climb on the Sunday. I took her up the Drindelhorn when she was tired for a selfish reason, and I brought her to Drindel for a selfish reason— because my friend had fallen ill and I didn't want to go climbing alone. I took her knowing that she would come with me, and that if I didn't take her she would never climb with anyone else. All my life I must know that if I hadn't taken Cathryn to Drindel whatever way she died it wouldn't have been on a mountain." He drained his glass and looked round for the waiter.

"Odd that an unimportant mountain like the Drindelhorn should be my last mountain."

"How do you mean—your last mountain?"

"I shall never climb again. Do you suppose I could come down another snow-slope without living that particular descent all over again? Do you think I could come down another glacier without remembering that descent with Heinz? As it is I've only to close my eyes to see it all again. . . ."

The waiter brought the drinks and added another saucer to the pile.

Johann said, with sudden excitement, "But don't you see that by not climbing again you are running away again? Don't you see that the only way to stop living it all over and over again in your mind is to face it in reality—not merely to climb another mountain, but to climb that particular mountain?" His deep-set eyes had the brightness of inspiration. "Yes, yes, don't you see that that is what you must do? You are still running away, and so long as you run away the pain will follow you. Because you ran away from Drindel you must make this expiation—you must go back! Herr Francis, you must believe that I am right!"

"You want me to go back and live every moment of that hell over again?"

"There's no other way, I'm convinced of it! You will go

back in the way that people who have committed a crime sometimes give themselves up after having first tried to escape."

"I thought you considered me innocent of any crime?"

"It is not what I think, Herr Francis. It is between you and
your conscience. You are weighed down with a sense of guilt,
and I say that you cannot be rid of it except by facing it with
courage. You say that you used your sister for selfish ends,
regardless of the cost to your mother; very well then, for your
own peace of mind you must face the consequences—you have
no right to try and evade them. That is how I see it."

Francis said, bitterly, "Don't you think I've been punished
enough—without self-flagellation?"

"Atonement is not self-punishment. It is wholeness. If
you do not believe in being at one with God, as an artist you
must believe in being at one with yourself—in being whole-
integrated. . . ."

Johann twisted his glass between his fingers, frowning with
the intensity of his will to convince the other man.

"You must believe me! I have never been more sure of
anything in my life than I am of this. I *feel* it! If you achieve
nothing else by coming back you will have made expiation for
running away—for deserting your mother when you could have
comforted her by remaining with her. That will be something.
But I believe that it will go beyond that."

Francis was silent for a few moments, then he murmured in
English, "Almost thou persuadest me!"

Johann said quickly, "We can go by the day-train tomorrow.
All your climbing-kit is there, ready."

"But you won't be able to come on to Drindel—you have to
be at your bookshop——"

"That is so. We shall arrive late in Salzburg and you can share
my room, and in the morning you can go on to Schultzburg."

"You're not asking me to walk from Schultzburg—to retrace
every inch of the way I went with Cathryn?"

"That is for you to decide. It is not necessary. What is
necessary is that you shall climb the Drindelhorn at least as high
as the foot of the Schwarzkogel . . . and it is better you do it
alone. There are some things I think we do best alone. Making
peace with ourselves is one of them, I think."

"I wish I knew what made you so sure you were right," Francis said, half to himself.

"I cannot give you any reason, Herr Francis. It is something I feel so strongly that I am sure of it."

Francis said, with the old ironic smile, "A matter of faith—is that it?"

Johann answered, simply, "Yes. It is that—a matter of faith."

5

Before leaving Paris Francis wrote to Sue.

Johann came to see me this week-end, sent by Lotte. I am going back to Austria with him. He has persuaded me that I should climb the Drindelhorn again, alone. It is probably all in line with the best modern psychology; I don't know. I only know that whether it helps or not I have made the-journey-to-the-end-of-the-night here and there is no point in going on with it. In fact it's finished. I have got to the end of the night, and this is the night between nights—that is not my phrase; I wish it were! Cathryn gave it to me the night we spent in the Hütte below the Drindelhorn peak. She said once it was better to die on a mountain than in bed; it may be that it's easier to come to terms with one's conscience on a mountain than in the treadmill one makes for oneself in cities. I don't know. Johann, quoting St. Augustine, declares that believing is consenting to the truth of what is said, but I do not believe, for I recognise no truth and yield no consent to Johann's assertion that only through expiation of the sin of my moral cowardice can I find peace. I am not convinced of that, but I needed, badly, to be given a direction, and Johann has given it. In the night of the heart all roads are equally dark. What happens after Drindel I have no idea; nor has Johann, it seems; he says that it will be 'revealed', but he seems confident of the dayspring from on high. If it is indeed ever day again I shall send you word; if not there will be no point.

I would like to give you a message for Johnny, but I cannot think that any message I could send would be welcome. I am deeply ashamed of my treatment of him, though I don't expect him to believe it; I hope that he will be happy again, and I wish that I could contribute in some way to that happiness, but I don't think that is possible, and I doubt if he

*would wish anything from me but silence, or anything in connection with
me but to forget me. I thank him for everything he did for me and tried
to do—I think I would like you to tell him this even if he cannot accept
it as worth anything. I expect you and I will meet again, but when or
where or how I have no idea, for I am moving through darkness, but
perhaps it is something that at least I move in a forward direction instead
of going round in circles. For what it's worth I send you my love.*

Salzburg and the rushing torrent of a river; the tumble of
bells from the Glockenspiel, an awareness of the presence of the
mountains even in the darkness. A blue-washed room above a
cobbler's shop; Johann's bed with the crucifix above it, the rosary
beads twisted round a brass knob; Johann kneeling on the bare
boards saying his prayers. The clean pine smell of the floor-
polish; the brown smell of the river below the window; the
snow-smell of the mountains. . . . Lying listening to the river,
listening to Johann's deep quiet breathing; listening to the clocks
striking the quarter hours, the half hours, the hours. Wishing
you could get to sleep before they struck again; trying desperately, but being overtaken by them. The insomniac nightmare of
striking clocks. . . . Wishing you had a drink. Wondering if it
would waken Johann if you got up and lit a cigarette; deciding
against it; telling yourself it didn't matter whether you slept or
not. . . . *We'll spend some time in Salzburg on the way back.*
This is the way back. Odd how things work out. . . . Odd of
God. Not that you believed in God. Or that you believed in
anything . . . working out . . . Drowsiness confused the thought,
and he slid into sleep. . . .

Then there was morning sunlight, and a clatter of cartwheels
and horses' hooves on cobbles; there was the early morning freshness on the air, and a smell of coffee, and a sense of hurry. Johann
took his *Frühstück* at a small café next door to the cobbler's, a
small dark little place, but it served well enough, he said, and
it was patronised by workers like himself who lived in rooms
in which there was no service.

When they had taken coffee and rolls Francis walked with
Johann to his bookshop some distance along the other side of
the river; there was no train to Schultzburg till midday. On the

bridge they stopped and looked across to the hulk of the Unters-berg range a few miles out from the town, across a meadowy plain. The chestnuts were in bloom along the river, and there was a scent of hawthorn on the fresh morning air.

Johann sighed. "One does not wish to go inside on such a morning."

Francis leaned on the parapet of the bridge and looked one way across to the wooded slopes of the Kapuzinerberg, the other way to the *Schloss* perched up on its hill above the *Innere Stadt*.

"I was going to bring Cathryn here—on the way back," he said.

"We were going to live here."

"Yes. I'd forgotten."

Johann straightened himself. "We'd better be going—I must, at least."

They went on across the bridge and parted outside the bookshop. Francis declined Johann's suggestion that he should pass a little time there; it was not the kind of bookshop that interested him.

"I shall be home at the week-end," Johann said. "You won't leave Drindel before then?"

"No. I'll wait."

"We might climb something together?"

"We might."

Johann held out his hand. "*Aufwiedersehen*."

"*Aufwiedersehen*."

When he left the shop in the evenings Johann always had his evening meal before going home. On fine evenings when he had eaten he sat at a café on the Glockenspielplatz for a time, or took a stroll along the river. Sometimes he took a book and sat up on a terrace below the monastery woods, which meant that in the summer it was always getting dusk before he returned to his room. The day that he parted with Francis he followed his usual routine. When he opened the door of his room and switched on the light he was startled to see Francis lying on his bed. It flashed into his mind that perhaps Francis had spent the day drinking after they parted, then he saw that he had evidently fallen asleep reading, for a book lay on the bed beside him. Johann went over to the bed, but he did not need to pick up the shabby old black-covered book to know that it was his copy of Pusey's translation of *The Confessions of St. Augustine.* . . .

The opening of the door and the snapping on of the light wakened Francis. He raised himself on an elbow, confused.

"Oh, hullo, Johann. Is it very late?"

"About ten. What happened? Did you miss the train?"

"Yes. After I left you I walked about for a bit, but I felt tired—I slept badly last night; in fact it was getting light before I got to sleep. I thought I would come back here and sleep for an hour before the train went—I had to come back for my things, anyhow. When I woke up it was the middle of the afternoon! I went out and got something to eat, and asked at the station about trains, but the evening train to Schultzburg doesn't arrive till eleven at night. So I came back here and began looking at your books. I picked this one up out of curiosity. I got interested and read for a long time. I must have dozed off—I seem to have a lot of arrears of sleep to make up!"

He swung his legs over the edge of the bed.

"Do you mind if I stay another night, Johann? Or I could go out and get a room somewhere if you'd rather——"

"Stay as long as you like. Spend the rest of the week here and we'll go to Drindel together on Saturday."

"Better I should go Thursday and climb Friday and come down Saturday—get it over before you come!"

"You'll go all the way to the *Hütte*?"

"I think so. Would you like to lend me St. Augustine to take with me? I'll need something to read up there."

"If he interests you take him by all means."

"He does interest me. He seems to have been"—Francis smiled—"a very human sort of person! And I like his literary style! Though that may have been Pusey, of course. . . ."

"It's even finer in the Latin. It's there if you want it, and the *De Civitate Dei*. And the Sermons and the Soliloquies in English. You noticed perhaps?"

"No. I picked up the *Confessions*, and time, as they say, passed. . . . Are you too tired for us to go out for a drink now?"

"I'd like it."

Francis dashed cold water on to his face, put on his coat, and they went out.

As they walked towards the *Innere Stadt* Francis said, "You got Cathryn interested in Augustine, didn't you?"

"Yes. It was by chance. I quoted something once and she liked it and asked me where it was from. You may have noticed it at the beginning of the *Confessions*—'Thou madest us for Thyself, and our heart is restless, until it repose in Thee.' She had read the *Fioretti* of St. Francis and the life of St. Teresa of Avila, but Augustine was new to her. She borrowed that copy of the *Confessions*." He turned to Francis suddenly. "I think you should keep that copy—if you would care to. I have it in the Latin." Then, as Francis protested, "Yes, yes, keep it! Take it to the mountain with you. There was something else Cathryn specially liked. 'Too late loved I Thee.' You may find it. It may mean to you what it meant to her."

"That I doubt. Cathryn was a Christian. I am not."

"Neither was Augustine of Hippo for the first thirty-three years of his life!"

"He interests me as a philosopher, and a mathematician—and as a vital personality. He had passion."

"Yes. Herr Francis. He had passion."

For two days Francis sat under the chestnut trees beside the river, and on the terrace under the Kapuzinerberg woods, and among the roses of the Mirabellengarten, and at cafés in the *Innere Stadt*, reading of Augustine's youthful lusts and 'various and shadowy loves', of Augustine weeping for dead Dido, who killed herself for love, and delighting in his own passionate need to love and be loved, Augustine running wild with companions as young and reckless as himself in the streets of Babylon, Augustine in Carthage with his wild loves, and his wild longing—'I loved not yet, yet I loved to love'—Augustine who did not fall in love but was in love with love. . . .

There were moments when Francis closed the book with the feeling that it was all too personal and intense and that he could stand no more . . . it came too close. Those shadowy loves of Babylon and Carthage; those shadowy loves of Paris and the Riviera; the fourth century or the twentieth, the human hunger remained the same, and the human emptiness. For though we are clad in the garment of the flesh, our spirits move among the stars.

Always at some such point Francis Sable would thrust the book into his pocket and sit staring at the river rushing past, or at the distant mountains, or at the roses showering over their pergolas, and he could not see the river or the mountains or the roses, but Merrilee with her dark cloud of hair, Sue with her troubled eyes, Lotte with her laughing face like a happy child's; and his mother with a gloved hand over her face, and a boy called Johnny blundering blindly out of a room. The pattern of your nights and days; your hollow loves, and your rejections of love; all a feeding of the wind, a confused pattern, formless, devoid of design. You made the dark journey to the end of the night, the dark night of the soul, but it left you still engulfed in darkness, in the night between nights. You were restless, restless. Augustine discovered Cicero and you discovered Augustine, and what you were seeking you hardly knew; but there was this disintegration of self, this dissatisfaction, this consuming restlessness. And Augustine knew it all in the fourth century—even the popular success, down even, he thought, ironically, to the prize poem. . . .

There was nothing, it seemed, which Augustine did not know of the spirit's unrest or of the body's needs. The passage in which Augustine wrote of his grief over the death of his beloved friend, with whom he felt himself 'one soul in two bodies', moved him deeply, spoke to his condition touching Cathryn: 'For I wondered that others, subject to death, did live, since he whom I loved, as if he should never die, was dead; and I wondered yet more that myself, who was to him a second self, could live, he being dead.' The death within life of life as a habit, and the spiritual disintegration, and the crushing weight of misery which nothing could dispel—not 'the pleasures of the bed or couch, nor books or poesy', and a turning away even from the light of day, and the earth under one's feet 'a hapless spot, where I could neither be, nor be from thence. For whither should my heart flee from my heart?' Augustine, hounded by the restlessness of his misery, went from Thagaste to Carthage . . . and you, Francis Sable, go from France to Austria, and your unrest goes with you, but Augustine went away and you are going back. . . .

He left Salzburg on the Thursday and caught the mid-day train to Schultzburg, and from thence he walked, and it was both only yesterday and a lifetime ago that he did that hillside walk with Cathryn. Across the valley, towering above the other peaks in the range, the Drindelhorn stood out white against the clear blue of the sky. It looked so calm up there, viewed from the valley, a serene white stillness; there was no intimation of the blinding wind that tried to tear you from your holds, or of the remoteness of a world above the clouds.

He walked slowly through the bright afternoon sunlight, thinking of the man who had lived and loved and suffered and known remorse sixteen hundred years ago, the man who had loved beauty and was drawn by it, and wrote upon 'the fair and fit', the beautiful and the fitting, and despised a vulgar popularity, and would rather have been unknown than so known, 'and even hated, than so loved', Augustine, the writer, composing his 'corporeal fictions', repelled by the idea of God, reading Aristotle and pondering the Predicament of Substance. . . .

Augustine, man-of-letters, scholar, philosopher—and *bon vivant*. Augustine seeking distraction in people, and discovering the great fable, the protracted lie, of the social world, the external, material world . . . perhaps you had always known that it was a lie, all the parties, and the amusing talk, and the success. There was the Good Time lie; and the I-Love-You lie which sprang to your lips when you held a lovely body in your arms and desire beat in your blood; there was the answering lie, and the face of lust, and the after-emptiness, the *post-coitus triste*. There was the Romantic Lie and the Sentimental Lie, the lies you told to yourself . . . and there was the white peak of the Drindelhorn, as clean-drawn against the sky as when Augustine of Hippo wrote of first and last things whilst the Roman Empire cracked and the Vandals were at the gates of his native city. Empires and wars and revolutions came and went, like the coming and going of the things of the imagination and of memory; civilisations waxed and waned and crumbled, but still the Drindelhorn stood white against the sky, symbol of eternal truth, the unchanging order of time.

Herr and Frau Amanshauser greeted him as though he were a son. They behaved as though they had lived only for the moment when he should return. They were expecting him, for Johann had written them from Salzburg, and Lotte had told them that she had found him 'ill with unhappiness' on her visit to Paris. It had no more occurred to Lotte, he realised, to describe exactly the condition in which she had found him than it had occurred to Johann to explain why he was coming back to Drindel.

"You will rest, now that you are here?" Frau Amanshauser urged, setting an enormous *Aufschnitt* before him, at a table in the window of the *Speisezimmer*. "You will do no writing or climbing, but just take things quietly?"

"I came back to climb the Drindelhorn again," he told her.

She looked distressed. "But that mountain, of all mountains, Herr Francis—is that a good thing to do?"

He smiled at her. "It is a good thing to do, Frau Amanshauser."

She shook her head, and he patted her plump hand.

"You don't understand? But you are a Catholic, so it should not be difficult for you to accept without understanding."

Frau Amanshauser consulted her husband.

"Why do you suppose that Herr Francis must climb the Drindelhorn again—so soon on top of the tragedy?"

"It is no doubt something to do with his conscience," Herr Amanshauser told her. "Something to do with running away after the inquest."

"He didn't run away from the mountain!"

"How do we know what is between a man and his conscience?"

"You think it's a penance?"

"I think nothing. There is something Herr Francis feels he must do. No doubt he does it for the good of his soul. Why that should be is not for us to inquire."

Francis climbed up to the cornice above the ice-fall into the full force of the wind along the ridge . . . and then he saw the great boulder he had seen so often when he had sat in his apartment in Paris, or at the Montparnasse cafés, or walked the boulevards and the gardens of the Luxembourg. It stood up massively in the clean sweep of the snow. There was no dark huddle at the base of it, and no brown patch spreading in the whiteness. Virgin snow, everywhere. He stood leaning on his ice-axe and looking at it, at the boulder, and the steep white waste of snow. That was how it was, white, empty, untrodden. He slipped the rucksack from his shoulders and took out the crampons and strapped them to his boots, then began to hack his way up the frozen snow.

When he came out on to the terrace at the top the sun was just clearing a long stratum of cloud; the crags and spires and buttresses of the Schwarzkogel *massif* were caught in a crimson glow, and the Drindelhorn peak was ice reflected through fire.

You could not merely say, Francis thought, that the rocks and the snow and ice reflected the sunrise; it was more than a reflection of light; something was happening; it was a performance; you felt yourself in the presence of a ritual. That crimson glow on that particular mountain was light reflected from a source unimaginable millions of light-miles away, and of all the earth's millions you, Francis Sable, were the only one to see it at that particular point, at that moment in time. And you could use up all the adjectives in your writer's repertoire and still fail to convey its immensity and splendour. You felt that tremendous light somehow flood in yourself, in that non-physical part of yourself you called your soul. Something was happening in yourself as well as on the mountain. All the crags and couloirs of your spirit's desolation were touched with light. You felt that you knew at last the meaning of being visited by the dayspring from on high. Something in you knelt down and prayed—to that God in whom you did not believe. . . .

He went on over the ice-hard snow of the terrace and on to the ridge. The clouds swirled over it like smoke, and when they parted in their endless folding and refolding the spires of crags thousands of feet below were visible. The wind tried to tear you from the glassy knife-edge, but you clung on with hands and feet and knees and the force of your will. You gripped with your will and with your body, and somehow you came out eventually on to the terrace at the foot of the Schwarzkogel, rested in a snowy hollow for a few moments comparatively out of the wind, then removed your crampons and started for the citadel of solid rock ahead of you.

He reached the hut in the middle of a brilliant afternoon. He had climbed up out of the clouds into a world of clear blue sky, blindingly white snow, and a dazzling sunlight. In the hut he unpacked, and started the Primus.

When he had eaten he put on his sun-glasses and walked to the foot of the peak. It was good to walk without carrying a pack. He had no intention of climbing the peak. He had done it twice already and it was a bore. He had a sense of lightness that was more than the physical lightness of walking without a pack. He picked his way between ice-covered rocks that thrust up like stalagmites with a feeling of walking, in that white world, in the illustration to a child's fairy tale. Below that floor of thick fleecy cloud there was a world of pastures, hay-huts, huddled villages and little towns of wooden houses; a world of streets and traffic, of railway lines, docks, ant-like swarms of people; a world of newspapers, wireless, cinemas; there were cars and taxis darting in all directions across the Place de la Concorde; there were the red 'buses like top-heavy galleons in Piccadilly; there were crowded café terraces, and shops stuffed with all the inessentials with which people cluttered up their lives. All down there under the clouds; here you were cut off from it by a tight-rope of snow and ice stretched in space; by a sea of clouds; by bastions of rock . . . and by something in yourself. You climbed up out of the world, and out of the self that inhabited that world.

When he got back to the hut the light had gone from the peak and the crags of the Schwarzkogel were grey and desolate. He heated soup on the Primus, put out bread and *Würstchen* and made his evening meal. Then he lay on a bunk and pulled the blankets over him and went on reading the *Confessions*, first in the fading light, the book held close to the window, and then by candlelight.

He was fascinated by the story of Augustine, as Professor of Rhetoric, reciting before the consul a panegyric of the Emperor, 'wherein I was to utter many a lie, and lying, was to be applauded by those who knew I lied'.

That appealed to the sardonic in him; one had oneself so often been applauded as brilliant and witty in one's clever and amusing lying by people who knew, if they thought about it—which they avoided doing—that it was all lies. Of course it was all lies, all the witty generalisations and brilliant paradoxes, and it perpetuated the biggest lie of all, the intellectual lie, the lie of progress. . . .

He read on and came to Augustine's observation of a cheer-fully drunk beggar in the streets of Milan, and his reflection that that lightheartedness the beggar had attained 'by means of a few begged pence, the same was I plotting for by many a toilsome turning and winding—the joy of a temporary felicity. For he verily had not the true joy, but yet I with my ambitious designs was seeking one much less true. And certainly he was joyous, I anxious; he void of care, I full of fears. But should any ask me, had I rather be merry or fearful? I would answer, merry. Again, if he asked had I rather be such as he was, or what I then was? I should choose to be myself, though worn with cares and fears; but out of wrong judgment, for, was it the truth? For I ought not to prefer myself to him, because more learned than he, seeing that I had no joy therein, but sought to please men by it, and that not to instruct, but simply to please.'

At that point Francis closed the book. It all came too close. He had the feeling of something cracking within himself, cracking and crumbling and dissolving; the feeling of being all broken up inside, of utter spiritual disintegration. One had been possessed of something one chose to call a soul, by which one understood all the non-physical part of oneself, consciousnesss, mind, emotion; it had all been as compact as the body that housed it; one knew what one thought about most things, what one felt; one had certainty. You called yourself a rationalist; you demanded a scientific explanation for everything; metaphysics were merely higher mathematics, God merely a matter of definition and bio-chemistry. You arrived at truth by a process called logic. You explained life in terms of protoplasm, truth in terms of numbers; beauty was of the senses; it was something you heard, something you saw; it was an Attic marble of Aphrodite; it was the Ode to a Grecian Urn; it was the second movement of Bach's Concerto for Two Violins; it was the splendour of mountains; it was moon-light on water; it was the rhythm of a bird's wings, the curve of a young girl's breast. It was all that Augustine meant by the 'fair and fit'; it was all in terms of the sensible world. You did not need to ask yourself what is truth, what is beauty, for you had certain criteria, certain values, which you did not question. Your mind, like Augustine's, ranged through corporeal forms, and you did not inquire into the nature of mind, and were as impatient as the unregenerate Augustine of 'incorporeal substance', preferring 'lineaments and colours and bulky magnitudes' . . . and 'the gales of tongues blew from the breast of the opinionative'—and how they did blow!—and what you were pleased to call your soul was driven forward and backward, and the light was overclouded and the truth unseen, and you were restless, restless. Inside yourself you were integrated; there was a solid, compact, unity that knew what it thought and felt and believed; it went everywhere with you; it was your soul, your personality, your particular ego, as whole as the body it inhabited; it had its specific reactions, mental and emotional; it was the essential *you*. *C'est moi*. Like Augustine you were possessed of a nimble wit and were well-versed in all the liberal arts, and as with Augustine it profited you nothing; you were restless, dissatisfied, perpetually seeking, without knowing what it was you sought.

> 'I shall seek until I find
> Something I may never find;
> Something lying on the ground
> At the bottom of my mind.'

It was all so much weariness and disillusion, so much emptiness of heart and impotence of spirit. You held a lovely body in your arms and knew ecstasy, but it was an ecstasy of the flesh that was destroyed in the very moment of fulfilment. There was the ecstasy of music and the sense of the soul taking wings, but the violins swept onwards and upwards and into silence, and then there were only men and women with digestive troubles and money worries, Schopenhauerian figures 'stung by appetite, goaded by desire', replacing their instruments in their cases, or so many blobs of faces bobbing in a sea of applause, and you were engulfed again in the material world. 'Man himself is a great deep,' declared Augustine, and 'the hairs of his head are easier to be numbered than are his feelings, and the beatings of his heart.' And Augustine had an ambition to be a great orator—as great an orator as Hierius, of Rome, to whom he dedicated his books on the fit and fair, and whom he loved with an ardent hero-worship for his fame and philosophical learning, for it seemed to him most wonderful that a Syrian, first instructed in Greek eloquence, should become a brilliant Latin orator, and he was such a man as Augustine would be himself—Augustine in his late twenties, proud, brilliant, successful, ambitious . . . and 'tossed about by every wind', perpetually subject to change, yet longing for permanence, rich in scholarship yet empty of understanding, encompassed by an aura of brilliance, yet standing with his back to the light, accusing the flesh for all dissatisfactions, seeking unity in corporeal forms and immutabilities in the mutable . . . and Francis Sable in the twentieth century no less than Augustine in the fourth. . . .

He lay watching the light fade and the stars come out, at first faintly, and then in a brilliant blaze of splendour. Heavens, what splendour! Were there really millions of human beings somewhere down below streaming in and out of cinemas and cafés and only vaguely aware of the stars, if at all, devoid of any sense of wonder, never looking at the miracle of the firmament and asking themselves Why? How? Whence? What am I? What is this universe? What is truth? What is God?

But you, Francis Sable, if it comes to that, how often have you in your thirty years of living asked yourself what is truth, what is God? Oh, you have read philosophy—you have read Hegel and Descartes and Plato and Spinoza and Schopenhauer and Epicurus, with all the eagerness with which the young Augustine read Aristotle, but were you seeking truth, 'the philosophy of sunrise', or merely intellectual exercise? Were you concerned with Ultimate Truth and the Supreme Good, or merely academically interested in philosophy? Your wisdom like your ecstasy was precarious, balanced on the uncertain edge of the material world, whose margins faded forever and forever as you moved, Ulysses-wise. Yet how you pursued those horizons, and how you clung to your rationalism, your earth-bound certainties, with a kind of defiance, as though asserting that it were possible to mock God—making it, in fact, your moral duty to do so, as proof that you were a free-thinker. You chained Prometheus to the rock of materialism and called it freedom! But it was Prometheus unbound who stole fire from the gods. The Promethean fire. You loved Shelley as Augustine loved Virgil, but Shelley, for all his fire and music, no longer spoke to your condition; you needed something beyond corporeal beauty and the ecstasies of the senses. You needed the beatitude of spiritual peace, and the peace of that beatitude and the certainty of eternity.

Last time he had lain in this hut, he reflected, ten thousand feet above the culture of cities, he had pondered the life of Francis Sable and come to the conclusion that it was a problem in ciphers, adding up to nothing. Since then he had made the 'journey to the end of the night', and it too was a dead end, and a night between nights. Now there was this sense of emergence into the daylight, of the dayspring from on high visiting the heart, breaking up the hard crust of materialism, and the beginnings of belief in something beyond the material, that the order of the universe, and the government of human life, belongs to something beyond any materialist explanation. And this you must believe, for there is no other way out of the darkness. If there is no ultimate truth, no truth higher than the materialist conception, then there is no light on the mountain, no dayspring from on high, no day to follow the heart's night. Materialism having failed you, despair has driven you to give assent to the idea of a profounder meaning to life than materialist reasoning; all the non-physical part of your being insists that there must be something immutable and therefore eternal, and that higher reality is truth, ultimate and absolute. And this absolute truth is God. . . .

With the impact of that thought Francis Sable had a sense of perspectives opening out in all directions, of limitless life flowing through all the centuries of the past and to come; flowing with the wind through immeasurable space, flowing through the meadows of the stars. He had climbed up through the clouds above the material world, so small and narrow and limited, into the boundless fields of light. The night between nights was over. Whatever happened now there would be day.

He turned and extinguished the candle, pinching the wick between his thumb and forefinger, and suddenly the childish question sprang at him from the darkness, Where does the flame go when it's out? It no longer exists; but nothing created can cease to exist; there is no such thing as nothingness. Where does the flame of the spirit go when physical death extinguishes it? Your life of the flesh is quenched, Cathryn, but you were mind and spirit too, and the soul is more than flesh, as the flame is more than the lamp; the body returns dust to dust, and the soul—it came to him suddenly, in a flash of revelation—returns to God, the author of its being, the Supreme Spirit of which it is a part, since God made man in His own image.

'*And I heard, as the heart heareth, nor had I any room to doubt.*' Thus it was with Augustine of Hippo; and how else should revelation come? '*Too late loved I Thee, O Thou Beauty of ancient days, yet ever new! Too late loved I Thee!*'

Cathryn, his heart exulted, Cathryn! This is why I had to come back—to find you! I had to see the light on the mountain! I had to know the dayspring from on high!

He lay in the darkness looking at the stars, listening to the wind, with a sense of his whole being flooded with the light of revelation, a light both brilliant and soft, like the light at evening, when he and Cathryn had walked in from Schultzburg, like the light in the Champs-Élysées when there had been that strange pervading happiness, and she had sung under her breath the last aria from the St. Matthew Passion. . . .

With the memory it began to run through his head, the softly flowing music and the soothing words—'*Lie Thou softly, lie Thou softly, softly here. . . .*'

Behind closed eyelids he saw her smiling.

"It's going to be a good day tomorrow," he murmured drowsily, and slipped into sleep.

PART III

THE LIGHT ON THE MOUNTAIN

'I see His blood upon the rose
And in the stars the glory of His eyes . . .'
(JOSEPH PLUNKETT.)

I

DOROTHEA was at Victoria to meet Francis off the boat-train. He had not written her; she knew nothing of his return to Drindel or what had happened to him after he had left there on the day of the inquest. Eventually she had heard from Sue that he was back in Paris; that was all she knew. Then, suddenly, the telegram from Paris with the time of his arrival at Victoria. She had a room prepared for him; even if he were going on to Crag House he would perhaps spend a night with her, she thought; and as he had given the arrival time of his train presumably he had wanted to be met. She had not been to Victoria since she had seen him and Cathryn off, the pair of them so young and good-looking and alive. But that was the Continental departure platform; this was something quite different; this was the arrivals platform; one of them was coming back; one of them . . . God had taken the other to Himself, the ewe lamb. But upon the Cross had died the Lamb of God.

Francis was coming back. Her heart beat painfully between excited happiness and a kind of fear. He was her beloved son, difficult sometimes, and always a little aloof, but never his father's son, as Steven had always been; he had never been as close to her as Cathryn, but still she felt that there was something of herself in him, whereas even as a child Steven had always seemed alien to her. Sue had been angry with him for running away after the inquest, but she, his mother, felt that she understood. It was he who had taken Cathryn on that fatal journey. Remorse was something she understood; she knew what a tearing, tormenting thing it could be in its futility. If Sue had ever known remorse she could not have judged Francis as she did. In her own heart there had been no judgment at the time or ever; she had pitied him, deeply, and it had comforted her that Johann too had understood and joined his prayers to hers that Francis might find peace. Sue had written her from Paris that Francis still seemed to be suffering from the shock of the tragedy. That was all Sue thought fit to say, and all Dorothea knew as she waited at Victoria, sick with anticipation that was all eagerness and dread. To be nervous of meeting one's own son was absurd, she told herself, and yet the fact remained that she was sick with nerves. The train was half an hour late and she lived an eternity of agitation in that time.

Then at last the train came in and in a moment the passengers were swarming out on to the platform and the people waiting with her began to move forward, eagerly. Only she, it seemed to her, stood still, with the dark waves of movement washing about her. She stood still, straining a little on her toes to see, her handbag under her arm, her hands locked together. Then she saw him, tall, hatless, distinguished-looking as ever, caught in the crowd yet somehow not of it. He saw her quickly, and smiled a little. She realized before he reached her that he was thinner in the face, a little haggard.

He came up to her, put down a pigskin valise, and kissed her.

"Thank you for coming to meet me," he said. "I hoped you would. I'm afraid we're a little late. . . ."

He was gentle, she thought, relieved, curiously gentle. She hardly knew what she said. All was confusion; baggage to be retrieved from the guard's van; a taxi to be found. There was a great deal of baggage. He apologised for the quantity.

"It's really all memoirs of my dead life," he said, with a touch of the old irony. "I'm not going back, you see."

In the taxi she asked him, "Do you really mean you're not going back to Paris?"

He smiled. "I really mean it. One can't go on forever repeating the pattern."

"Does that mean you'll settle in London?" He had always declared that he hated London—that there was only one city more basically uncivilised and that was New York.

"I don't know. I don't know at all. I've no plans. I've given up the Paris flat and packed all my books and here I am—and that's all I know. I should like to stay with you for a time—if I may."

"Of course. I hoped you would."

"I should like to meet Father Connor."

She said again, a little faintly, "Of course."

"You still see him?"

"Yes. He has been very kind. He comes to the house once a week. He has helped me—greatly." She was silent a moment, then she asked, "Shall you go to Crag House?"

"I hadn't thought of doing so."

"You know Cathryn is buried there?"

"Yes, I knew that. Sue told me."

"I put some white roses on the grave from you."

"Thank you."

They finished the journey in silence. He is different, she thought, exultantly, he has come close to me—at last.

At the house she told him, as they went up the stairs to his room, "Cathryn's room is just as she left it. I keep the windows open and put fresh flowers in. I hope you don't think it morbid—I don't do it morbidly." She spoke nervously, a little fearful again.

He smiled. "I'm sure you don't. I'm sure the flowers make her spirit welcome."

She said, eagerly, grateful to him, "I think of it like that. I feel her close, you see. She's gone only in the flesh. She still *is*. She has found eternal happiness, so why should we mourn? The priest at Drindel said a Mass for her—I don't know if you knew?"

"Johann's sister told me. I was glad."

They came into his room. There was a musky scent from a bowl of roses on a table. The room was full of a mellow evening light. The window opened into a green-gold sea of plane-tree branches. Dorothea moved about murmuring about the bathwater being hot, making sure he had towels, adjusting a curtain. Francis went over to the window and stood there looking down into the walled garden.

He heard his mother saying, "Dinner isn't till eight, so take your time."

She was on the point of leaving the room when he said, "You didn't know, perhaps, that I went back to Drindel?"

She turned, her hand still on the door-handle.

"I didn't know."

"I wondered if Johann told you. He probably thought I'd prefer to do so myself. I went back and climbed the Drindelhorn again."

She was silent a moment, then she said, with difficulty, because of the ache in her throat, "You felt you had to?"

"Yes."

"And it helped?"

He nodded.

"I'm glad."

She went out, softly. They were close at last, her heart exulted, there was no need for explanations.

Francis was grateful to her that she understood without explanation, yet that she asked no questions and offered no reproaches wounded him. If she had reproached him for selfishness and heartlessness in his flight from Drindel, and in leaving her to the loneliness of her return to London, it would have made his remorse easier to bear; he could have built up round himself, then, some sort of self-protective barrier; as it was he felt himself defenceless utterly and the passion of his desire for atonement was intensified. He was painfully aware that the question of forgiveness did not come into it for his mother; he had robbed her of her ewe lamb, and the daughter she had hoped to have given to the Church, but she attributed no blame to him, any more than she blamed him for deserting her in the midst of her pain; he had been selfish before the disaster and a moral coward after it, but she loved him, and because she loved him she was on his side, as Lotte had been; she loved him and accepted him, all that he did, all that he was, and all the pain that loving him might entail, because love is selfless, seeketh not itself. All over the world, at every minute of the night and day, people were asserting to other people that they loved them, asserting it passionately, asserting it earnestly, unconscious that they lied, unconscious of the blasphemy. I-love-you, the universal lie. Love, the eternal truth. And when you had sinned against those who selflessly loved you the pain of it was almost more than you could bear, yet that you should suffer it was just. You had somehow to make atonement. You had somehow to come to that at-one-ment with

God in which alone was peace. Again and again you came back to it—'Thou madest us for Thyself and our heart is restless until it repose in Thee.' So simple the truth was in its profundity.

When he retired to his room for the night he lit the candles in the Georgian silver candlesticks set either side of the bowl of roses, drew the shabby volume of the *Confessions* from his pocket, and sat down at the table. He turned the pages till he came to the chapter in which Augustine and his mother stood at a window overlooking the garden of a house in Ostia, where they rested after a journey. They were blessedly alone and talked together, in a sweet intimacy of understanding, of eternal wisdom, their spirits soaring beyond the need of words, beyond mind, then coming to earth again, to vocal expression, 'where the word spoken has beginning and end'. Francis read slowly, savouring anew the familiar passage, and he drew a pencil line under the lines, 'If to any the tumult of the flesh were hushed, hushed the image of earth, waters, and air, hushed also the poles of heaven, yea, the very soul be hushed to itself, and by not thinking on self surmount self, hushed all dreams and imaginary revelations, every tongue and every sign, and whatsoever exists only in transition, since if any could hear, all these say, We made not ourselves, but He made us that abideth for ever.'

He sat musing after that, smiling a little. Heavens, but the man could write! What poetry! And what good commonsense for all the neurotics who seek to cure their preoccupation with self by a disintegrating psycho-analytic orgy of indulgence in it! Fifteen hundred years before Freud Augustine of Hippo knew the answer—'and by not thinking on self surmount self'.

He smiled, too, over the passage in which Augustine, stricken with grief at his mother's death, decided to go and have a bath, having heard that the word is derived from a Greek word which means to drive sadness from the mind. But Augustine felt no better after his bath, though a lot better after a night's sleep . . . proving, Francis thought, as he closed the book, that human nature was very much the same in the fourth century as in the twentieth. And that, he thought, brings us to the other lie, the lie of 'progress'. . . .

In the morning the maid brought him coffee and rolls and a selection of Sunday papers.

"Breakfast isn't till half-past nine," she said. "Her ladyship always goes to early Mass."

He asked quickly, "Has she gone yet?"

"She doesn't leave till quarter to eight," the maid answered. "It's seven-thirty now."

When the maid had gone he leapt out of bed and washed and dressed hurriedly. He would have no time to shave, but as he had shaved after his bath last night that was not important. He ran down into the hall just as his mother was leaving.

She smiled at him. "There was no need to get up so early. I thought you would have coffee and read the papers in bed and we'd have breakfast together when I get back."

He said, quickly, "I want to come with you—if I may."

He saw her eyes fill with tears, but she said, not quite steadily, "Not just to please me, Francis . . ."

"No. Though if it pleases you I'm glad. But I went in Drindel with Johann, and last Sunday in Paris by myself."

She made no comment, merely laid a hand for a moment on his arm, then they went out together into the freshness of the early morning.

She asked him nothing, but her understanding was measured by the fact that a few days later she gave him for his thirty-first birthday present the carved ivory crucifix which she had given Cathryn at Easter.

"I thought you should have it," was all she said.

He knew that it had been Cathryn's; she had taken it with her to Drindel. He was deeply moved, almost to tears, and he had not wept since he was a child. He had not wept for Cathryn, though inside himself he had never ceased to weep. But now, suddenly, he could have wept childish tears. She had, he thought, almost too much understanding, this patient bereaved woman.

He said, with difficulty, "I can't thank you—you know that."

"You don't have to. Cathryn would have wanted you to have it."

The following day he met Michael Connor for the first time.

2

When they were not discussing Catholic theological points,

and Augustinian metaphysics, mysticism, and system of morals, Michael Connor talked about Ireland. He came from Galway and had a passion for the West; he spoke of it with a wistful nostalgia. He was a Gaelic scholar and had made his own translations of many of the ancient songs and poems; he had a tremendous feeling for all things Irish. He had served his novitiate in Ireland, but done his philosophy and theology in England; he had gone back, according to the rule, for his tertianship, but he knew that he was not likely to be in Ireland again. He could have been appointed to a Jesuit college in Ireland, but he had no vocation for teaching, whereas he had a flair for preaching; when he was sent to England he returned to a country for which he had formed an affection, but he could not root Ireland out of his heart. He loved it not merely for its physical beauty, and because it was a land of poets and saints and martyrs, but spiritually, because in a cynical materialist world it seemed to him the one country where Christianity was a living reality, a vital living factor in the everyday lives of the mass of people. It was a long way off perfect, he acknowledged, but Irish people in the main, he insisted, did at least aspire to Christian conduct.

"At least," he told Francis, smiling, "they know the difference between right and wrong! There isn't that cynicism and materialism which pervades and corrupts the rest of Europe. The mass of people of all classes accept the authority of the Church and its spiritual discipline. In Ireland the purely nominal Catholic is an exception to the rule."

He spoke with nostalgia of a Franciscan monastery beside a lake at the place in the West called Ballyroon. He had himself been attracted to the Franciscans before he finally decided to serve his novitiate for the Society of Jesus. He had been attracted by their austerity and simplicity, and by the fact that he had a great devotion to St. Francis of Assisi, but the Jesuits were the Soldiers of the Church, and as such their order made the greater appeal; the same vows of poverty, chastity and obedience were involved and one could live as austerely within the Jesuit order as in the Franciscan.

All this he discussed with Francis in Lady Sable's quiet little house in Kensington, or walking under the trees in Kensington Gardens. Francis liked Michael Connor both as man and priest.

He enjoyed their philosophical discussions and admired the cool clear mathematical quality of the Jesuit's mind, and his capacity for poetry as well as the mathematical precision of logic. It was an Augustinian mind. Temperamentally, he felt, he had more in common with Augustine than had Father Connor; the priest gave the impression of never having been touched by carnality, whereas Augustine had known all the fires, all the carnal hungers, and all the joys; Augustine had loved love, he had loved music, he had delighted in colours, poetry, all the corporeal aspects of beauty; he had loved good food, known and indulged all the carnal appetites. He had been of his world—as Francis Sable was of his. But Michael Connor had known since he was a boy of sixteen that he had wanted to be a priest; he had known from the beginning of his adult life that the world was not for him; that his life was dedicate. By the time he was eighteen he had known that he wanted to be a Jesuit. His mother had wept and implored. Let him be a priest by all means; she would be proud for him to be a priest, but not in the Society of Jesus. It was too drastic; too rigid an order, and his health, she was convinced—for he was a delicate boy—would never stand up to the strain of all the hard manual labour involved in the novitiate, and the long gruelling year after year of study and examinations. And one slip or failure and he would be disqualified, and all the years of physical, mental and spiritual labour be lost. It would be fourteen years before he took his final vows; it was too long and exhausting, both for him and for those who loved him.

Father Connor smiled, recounting it to Francis. "I too was the ewe lamb, you see. I was the only son, and my mother had prayed for a son as your mother prayed for a daughter. She begged of me if I must serve the priesthood in an order to let it be the Franciscans to whom I had first been drawn, and when I answered that the intellectualism of the Society of Jesus attracted me she reminded me that the Dominicans maintained a very high standard of learning. Why had it to be the Society of Jesus?"

"And why had it?" Francis had asked.

"It's not easy to say in so many words. I had been to a retreat conducted by a very distinguished Jesuit and been very much impressed. I had read a good deal of Jesuit writing. And all the time there was this persistent feeling that it was the nearest approach to Augustinianism in the modern world. And if you ask me why St. Augustine meant more to me than any other of the saints—more than St. John of the Cross, or St. Teresa of Avila, or St. Francis of Assisi, for all of whom I had quite early a great devotion—I can only say that he came closest to my heart and mind."

"So in spite of your mother's entreaties you persisted in this idea of becoming a Jesuit?"

"When my mother saw that my heart and soul were set on it she made no more objections. But first she had my father take me to meet a Jesuit friend of his who taught at Clongowes. 'I want you to tell my son exactly what it means to become a Jesuit,' he said. My father's friend looked at me very sternly and asked me what sort of a romantic notion had I got into my head? Didn't I know that it was a killing life, an insupportable drain upon body and spirit? It was fourteen years' hard labour, he said; it was penal servitude; people nearly died of homesickness and heart-sickness and despair long before their novitiate was up. 'But you didn't die of it, Father,' I said, boldly. 'Some of us are stronger in body and soul than others,' he replied. I said, stubbornly, 'Even though it's all the hardship and struggle you say it is, Father, I still say that this is what I want to do.' Then the stern-looking man smiled, first at me and then at my father. 'He will be all right,' he said."

"And you were?"

"I was homesick and heartsick and I despaired, but by the grace of God I survived to take my final vows, and I have had no regrets."

"Even though it means you may never see Ireland again?"

"If that is God's will. God made other places besides Ireland —which is something we Irish tend to forget! But you should go to Ireland—it would have something for you. You might do a retreat there. At the end of the month Father Halloran is giving a retreat at the Franciscan monastery at Ballyroon. He is one of the most eminent Jesuits of the Irish province. You might consider going. It would be a good introduction to Catholic Ireland."

Francis felt that he did not need to consider it. He had been waiting for direction and now he had received it.

3

From that point onwards, until the day of his death, he had a sense of his life being ordered by a power outside of himself, and he surrendered himself to it. There was in him a conscious and willing submission, and the feeling of moving in a dream from which he could not wake and from which he had no desire to wake. Everything material assumed a curious unreality. His mother wanted to know whether she should send a certain suit to the cleaners whilst he was away in Ireland. He gave her what she thought of as his 'lost' look and said vaguely, "Suit to the cleaners? I don't know . . . Do as you please." It was so completely unimportant; all that life in which one sent suits to the cleaners had no reality any more. There was a letter forwarded from Paris from his publishers inquiring as to whether he could let them have a 'blurb' for their autumn catalogue concerning his new book. He stared at the letter as though he did not understand it. Blurb . . . new book . . . autumn catalogue. That strange remote world in which one wrote books, and wrote descriptive pieces about them before one had composed a word of them, that world of autumn catalogues and spring lists, of 'blurbs' and galleys and page-proofs, of committing thousands of words to paper . . . he had the feeling that it had nothing to do with him, as though he had inadvertently opened a letter addressed to someone else of the same name. That was it, he thought, someone else of the same name. Francis Sable, the writer. Unfortunately you couldn't readdress it. He took his fountain-pen and wrote on the envelope 'Gone away', resealed it, and when he went out dropped it into a letter-box. When he had indeed been gone away some days his publishers rang up; there was some mistake, they felt; they had received their letter back marked 'Gone away'. Lady Sable told them, bewildered, that her son had gone to Ireland and she had no idea when he would be back, and she was not able to forward anything. He was not writing anything just now, and so far as she knew had nothing planned. . . .

A long time after—weeks measured in the artificial computation of hours and days—when he was walking beside the lake at Ballyroon, in a stillness so deep that the blood—listened to it,

Francis thought of all that world as of something enacted on a stage; certain emotions in oneself had been roused, but one was not of it; one had witnessed it all, been somehow emotionally involved in it, in a sense lived it for the time being—but only in a sense; it was not truth but fiction. Truth was something true yesterday, today, and forever. Truth was these mountains which had been there since the timeless beginning; truth was this wild land where the stones were as old as God. Truth was the brothers reciting the Rosary in the monastery chapel when lake and bog and mountain were held in the benediction of the evening light; truth was the sacred mystery of the Mass. Truth was eternal, and only truth had reality. A living part of himself had been the night alone in the hut below the peak of the Drindelhorn, the unearthly light, and the rising tide of revelation. The Irish mail and the night-boat to Dublin were unreal as suits for the cleaners and publishers' lists and the train-journey across the flat Irish midlands. Reality began with the hills of Clare blue-grey across Galway Bay, and the first breath of burning turf on a salty wind, and the brown and grey and golden mountainy land rolling away to the massive blue range of the Twelve Pins; reality was the strewn boulders and the stacked turf and the low-built cabins almost invisible among the stones; reality was the crimson tide of the fuchsia hedges, and this lake with the brown moorland of bog flowing away to the foot of the blue mountains, and the lost cry of a curlew, and the sudden wild sobbing of a donkey, then the silence closing in again so deep you grew aware of the stir of one leaf against another, that silence of a land in which for mile upon mile nothing moves but a leaf in the wind or a bird drifting on the air. A silence which is made of stillness; the silence which is peace.

Behind him a hayfield flowed down to the narrow beach on which he walked; the hay had been gathered and cows grazed on the short grass. At the far side of the field the monastery, old and grey, huddled in its belt of trees and looked sleepily across to the mountains. One had somehow arrived, Francis thought, in the land where it was always afternoon. When the monastery clock in its square tower struck the hour the sound was laid so softly on the thin golden air as to be merely part of the silence, like the cry of the curlew along the lake.

It was strange, he reflected, how eventually the chaos of living evolved into a pattern; and there was the complex interweaving of one life with another. Because a twentieth-century Irish boy called Michael Connor found that a fourth-century Numidian, citizen of the Roman Empire, Augustine of Hippo, spoke to his spiritual condition more than any other philosopher he had become a Jesuit, feeling that the Jesuit order came closest to Augustinianism; an Austrian boy had become interested in St. Augustine, and read a treatise on him by an Irish Jesuit working in London—Father Connor. And then an English couple, brother and sister, had gone to the Tyrol for a wintersports' holiday and had stayed at the inn run by the Austrian boy's parents, and he had talked to the English girl of St. Augustine, and had recommended her to Father Michael Connor. So the wheel had turned till now the brother of that girl had become interested in St. Augustine, through the Austrian boy, and the Irish priest, and now here he was in the West of Ireland, living in a Franciscan monastery, staying on long after the rest of the visitors for the retreat had gone, with no plans, and life assuming the quality of an endless dream. If Michael Connor had not been drawn to St. Augustine some thirty years and more ago Francis Sable would not now be at Ballyroon. Was that the first link in the chain? Or did it go back fifteen hundred years to the day when Ponticianus called on Augustine, and found him sitting with his friend Alypius at a gaming-table at his house, and told him the story of the Egyptian monk Antony, so that Augustine saw himself face to face as it seemed to him, as in a mirror, and was filled with horror and shame, and after a fierce spiritual struggle, was converted. . . . If Ponticianus had not called that day, or if there had not been that copy of St. Paul's Epistle to the Romans lying on the gaming-table, so that he had been moved to tell the story of Antony—would Augustine have been converted at some other point, through some other experience? Was the conversion of the writer, Francis Sable, in the twentieth century determined back in the fourth, by the lawyer, Ponticianus, determining to call upon Augustine? Francis smiled at the speculation. Pursuing that course you could go back to the beginning of creation; for what chain of events determined Ponticianus to go to Augustine that day? You could go back and back, until you came to God and timelessness and eternity. It was simpler, therefore, to accept all things as the will of God, for in that all things were unified.

He had understood very little of the spiritual exercises of the retreat; Father Connor had warned him that this would be so, but had said that it would not matter, and it had not mattered. He found the personality of the ageing Father Halloran sympathetic, and he got something of value from his lectures, and from talks with him. He confessed to him that he had been astonished to find that he did not know how to pray.

"My heart prays all the time, but I have no words—it's as though," he smiled ruefully, "I didn't know the formula."

The old priest smiled. "What did you learn as a child?"

"Oh, just the usual things—Our Father——"

"It was how our Lord taught us to pray. Try saying it again and thinking about it—as though it were a very fine and beautiful poem you had discovered for the first time. Read it as you first read Shelley, or Francis Thompson. Devote an hour of meditation to it."

It was strange, Francis thought, how the truth and beauty of something could be submerged in over-familiarity, the way the finest passages of Shakespeare were spoilt for one by forcible memorising at school. Millions of so-called Christians of all denominations gabbled the Lord's Prayer in their churches and tin tabernacles on Sundays and it meant nothing to them. How they would hate it, most of them, if God's will were done on earth, if His kingdom did come! And how little intention most of them had of forgiving them that trespassed against them, of forgiving their debtors as they hoped to be forgiven their debts. How few of them really wanted not to be led into temptation, or to be delivered from anything but the most material of evils!

He came and went with an increasing confidence in the monastery chapel, and ceased to feel an outsider at the Mass. He began to take his part unobtrusively in the monastery life, working in the garden, doing odd jobs about the farm—whitewashing a cowshed, mucking-out byres, tending the poultry—and finding a curious satisfaction in these humble chores. He no longer wore the lapis-lazuli ring, and he regarded his stained and roughened hands with pride. They were no longer beautiful

hands, he thought, but they were honest hands, that had contact
with the earth and were at home with axe and spade. Almost
invariably women had remarked on his hands. 'You have
beautiful hands,' they said. One after another, they said it. Sue,
Merrilee, the princess, all of them; Merrilee had been the last
to say it. Lotte had not said it; Lotte did not say that sort of
thing; she had been blessedly free of coquetry. Well, no one
would ever say again that he had beautiful hands. His hands, he
thought, were the outward and visible sign of his inward and
spiritual change. He looked sometimes at the lapis-lazuli ring,
and as he turned it in his fingers it was as though curtains were
drawn back in his mind and the whole landscape of the past
stood revealed. He saw again the tall chestnut trees of the Avenue
de l'Observatoire, and the faded grey-painted shutters of windows
that opened into them. There was the smell of coffee that was
the morning smell of Paris, and the morning sounds of mattresses
and mats being beaten. There were the crowded boulevards and
the chattering café-terraces at the *apéritif* hours; there was the
amused interest in human frailties, neuroses and eccentricities;
you were amused and you were amusing; and always in front of
you, on café-terrace, in *bistro*, in American bar, the mounting
pile of saucers. . . . There were the Biguine cabaret places in
Montparnasse and the Bal Nègre, there were the tough places in
Montmartre, there were tails and white ties at the princess's.
There was the amusing riff-raff of the Quarter; and the amusing
elegance of the Étoile. There was Jimmy's, and the Jockey Club;
and the Ritz bar. There were the afternoons drowsy with wine
taken at midday, and shutters closed against the sunshine, the
bright noisy day shut out, and an artificial twilight stirring with
sensual secrets—the amorous siesta of the Paris afternoon. All
that tense febrile excitement that expended the spirit in a waste
of emptiness. All those explosions of nervous energy into
nothingness. All those hot lazy summers on the plages of the
French and Italian Rivieras, and in the fishing villages of the
Balearics—the cheap red wine, *vin rouge, vino tinto,* as rough in any
language, and as insidious. There were the little cafés with the
red-striped awnings, and the sun—the hot strong sun day after
day, and the sea almost purple it was so blue—the authentic
wine-dark sea. You drank too much and were madly gay and

correspondingly promiscuous. It was rakish and raffish and terribly amusing. Your body was drenched in sun and wine—and Pernod—and sex. Your mind was drenched—to saturation point —with D. H. Lawrence, the Russian Ballet, and sex.

There were winters in Rome and Florence and Venice; and except that there was less sun it was all much the same; you led the same sort of life—the same amusing malicious talk, the same cliques, the same sort of *affaires*, the same self-conscious gaiety, good-humoured cynicism, the same sex-and-*apéritif* sophistication. Somehow, betweenwhiles, you got some work done. It didn't take much out of you; you didn't put much into it because you hadn't much to give. You had this surface brilliance, a kind of perverted genius. Sometimes in spite of yourself you were serious; sometimes the poet in you escaped. But for the most part you were witty-at-all-costs, and the cocktail-crazy post-war world wanted what you had to give, and what you uniquely gave, so that success was easy and productive effort didn't interfere with the good times, the chronically good times. . . . There were moments, even at the time, when you had known how trivial it all was, when something in yourself had stood aloof and contemptuous, but you were of your world, and its Neon lights were all the illumination you recognised. A decade of ginned-up, jazzed-up gaieties, of Bright Young Things, and Wild Parties, of *nouveau-riche* vulgarity, of the brilliant witty superficiality of the novels of Francis Sable, with their odd, disconcerting flashes of bitter poetry. . . .

There were times when the sense of the futility and the tawdriness of his past life almost overwhelmed him, so that he seemed to himself the most despicable of all things living, and he would bury his face in his hands, pressing his fingers against his eyes as though he would press out the inner vision of selfishness and materialism which had been his life for thirty-three years. He felt that he understood why Oedipus gouged out his eyes when he realized the enormity of his sin. He understood all too deeply the storm of bitter weeping which had swept Augustine under the fig-tree in the garden, the torment of sick self-disgust. Too late loved I Thee, in truth, O God, 'O Thou Beauty of ancient days, yet ever new! Too late loved I Thee!'

If Francis Sable had found that beauty which is truth six years ago, he thought, he might have written that really great book. Now it was too late. Greatness came out of something deeply felt, Cathryn had insisted, the heart torn up by the roots. She had had to die for that to happen, and what would come out of it it was impossible to foresee, but it would not be another book, because Francis Sable the writer had not survived his heart torn up by the roots; he had died in the spirit and descended into hell. The man who had been spiritually reborn had only one desire—a consuming desire for atonement; to that his whole life was now dedicated. And increasingly it seemed to him that it could only be made through the complete holocaust of self. On the negative side the course was clearly indicated; on the positive side it was still dark. Father Halloran, with whom he had discussed his problem, had said that in due course grace would be given him to see what was required of him; only let his heart remain open to receive that grace, for it would surely come. Just as now the Ignatian exercises were incomprehensible to him; in time he would understand them and benefit by them; only let the heart remain open.

He would remember him always, he thought, the good old man with his worn face and kindly eyes and shabby soutane; there was in him, surely, the fabric of a saint. When he was not addressing the community he seemed to spend all his time on his knees, at all hours of the day and night, in the chapel, Francis had observed. He had seen him there once at midnight when he had come in from walking beside the lake in what was for him the insomniac moonlight; he had gone into the chapel to pray before going to bed and seen the old man kneeling there, his eyes closed, the crucifix in his clasped hands, tears rolling down his face. He had been unaware of Francis's entry, and Francis had tiptoed out and gone up the polished bare boards of the wide staircase to his cell-bare room; he was deeply moved. The incident made a profound impression on him. In his room he took his own crucifix from above his bed and knelt a long time on the bare boards with it in his hands; he did not pray, and yet his whole being prayed in a passionate penitence; it was as though he were involved in a tremendous act of contrition. Blessed Saint Augustine, his heart prayed, help me, for I too have

come late to the ancient and eternal beauty that is truth. Help
me, O my God, for late have I loved Thee. . . .

4

On a wild wet morning he walked with Father Halloran to the
station. The old man had refused to have a car sent for him,
protesting that he had no luggage, as indeed he had not, all
that he needed being stuffed into the sagging pockets of his
threadbare coat. He trudged along in his old-fashioned down-at-
heel boots, his thin body bent to the wind, his eyes watering, his
shoulders hunched under their inadequate covering, but his
expression was cheerful and kindly as ever; he counted it a sin
to complain about the weather in any circumstance; the weather
was an act of God, and it was not for man to criticise God's
actions. When the clouds broke for a few moments and the
hulks of the mountains stood revealed grey and distant he
inquired of Francis as to whether he had been up any of them.

"There'd be no real climbing to it," he added, "but there'd
be a grand view from the top."

"I'm a rock-climber," Francis told him. "Anything else
seems tame. I've collected peaks in my time, but never views."

"There's rock-climbing in these parts, too—I understand it's
as easy to break your neck here, if you choose the right rocks,
as in the English Lake District. I've never been attracted by
climbing for its own sake; I'm the sort of person you mountaineers despise—I always go up mountains by the easiest route,
and purely for the sake of the view from the top."

"So long as you don't go up by train or car or funicular we
mountaineers don't really mind, you know!"

The old man's sunken grey eyes twinkled. "Do you
mountaineers ever go up barefoot?"

"Good heavens, no!"

"Then we amateurs beat you. In this country every year
thousands of people climb Croagh Patrick barefoot—and fasting.
Men, women and children, young and old. At the top some of
them do the Stations of the Cross on their knees in the loose
flints."

He smiled at Francis across the upturned collar of his coat.

"Mind you it's not real climbing. But it's steep going, and the peak is just a cone of loose stones—you had better add it to your collection!"

Francis returned his smile. "Is the view from the top added to your own collection, Father?"

"I've been up it a score or so of times, but as often as not there's no view, only a great wet cloud. But you don't climb Croagh Patrick for the view, though it's a fine one when it's visible, or for the glory of it, but for the grace of it. It's a holy mountain. If you go with the pilgrimage in July you attend Mass in the little chapel at the summit. There are many who spend the night shelterless on the mountain and hear the first Mass at five in the morning."

"And they've gone up barefoot and fasting," Francis murmured.

"Many of them. Why don't you try it? Climb for humility instead of glory! Nothing but grace could come of it."

"I'm sure. Even climbing for personal satisfaction, for nothing more than to be able to say one's done it, for the conquest of fear and height and difficulty—all the things one sets out to triumph over in climbing a mountain—climbing for no more than this, for glory, if you like, it's always a good thing to do. For one thing you climb up out of the world, and in a sense out of yourself. It's good for the soul. If I were one of those people who believe in campaigns and associations and all that sort of thing I'd organise a Climb More Mountains campaign, run by the Climb for Grace Association!"

"There should be a special sub-committee for holy mountains," Father Halloran suggested.

"I'll go up Croagh Patrick before I leave here," Francis said.

"Perhaps it'll give you the sign you're waiting for."

"Perhaps. My spiritual destiny seems to be bound up with this country—an Irish Jesuit sent me here, where I meet another Irish Jesuit who sends me to Croagh Patrick. It could have some significance."

"It could so."

They walked on in silence, heads bent to the rain, Francis preoccupied with this idea of Ireland and his spiritual destiny, the priest aware of the other's preoccupation and not wishing to intrude on it.

At the little station there was the usual crowd of people gathered to see the train go out; most of the people travelling on it were only going into Galway for the day, but still it was an excitement to see who was going, and guess at or discover the reason why, and to see them go; it was activity; it was something happening; it was life. In the evening an even bigger crowd would gather to see the train come in; that was the regular evening's diversion, and more exciting than the morning one, for who could tell what stranger might come off the train? But morning or evening there was always that exciting chance of the strange face. The tall handsome Englishman who had gone to the monastery for the retreat had been an excitement; so had the Jesuit priest who had come to conduct the retreat. Now everyone knew the retreat was over, and here was Father Halloran departing—"Good day to ye, Father." " 'Tis a soft day, Father"—but it looked as though the Englishman wasn't going with him, and wasn't that very strange now? And what would be the meaning of it, at all? And there was the reverend father getting into a third-class compartment, and wouldn't that shame some of them that never travelled anything but first-class, and they wearing the habit of Franciscans? True they got their first-class tickets for the third-class fare, but all the same it was difficult to imagine Our Lord travelling first-class . . . or St. Francis.

The little mountainy-looking train filled up as soon as it came in, and it looked as though Father Halloran would have no seat, but an old woman in a black shawl, with a hen in a sack in her lap, the mouth of the sack tied round its neck, moved up, patting the seat beside her.

"There's plenty room, Father, plenty room."

"I won't be taking your corner seat," he protested.

"Ah, why wouldn't you, Father? There's many a reverend would be travelling in comfort."

Father Halloran smiled. "All the same, thanking you kindly, but I am not taking your seat, so—please——"

The old woman moved back, reluctantly, and the hen clucked discontentedly.

" 'Tis all wrong, Father. 'Tis not respectful."

Father Halloran placed his breviary in the place she had vacated, then leaned from the window to speak to Francis.

"Don't wait in this rain," he urged.

"I must see you off," Francis told him, and added, smiling, "It wouldn't be respectful not to!"

"I'd sooner have a man's affection than his respect!"

"Then I'll go." He held out his hand. "Good-bye, Father. Thank you for all your help."

The priest took his hand in both of his. The rain dripped off the brim of his battered hat as he leaned forward.

"Don't worry," he said. "It'll all be made plain in time. Just keep on praying and doing whatever comes to hand. A Hail Mary or two at the top of Croagh Patrick would do no harm—no harm at all!"

He released Francis's hand and took off his dilapidated hat and shook the water from it. Then he regarded the sodden shapeless thing and smiled.

"You have to be a scholar to wear a hat like that!" he observed.

Some people standing by the compartment laughed.

"Glory be to God, you do so!" a woman declared.

Francis laughed. "Good-bye, Father," he said again, and walked away. At the exit he turned for a final salute. Father Halloran, smiling, waved the scholarly hat after him.

Francis, bareheaded as always, his coat collar turned up against the rain, his hands thrust into his pockets, walked away smiling. Ah, the good old man! The kindly, humorous, saintly man—it would have been worth obeying Father Connor's injunction to go to Ireland if only to have met him. Meeting some people was an experience of positive spiritual value.

The rain lifted as he neared the monastery, and the mountains emerged again, near and darkly blue, their outline boldly drawn against the cloudy confusion of the sky. You have climbed so many mountains, Francis Sable, he thought, for the adventure of it, and the satisfaction of it, for the pride and the glory of it; now the time has come to climb a mountain for the humility of it, a mountain that hundreds of thousands of men, women and children, of all ages, the very old and the very young, have climbed before you, through the centuries; a mountain that offers no mountaineering honours; in all material senses a completely unrewarding mountain; you will climb it for the good of your soul, and in the belief that somehow grace will come of it. . . .

5

He decided that instead of trundling back to Galway in the small mountainy train, and then going back along the main line to Athenry and up to Westport, it would be simpler to walk the thirty odd miles, through Letterfrack, past the Goat Mountain, and the Devil's Mother, and up the Erriff valley. He started out soon after it was light, and he arrived in the little town of Westport just before it was dark. During some twelve hours of walking he met three adults and some children. When he had been going about four hours an old woman greeted him from the door of a whitewashed cottage at the side of the road. She was full of curiosity as to whither he might be going, with the dust of the miles on his boots, and the pack on his back; when she learned that he was going to Westport she bade him come in and take a glass of milk. He went into a dark stone-floored interior with a brick fireplace at the far side and a turf fire on the hearth; there was a long deal table, grey with age, and rough chairs either side of the fireplace; the hens ran in and out, and an old sheep-dog lifted its head from its paws in front of the fire at his entry, then dozed again. The smoke blew down the wide chimney and misted the room. There was the strong sweet smell of the burning turf; above the door was the emblem of the Sacred Heart.

The old woman shooed out the hens, flapping her apron at them.

"Máira!" she called.

A young girl came from an inner room; she was slender and barefoot, with a whorl of thick tangled dark hair. She had an oval face and delicate features. With the wild look of a young gypsy, she had none of a gypsy boldness. When she saw the tall stranger the colour came into her face and she looked confusedly back from him to the old woman.

"He's walking to Westport, God help him," the old woman told her. "Bring him a glass of milk to take the dust of the road off his throat." To Francis she said, "Be seated now."

Francis removed his pack and sat on a chair by the fire.

The old woman seated herself opposite him and regarded him with awe and wonder. She began asking him questions; was he from England, was he long in Ireland, would he stay long in Westport.

"Two nights only," he told her. "I want to climb Croagh Patrick tomorrow, then I shall walk back, but I shall go back the other way, through Louisburg."

"Aren't you great!" she exclaimed.

The young girl came back with the milk. Francis smiled at her as he took it from her.

"You'll have climbed Croagh Patrick, I suppose?"

"Five times," she told him.

"Barefoot?"

"Yes."

"How long did it take you?"

"About an hour."

"Is that all?"

"Ah," said the old woman, "you should allow yourself two hours, in all fairness, not being used to it."

They both stood at the door of the cabin when he left and watched him till he was out of sight. He walked away wondering about the girl, what her life was with the old woman in that lonely place. She had the combination of wildness and shyness of a wild creature, but there was also in her manner, he thought, a quality of restlessness and suppressed passion. . . . He felt that she had been as acutely aware of him as a male as he had been of her as a female, that subtle sex awareness that can charge an atmosphere though nothing has been said, no gesture made. Once, almost certainly, he reflected, he would have gone back by the same route, to call at the cottage and see her again; once there would have been a delicate, tentative excitement in the encounter; once he would have allowed himself to speculate upon her psychology and her life, and probably have evolved a story out of the brief interlude, the flash of awareness. But now he could go back by another road, and if she haunted him for so long as a day almost certainly she would be lost to him by tomorrow.

Two hours later he passed a man cutting turf; here the road ran for miles between undulating brown bog. The man straightened himself as Francis approached.

"It's a grand day, thank God!" he called to him.

"It is so," Francis called back.

It was a grey, sunless day, with a wind that seemed to come from all directions. But it was not raining, so it was a grand day, thanks be to God whose handiwork all days were; all days were good, since God made them, but the days when there was no rain and you could walk the roads dryshod, and cut the turf, and generally go about your business in comfort, those were the grand days. It was Father Halloran's philosophy, too, Francis reflected, and a good working one, since it obviated all the complaining about the weather which was so tedious because so futile. What had to be accepted in any case was best accepted with a good grace. Since God's will would be done it were better to say Amen to it.

In the middle of the afternoon he ran into some barefoot children who came out of a side-turning. When he sat down on a stone wall by the roadside to eat some bread and cheese they leaned in a row against the wall opposite and silently stared. They were very ragged; the dresses of the little girls were so patched that it was almost impossible to tell the original material. They all had straight fine hair that looked as though it never knew brush or comb, and their eyes had the dark secret look peculiar to children and animals. The wind blew a small sour-sweet smell from their warm bodies. Children, Francis thought, natural children who ran wild, smelt the same wherever you encountered them—in an English street, an Italian village, an Irish bog. And they had the same half tentatively hostile, half tentatively friendly, curiosity about them. You, as an adult, were their natural enemy, but the enemy was sometimes friendly; you waited for a sign either way; you were on guard; it was more exciting and interesting if you were a hostile enemy; anything else was rather boring; it led to inquiries as to how old you were, what your name was, how you liked school, questions of a fatuity beneath the contempt of any natural child. And these, Francis thought, were natural children—quite terrifyingly natural. He smiled at them, but they did not smile back. They watched his every movement as though it were something infinitely strange. They shifted from one foot to another, they made little skips and jumps where they stood, they nudged each other, but they did not speak, and they did not take their eyes off the strange man sitting on the wall eating his bread and cheese with as much nonchalance as he could affect in the circumstances. There was nothing for it, he felt, but to pretend they were not there.

When he had finished eating he restrapped his rucksack, a process they seemed to find so fascinating that they advanced a few steps closer. Reshouldering the pack he turned to them.

"Good-bye," he said, smiling.

Several of them replied instantly, "Good-bye!"

A few yards along the road he looked back; they were all walking backwards so as not to lose sight of him. He waved, and they waved back.

Well, it was one form of human intercourse, anyhow; and, provided you had plenty of self-possession and were not self-conscious, had points in its favour; at least it made no conversational demands. . . .

The light was failing when finally he toiled up a long hill, came out on to a main road, and dropped down into Westport. There were, he knew, at least two good hotels, but he did not want an hotel; he wanted merely something to eat, and a bed for a few hours, and as soon as it was light he would be away again.

He went into a dark little pub, drank a glass of stout, and inquired for a room. A stout shirt-sleeved man behind the bar said that that would be all *right*, and did he want something to eat. Francis replied that he did, and this also was all *right*, and he was taken behind the bar and into a small restaurant where each table supported, in addition to cutlery, a bottle of brown sauce, and a narrow vase of faded and dusty red and yellow artificial flowers of no recognisable species. There was a strong smell of fried fish. The menu was that or hamanneggs. Francis said that he would have hamanneggs, and shirt-sleeves shuffled out. At the far end of the room two young men were having fried fish and chips and tea, also stout. One of them was a little drunk and was engaged in an interminable monologue which had something to do with football and a grievance, Francis gathered. There seemed to be somebody called McCullagh who was a fine footballer, and of whom the man with a grievance was afraid.

"And aren't I man enough to admit that I'm afraid of him, and isn't that honest now? If I can come off the field walking on me two legs I can go back to work in the morning. Isn't that right now? And haven't I the right to go to work? I can earn ten bob a day, and haven't I the right to earn it? But if I come off the field with a broken ankle and I'm up in the lodgings above drawing thirty shillings a week, I'm not worth a sausage. Isn't that right now?"

The other man grunted, "Eat up your supper now; we must be going."

He glanced uneasily in Francis's direction, but the man who was afraid of McCullagh knew no such embarrassment in the presence of a stranger. He flowed on :

"McCullagh's captain of a fine team. They've never been equalled. Aren't I admitting it? They've been beaten but they've never been equalled. I'm man enough to admit it! McCullagh's a better footballer than I am. I acknowledge it! I'm afraid of him. I keep out of his way. If I can come off the field on my two feet——"

"You're no footballer, Joe," the other man cut in, bitterly, and repeated, with increased impatience, "Eat up now!"

Francis's attention was distracted by the return of shirt-sleeves with a tray laden with ham and eggs, bread and butter, tea, and more stout.

"And what time would ye like to be called in the morning?"

"I'm walking to Murrisk Abbey as soon as it's light," Francis told him, "so I'll get myself up. I'm going up Croagh Patrick."

"It's a long walk from here to the Abbey," shirt-sleeves pointed out.

Francis smiled. "That's all right. How long do you reckon it takes to go up?"

"Three quarters of an hour. But the Stations of the Cross put another half mile on to it. But it's the wrong time of the year to be going up the Reek. There'll not be a soul on it. It'll be terrible lonely up there now. Back in July, now, there was ten thousand, they reckoned, on the mountain on the day of the pilgrimage."

"Ten thousand is a lot of people to be on one small-sized mountain at a time," Francis observed.

"All the same, it's more companionable that way, and all going along together ye don't notice the steepness so much, and it passes the time quicker. Also if a mist comes down ye could get lost on your own."

"I've climbed quite a lot of mountains," Francis assured him. "Big tall high large ones—Swiss ones."

"Is that so? Ye'll be all *right* then?"

"Sure," said Francis, "I'll be all *right*."

And you were all right, Francis thought, some sixteen hours later, provided you had a good pair of climbing boots; but when you had left your shoes beside the statue of Saint Patrick at the foot of the mountain, and went over very flinty scree on your quite unaccustomed bare feet, it was quite another matter. And you were not used to climbing on an empty stomach. . . . Admittedly a mountain, large or small, was nothing if it was not an endurance test; it was merely that there were various kinds of endurance tests, and this happened to be one he had not previously experienced. You have been frozen on exposed snow-slopes, you had been nearly blown off knife-edge ledges, you had clung to rock-walls by little more than your finger-nails, will-power, and the friction of your clothes, you have been exhausted, physically, mentally and morally, and gone on; you had, in fact, known every kind of mountaineering endurance test except this one of going over scree on your naked feet. And it demanded a greater endurance, because with the other things there was the feeling of fight which kept you going; you persevered and struggled and won; here nothing heroic was called for, merely a painful dogged business of putting one foot before the other and every step was a dull uneventful misery, and it was all so exhaustingly monotonous. They could call it a mountain if they liked, but it was nothing but a very steep hill made of stones and a drizzling rain and a blinding mist, and it went on and on, and up and up, the stones sliding under your feet, and it was utterly and completely and soul-destroyingly uninteresting. There were mountains which, if they killed you, fought you to death; this mountain if it killed you would do you to death in a long-drawn-out dull misery.

For a time heathery moorlands fell away on either side of the stony track to the valley. After the first Station of the Cross at the foot of the cone-shaped peak there was nothing but stones and boulders. From the base, when the clouds broke, it had been possible to get a glimpse of the tiny chapel at the summit, and all the way to the first Station there had been an occasional view of the valley in the drifting mist; but now you toiled up steadily into thick grey cloud, and all you could see were the stones under your feet . . . and your own blood on the stones. You were no longer aware of the pain in your feet; you had grown accustomed to it; there was the old mountaineering capacity for doggedly going on, for putting one foot before the other, one foot above the other, for as long as need be. Somewhere down below, out of sight in the mist, a sheep bleated, mournfully. Stones slipping and sliding under your feet; stones lying grey and heavy in your head, so that thought could no longer move there.

Suddenly he saw something that was not a stone. In a little heap at the base of a boulder lay a rosary. He picked it up; it was a cheap humble thing of wood, the chain of thin wire, rusted now by the weather; a poor person's rosary; some old woman's, perhaps, or a child's. . . . It must have lain out a long time in the rain to have become so rusted, the beads so soaked and muddied; one of the perforations of the little bone Sacred Heart was broken; the tiny crucifix was swollen. He thought of his mother's beautiful ebony and silver beads; Cathryn's had been beautiful, too, of polished horn. . . . Well, but the first Cross was made of wood, and a poor person's prayers counted on wooden beads stood no less chance of being heard than the rich person's told on ebony or ivory. And whoever lost this rosary on the holy mountain would grieve as though it had been the costliest ever made. It had its value in love and sorrow and suffering and devotion. He tugged his handkerchief out of his pocket and dried it as tenderly as though he were wiping tears from a face, then twisted it round his wrist and holding the crucifix in the palm of his hand went on and up over the stones.

Now the stones were lifted from his head and he could think again. Father Halloran came back into his mind, suggesting that perhaps Croagh Patrick would give him the sign he sought. . . .

Preoccupied with his thoughts he did not see the chapel until he was almost on it; it loomed up suddenly like a ship in the mist. The door was locked and there was no shelter from the driving wind. The mist was so thick that the Stations of the Cross could not be seen, and even the stone walls of the chapel looked shadowy. He glanced at his watch and saw that he had taken an hour and a half to make the ascent—Francis Sable, member of the Alpine Club, had taken longer than the average to make an ascent of two thousand five hundred feet in which no climbing was involved, nothing but putting one foot before the other. Certainly one didn't go up Croagh Patrick for the glory of it! He smiled at the thought, and heard Father Halloran saying, his eyes humorous, "Climb for humility instead of for glory!" Well, the experienced mountaineer had been beaten by a girl called Máira, and by a stout man at a pub, and no doubt by thousands of others—probably by an old woman whose rosary he now held in his hand. An exercise in humility—that was Croagh Patrick.

He reflected that last time he had climbed a mountain he had done it as an act of expiation; why had he climbed this one? As an act of faith? 'My God, I believe in Thee, because Thou art Truth itself.'

He heard Father Halloran saying, "A Hail Mary or two would do no harm at all!"

He knelt down on the stones beside the chapel door and with the rain-sodden crucifix in his hand repeated the *De Profundis*, a *Pater*, and an *Ave*.

When he rose from his knees it came to him that he had said part of the rosary for the dead.

Cathryn, his heart cried, Cathryn!

What more natural than that she who had loved mountains, and died on one, should be present in spirit here on this holy mountain? Now it seemed strange to him that he should not have realised why he had to climb Croagh Patrick—that it was to keep a tryst with her as he had kept it when he had returned to the Drindelhorn. He was filled with exultation. He felt her presence so strongly that it was as though only the mist hid her from sight.

He made the descent slipping and sliding over the stones quite unaware of any pain from his cut and bruised feet, or of the sting of rain in his face. His whole being was a *Te Deum Laudamus* of love and gratitude and joy.

Now it seemed to him that he had received the sign for which he waited, and that whatever course it took his spiritual destiny lay in this Catholic country, where, as Father Connor had said, the people at least knew the difference between right and wrong.

6

He stayed on at the monastery as a kind of lay-brother, sharing the duties of the lay-brothers, and accepted without question by the whole community. He had no plans; his course was still dark, but he was confident now that eventually the path he must follow would be revealed. The interim, he felt, could be regarded as spiritual preparation for it.

The last of the roses bloomed and faded on the monastery walls; a chill crept upon the morning and the evening air; the leaves of the sycamores crowding in among the pines in the belt of wood protecting the monastery yellowed and fell, and wild westerly gales with sudden rains swept along the lake.

Brother Anselm, stacking turf in the yard with Francis one wild wet day inquired, "Shall you stay with us through the winter, Brother Francis?" In some unaccountable fashion he had become one of them, and it was thus they always addressed him.

Brother Anselm was old and thin and wiry. He had been at the monastery forty years.

"I don't know. I can't see ahead. I live from day to day."

" 'Tis better so. Take no thought for the morrow, our Lord said."

"I have a curious feeling of waiting for something, but I don't know what. Like expecting a letter, you don't know from whom." He smiled. "Waiting for a sign, I suppose you'd call it?"

"What else?" Brother Anselm said, simply.

The wind blew the turf dust into their eyes.

Francis said, straightening himself a moment and blinking, "I wonder why the good God always sends a wind when there's a load of turf to stack?"

"Maybe 'tis to give us a chance to be saints," the old man said, drily.

"I can't say it makes me feel very saintly."

"There was a Jesuit Father came here once who told us that

to say *Deo Gratias* to all things was to be a saint. Did ye never hear of Father John Sullivan now?"

"I did not, then." Unconsciously Francis would drop into the idiom.

They continued stacking sods, and Brother Anselm recounted the story of John Sullivan, son of Sir Edward Sullivan, Lord Chancellor of Ireland—'that was in the bad old days of the Lord Lieutenant'—and distinguished Dublin barrister, who became a convert to the Church in his thirties and entered the Society of Jesus at the age of forty, and how from being the best-dressed man in Dublin he became the shabbiest priest in all Ireland, with his clothes patched and green with age, the way you'd think he was a silenced priest instead of a master at Clongowes and one of the saintliest men walking the earth. "He has the great gift of prayer," said Brother Anselm, "and many a dying person he has prayed for recovered and is alive to this day."

"You mean he is a faith-healer?"

"Ah, no. He wouldn't thank you for calling him a faith-healer or miracle-worker. 'Don't thank me, thank God' is what he tells those who try to thank him. He is a great believer in prayer. The power of prayer is the greatest power on earth, I've heard him say. Like yourself he has a great devotion to St. Augustine."

Francis's heart quickened at the name. Was this another thread woven into the pattern? Brother Anselm went on talking about John Sullivan, recounting anecdotes, and sayings attributed to him, and Father Sullivan could not be accounted a modern Augustine, Francis thought, for the African had been of the world worldly and the flesh fleshly, and the Irishman had never been that, but the lives of both after their conversion had been in terms of the complete holocaust of self, a complete renunciation of material joys and satisfactions. Both had been rich in the things of this world—social success, distinguished careers, prestige. Both had fulfilled the most cherished dream of a devoutly Catholic mother when they had been received into the Church. Francis felt that he could understand John Sullivan's interest in Augustine of Hippo, and his own interest in Augustine made him interested in Sullivan. It gave him a curious satisfaction that in this twentieth century no less than in the fourth some rare spirit should find the holocaust of self possible.

He lay in bed that night, staring out at the moonlight almost day-bright on the lake, and the links with St. Augustine seemed to him like the beads of a rosary, each with its own significance, yet making a whole. He had a sense of something shaping to a pattern whose design was not yet clear, but which was something begun in his night of solitude in the hut below the Drindelhorn peak. A whole new world had opened up then, with the realisation of something beyond the material; there had been a vast, bewildering, but wholly exciting contemplation of endless new vistas; you became involved in the new perspective but you could not yet comprehend it. There was this sense of unreality, and yet it was the only reality; all else was meaningless.

When he finally slept he dreamed he was on an almost vertical rock-face, gripping the smooth surface with the toes of his boots, finger-nails, and the friction of his clothes. With his arms full-length above his head he groped in vain for handholds and only a sweating, straining will-power saved him from slipping; he could move neither up nor down and it came to him that he was done for. Then there was somehow someone beside him, and half turning his head he saw a man in ordinary lounge clothes. With the inconsequentiality of a dream it did not occur to him to ask how this man came to be there, or upon what he stood with such ease on the smooth rock-face. The stranger said, "Let me help you," and suddenly it came to Francis, with a shock, that the stranger was God. He said, "You're God, aren't you? That means you know everything." The Stranger said, "You will be all right now," and Francis knew that this was so and he began to climb, finding holds and climbing up steadily, and all the time the Stranger was somehow beside him. As he climbed the realisation grew on him that something tremendous had happened to him, that this pleasant and ordinary-seeming Stranger in conventional clothes really was God, and he was overwhelmed by a sense of unworthiness. "I am so full of sin!" he said, and began to weep. . . . and wakened. He lay with the tears streaming down his face and the room seemed to be full of a voice crying, "St. Augustine! St. Augustine!"

Then he knew that the voice was crying in his mind. The moon had gone and the room was dark, and the darkness was alive with the reiterated cry, and his whole being was full of it,

He lay in the borderland between waking and sleeping, disembodied somewhere in time and space, in the spirit's eternity, and there was the unfathomable immensity of space inhabited only by the winds that ranged it and the suns and moons and stars and planets poised in it; there was a terrible unendurable loneliness that drove the escaped spirit back into the body in search of the known, comprehensible, material world. Not lightly, it came to Francis, now fully awake, could the spirit trouble 'the gold gateways of the stars' or besiege 'the pale ports o' the moon'.

But as time went on, and he learned to pray without self-consciousness and with confidence, he had very often this experience of the spirit disembodied in space, and transcending time. Without realising it he touched the edges of mystic experience. He discovered how to go out of his corporeal being and into his inward self, that elevation to a level above the mind and into pure spirit which Augustine and his mother experienced the evening at Ostia when they rested after their journey, in a room looking into a garden. There was that Augustinian momentary flash of arrival at 'that which is' described in the *Confessions*, beyond any intellectual process, and remote from normal consciousness, a transient intuition of God and eternity, but this side of ecstasy, a swift touching of Eternal Wisdom in a moment of contemplation. He began to develop a capacity for infused contemplation and prayer, and was able to sustain the *contemplatio* for longer and longer periods.

He had little sense of the passing of time. The last of the leaves were stripped from the trees, and it was winter, with driving rains, day after day, and great Atlantic gales. The mountains smoked with low cloud, or were lost altogether. The days flowed into each other with their routine of religious duties, and domestic, farm, and garden chores. There was Mass and the Holy Office; there was the intensity of mystic experience of the supreme sacrament of Holy Communion; there was livestock to tend, dishes to wash, floors to scrub or polish, and always a cattle-shed to be mucked out, something in the garden that the wind had torn down to be nailed up or staked. He did all the routine tasks and duties, all that came to hand, quietly, unobtrusively, not even conscious of the humility he had assumed, and when he was free of all duties, spiritual and material, walked in solitude beside the lake, or over the wild brown mountainy land. He spent a great deal of time on his knees in the chapel meditating before the Blessed Sacrament, and knew a deep peace. He withdrew more and more into himself. He had no part in the talk in the refectory. It was not that he was shut out, but that he preferred to stay outside, not from lack of sympathy or interest, but because what was happening to him spiritually made everything external unreal. Life continued to assume the quality of a dream, but only the dream had reality.

His mother did not break in on his long retreat until in December she wrote to ask if he had considered coming home for Christmas. If such was his intention she would remain in London; otherwise she would accept the invitation of Steven and his wife to go to Crag House. She added that Sue Lester was coming to London for a week or two to arrange an exhibition of her work in London before Christmas; she had expressed the hope that Francis would be in London when she arrived.

It was the first intrusion from the outside world he had had since he had arrived in Ireland. He found that it required quite an effort of will to think in terms of material things. To go to England or not to go; to decide whether he wanted to meet Sue again or not. He had not seen her since the night she had come to his apartment and he had returned in the early morning after seeing Lotte home and had found her there. There had been a letter from her awaiting him when he got back from Drindel, in answer to the one he had written her before going. He still had it, because it was his custom to keep letters until he had answered them and then to destroy them, and this one he had not yet answered. He took it out of his wallet now and reread it. It began, *My Darling,* and he frowned then as he had when he had first read it, asking himself as then why she had to write so extravagantly and so intimately; he had once asked her to be his mistress and she had refused; that left them, surely, on the level of simple friendship? She would say, he supposed, that she was still in love with him, and that a certain degree of intimacy had been established between them through her admission of her feeling for him and his advances to her, but that she used the possessive endearment was indicative, he felt. She wrote that she was grateful to him for writing her, and that she hoped that the return to Drindel would give him what he wanted—*'for your sake that you may find peace, or whatever it is you need to enable you to get back to work, and for my sake that I may hear from you again, since you say I shall hear from you if it is ever day again.* She added, *I showed the relevant part of your letter to Johnny and I'm afraid his reaction was cynical. He said bitterly that words were cheap. I told him I was sorry he couldn't feel the sincerity behind the words, and he replied that Francis Sable didn't know the meaning of the word. I am afraid that for the time being at least he is very bitter, but he is young and he will grow out of it, though of course I can't tell him that. When you are back in Paris if you feel you would like to see me again you know that it would make me very happy. Thank you for sending me your love "for what it is worth". It is worth very much to me, because, you see, I love you much more than is meet or wise. À bientôt—j'espère.'*

He sighed as he refolded the letter and replaced it in his wallet. Poor Sue! But how could people be so lacking in pride as to make others sorry for them? The mere thought of anyone saying 'poor Francis' was repugnant. It was a question of one's *amour-propre.* One could have humility without losing that. It was the difference between humility and abjectness. Love suffereth long and is kind, is not puffed up—but it needn't grovel. Humility was something different; it had its own dignity.

But the damage he had done to Johnny—that was very grievous. It was a terrible thing to make another human being bitter, to replace faith with cynicism. It showed lack of understanding on Sue's part to say that he would probably grow out of it; youth did not necessarily grow out of the bitterness of its disillusions; it very often grew deeper into them; the psychological hurt in youth could very easily produce misanthropy in maturity. Sue, he thought, was like the people who lightly dismiss the sorrows of childhood; a child soon forgets, they asserted, but the truth was that a child never forgets, because everything that happens to one happens to one for life; memory thrusts something out of sight, but nothing is ever forgotten; it is always there, deep down, and we are what we are because of it. St. Augustine was good on what he called 'the vast court' of memory, in which one met oneself. He spoke of 'recollection' as the re-collecting of that which had been buried in the deeper recesses of the mind, 'whence they must, as it were, be collected together from their dispersion; whence the word "cogitation" is derived. For *cogo* (collect) and *cogito* (re-collect) have the same relation to each other as *ago* and *agito*, *facio* and *factito*. But the mind hath appropriated to itself this word (cogitation), so that, not what is "collected" any how, but what is "re-collected", i.e. brought together, in the mind, is properly said to be cogitated, or thought upon'.

He brought his mind back to Johnny, and the sense of guilt and remorse, which was always with him, pressed heavier still. There was no cure for remorse because there was no undoing what was done. There could be no absolution within yourself, however deep your contrition, however passionately you sought to atone. You could not expiate the wrong done to the other person or the guilt within yourself. You could pray for those you had wronged; it was the most you could do, and the least. He could pray for Johnny—who, if he knew, would despise his prayers and account him a hypocrite.

And he could go to England for Christmas—that would be something he could do for the other person against whom he had grievously sinned. That it would also make Sue happy was another reason for going—as was also the fact that he would prefer to stay where he was, held in his endless dream.

But in England there was Father Connor. He felt that he was ready to be received into the Church, and that he wanted Father Connor to be the priest to receive him—that it was something he owed to him, and to Cathryn.

7

Dorothea had warned Sue that she would find Francis changed, but Sue freely admitted that her imagination would not reach to the Francis Sable she had known so changed that he was about to be received into the Church. He had written her that he had made the journey to the end of the night; now, it seemed, he had come out the other side and into the morning; she recognised that the process must have involved some tremendous spiritual crisis, but she found herself hoping that it would not be obvious, that in spite of his mother's warning she would find him outwardly, at least, the Francis she had always known, whatever his inner beliefs and attitudes to life might now be. She had known other converts to the Church, and for all practical purposes of friendship and social intercourse they seemed unchanged after their conversion—which was a relief. Having ascertained from Dorothea that Francis had not grown a beard or adopted any eccentric style of dressing she went to meet him at the house in Kensington confident that however different his moral code might now be he would still be, somehow, the Francis she had always known.

She had refused an invitation to luncheon or dinner on the pretext of lack of time; she would just look in for a drink before dinner, she told Dorothea. "I suppose," she added, nervously, "he does still drink?" His mother smiled. "Why not?" she said, simply.

She felt reassured. That was all right then. His Catholicism would be just a private peculiarity; they would drink and talk together as they used to in Paris. It would all be quite easy and simple.

When he opened the front door to her himself she was momentarily disconcerted. She had not expected that informality.

"I saw you coming," he offered in explanation, and even in her confusion she felt the old familiar charm of his smile.

He took her fur coat from her, holding the fox collar a moment against his cheek.

"You always have nice furs," he said, smiling.

He led the way into a small panelled room full of books. There was a fire, with logs, and bronze and yellow chrysanthemums. On a small table were a decanter, a cocktail-shaker, glasses, a dish of ice-cubes, another of olives. Francis was thinner in the face, she thought; he had always had that fine-drawn look, but now it was intensified. She felt the old pain rise in her, the despairing realisation, I'll never be less than in love with him!

"Will you take sherry or a cocktail?" he was asking her.

"I'd prefer a cocktail, thank you." You went further on gin; sherry didn't help much when you were nervous. Ridiculous to be nervous, of course, but there it was. . . .

He dropped ice-cubes into the shaker and stood shaking the concoction. He poured the coloured liquid into two glasses painted with red and yellow cocks, handed her cigarettes in a shagreen box, held the lighter for her. She remembered the last occasion and the unsteadiness of his hands. She missed the lapis-lazuli ring.

When they were settled at either side of the fire with drinks and cigarettes she took the conversational plunge.

"You never looked me up when you got back to Paris. I hoped you would."

"I came back only to pack."

"I'd have helped."

"That's sweet of you, but I needed to be alone."

"You promised to send me word if it was ever day again."

"I should have, eventually. I had your last letter with me in Ireland. Then my mother wrote and asked me if I would be coming home for Christmas, and said you would be in London. I knew we'd meet then, so there was no need to write. I knew, too, that you would have had news of me from my mother."

"She wrote me that you were receiving instruction from Father Connor. I could understand Cathryn turning to the Church, but not you. With you it doesn't make sense, somehow."

He smiled. "Not even after the dark journey?"

"I should have thought when you came out into the light again—at the end of the tunnel—you would have found refuge in work, not in the Church."

"Work was never a refuge for me. It was merely a symptom."

He bent forward and refilled her glass. She noticed that he had barely touched his own.

"You don't mean you don't intend to go on being a writer?"

"I've nothing more to say."

"I should have thought your religion would have given you new things to say."

"I'd sooner do than say."

"How can you—without becoming a priest?"

"I don't know—yet."

She made a gesture of impatience. "Francis, I don't understand all this! How can you? You had such a good clear rational brain—how can you accept all this mystical stuff, the Immaculate Conception, Transubstantiation, and the rest of it? It completely baffles me!"

He smiled. "There's something called revelation, Sue. Once you get off the materialist plane it can happen to you. It happened to me. It has happened to many people. I used to wonder what people meant by having been given grace. Now I know."

"Now you can swallow everything!" Her voice was bitter.

He replied, simply, "Now I understand. It's as though one were suddenly given the key-word that explains everything."

"If it's as simple as all that why can't you give us all the key-word and have us all converted?"

"Because without faith there's no understanding. In your present mood, for example, you'd never understand anything. Your mind is closed—with an enormous great padlock of impatience on it! Let me give you another drink and then tell me what you are doing. I gather you're having an exhibition over here. . . ."

She said, as he refilled her glass again, "You're not drinking yours. Have you given up drink—along with all other carnal pleasures? Oh Francis, how ridiculous all this is! What happens now about all the things you used to enjoy? You were such a *bon vivant!*"

"It was all such bad living, really, if you mean all the parties and the so-called good times and the so-called love-affairs."

"Leave out the wild parties—I'll agree they were a waste of time, and that most good times were not worth having, but leaving the *affaires* out of it, what becomes of love now?"

"I'm beginning to understand it for the first time!"

"Oh, I don't mean all that diffused Christian love! I mean love as ordinary people understand it—love between men and women. Let's call a spade a spade—I mean sexual love!" There was something to be said for having had three cocktails; it enabled you to say what you meant, anyhow!

He smiled. "If we're going to call a spade a spade, let's really do so, and call it lust! That, I hope, goes the way of the wild parties and all the rest of the wastes of energy!"

"You really think you can—at thirty-one! You—Francis Sable, of all people!"

He laughed. "Sue, dear, why do you try to discuss this? You're so violently opposed to the whole idea that it's quite useless for me even to attempt to help you to understand!"

She persisted. "Even if you succeed I don't see the good of it! It all just seems a waste of life to me!"

"I know it seems like that to you—that's why I don't want to discuss it. I know I can't make you understand, any more than at one time anyone could have made me understand."

He offered her the cigarettes again, but she waved them away. "I must be going. There's no point in my being here. We've nothing to say to each other any more."

"I'm sorry you feel that, Sue. Actually, if you'd allow it, we can talk to each other for the first time. In Paris we couldn't because then you were merely a lovely body I wanted to possess." He smiled again. "Aren't you being rather difficult, Sue darling? When my approach to you was purely physical you'd have none of me—for that reason. Now that my approach to you is strictly non-physical you put up that as an obstacle to friendship! Aren't you being a quite unnecessarily unapproachable lady?"

She felt herself surrendering to his charm, and resisted it. She said, bitterly, "You have to go from one extreme to the other, don't you? It couldn't occur to you, I suppose, that a normal woman doesn't want either the purely physical or the purely spiritual approach from the man she loves? In Paris I wasn't prepared to be just one more of Francis Sable's *affaires*. I would have gone to bed with you without being married to you if I'd felt you loved me—but I didn't feel that. Now, apparently, you're completely indifferent to me physically and I'm supposed to meet you on some fine and pure and noble plane. Well, I'm not that sort of woman, either!"

She rose. "I've had three cocktails and I'm full of gin and could very easily cry! Only a very threadbare sense of humour holds me together, I warn you, so you'd better see me off the premises while the going's good!"

He got up and put his hands on her shoulders. "I don't want you to go, Sue, and I certainly don't want you to cry! I'm not indifferent to you, physically. You still seem to me a very lovely woman, and I've never loved you so much as now." She turned away, with a movement of impatience, and his grip on her shoulders tightened. "Don't smile in that cynical way, Sue, and please forget the bitter thing you were going to say! Look at me!"

She turned to him and looked at him and saw the intensity in his eyes, and, with a sense of shock, all the suffering and spiritual

struggle of the last few months. She suddenly realised that
it was not merely that his face was thinner, but there were lines
there that had not been there before; there were lines across the
forehead and between the brows and at either side of the mouth
that had nothing to do with age and everything to do with a
tremendous crisis of spiritual suffering and conflict. All resentment and hostility and impatience collapsed in her. She leaned
her forehead against his shoulder.

"I'm sorry, Francis," she murmured. "You see, I've always
loved you so much, and now it seems that you love me too late."

"Too late for us to be lovers, but that's reducing everything
to that purely physical level we're both agreed is a bad thing!"
He took her face in his hands. "Please don't be unhappy, Sue.
Let's pretend we're in Paris and go and have dinner in a first-class
French restaurant and get to know each other—it's high time!"

With part of herself she wanted to refuse, feeling that it
would be unbearable, dining with this man who looked so like
Francis Sable and yet who was so different from the Francis she
had known; but another part of herself insisted that just to be with
him would be as near to heaven as she was ever likely to reach.
She accepted the invitation.

"We'd better dress," Francis said. "I'll 'phone for a taxi
for you now, and meet you at Chez Bellini in about an hour's
time. Will that do?"

Fifteen minutes later, sitting in front of her dressing-table
in her mother's house, she buried her face in her hands in a
sudden rush of tears. O God, she said, O God!

But it was no use crying when you were just going out to
dinner. She pressed her finger-tips hard against her eyes, made
an effort at control, and went on dressing. Why not be happy?
You were going to spend an evening with the man you loved,
and who loved you. What was there to cry about? Too late to be
lovers . . . but at least an unsublimated love could never let you
down! There was at least that about it. It would be forever
changeless and forever new. . . . Here was the unheard melody,
the happy boughs that could not shed their leaves nor bid the
spring adieu, and she, O God, would be till the end of her days
the still unravished bride of quietness. . . .

Francis, on the contrary, felt at peace in their relations

for the first time. Now Sue was all sweetness and undemanding gentleness, he thought; now there could be nothing but gentlest and sweetest friendship between them. And again the last aria from the St. Matthew Passion ran through his head.

He slipped the worn copy of the *Confessions* into the pocket of his dress overcoat, then went downstairs to telephone for a taxi. Whilst waiting for it to arrive he opened the book at random. He ran his eye down the left-hand page, but it had no immediate message for him; then almost at the bottom of the right-hand page he found, 'Let me not be mine own life; from myself I lived ill, death was I to myself; and I revive in Thee. Do Thou speak unto me, do Thou discourse to me. I have believed Thy Books, and their words be most full of mystery.' He smiled and closed the book. Blessed Saint Augustine!' He had, increasingly, this sense of personal relationship, of friendship.

He reached the restaurant before Sue and when he had disposed of his coat strolled over to the flower-stall and regarded, critically, the display of roses, carnations, orchids. Carnations were too ordinary, he thought, and roses too sentimental; the mauve orchids were vulgar; he decided on a spray of small brown and green orchids; they looked like Sue, he thought; they had a kind of cool elegance; they were *chic*, and Sue was nothing if not that. Whilst the spray was being made up he reflected that had his guest been Lotte he would probably have chosen carnations—pink, probably—made up with plenty of fern; he might even have allowed himself to make it red roses. . . . But if it had been Cathryn . . . there was no single flower you could buy Cathryn. You bought them all, or none. You never wore evening clothes, did you, Cathryn? You didn't lead that kind of life. In Paris you spent your evenings in your garret studying Cennini by candlelight. Did no one ever buy you flowers, Cathryn? There were the roses you were to have had from your faithless Francis on your twenty-first birthday . . . but—ah, *mea culpa, mea culpa !*—the only roses you ever had from him were the white roses placed in his name on your grave. . . .

He took the finished spray from the girl in charge of the stall, paid for it, and turned away, and a moment later Sue came round the swing doors. She wore a shimmering golden gown and a jade necklace.

"You look very beautiful," he greeted her. "I'm glad I chose orchids for you."

She took the spray from him with an exclamation of delight and fastened it below her right shoulder. He observed with satisfaction that it was perfect for the dress. Sue too was aware of its perfection—and of its impersonalness. They went into the restaurant that was all old rose brocade, Venetian mirrors, cream and gold paint and soft concealed lighting. It was probably the most beautiful as well as the most expensive gourmets' restaurant in London.

Sue sat beside Francis on the rose-brocaded *banc*, and she thought, I am with the best-looking man in the room, I am with the distinguished Francis Sable, and I am wearing his orchids, and there is no one else in the world I would sooner be with; we are eating exquisite food, and drinking champagne, and Francis is being as charming as only he knows how; he is being more than charming; he is being almost lover-like; he has said that he loves me; he has said more than once that I am beautiful, and of all the people in London he might have dined with tonight he has chosen to have me as his guest. . . . I ought to be the happiest woman in the room; I ought to be the happiest woman in London tonight; and I could cry and cry. . . .

Francis looked round the room, and the whitewashed walls of the refectory of the Franciscan monastery came into his mind; he saw the brothers in their shabby habits; he saw the long table of scrubbed wood, and at the head of the table, shabbiest of them all, Father Halloran, with his lined face, Father Halloran dipping dry bread into salt, insisting that having taken a small bowl of soup he needed no more. The waiter brought a basket of peaches and black grapes to the table, and he thought of Brother Anselm setting upon the refectory table a wooden bowl of apples from the few old trees in the monastery orchard. The apples were small, and a little withered from storage, but everyone said what good apples they were, because all God's gifts were good.

It came to him that this was the last time he would eat in such a place as this; the last time he would wear the clothes he then wore; the last time he would buy a woman flowers or tell her she was beautiful. It was his farewell to the world. There crept upon him a nameless sadness. He could not have said why he was so sad. 'In sooth I know not why I am so sad.' Perhaps it was that all farewells were sad; all farewells and all renunciation. Renunciation? Was he, then, renouncing the world? To some extent he had renounced it already; beyond that he did not know. Only there persisted this feeling that all that he was doing now he was doing for the last time, and that it was not merely this particular thing of wining and dining in a fashionable restaurant, but everything that went with it—the whole of a life in which one did that sort of thing.

Sue had also this feeling that she and Francis would never again be together in that way, and for all the pain in her she wanted that the night should never end. But well before midnight it came to its inevitable end, and he took her by taxi back to her mother's house in Chelsea and excused himself from coming in with her. He felt a need to be alone. He offered no explanation.

"I won't come in," was all he said.

He opened the front door for her, then took her face between his hands.

"You've been sweet," he said, and kissed her forehead. "We'll meet again," he added, then he was running down the steps, across the small paved garden, to the road. She waited till the gate closed on him, he waved to her, then walked briskly away.

Sue went slowly up the stairs to her bedroom. It was early yet, barely ten-thirty, but her mother always retired early, and she crept past her room anxious not to wake her. Tomorrow she would have to answer all the questions as to how she had 'got on' with Francis Sable—the tiresome eager questionings of a mother who still hopes to see her daughter make a good marriage, even though she has turned thirty and shows no signs of doing it. Sue was all too well aware that her mother cherished a persistent romantic hope that her only daughter might eventually become Mrs. Francis Sable. In her own room Sue took off her fur wrap, then unpinned the orchids, removed the silver paper, and put the spray in a glass of water on her dressing-table. They were the first flowers he had ever given her, and were likely to be the last, she thought, sadly.

She turned on the electric fire, pulled off her golden dress, and put on a dressing-gown, then sat in a low chair beside the fire and lit a cigarette. She couldn't go to bed yet; it was early, and she felt wide awake. She felt a little resentful at having been brought home so early. But what, really, could you do in London? In Paris—or Vienna, or Berlin—you could always 'go on' somewhere after you had dined, even if you did no more than sit on a café-terrace. There were night-clubs in London, of course, but it wasn't the same. You didn't go on to places like Ciro's or the Embassy unless you wanted to dance. It would have been heaven to have danced with Francis, but he obviously wasn't in the mood. For all she knew he now considered dancing 'sinful'. He had become a little silent during dinner, and she had a feeling that a good deal of the time he was hardly present in his body. He had never been so gentle, so sweet, yet never more remote. The tears mounted in her again. At one time I could have had him for my lover, she reflected, bitterly, and now it's too late. If they had been lovers in Paris, how much difference would it have made? Very little, probably. It would have been no more than an *affaire*. It couldn't have rescued him from his ordeal of 'the dark night of the soul'. He needed more than a purely physical *affaire*, but his relationship with her could never have been more than that; she had always known that. Perhaps it was true that he had always loved her more than anyone, but still it wasn't enough. Not enough to satisfy the emotional hunger in her, or give him what he spiritually needed. He needed love, but for him it wasn't to be found in the man-and-woman relationship; he had loved Cathryn, but he had needed more than that, too. Yet through Cathryn, it seemed, he had found at last the love he needed, and fantastic as it must appear to those who had known him at Oxford and in Paris, it was not any human love, but the love of God.

She lit another cigarette from the stub of the first one. Now he loved her deeply, tenderly, but passionlessly. Now he who had always had something *noli me tangere* about him was more remote than ever. He was closer to her than he had ever been, emotionally, but no nearer to making her happy than he had been in Paris. But to feel that he was close to her, that now he really cared about her—wasn't that something? Wasn't that more to be desired than the realisation that he wanted her purely physically? Something in her cried, despairingly, I don't know,

I don't know. . . . If with her present knowledge, and in her present mood, she could be transported in time back to his apartment in Paris, feel his arms round her again, and his mouth on hers, as then, hear him saying to her, "You can help me, Sue. I need someone. Someone close to me," she knew that she would take him to herself, gladly, proudly—ecstatically. But life as it was lived did not offer those Barrie-esque second chances. You behaved in a certain way at a certain time for one reason or another, and that was that. Now it seemed to her that she had behaved selfishly and cruelly to him at that time, when he had so great a need of her, and this torment of regret was her punishment. You didn't have to believe in God and sin and punishment for that to be true; we had it in us to create heaven or hell, and in our human selfishness and stupidity we mostly created hell. If you were a materialist you thought of sin in terms of unhappiness, because it was anti-life, and as such evil; and just as happiness, the good life, was its own reward, so unhappiness, all that was anti-life, was its own punishment. Unfortunately there was no absolution, and you could not make expiation. It came to this, then, that if you were a materialist you were doomed and damned in inescapable hells of your own making. There was no help for you. God was merely an exclamation of despair, instead of as, for believers, an aspiration of hope. It must be very comforting, she thought, half way between bitterness and regret, to be able to escape into the comfortable and comforting doctrines of Mother Church. . . . Francis was to be envied. Oh, most passionately Francis was to be envied! Being a materialist was a desperately lonely business. No wonder religion had been called the opium of the people. It was a drug, all right, like cocaine or heroin—or alcohol, or sex, or even, in some aspects, work—yet, when you came to think about it, it was a drug most people managed without.

Perhaps, she thought, wrily, that was what was the matter with them; they were all going round doomed and damned and hopeless. Perhaps it was better, after all, to be doped into some sort of faith and hope. . . . But if you weren't given the grace, as they called it, you couldn't come by the dope, and how did you come by the requisite grace? Her mother, and the dowager Lady Sable, and Cathryn, through a natural leaning in that direction—the direction of religious mysticism—other people, like Francis, as a result of some tremendous spiritual crisis. But if you had no leaning towards religiousness, and experienced no spiritual crisis. . . .

She pressed out the end of her cigarette. Oh well, when all else failed you there was always work; if you were what they called a creative artist you had your own brand of dope. All art, it had been said, was neurosis; no really happy person would want to do anything as unnatural as spend hours, days, weeks, months, painting a picture or writing a book or chipping a piece of stone or wood into a particular shape; we translated our neuroses into pictures, books, sculpture; we got our tormented souls somehow on to the canvas, into the written words, the carved wood or stone, we worked our conflicts out into some sort of pattern; we derived a certain satisfaction from it; it was perhaps all the satisfaction there was; and it offered an incentive to the business of going on living. . . .

She was a long time in getting to sleep when she finally went to bed, and when at last she slept she dreamed of Francis. No Freudian analysis was necessary to explain the dream. There was no strange symbolism in it. It was all very simple and clear and vivid. Her unconscious took her straight back to Francis's apartment in Paris and that particular incident which she so bitterly regretted. The dream gave her what life had denied, the second chance. Francis was her lover and she lay with him in intense happiness. "Now," he said, as he kissed her, with deep tenderness, "now everything is all right."

She wakened with tears streaming down her face, and lay for a little while with her mind repeating his words, savouring their comfort. "Now everything is all right." Now there was an end of hunger and grieving; everything was all right between her and Francis, at last.

Then, gradually, the dream ebbed and reality encroached, like the relentless brightness of day overtaking the twilight of dawn. Gradually realisation invaded her. It wasn't true; everything was not all right; everything was as full of dissatisfaction as it had always been. Francis was as remote from her as ever, and there had been and would be no second chance.

She buried her face in the pillow and wept all the futile,

hopeless tears that had been dammed up in her for so long, and for so long demanding to be wept.

When the tidal wave of grief had spent itself she got up, telling herself, resolutely, that whereas tears were merely so much dissolution of spirit, it was wonderful what hot coffee and a hot bath would achieve in the essential business of holding body and soul together through yet one more difficult day. . . .

8

That dinner with Sue could be said to be Francis Sable's last public appearance. He never again ate in an expensive restaurant, and he never again touched alcohol. He had known when he looked round at the rose-lighted luxuriousness of Chez Bellini's, and the whitewashed refectory of the Franciscan monastery had come into his mind, that that was the end. After that he had only toyed with the delicate food on his plate and had left the wine untouched in his glass.

"You're not eating," Sue had protested, noticing.

"I'm not hungry," he told her. And it was true. He was consumed with hunger, but not for food for the body.

Father Connor received him into the Church a few days later, with his mother and Mrs. Lester as witnesses. He left them outside the church, immediately after the ceremony. He felt an intense desire to be alone. It was a cold wet day, with a sleety drizzle, but he turned up his coat collar and strode away in the direction of the park. He thought of his walk to the station with Father Halloran in the wild wet wind of Connemara, and suddenly it came to him that he loved that good old man, and that he loved Ireland, and he was filled with nostalgia. He must get out of this God-forsaken country. God-forsaken because God-forsaking. He walked through the empty park, along Piccadilly, heading Eastward, through the City and out to the grey dock walls and interminable drab high street of Wapping. It did not matter to him where he walked; he was hardly aware of his surroundings. He crossed the river into Rotherhithe and spent a long time leaning on the embankment parapet staring at the grey water slipping past, and he had the sense of everything in him flowing,

flowing like the river, taking him with it, a strong deep tide moving steadily on, though he did not as yet know where. He remembered being told that after his reception into the Church John Sullivan had gone home and taken up the carpet in his room and stripped it of all but the barest necessities, and always he had preached, 'Live comfortlessly. Every victory over self is a victory for God.' Live comfortlessly, live comfortlessly; his mind repeated it like a prayer and all his being gave assent, but to what end? To live with a Franciscan simplicity and austerity in the service of God—but where, how? There was this sense of waiting for direction. Johann Amanshauser came into his mind; talking with Johann had clarified everything once; it might again. By the time he had got back to the West End he had resolved that he would go and see Johann . . . and say good-bye to Lotte, gay, lovely Lotte, for she too belonged to a world he was bidding farewell. You went with the tide; you submitted yourself to the will of God. In that submission there was peace.

His first Mass as a member of the Church was on Christmas Eve, and it made a profound impression on him. He had the feeling that it was for this he had hungered all his adult life without realising it. He knew an intense relief. He remembered the 'terrible longing' of which Cathryn had spoken on a spring day in Kensington Gardens when he had suggested that she should go back to Drindel in time for the apple-blossom; it would hardly delay her entry into the Church, he had urged, adding, "You're as good as in it already!" She had replied, he well remembered, "Would you say that to be within sight of a meal for which you hunger is as good as having the meal?" He had demanded, was it so great a hunger, and she had answered, Yes, the most terrible longing, and half to herself had quoted St. Augustine—though he had not known then that it was St. Augustine—'What the parched soul longs for lies hidden in a secret place.' He had felt then as she had that they did not speak the same language. She had had to die in the flesh before that could happen. Now that she was all spirit they could come close. He had fled from the pain and horror of her death; but he had gone back for her, gone back *to* her. On the mountain on which she had died he had found spiritual life. The parched soul had found the secret place for which it thirsted almost unto death. There was the tremendous mountain sunrise, the sense of dayspring from on high; there was the revelation that had come with a blaze of stars, the realisation of endless perspectives opening out, of the soul escaped at last from the chains of the materialist conception of truth and being; there was the light in Cathryn's face that Christmas Eve at Drindel when she had set out for the midnight Mass. . . .

All this was involved for him in that Christmas Eve Mass in London. His whole being cried then in a passion of love, in the presence of the Blessed Sacrament, " 'Too late have I loved Thee, O Thou Beauty of ancient days, yet ever new! Too late I loved Thee!' Late, late I loved Thee, O my God, but I am come at last. Late have I loved Thee, yet never loved I till now! O love who ever burnest and never consumes! O charity, my God! kindle me. Kindle me!" The tears streamed down his face, but he did not know. His body knelt in a church made with hands; his spirit was released into eternity to become one with its Creator.

For the first time he knew Christmas as a religious festival; for the first time it had significance and beauty, was a feast in the true sense.

Dorothea felt no distress when he announced his intention of going to Austria immediately after Christmas.

"I need to see Johann, and I want to see Lotte," he told her.

She asked no questions as to his plans or when he would return. Whatever he did now, she was deeply convinced, all would be well.

When Sue telephoned her during Christmas week he had already left for Salzburg. Sue was disappointed and hurt.

"He said after we dined together that we should meet again, and then he goes off without saying good-bye even!"

"He didn't say when you would meet again," Dorothea pointed out.

"That's merely being Jesuitical!" Sue objected.

Dorothea smiled. "Perhaps. Nevertheless if Francis said you would meet again he intends that you shall."

"I hoped he'd stay for my exhibition."

Dorothea felt that it would be otiose to point out to Sue that for Francis just now there were things more important than Sue Lester's exhibition.

"It may still be on when he gets back," she suggested, and changed the subject. She felt that she understood Francis's need to see Johann, and that Sue wouldn't. Sue loved Francis, but she completely failed to understand him, it seemed to her. If she had any understanding of him she would not have judged him for running away after Cathryn's death, or been so startled by his joining the Church. There had been a time when she had hoped that Francis would marry and 'settle down', and then she had shared the hope of Sue's mother that he would marry Sue; Sue had seemed 'suitable' then; but not now. Now he was the beloved son she had borne for the Church, and he had something more important to do with his life than marry; she believed that he would discover within himself a vocation for the Society of Jesus, as John Sullivan had when he turned his back on the world in which he had been so brilliant and successful. She was well aware that if he became a Jesuit he would be lost to her as a son, for all practical purposes, but this was not something which could weigh with her. If he should become another John Sullivan, she felt, her cup would be full and running over.

When he left for Austria he asked her to give no information about him to inquirers, but to say simply that he had gone abroad and she did not know when he would be back—and this was true, for he did not know himself. He did not want any letters forwarded; they none of them had any interest for him any more. She could do as she liked about them. He recommended she should simply drop them all into the waste-paper basket. She could not bring herself to be as drastic as that, though she was in complete sympathy with his fading out from the world he had always known. She dealt with his mail as best she could; the fan-mail she felt she could do nothing about, and it was not important; to his publishers, and his agents, and sundry editors, she said simply that he had gone abroad and did not wish correspondence forwarded. The cheques that came in she paid into his account. Invitations to give lectures to various literary and debating societies she ignored, except when there were stamped and addressed envelopes enclosed, and then she wrote saying that he was away. She was conniving, she knew, at the death of Francis Sable the writer, but she was convinced that by so doing she was assisting at the bringing to life of Francis Sable the priest. If it came to a choice between having a son who was a brilliant successful writer, and a son who was a brilliant and saintly priest, there could be no question as to which had the higher value; it was a choice between Augustine's two cities—the city of the world, and the city of God.

Apart from Father Connor she did not discuss the matter with anyone, but kept all these things in her heart.

9

In Salzburg it did nothing but rain, and it was bitterly cold. The Untersberg range was blotted out as though it did not exist behind the unlifting grey pall of cloud. Francis sat with Johann beside the tall tiled stove in the room above the cobbler's shop, and the rain beat against the window and the river was a brown and yellow torrent racing high between its narrow banks, and they talked. Francis told Johann of the months he had spent in Ireland, of his stay with the Franciscans, and the finding of the rosary on Croagh Patrick.

"I was at peace with the Franciscans, and I have a great regard for St. Francis of Assisi, yet I don't feel myself drawn to the Order. I can't get away from the feeling that somehow my destiny lies with the Jesuits. My first contact with the Church and the Jesuits was through you. You put me on to the Jesuit Father Connor. It was through him I went to Ireland and a retreat conducted by another distinguished Jesuit—Father Halloran. There I learnt about yet another Jesuit, Father Sullivan —only to find he had a great devotion to St. Augustine. It all seems to add up to something, only I don't yet know to what. Except that Ireland is involved. I thought you might be better at this spiritual arithmetic than I am. I felt if you couldn't help no one could."

Johann shook his head. "I cannot help you, Herr Francis. You are free. You have a wonderful opportunity to do something of importance with your life in the service of God, but no one can tell you what it should be. If I were in your position— that is to say if I had your gifts—I should join the Society of

Jesus, but then I am not you. If I recommend you to become a Jesuit it is because I have a special feeling for them—but that does not make it valid for you. For the time being I think you should do nothing. Presently you will know."

Francis insisted, "I must do something—I can't just be a parasite on society, and writing is finished for me. I must have work of some kind. I feel that whilst I am waiting for the will of God to be revealed to me I should like some quite humble job—washer-up in a restaurant, or something of the kind."

Johann told him, "There would be no chance of your doing that now that the tourist season is over and the restaurants are slack. But if you are really serious about a humble sort of job we need a packer at the bookshop—only of course you are a famous English author and it is a mere office-boy's job. . . ."

Francis said eagerly, "But don't you see, just because I am the celebrated Francis Sable I must have such a job? If I were obscure it would have no value. I want to be nothing and nobody and work with my hands, as I did with the Franciscans. If your employer really wants a packer take me to him and vouch for my honesty and reliability, but say nothing of Francis Sable the well-known writer. Let me be just an Englishman down on his luck and willing to turn his hand to anything." He smiled, and added, "You can say, if you like, that I'm quite knowledgeable about books—not that it matters for the packing department, but it would account for my being attracted to the idea of working in a bookshop, perhaps, and might dispose the boss in my favour."

"I'll speak to him today," Johann promised. "As a foreigner you'll need a labour permit, I imagine, but no doubt it can be arranged."

In this way Francis Sable spent a year of his life as packer in a Catholic bookshop in Salzburg—the bookshop that once had been 'not the kind of bookshop that appealed to him'. He had a room in a ramshackle old house halfway up a street climbing up behind the Dom. His landlord was a railway worker called Meisel, a pleasant, good-natured, intelligent man of about thirty-five, with a sweet-faced wife a few years younger. They had four children, the eldest of whom was a bright sensitive boy of thirteen called Gustav. Francis was fond of all the children, but was particularly interested in the eldest boy because of his feeling for music and poetry. The Meisels were good Catholics and a happy united family, and they very quickly accepted Francis as one of themselves. Herr and Frau Meisel loved each other and the children; the children got along well with each other and loved their parents. There was no bickering or conflict, or the irritabilities all too common in family life. There was a wholeness about the family, Francis felt; Frau Meisel was a good mother because she was a happy wife, loving her man and confident in his love for her. She had no dissatisfactions and frustrations to work off on her children in scoldings and naggings. The children in turn gave no trouble because they were free and happy; free of frustrations they had no grudges to work off against their parents. Gustav, and Mirabelle aged nine, had easy natural good manners; Laura, aged six, was a shy dark elusive little creature whom Francis never got to know very well; Bruno, aged three, wandered about singing little songs to himself and living in his own private world. Mirabelle was high-spirited, but inclined to be shy of Francis even after months, but Gustav was ripe for friendship, and for all the knowledge on books and music, places and history, birds and flowers and stars, that Francis could give him. There was something quick and eager about him. He wanted to know all about England, how high the mountains were there, what sort of food the people ate, whether St. Paul's Cathedral was as fine as the Dom. He wanted to learn English. He wanted to travel—like Herr Francis.

Francis taught him English, and found him an apt pupil. They went walks along the river together, and up into the mountains ski-ing. Sometimes on a Saturday afternoon, when the bookshop was closed, Johann came with them. Ski-ing with Johann in the Austrian mountains revived memories in Francis, not merely of Cathryn, but of Lotte—Lotte in her scarlet ski-suit, flashing past like a spurt of flame; Lotte graceful as a bird on the wing—and himself spurting after her, and the collision and the tumble, and the kisses mixed with snow and laughter. . . . Heavens, how far away and long ago it all seemed now, life lived in another lifetime in another world! Something stirred in him with the recollection, and he tried not to think of her. During the daytime, by an effort of will, he could banish her from his thoughts, but she came to him, disconcertingly, in his dreams at night. Strange, he thought, that of all the women he had known and possessed, Lotte, who was all chastity, should be the symbol of carnality. Well might Augustine of Hippo cry to God to deliver him from the 'birdlime of concupiscence'. Ah, those soft seductive hands plucking at the garment of the flesh, those voices of memory conspiring with habit to demand, 'Thinkest thou, thou canst live without these things?' After his encounter with Sue in London he had begun to think it was not difficult to do so; here was a woman he had once desired intensely and to whom he was now dead, though he still found her beautiful. He had believed then that sexuality was dead in him, burned out of him in the intensity of his spiritual fire. With the revived memory of Lotte he realised, to his mingled dismay and humiliation, that he was not to be let off so lightly.

Then in the summer she came to Salzburg for a week-end, on her way to spend her summer holiday at Drindel. She was as gay and vivid as he had remembered her, and it seemed an eternity since he had parted with her in Paris. Then in his nervous and emotionally exhausted state he had known only tenderness for her; now she disturbed him profoundly, and because that was so he contrived that they should not be alone together. With Johann they walked in the woods on the Kapuzinerberg, wandered along the river, and walked up the Untersberg, spending the night in the Zepperzauerhaus below the peak . . . and when she was gone he hardly knew which he felt most, relief or desolation.

Lotte, for her part, accepted quite simply the fact that he did not wish to see her alone; after all, why should he? Just because he had once lain with his head in her lap, and at the end of that light-hearted day had suggested she should marry him. . . . Had she not spent a year in insisting to herself that these things did not count? He had been glad of her company on a day in Paris when he was desperately lonely, at the very bottom of a deep dark well, and purely sentimentally the idea of marrying had come to him, and she had pointed out the unsuitability of the suggestion. Very well, then. There was not and never had been anything between them but simple friendship, and there was completely no reason to suppose there ever would be. He was in any case a very different person from the Francis Sable of those

Paris days. This reborn Francis, she told herself, would not have even for a day sentimental romantic notions about her—or any woman.

He was gratefully aware of her simple acceptance, and glad that she could not know that he thought of her continuously when she had gone, so completely unable to banish her from his mind even during the day that he began to question the wisdom of the celibate course he had set himself—and even his strength to continue in it. That Augustine had had similar struggles and conflicts and finally triumphed over them greatly comforted him. He invoked St. Augustine continually to give him strength and guidance, but there were the bad times when he had the feeling of his beloved saint having deserted him, and depression and hopelessness would close in on him. Then all friendship would seem to be withdrawn from the world, and all light, and all purpose. It would seem to him then that he was between two worlds—unable to live on the purely materialist plane as before, yet unable to inhabit the spiritual world of faith.

There would come to him at such times the thought that now there was no obstacle to his marrying Lotte, if she would have him. Once it had been out of the question for her because he was not a Catholic, apart from the fact that what he felt for her was not a good basis for marriage; he could feel as much for any charming, sweet-natured pretty young woman— though she evoked in him a curious tenderness which he had never known for anyone else. Now when he was perhaps on the way to saying good-bye to her for ever everything in him insisted that there was no need. The idea offered itself to him like a reprieve. Married to Lotte, who was sweet and gentle and good, he could live as a good Catholic and bring up a family as Christian and as happy and united as the Meisel family. There would be lovely little girls like Mirabelle and Laura, and a bright intelligent boy like Gustav. He could be a writer again, under an assumed name—a different kind of writer. They would have a little house outside Vienna, with a garden for the children. They would hear a lot of good music, and they would spend their holidays in Salzburg and Drindel. All such quiet happiness and content-ment could be his, if Lotte were agreeable, and he did not feel that it was conceited to believe that now she would be.

The picture would outline itself in his fevered imagination in all its completeness of material and spiritual satisfaction, but just as at Chez Bellini's with Sue the Franciscan monastery refectory had come into his mind, so now there was always superimposed on this picture of family life a sudden vision of Father Halloran in his shabby black habit, on his knees at midnight in the monastery chapel; Father Halloran with his lined face and his slight thin body battling against the driving wind and rain as he tramped back from the monastery into Ballyroon. With that memory he would always grope in his pocket for the weather-beaten rosary with its little wooden cross; his fingers would close over it and a passion of prayer rise in him. To accept this reprieve which marriage with Lotte meant would be to go back on the supreme act of atonement he felt impelled to make, the complete holocaust of self. Lotte who was gay and lovely represented all those joys of the flesh—including that of parenthood—which he had set himself to renounce. His deepest spiritual need was not for reprieve but for the strength to make the final acts of sacrifice. It must be like that, or everything that had begun that night in the hut on the Drindelhorn would be betrayed.

Towards the end of that restless tormented summer something happened. There was a sunny Sunday when with the Meisel family he climbed up the steep cobbled path of shallow steps on the Kapuzinerberg, past the tableaux of the Stations of the Cross to the great Calvary at the top, and on into the woods that laved the Capuchin monastery like a green sea. Francis and Gustav walked together; the two little girls in their blue dresses raced ahead, darting in and out of the trees like kingfishers. Their shrill cries seemed a natural part of the woodland sounds of bird-song and the sea-murmur of wind in the tree-tops. The woods were full of a green twilight broken by sudden splashes of sunshine. Herr and Frau Meisel were some way behind, setting their pace to suit Bruno, who even charging up the hill in the impersonation of a train did not go very fast. It was a warm, gentle day, with a summer's-end mellowness about it. Francis had a sense of grace he had not known for a long time. His spirit flowed serenely with the soft warm serenity of the day.

When they reached the iron gates of the monastery Gustav paused and peered through into the garden with its sun and shadow-dappled paths.

"It's a good life they live in there, Herr Francis." There was a curious note of yearning in the boy's voice. He asked, as they walked on, "Have you ever wanted to be a monk?"

"I have thought of it often," Francis told him, and added, "I lived some time with the Franciscan brothers in Ireland."

Gustav looked at him, eagerly.

"The Capuchins are closer to St. Francis. I would like to be a Capuchin. I pray to Our Lady and St. Francis about it all the time."

"Do your parents know this?"

"Yes, Herr Francis, but they say I am too young yet to know my own mind. All the same I won't change. I know I won't change! Ever since my first Communion I've known this was what I wanted."

The boy's dark eyes were bright with the intensity of his conviction. Why shouldn't he know, Francis thought; there was a thirteen-year-old boy called Francis Sable who had insisted at his public school and to his family that he was going to be a writer; and a thirteen-year-old girl who had declared that she was going to be a painter. . . .

"You believe me, don't you, Herr Francis?" the boy beseeched.

"Yes, Gustav, I believe you."

They walked on in silence through the woods. Francis felt a curious tenderness for the boy at his side, a spiritual flowing-out to him, and a kind of heart-ache. What was that prayer they taught you as a child—'Pity my simplicity, suffer me to come to Thee.' Sweet Jesus, let it be so; suffer him to come to Thee in the way his young heart is set. . . . There was nothing one could do but say 'I believe you', and pray. . . .

They went on up past Mozart's little house through more woods to a dark ivied *Schloss*, where the little girls ran back to their mother and drew close to her, and the stalwart Bruno suddenly wanted to be hoisted to his father's shoulders. Here were cobwebbed windows, a drawbridge with rusty chains, a tower with a spiral staircase twisting up into darkness, and a chill atmosphere of dampness and decay. From a terrace bounded by a rough stone wall they looked down into the valley, brimming with sunlight.

Suddenly the stillness was invaded by the rich full swell of organ music; it swept over the dark woods and the sombre *Schloss* in a great golden tide, then, as the tide receded, like a shaft of light came a clear pure voice, with the reed-like quality of a flute, lifted in triumphant proclamation:

'I know that my Redeemer liveth.'

Thin and clear as a reed yet full of confidence the voice seemed to climb up out of the golden valley and fill the dark woods with light.

Francis looked at Gustav. The boy stood with his head raised, his listening face rapt with ecstasy.

Mirabelle in her shrill little-girl's voice demanded to know where the music came from. Frau Meisel hushed her, murmuring that it was from a radio in the *Schloss*. Laura wanted to see and was commanded to hush. Frau Meisel held the little girls close to her and looked anxiously in the direction of Francis and Gustav; they were the two musical ones and their pleasure must not be spoilt. She need not have worried, for both Francis and the boy were in another world—a world that held nothing but the rise and fall of the flute-like voice, the deep ebb and flow of the organ notes. In the passionate conviction of the words there was adoration bordering on ecstasy. . . .

'Though worms destroy this body,
Yet in my flesh shall I see God.'

When the last note had vibrated into silence Gustav said in a low voice, a little unsteadily, "What was it, Herr Francis? I couldn't follow the words very well in the English. . . ."

"It is from Handel's *Messiah*," Francis told him, and translated. "We Catholics haven't all the beautiful sacred music," he added, with a smile.

"We've nothing as beautiful as that!" the boy asserted, fervently.

"Nonsense," his father said, as he came up, "we've Mozart's *Laudate Dominum*! Don't you agree, Herr Francis?"

"I do. But there's a peculiar quality of passion and triumph in this thing . . ."

Gustav gave Francis a quick look of gratitude, and they all went on, away from the dark grounds of the *Schloss* and into the green and gold woods.

Later in the day, when they were coming back down the hill, Francis found himself walking with Frau Meisel; Gustav was ahead with his father.

Frau Meisel said, "I couldn't help noticing how interested Gustav was in what you were telling us about Rimini and the Church of St. Francis, while we were having lunch. He hangs on every word you say! You've taught him a lot, Herr Francis. You should have been a teacher!"

"Perhaps. Though it's only since I've known Gustav that it's occurred to me that I might have something to give to the young."

"You have a lot to give!" Frau Meisel said, firmly.

"I don't know. I don't know! When I was listening to that music it came to me that perhaps if I were to join a teaching order——" He broke off and finished quickly, "Let's not discuss it, Frau Meisel. I've got to wait until I know."

"Meanwhile you're wasting your time as a bookseller's packer! Do you think we don't know you are an educated man, Herr Francis? You do not speak about yourself, but we are not so simple and ignorant that we do not know an educated person when we meet one! We hear you talking to Gustav, and you have been all over Europe, and in America—the ordinary working man isn't able to travel like that, and his education doesn't run to so many subjects. We think, my husband and I, that you are a gentleman. Why you do the work you do, and why you share our humble life, we do not know, and it is not our business. You have your reasons, obviously."

"Yes, I have my reasons, and one day no doubt I shall tell you, but not now. Not until it is all clear to me what I must do."

"You are waiting for a sign, Herr Francis?"

"Yes, Frau Meisel, I am waiting for a sign."

10

Walking by the river with Johann that evening Francis said, "Frau Meisel has observed that young Gustav regards me as a kind of human encyclopaedia and considers on the strength of that that I am wasting my time as a bookseller's packer and should be a teacher!"

"She's perfectly right. As a Jesuit teacher you could be of great service to Catholic youth—boys like Gustav Meisel."

"I wish I could be convinced of it. But the fact that one thirteen-year-old boy finds me an acceptable teacher proves nothing."

"Do you think that the ex-barrister John Sullivan had any more reason to suppose he would make a good teacher? You seem to have made remarkable progress with young Gustav in six months."

"He is a rather remarkable boy."

"He's quick and sensitive, but not brilliant. With anyone else he would probably be much less remarkable. You have too low an opinion of yourself, you know!"

Francis sighed. "I've no opinion of myself at all! If teaching were merely dispensing information I am probably as good a human encyclopaedia as any other over-educated intellectual. But the handling of anything as delicate as a young human soul— that is another matter. I am not a John Sullivan. I only wish I were!"

"Doesn't it occur to you that it is a very important calling— the spiritual guidance of the young?"

"It does occur to me, very strongly—so much so that I feel it's a vocation demanding the highest qualities!"

"If you took on the job you might develop the qualities," Johann suggested, smiling. He added, "If you felt you had the qualities it would be pretty certain you hadn't them! Why don't you discuss it with Father Connor?"

"No. I must know from within myself. I need to be as certain as young Gustav is of his vocation! Today, when I saw that boy's face as we stood listening to that aria from the *Messiah*, I had the feeling that it was my mission in life to help him and all boys like him—the feeling that I really had something to give youth . . ."

"It didn't occur to you that hearing that music suddenly like that, with young Gustav, was the sign for which you waited?"

"It did occur to me. But afterwards I thought perhaps that was arrogance on my part. How is one to know?"

"The first thing you have to know is whether you have the vocation to join a religious order. After that which order. If the Jesuits, whether you will join the English or the Irish province——"

Francis said quickly, "Oh, the Irish! It is indicated surely—Father Connor, Father Halloran, Father Sullivan, have been my signposts—and then the finding of the rosary on Croagh Patrick—my spiritual destiny surely lies in Ireland!"

"And in the Irish province the Society is mostly a teaching order. Doesn't it add up?"

Francis smiled. "Perhaps."

But the summer passed, and the autumn came with its endless rains, and the winter with snow banked three feet deep along the sides of the roads, and the little red-coated figures of 'Grampus', like the English 'Santa Claus', but carrying a birch for the punishment of naughty children, began to appear in the windows of toy-shops and confectioners, and a little later on the robed and mitred figure of St. Nicholas, and once again the dowager Lady Sable wrote to her son to ask if he would be home for Christmas. . . .

Francis had the feeling that if he went he would not be in Austria again, ever. He would not see Johann and Lotte again, or Herr and Frau Meisel, or young Gustav, or Mirabelle and Laura like bright lovely birds, or the self-contained little Bruno. Yet he felt within himself that he must go, and the deeper this conviction grew in him the deeper became his sadness.

"We shall miss you," Frau Meisel said, "but it is right you should go home for Christmas. Only why do you say you will not be in Austria again? Could it be——"

She broke off and the colour beat up into her face.

"Forgive me, Herr Francis. I have no right to ask. It is just that sometimes you seem like one of ourselves, one of the family——"

"It seems like that to me too," he assured her. "And you are right—it could be that I shall join an order; a teaching order. I shall offer myself to the Irish province of the Society of Jesus."

"You will become a Jesuit teacher?" Her eyes were bright.

"By the grace of God, and in the fullness of time," he said, smiling.

"But that is wonderful, Herr Francis! We shall pray for you." The tears were in her eyes now. "We shall never forget you—never!"

For Gustav it was not so easy; he kept telling himself that it was fine that Herr Francis was going away to become a Jesuit, but he could only feel desolate. There would be no more ski-ing in the mountains, no more walks and talks along the river and in the woods. Herr Francis would go back to a remote place called England and they would never meet again on this earth. That, he knew, was not the right way to feel about it; nevertheless it was how he did feel about it, and, very secretly, he wept.

Nevertheless, when the dreaded day came he trudged along beside Herr Amanshauser to see Herr Francis off on the train for Vienna. Francis felt that he could not leave Austria without saying good-bye to Lotte, whom he had not seen since the summer.

Johann was delighted by Francis's decision to go to England and after Christmas offer himself to the Society of Jesus. That they would not meet again seemed to him quite unimportant. He had a deep affection for Cathryn's brother, but he had a considerably deeper devotion to the Church. Nothing but good could come of Francis's decision, he felt. He knew something of the exultation he had known when Cathryn's conversion was complete, and she had come back to Drindel . . . and on a summer night had promised to marry him when the snow came again. . . . But God of His infinite wisdom had willed otherwise, and now through her death her brother had saved his soul and dedicated himself body and soul to the service of God. Here, then, was no occasion for sadness, but for rejoicing.

He walked with his head held high, his eyes full of their unquenchable dark fire. Francis kept his eyes on the ground, and there was no exultation in him; only a heaviness of spirit. He put an arm round the boy's shoulder, and they walked in silence.

At the station he turned to Johann, "If you would be a friend to Gustav in my place . . ." he suggested, in a low voice.

In spite of the low tone the boy heard him and gave him a stricken look.

"Herr Johann will be your good friend," he said firmly.

"*Ja*, Herr Francis." He turned away, his eyes swimming with tears. Francis pressed his shoulder.

"You, too, have a work to do in a few years' time," he reminded him.

"*Ja*, Herr Francis," the boy whispered.

Francis felt his throat aching, but there was nothing he could do, and nothing more to say.

It was a relief when the train came in. Gustav took out a grubby handkerchief and blew his nose and made a desperate effort at composure.

"Think of me scrubbing floors in the seminary when you pass the monastery in a few weeks' time," Francis said, smiling.

Gustav smiled back, wanly, and almost inaudibly he said for the last time, "*Ja*, Herr Francis."

Francis shook hands with Johann, then placed his hands on Gustav's shoulder and bent and kissed his forehead.

"God keep you," he said, and felt the boy's body quivering with suppressed sobs.

He stood waving at the window of the compartment. Johann had an arm round Gustav's shoulder. . . .

For a long time Francis sat slumped in his seat in the hot crowded third-class compartment, his eyes closed, engulfed in sheer wretchedness. Scrubbing floors in a seminary. . . . If John Sullivan could do it when he was forty Francis Sable could do it when he was thirty-three. But then Francis Sable was not of the stuff that saints were made of, which John Sullivan clearly was. . . . Well, but there was no need to go through with it; he need not be going to say good-bye to Lotte; he could be going to Vienna to ask her to marry him, to secure for himself all the loveliness and peace and fulfilment she represented. There was still that reprieve possible. Lotte who had rescued him once from the dark tunnel could rescue him now a second time, and for the last time. It was not too late. Why try to go through with something for which you hadn't the spiritual strength? The nearer the train drew to the capital the more insistently, like the hammering of a heart, did the wheels in their revolutions insist, Marry her, marry her, marry her. . . .

When he arrived at the Westbahnhof he went straight to St. Stefan's. Low walls of snow were banked along the sides of the streets, and icicles hung from the feet of Christ crucified in the shrine outside the cathedral.

All over the big dark church people knelt, shut in their own private worlds of supplication or meditation. The darkness of the day deepened the always twilight dimness of the church, but intensified the glow of the lighted candles. Francis slipped into the nearest pew and knelt down, but for once he could not concentrate; he was uneasily aware of the footsteps and dark hurrying forms of people using the cathedral as a short cut, of sightseers who came and went without genuflecting, of an old shawled woman in front of him fumbling her rosary beads, of an old ragged man shuffling in to sit down out of the cold. He buried his face in his hands and tried to pray. 'Sweet Heart of Jesus, be Thou my love. Sweet Heart of Mary! Be Thou my salvation!' And still he was aware of metallic footsteps, of rustling movements. 'Blessed St. Augustine, who knew well how the flesh lusteth against the spirit and the spirit against the flesh, help me to achieve the chaste dignity of continence, to the glory of God. Pray for me, I beseech thee.' There was a whispering in the aisle flanking the block of pews in which he knelt. He pressed his fingers deeper into his eyes in an attempt to shut out the world, to lose himself in prayer, and began to repeat the *De Profundis*. '*De profundis clamavi ad Te, Domine; Domine, exaudi vocem meam* . . .' He got no farther; it was no good. Lotte's face swam smiling before his inward gaze.

Outside on the St. Stefan's Platz the wind had an edge like a knife. He huddled deeper into his overcoat and strode off down the Kärntnerstrasse, thronging with eager Christmas shopping crowds. At the corners of the side-streets twigs of laurels and sprays of mistletoe dipped in gold or silver paint were being offered for sale, and there were baskets of silvered or gilded or frosted fir-cones. The shop windows were bright with lights and decorations and ornate gifts. The crowds gazed and loitered in spite of the bitter wind. By the main entrance of the Opera House stood a tall Christmas tree strung with coloured electric lights.

In a café on the Ringstrasse Francis telephoned to Lotte.

When she came to the telephone, he said, speaking in French, "Is that Mademoiselle Amanshauser? It is? Good. This is Francis Sable. Yes, I am here in Vienna. Don't you remember a conversation one Christmas at Drindel, when you spoke of the pleasure of surprises and the excitement of uncertainties? I said I might one day turn up in Vienna and take you to dinner. You were charming enough to say that even if it didn't happen it was still a sweet thought. You remember?"

She laughed softly. "I remember very well, Monsieur."

"Good. The sweet thought has taken shape. Can you dine with me tonight? I am getting the night-train to Paris."

"You are going tonight? But no, that's impossible! That's not kind, Francis!"

"Nevertheless, I must go to England, and I must see someone in Paris on the way, and I must go at once, or I shall never go!"

"Then obviously you should defer your going!"

"And spend the rest of my life in self-reproach! Now it is you who are not kind! Tell me where you will meet me—there are only a few hours. I'd prefer somewhere small and quiet."

"There's a small Polish restaurant off the Graben—anyone would tell you. They have delicious open sandwiches and you can drink vodka to keep out the cold!"

"I don't drink these days, but that's no reason why you shouldn't. What time shall we meet?"

She promised to meet him within an hour, and he spent forty-five minutes in the café over a glass of coffee. There were English, French and Austrian newspapers available on long sticks, and a tolerably good orchestra playing light Mozart pieces. Three times during the three-quarters of an hour he sat there his waiter replaced the glass of water he had brought with the coffee for a fresh one. . . .

When he left the café he went back up the Kärntnerstrasse and cut through into the Graben, reaching the Polish restaurant a few minutes before Lotte arrived.

She wore the round fur hat and the full-skirted wine-coloured velvet coat with fur at the neck and hem and wrists in which he had first seen her when he had stood with Cathryn at the upper window of the Amanshauser *Gasthaus* and she had stepped out of a taxi into the snow. She was like a Russian princess, Cathryn had said, 'Straight out of the fair scene in *Petrouchka*!' And he had blown her a kiss and murmured that she had a lovely face, and God in His mercy give her grace. . . .

He smiled as he took her gloved hand and raised it to his lips.

"It was nice of you to come," he said, as they went over to a high-backed settle in a corner. "I used to think I would one day take you to the *Drei Husaren*, but one needs to be gay and of the world for that, and I am no longer gay, and less and less of the world. But I had to see you before I left Austria."

"Shall you be long away?"

"From Austria? It's unlikely I shall return."

He took off his overcoat and hung it on a stump of a mutilated tree—the usual café hat-stand—near the door. He went over to the counter and looked through a glass screen at the assortment of open sandwiches—caviar, smoked salmon, scrambled egg with chopped onion and a sprinkling of paprika, salami sandwiches, cheese sandwiches. . . . He made a selection and carried the piled plate back to the table with a glass of vodka.

Lotte lifted the glass.

"Here's to your return, in spite of what you say!"

He frowned. "No, my dear, I'm not returning."

"*Aufwiedersehen*, then!" Pain gave an edge to her voice.

"*Aufwiedersehen*."

She drained the glass.

"It's a depressing toast," she protested.

"I'm sorry, but I am depressed. You must bear with me this once."

She was all softness again immediately.

"Why are you depressed, Francis?"

"I suppose because saying good-bye is a depressing business. I suppose one always shrinks a little from finality."

She sat looking at the plate of delicacies for which suddenly she had no appetite. She said after a long moment, "You mean you are going home to join an order?"

"Yes."

"The Jesuits?"

"If they'll have me."

She was silent. He took a caviar sandwich from the pile and set it in front of her on a little paper napkin.

"You must eat," he said.

"Thank you. Yes." She took a bite from the sandwich.

"I'll get you some more vodka."

She protested that she didn't want it, but he went to the counter and returned with the glass refilled.

She raised the glass and forced a smile.

"*Bonne chance!*"

"Thank you."

She drained the glass.

He said, selecting a sandwich, "You know, Lotte, you were very nearly my undoing! Ever since you came to Salzburg in the summer I've been fighting the temptation to ask you if you would marry me. Even on the train coming here. Even now it would be desperately easy to say to hell with everything—given the encouragement!"

She said in a low voice, "If you did that you'd regret it. You'd despise yourself."

"I suppose so. But if I'd asked you in the summer and you'd agreed?"

"I think you'd have regretted it—later on."

"You'd have married me if I'd asked you?"

She looked at the table. "I expect so. I've always loved you." She added, with difficulty, "I expect—I wouldn't have been able to refuse you . . ."

She looked at him and her eyes had a stricken look.

"Oh, Francis, why are we talking about it?"

"I wanted to know. If you'd have had me it makes the sacrifice that much the greater." He smiled, bleakly. "It's easy to make sacrifices with nothing much to sacrifice!"

"It could be argued that you'd no right to sacrifice my happiness along with yours!"

"I could counter that with the argument that I should probably not have made you happy and therefore I was not really sacrificing your happiness, but actually protecting it, by my own sacrifice! I could also argue that my need for you was much greater than yours for me—that I should have got much more out of the marriage."

"I don't know why you should assume that."

"I'm much too complicated a person to make any woman happy. I'd have had all your loveliness and sweetness and goodness, and in exchange you'd have had my self-disappointment, spiritual frustration, egotism, and the rest of it!"

"Then you wouldn't have been happy if we'd married, so it's not really a sacrifice after all!"

"Perhaps. But it feels like a sacrifice, I can assure you! It feels horribly like one! It seems I've not yet reached the stage at which I can get a kick out of self-abnegation. I merely find it depressing."

"The fact remains you go on with it. Grace must come of it in the end. I wish I could help you. But there seems nothing I can do for you except pray for you."

He said, violently, almost bitterly, "You'd better pray—hard!"

When they came out into the Graben the coldness struck them like a blow in the face. He pulled her arm through his, drawing her close to his side.

"It's slippery underfoot," he warned.

In the Kärntnerstrasse they picked up a taxi with chains on its wheels. In the lamplight the icy roads glistened like glass. As they drove off Lotte asked, "You left your baggage at the station?"

"Yes. I only had a rucksack."

"You travel light these days! I remember you used to have such imposing-looking pigskin suitcases, with your monogram on!"

"I'm not that sort of traveller any more." With a sudden flash of the old Francis he declaimed, in English:

'Gone now the pigskin suitcase,
The opulent valise;
Farewell the first-class travel,
The *rentier* at his case—— '

And that reminds me, he told himself, I must make arrangements about that *rente*. Between the unearned, and the royalties which I suppose will go on for a while, I ought to be quite an asset to any order. . . .

Lotte brought him back to the present by protesting that she was sure it was very fine poetry but didn't he know something in French, or would he translate?

"I was thinking aloud," he told her. "Forgive me!"

He kissed her finger-tips, then kept her hand in his, and they sat in silence. The taxi crossed the boulevards and slid forward into the garish brightness of the Mariahilferstrasse. In a few moments, Lotte thought, we shall be at the station; in half an hour the train will go, and Francis will be gone, and we shall not meet again, and it's better this way; I must hold on to that thought; it's better this way. He has to make his act of atonement; there has to be this expiation. . . .

Francis thought, Even now it's not too late. I could take her in my arms. The train for Paris could leave without me. I need not go on with the holocaust. It is too much.

But to go back now—wasn't that too much, too? Could he face that? Face the Meisels again, Johann, Father Connor, his mother, all the people who believed in him? Say to Frau Meisel, "I couldn't go through with it. I am in love with a Viennese girl"? Say to Johann, "It's no good; I'm not cut out for celibacy. All the Gustavs will have to get along without me"? Say to Gustav, "You will become a Capuchin, but I shall never become a Jesuit. It was all the merest emotionalism when I was moved by that hymn from the *Messiah*. It went to the very bottom of your young soul, but it only touched the surface of mine. You are the young and pure in heart; I am old and steeped in worldliness and its corruption. I have nothing to give you. I love a girl more than I can ever hope to love God"? Say to Father Connor, "I hadn't your singleness of purpose. I have failed you"? Say to his mother, "Behold your second disappointment"? And to Cathryn—"It was all a lie, that night alone on the Drindelhorn"? Say to Sue, "You were right; I was deceiving myself . . . I have come back to your world—your sceptical, materialist world of unbelief . . . of which I can never again be a part, so that I shall belong no-where . . . and carry all my life the sense of failure, and the burden of unexpiated sin . . ."?

It could be, then, in spiritual matters, as on mountains, that there were times when you were compelled to go forward because it was even more difficult to go back. You held on because you dared not let go.

So there you were on a station platform once again, facing one more goodbye-for-ever, and once again you longed for the train to leave, because there was quite simply nothing left to say, and anything you said now could only be stop-gap stuff.

He found himself a seat in a wooden third-class compartment, dumped his rucksack, and rejoined Lotte on the platform.

He said, "I'm glad you wore this coat tonight, and the little Russian hat—you were wearing them the first time I ever set eyes on you."

She smiled. "And you blew me a kiss!"

Yes, my darling, I blew you a kiss; and I have never kissed you as I long to kiss you now, when it's all too late. It could all have been so different. But this is the way it is—farewells quite literally all along the line. . . .

He returned her smile. "It seems all as remote as childhood now. You've been sweet, Lotte. I'll remember with gratitude all my life."

Her eyes swam with tears, but she gave a little laugh.

"Monsieur est galant!"

"That is what you said that day we lunched in the Bois. It was all like a popular magazine story—at least it was like the beginning of one, but the end went wrong, and in the best Chekhov manner the hero and heroine part on a winter's night on a railway station, with tears in their eyes, despair in their souls, and cold feet. We need hardly add that the snow glistened on the roofs of the railway-station sheds, and lay in drifts along the sidings. All the same, the story should have had a different ending, my little one."

My little one, my love! But it's better this way. I must believe it's better this way. I wouldn't have made you happy, my little one, my love.

She said, resolutely, "It's a very good ending—the best ending."

"I want you to be happy, Lotte. I want it quite desperately." That at least was not stop-gap. "I like to think of you dancing and singing and ski-ing and kissing young men in the snow and finally marrying one who adores you."

"And who is rich and handsome?"

"Of course. And gay and witty."

"And a good Catholic?"

"Didn't I mention that? But of course!"

They paced up and down the platform making light conversation, and she thought, I shall never see him again, in a few minutes he will be gone, and it's right that he should go. Sweet Heart of Mary, help me to desire what is right. . . .

When they came back to his coach he said suddenly, "I am going to be very sentimental and ask you to accept a souvenir from me. I brought it from England with the intention of giving it to you." He pressed something small and hard into her hand and closed her fingers over it. "Look at it when I'm gone. It's a souvenir of my dead life, but when you look at it think only of champagne in the sunshine up in the Bois, and mulled wine at Drindel in the snow, not of dark tunnels and journeys to the end of the night. Now I'd better get aboard this train, for this is another journey to the end of the night—this night, anyhow!"

He bent and kissed her forehead.

"Thank you for everything—Drindel, and Paris, and for sending Johann to me, and for seeing me off!"

She smiled—a gay and lovely smile.

"*Monsieur est toujours galant!*"

Then he was aboard the train, leaning from a window, smiling, talking last-minute stop-gap nonsense. All along the length of the train people leaned and talked and laughed, or clasped hands, and said unimportant things because it was now all too late to say anything else.

Then at last the train began to move; hands fell apart; hands and handkerchiefs waved from carriage windows and from dwindling figures on the platform.

The girl in the wine-coloured velvet coat with fur at the neck and the flared hem, a round fur hat on her dark hair, waved until the train was lost in a cloud of smoke . . . then she stood a moment looking at a lapis-lazuli signet ring in the palm of her hand.

Kisses in the snow on the ski-slopes of the Drindelhorn; champagne under the trees in the Bois; his head in her lap under the willow tree beside the lake; sitting at the café opposite the Comédie Française; dancing till the dawn, parting outside the little hotel behind the Opéra. 'Thank you for everything'—he had said it then, too . . . but then he had kissed her lips, very gently, and held her a moment to him, and sighed. 'We will have other days like it,' she had said. 'You will come to Vienna.' There had been another summer, but he had avoided being alone with her. He had come to Vienna—but only to say good-bye. 'Thank you for everything,' he had said again, and 'It is a good ending,' she had answered him . . . and if there was a tightness in your throat so that it was a physical ache, and if your heart felt so full that it would burst, and your eyes burned with unshed tears, it did not alter the fact . . . *it was a good ending*.

She slipped the ring on to the third finger of her right hand because it was too big for her to wear as a signet ring, and walked composedly away.

II

Sue was wakened by the ringing of the telephone bell. Confusedly she switched on the bedside lamp and reached for the receiver. Who on earth should be ringing at this hour—the middle of the night? Then she glanced at her watch beside the lamp and saw that it was nine o'clock. All the same, on a dark winter's morning nine o'clock was an uncivilised hour at which to ring anyone, before body and soul were brought together again with the aid of hot coffee and a hot bath.

"Is that Sue? Oh, this is Francis. I've just arrived from Vienna. May I come along? I hope I'm not too early—I waited till it was nine o'clock. Are you up?"

"Up? Of course I'm not up! What do you take me for? It's not even *light* yet! By all means come along. Where are you? At the Lilas? Good Lord! All right, I'll go and open the front door. . . ."

She got up, brushed her hair, powdered her face, put on a dark plain dressing-gown, tailored and mannish—anything else would look coquettish, she thought. She drew back the curtains. The sky was a yellowish-grey and the huddle of roofs below the deep studio window shone with rain. She went into the tiny kitchen which opened out of the studio and plugged in the electric kettle and began to grind the coffee. She was still grinding when Francis arrived. He was unshaven after the night-journey and looked tired and rather old, she thought.

"I'm getting the eleven o'clock train to Calais," he said. "I just wanted to see you before I went. I'm going to London."

"I'll be there myself in the New Year."

"I'll be in Ireland by then, all being well. I intend to join the Irish province of the Society of Jesus if they'll have me."

"You've made up your mind, then?"

"Yes."

"The influence of the Amanshausers—*frère et sœur*, I suppose?" There was the old bitterness in her voice.

"You'd be nearer the truth if you said the influence of a thirteen-year-old boy who dreams of becoming a Capuchin. May I use your bathroom?"

"Of course. I'll make coffee."

He looked less haggard when he had washed, she thought, but there was a gauntness about him now, his cheeks thinned, his eyes a little sunken; it was a finer face now than in the days when he had been the Francis Sable that women found so attractive, but he would not readily attract them now, she thought; his face now was the face of an ascetic, and all the old easy charm had gone.

"What have you been doing all this time?" she asked, pouring coffee. "Your mother could tell me nothing except that you were in Austria."

"I worked in a Catholic bookshop, as packer."

"Whatever for? Are you going to write up the experience?"

"I don't write any more. I did it for a reason, but—forgive me—it's not one you'd understand, Sue, so let's not discuss it. Tell me what *you've* been doing——"

"Painting portraits of the *nouveaux riches* and making a little money. I spent the summer in the South. Paris gets so weary in the dog-days."

"The same people still move round in the same circle, I suppose?"

"Much the same. You heard Anna Kallinova died at Vence, I expect?"

"No. What happened to her?"

"She was t.b., it seems, but no one ever knew. Cathryn was very fond of her."

"I know." He crossed himself. "God give her rest."

She would never get used to it, she thought, Francis and all this Holy Roman business. It had all seemed natural enough in Cathryn; but in Francis . . .

She felt suddenly depressed.

"I suppose if you become a Jesuit you'll be lost to us all forever?"

"We shan't meet, if that's what you mean. Unless you come to Ireland."

"Do they allow females to visit monasteries?"

"Yes, but I shall be in various seminaries for some years," he pointed out.

"I thought a seminary was an educational establishment for young ladies!"

He smiled. "They are also establishments for the education of priests. Now you've learnt another fact of life!"

She was silent. Soon he would be gone and they might not meet again, ever, yet she was feeling hostile, the old irritation and resentment rising in her. He had promised they would meet again, and he had kept his promise—to say good-bye. Only it was all no use. They had nothing, really, to say to each other any more. . . . She had said that to him last time, at his mother's house; it seemed truer than ever now. Then she had been able to surrender to his charm; all that had gone now; it was as though in a year he had aged almost beyond recognition; this was not the Francis she had loved, this grey haggard man with the sunken eyes with their curious feverish look. She had loved Francis Sable the writer, but it seemed she had seen the last of him that night a year ago at Bellini's. . . .

"Did you see your shop-girl in Vienna?"

"Lotte? To be sure. It was why I went there."

"Does she still ravish you?"

"I still find her very sweet, if that's what you mean."

"Why don't you marry her, now that you've embraced the Church?"

"Because we are both agreed it's better not."

"You've chosen the far, far better thing?" Her voice was hard, derisive, but he refused to rise to the provocation.

"I believe so." He got up. "I must be going. Thank you for

the coffee—it was delicious. And," he smiled, "for the wash and brush-up."

"There's no need to go yet."

"It's better. I think perhaps I shouldn't have come."

"Perhaps." There was a curious deadness in her. What, really, had they to say to each other, she and this haggard ascetic suffering from religious mania—for what else was it?

Yet as he picked up his rucksack from the corner where he had dumped it a queer pity came to her. She longed with a sudden passionate longing for the old Francis to be restored to her—like a scene in a fairy-play or a ballet, in which the beggar throws off his rags and is revealed as a shining prince. If suddenly he should look up and laugh, ask her to come out and have a drink, ask her to sleep with him—oh, anything so long as it was the charming debonair Francis she had known, anything to end this nightmare of greyness and deadness, and pity like a cold rain. . . .

That Francis Sable of all people should arouse pity in one, should seem pathetic—it was preposterous.

"Francis," she cried suddenly, "oh, Francis—I can't bear all this——"

"I'm sorry," he said, helplessly.

"I know it was an awful shock about Cathryn, but still—I should have thought a balanced worldly person like yourself would be over it by now. All this Jesuit business—for you it's crazy——"

"Sue dear, what is the use of discussing it? I see that it was a mistake my coming, but you must believe I meant well."

He opened the door and looked back over his shoulder and smiled.

"Good-bye," he said gently. There was nothing else to say.

She answered him stonily. "Good-bye." For her too there was nothing else to say.

The door closed and she heard his steps going down the stone stairs. Exit Francis Sable, she thought, bitterly. It was the most awful waste; the most awful tragedy, really; a man who had had so much success, social and literary, a man who had had such brilliance and charm. He ought to be psycho-analysed. . . . If he'd been older you could have said he'd gone funny at forty.

But he was only thirty-three—though he looked forty and more. Poor old Francis! But how awful to be thinking of him like that! Francis Sable of all people.

Oh well! He'd got her up early, anyhow; nothing like a nice early start on the frightful day. At twelve o'clock the ghastly Miss Desirée Courtney was coming for a further sitting. Miss Courtney was a London typist who had won a prize in a beauty competition and now danced in the front row at the Casino de Paris. There was an elderly gentleman always referred to as 'my friend' who had commissioned the picture. He had been very anxious that 'the young lady' should be painted in evening dress. He liked young ladies in evening dress—it showed off their figures to advantage. He had made his money in women's corsets—cheap, very pink corsets—so he knew about the female figure; had a professional eye for it, so to speak. (Assuring Sue of this he had run an approving eye over her own figure. Miss Courtney had giggled. "Oh, shut up!" she had said.) So Miss Courtney was being painted in a kind of green snakeskin affair made of sequins that fitted her like a wet bathing-suit. Miss Courtney had twanging vowels and yellow hair and diamond bracelets. Miss Courtney was the girl who had made good. It was difficult not to let that creep into the picture. That would have been the really good likeness for which 'my friend' had asked—if not exactly what he was paying for. . . . One shouldn't let oneself in for such jobs, of course. But still, two hundred guineas was two hundred guineas, and when you had expensive tastes . . . Cathryn wouldn't have touched such a job; nor would old Anna—though Anna would have made a wonderful cruel satirical drawing both of Desirée and her friend. But then she, Sue Lester, hadn't Cathryn Sable's fastidiousness, or Anna Kallinova's capacity for satire; she was just an ordinary working artist who took her commissions where she found them, and, as they said in the advertisements, aimed to please . . . just as Francis once had. Or was that being unjust to him? Oh to hell with Francis! To hell with all the high falutin' stuff about artistic integrity; to hell with everything except the job in hand . . . because you were as miserable as hell deep down inside yourself, damned miserable, because your work wasn't what you wanted it to be, and your life wasn't what you wanted it to be, and your success as an artist didn't mean a dam' thing; it didn't mean as much as Anna Kallinova's failure. . . .

That was being morbid, of course, but it was a morbid sort of day—that began with being wrenched out of sleep by a telephone bell at crack of dawn, and brought you a religious maniac for breakfast, and Miss Desirée Courtney at noon.

Oh well! Sue Lester went into the bathroom and turned on the bath. Thank God for the man who invented plumbing, anyhow.

12

Francis could not shake off his depression. He felt none of the relief he had expected to feel in coming at last to a decision; he had a sense of taking leave of everything, and of the finality of that leave-taking. He had a feeling at times that it was almost like a preparation for death. His mother was bewildered by his melancholy; she herself was overjoyed at the step he was taking. The mother of Augustine of Hippo had not rejoiced more greatly or given more heartfelt thanks to God over her son's conversion, and Augustine himself had been filled with joy. But Francis seemed almost to regret the step he was taking. When Dorothea told Father Connor this he pointed out that it was a very solemn decision for a man of thirty-three to make, and a man who had lived as Francis had lived. It was the final gesture of renunciation, requiring the complete holocaust of self. His reward of joy and peace would come later. Father Sullivan, no less than Francis, was said to have appeared depressed when he returned to his family to say good-bye. He could assure her from conversations he had had with Francis that his intention was quite firm; he had no misgivings, nor had he any misgivings on Francis's behalf.

On a cold wet dark morning early in January Francis was seen off on the Irish mail at Euston by his mother and Father Connor. A small boy in a peaked cap came along the platform with a laden tray of newspapers, periodicals, and a few novels, strapped to him. He paused at the door of the third-class compartment by which Francis, the priest, and Lady Sable stood.

"Books, papers, magazines?" he demanded.

Francis glanced at the tray, then laughed.

"I see the books include Francis Sable's last novel."

"Seven and six net," the boy stated, hopefully.

"No, thanks, sonny."

The boy moved on.

"Odd how one's dead life pursues one," Francis said.

"At least it won't pursue you to Ireland," Father Connor suggested. "Not as far as Tullabeg, anyhow!"

"Thank God for that."

"Your dead life, as you call it, produced the person you are today," Dorothea said.

Francis smiled. "Paris as a kind of novitiate? Salzburg, perhaps, but not Paris. . . ." He thought, All these railway-station good-byes; first Salzburg, then Vienna, now London. . . . Thank God no one had seen him off in Paris.

They paced up and down the cold wet platform. There were Irish voices, priests . . . London was receding already like an outgoing tide. He slipped an arm through his mother's. She was a little pale, and silent. In spite of all it was hard for her, he thought.

"I shall be very close to you a great deal of the time," he assured her.

"I'll see she's not lonely," Father Connor promised.

"There's no need to worry about me," she protested, firmly.

For her, too, then, it was a good ending. . . . Thank God for that too.

"When I come to England for my philosophy we could meet," he suggested.

She smiled. "Perhaps."

"He has two years of floor-scrubbing first," Father Connor reminded her.

"After a year as a packer it'll at least make a change," Francis said.

Now that the time had come for starting on the new life his melancholy was lifting—as Father Connor had known it would. His only sadness now was the memory of the way in which he had parted from Sue. He turned to his mother.

"When you next see Sue give her my love, won't you? And if

you could tell her that none of this is as mad as it seems to her——"

"She thinks that?"

"Religious mania, she called it. She attributes it to shock." He smiled. "I suppose it must look like that to her."

Dorothea frowned. "With a Catholic mother she should know better."

He pressed her arm. "Don't blame her. Having lived for more than thirty years on a purely materialist plane myself I can understand. You and Cathryn were never on that plane, and anyone who hasn't been on it can't know the difficulty of seeing anything beyond."

"But to accuse anyone who is given the grace to get beyond it of religious mania——" Dorothea was thoroughly indignant.

"Francis is right," Father Connor said. "For people given to the purely materialist conception of life it puts a big strain on the imagination to conceive of anything else. It takes perhaps more imagination than this lady possesses."

"She calls herself an artist!"

Francis laughed. "She is not really a very good artist, you know."

Dorothea retorted, "That's probably the reason why—because she can't get off the materialist plane. No great artist is purely materialist, I'm convinced of it——"

"I think you're right," Francis said, "but we'll have to finish this discussion in two years' time—it looks as though I'd better board this train if I'm really going on it!"

She put her arms round him. "Good-bye, my darling. God bless and keep you."

He held her to him for a moment, then shook hands with the priest and boarded the train.

"Remember me to them all at Tullabeg," Father Connor said, his hand on the door of the compartment.

"Stand away there!" shouted a porter.

Father Connor stood away, and the train began to move.

This time there was no desolation in the heart of Francis Sable. There had been a good end, and here was a good beginning. He waved to the two who waved to him on the platform, until the smoke from the engine swirled down in a final act of separation.

PART IV

THE HOLOCAUST

'Naked, I wait Thy love's uplifted stroke!
My harness, piece by piece Thou hast hewn from me,
 And smitten me to my knees;
I am defenceless utterly.'

(FRANCIS THOMPSON.)

OUTSIDE of Ireland comparatively few people have ever heard of Father Francis Sable, S.J., any more than they have heard of another distinguished Jesuit of the Irish Province, Father John Sullivan, who died when Francis Sable was in the second year of his novitiate at Tullabeg. In Ireland Father Sable ranks with Father Sullivan for distinction of scholarship and for saintliness and, towards the end of his brief apostolate, the gift of healing through prayer. In England the name Francis Sable sometimes rings a bell in literary circles among the older generation—the post-World-War-I generation; in Ireland it is a living name, as living as that of John Sullivan, and that not because Father Sable died only recently but because he has become part of the country's long history of piety, of scholarly saints, and saintly scholars. It is as true of John Sullivan and Francis Sable no less than of Robert Emmet and Padraic Pearse, that 'they shall be remembered forever'. That Francis Sable's English name has gone into Ireland's national honours list of patriots and priests and poets is in the best Irish tradition; many who have nobly served Ireland have been of English stock. There was Erskine Childers, there was Parnell, there was the Countess Markiewicz—the lovely Constance Gore-Booth—and even Pearse had an English mother. In Ireland Francis Sable is not remembered as a writer; in England it is not known that he became a priest—indeed hardly anyone knows, or cares, what happened to him. He was just one of those writers who caused a stir in the 'twenties and faded out in the early 'thirties, and that tragic decade was not four years old before it had more important things to worry about than what had happened to a writer who was anyhow *fin de siècle*. The political activities of a man called Adolf Hitler began to impinge upon their consciousness. The gay days were over. Already by 1933 Europe was emptying as a playground, and there was the small cloud not bigger than a man's hand. In Ireland they kept a wary eye on the European scene, but they watched it through their 'foggy dew', which made the small cloud if not smaller at least dimmer. To Francis Sable the death of Father John Sullivan early in 1933 was more real than anything happening in Europe.

Despite the complete dissimilarity of their years before their conversion to the Catholic Church, their lives nevertheless had much in common. Both were of aristocratic families; both were converted in their thirties; both had devout Catholic mothers; both became novices in the Irish Province of the Society of Jesus in their early middle-age; both made a complete holocaust of self, renouncing successful and distinguished careers, Sullivan as a barrister, Sable as a man of letters, in order to follow the religious vocation; both were remarkable for their piety and asceticism, carried to saintly lengths; both had a great devotion to St. Augustine; both distinguished themselves as teachers and both eventually had what seemed like miraculous successes with the sick and dying for whom they prayed, though both repudiated the idea of faith-healing or miracle-working and insisted on that power of prayer in which both so passionately believed. Like John Sullivan, Francis Sable distinguished himself during his novitiate—in the old Georgian mansion at the edge of the Bog of Allen, where Sullivan also served his noviceship—by his humility and his austerity. Like Sullivan he was a great deal older than his fellow-novices, boys in their teens and early twenties—his 'Angelus', a second-year student put in charge of the thirty-three-year-old neophyte, was a boy of nineteen. Like Sullivan, Brother Sable's worldliness and knowledge and scholarship made him seem among all the young students like a university graduate back amongst undergraduates. And, also like John Sullivan, far from adopting a superior attitude because of this he took upon himself the humblest chores of sweeping and bed-making—"Let me do that!" became recognised as Brother Sable's slogan; and, as with Sullivan, the homesick, and those who despaired of staying the long difficult monotonous course, found a sympathetic and understanding friend in him. He discovered within himself a tremendous capacity for going out to the young—an extension and development of his feeling for young Gustav Meisel. Whenever a boy turned stricken hopeless eyes on him, and he felt the unshed tears in him, he would become aware of an ache in his own throat, a contraction of his heart, and hear Gustav's choked and final, '*Ja*, Herr Francis.' He was greatly loved.

When he took his first vows, two years to the day on which he arrived at Tullabeg, like John Sullivan he obtained permission to use the crucifix his mother had given him ... Cathryn's ivory crucifix. Like John Sullivan too, this was the crucifix he held in his hands when his soul left his body. And he never owned any rosary beads but the humble chaplet he picked up beside a boulder on Croagh Patrick.

2

Still following in John Sullivan's footsteps he was sent to Stonyhurst for his philosophy. Here his knowledge of the classics stood him in good stead, and he was able to help his young fellow-scholastics, with whom he was as popular as he had been with the novices at Tullabeg. He was always as willing to help them with their studies as with their chores. Their youth was somehow a wound in his heart—remembering Johnny, remembering Gustav. He remembered them both, constantly, in his prayers—the American boy that he might find the peace of Christ in the Kingdom of Christ, the Austrian boy that if it be God's will he should enter the Capuchin order. Lotte he remembered as he remembered a poem or a piece of music he had loved; she was part of the beauty of the world, like the St. Matthew Passion music, and Francis Thompson's *Hound of Heaven*, and El Greco's *Agony in the Garden*. He remembered her with tenderness and gratitude, and prayed for her happiness. Sue became quite early on merely a dim figure, part of the shadowy landscape of his dead life, peopled with ghosts; he prayed that she might be given the grace to see God, that like St. Augustine she might hear as the heart heareth, with no room to doubt, as he had heard and seen. Apart from his mother he had no desire either to write or to receive letters, and he had no visitors, nor any wish for them. His mother wrote occasionally with such family news as that Honor and Steven had a son; that she and Mrs. Lester were going on a holiday together to Switzerland, and then a postcard when they arrived there. He wrote his mother very briefly, knowing that she wanted only to know that he was happy and that his studies went well. At his request she made no reference to any publishing or literary affairs. Francis Sable the writer must be allowed to die.

At Stonyhurst he was back in the fell country of his boyhood and he was reminded of Cathryn, but without pain. The ghost who tramped sometimes with him through the heather, the wet brown earth squelching underfoot, was a leggy young colt of a thing, tireless, eager, her face lifted always to the highest crags of the highest hills. The little sister with whom he had climbed up into the clouds. "One day we'll climb an Alp together, Francis!" Even that he could remember now without pain. Ultimately, it now seemed to him, it was she who had taken him to the mountains, that he might find the light thereon, and climb up out of the world, finally and forever.

Physically the Lancashire fell country, with its brown and green and purple sweeps of moorland flowing away to the horizon, reminded him a little of the West of Ireland, with the 'mountain' and the bog, though he missed the strewn wildernesses of stones and boulders, and the indefinable quality of the light, which gave colour to the landscape and the sea even on a grey day. But there was something of the wildness of the Western Irish scene, and at times, especially when there was a soft small rain on the wind, nostalgia would stir in him.

When he arrived from Dublin his mother met him at Liverpool and travelled with him to Whalley. Their meeting was unemotional, for which he was grateful. It was unemotional not because no deep feeling was involved, but because both were at peace. He was doing what she was happy for him to do, proud for him to do; he was doing what he felt impelled to do; there could be no question, therefore, of the heartbroken mother meeting the homesick son. Each was moved by the sight of the other; love surged in them both, and each was filled with admiration for the other. They met as friends who completely understood each other and made no demands of each other.

They talked about Steven and Honor, as Dorothea had been lately at Crag House. Both, it seemed, were still horrified by the course Francis had followed.

"It has made Steven more rabidly Anglican than ever," Dorothea said.

Francis laughed. "Poor Steven! He really must feel that the Papist rot has set in in the family—first his mother, then his sister, and then his brother not merely joins the Church but becomes a Jesuit! It's enough to make him bring his son up a Plymouth Brother or a Jehovah Witness! What does Honor feel about this frightful Papist family she's married into?"

Dorothea shrugged. "She has no particular feelings, except that what she calls 'religious' people are a bore, and that anyhow one only goes to church to set an example to the tenantry and the servants. That it's the Church of England goes without saying—like reading *The Times* and voting Conservative."

"And playing bridge and riding to hounds! Isn't it odd, by the way, that in Ireland they call the Protestant Church the Church of Ireland—which is the one thing it isn't?"

He was thin, she thought, but looking much better than when she had last seen him. His eyes then had had a feverish look; now they were serene. His manner then had been nervous; now it was composed. She had the feeling that some conflict within himself had been resolved; that he was at peace.

He asked her about Sue. She had left Paris, Dorothea told him. The international situation looked too ominous. She had a very pleasant studio now in Chelsea. She seemed to be doing well. She was on the line at the last Royal Academy.

He laughed. "They all profess to despise the Academy, but it doesn't stop them submitting stuff!"

"I don't think Sue ever despised it, did she? I think it was always her ambition to be able to put R.A. after her name!"

"Perhaps. What else? Is she happy, do you think?"

"With people like that you can never tell, do you think?

Her mother seems to think she's having an affair with John Andley, the sculptor."

"Stonemason, you mean! Tombstones is about all he's fit for designing!"

Sue and her long-preserved virginity and that bearded poseur—it was too absurd. It was more, it was preposterous. It was the wrong of uncomely things, the wrong too great to be told.

"I hope it's not true," he added.

His mother gave him an odd look. "Is your objection moral or aesthetic?"

"Both. It would be wrong if he were a good sculptor; that he is a bad one makes it doubly wrong."

So the old Francis wasn't quite dead, she thought, amused. He had not yet acquired the completely Catholic habit of mind. His first reaction had been that Andley was such a bad sculptor, not that Sue, if it were true, had fallen from grace.

Francis was surprised himself at his first reaction—the sudden sparking to life of the old contempt for the bogus. It was not merely that Andley was a bad sculptor, but that he was pretentious, insincere. He considered Sue an inferior artist, but he did not despise her; she was not wilfully false, but merely lacking. Her integrity was not involved. If he regretted more her lapse of taste—if it were true that she was having an affair with Andley—than her moral lapse it was simply that he had never been able to regard her 'virtue' as other than nominal—a matter of pride rather than principle. He switched his thoughts away from the matter in sudden distaste and turned to his mother.

"Tell me about you," he said, gently, smiling.

"There's nothing to tell, really. I still see Father Connor regularly and we always talk of you."

"That's good news. Tell him how much Father Halloran meant to me. I love that man. I feel sure he's another Father Sullivan."

She thought, 'Perhaps you will be, too,' and her heart swelled with love and happiness. He was her beloved son, in whom she was well pleased, and just to sit beside him like this in a train for so short a time was great blessedness and joy.

Just before they parted—one more railway-station parting—

Francis said, quickly, "There's something you could do for me. Write to Johann and give him news of me, and tell him I remember them all in my prayers, and ask him to tell Gustav I pray for him specially."

"Johann sent a card at Christmas," she told him. "He wrote on it that they were all going along much the same."

"God keep them," Francis murmured.

He laid his hands on her shoulders in the moment of parting, and smiled at her.

"You're all right, aren't you?"

She returned his smile.

"Perfectly. I'm very happy."

He kissed her forehead; she held him a moment to her, with a murmured blessing, and they parted. They had no idea when they would meet again. It didn't matter. They were all right. They were at peace. Emotionalism was for shallow emotions; their deep mutual love and confidence called for no such surface display.

Francis thought about his mother a good deal during the time at Stonyhurst. His long solitary walks on the fells, in all weathers, in his free time, and the fact that he was not many miles from Crag House, brought all the old family life close to him. It seemed to him that living alone now in London his mother was much less lonely than in the life she had lived with her husband and children at Crag House. Her loneliness then must have been appalling, in her spiritual and emotional estrangement from her husband and eldest son, and her second son, Francis thought sadly, vaguely fond of her but never really coming close. She had had to wait so long for her ewe lamb, and even when she had borne her she had to wait for her to grow up before she had her companionship. It was something that she had the comfort of the Church. Something? It was everything. Looking back he was horrified by his own lack of imaginative sympathy. He seemed to have been quite incredibly blind and heartless—the quite unconscious heartlessness of youthful egotism. There were compensations in growing older. You became, gradually, just a little less preoccupied with self. Tramping the heather and thinking all this he would fill with remorse; life piled on life, it seemed to him at such times, would be all too little for the atonement he needed to make.

At Stonyhurst, with this intensified sense of guilt in relation to his mother, he increased his asceticism. It was now not sufficient that he should take on the humblest tasks, doing chores for youths some twenty years younger than himself, persisting in his 'Let me do that for you' principle, and helping them with their studies; now he felt compelled to live as austerely as possible, eating the minimum of food, walking out in all weathers on 'walk days' without an overcoat, never making up the fire in his room, training himself to make do with only a few hours' sleep at night, and devoting the hours of vigil to prayer. He had a horror of being thought ostentatiously devout, and made excuses about not feeling the cold, indoors or out, and not needing much to eat; it was a relief to him that he did not have to excuse his reduction of sleep. Nevertheless, in spite of the interpretation he put on his actions he acquired a reputation for piety, though he always shrank in embarrassment from any reference to his sanctity—it came to be said of him that what most men would accept as a tribute he seemed to take as an insult. The fact was that his sense of sin was so acute that any penance he could make seemed hopelessly trivial. He felt, profoundly, that if he could have another hundred years on this earth he still could not expiate his first thirty-three years of living as he had lived to himself alone; and after death through an unmeasured purgatory the expiation must go on. He longed to be able to say with Saint Augustine, 'Whatsoever I have been, in the Name of Christ, it is past'; it was past, but he could not escape the burden of self-condemnation. The Sacrament of Penance could give him forgiveness, but it could not ease his spirit of remorse, of the need for perpetual penance, for the remainder of his life, and beyond.

There were times when he was sunk in a deep depression, and at all times those about him felt a sadness in him, even when he smiled. But there were, too, times of prayer and contemplation, when he experienced profound peace, and the kind of pure joy which in the old days he had known when music had given his spirit wings. The joy he had known on the Kapuzinerberg listening to the flute-like voice triumphantly affirming an impassioned faith, the voice flowing into his ears, the truth distilled into his heart, as with Augustine, touched to the quick by the

hymns and canticles of the 'sweet-attuned Church'. Now he did
not need music to lift his spirit to the peaks of ecstasy; he could
reach it through prayer and contemplation, and through Holy
Communion, but the occasions were rare, and the occasions
when the *De Profundis* was indeed a cry from the depths were
many.

He gained also, at Stonyhurst, a reputation for brilliance in
examinations. Philosophy, with his classical background, came
easily to him, and he left Stonyhurst with honours. He returned
to Ireland, to take his theology at Milltown Park, Dublin, and
was seen off at Liverpool by his mother. She cherished the hope
that he might get through his theology as brilliantly as his
philosophy and be ordained at the end of the course, as Father
Sullivan had, but she said only, "I shall come to Ireland to hear
you say your first Mass."

He smiled. "It may be another ten years."

"It may be only three."

"I'm not John Sullivan."

"If I'm spared I shall come whenever it is. I shall pray it may
be soon."

Her prayer was answered, for as it turned out he was ordained
in the summer of 1939, at the age of forty, in the seminary chapel.
He said his first Mass in the People's Church at Tullabeg, and
his mother was present. Just as he had felt that he must be
received into the Church at the hands of Father Connor, so he
felt that he must go back to the house in which he had served his
novitiate for his first office as a priest. In the church that day the
dowager Lady Sable felt that now her life was fulfilled and she
could fold her hands and say from the depths of her heart,
'Lord, now lettest Thou Thy servant depart in peace.' . . .

This time Francis was able to reverse the order and see her
off on the boat back to England. She spoke of coming to Ireland
again early the following year. If, as he hoped, he was appointed
to the teaching staff of the famous Jesuit School, Clongowes
Wood College, she might even come and settle in Ireland, she
said . . . unless of course the war came. Did he think there
would be war? He shrugged. It looked like it, but who could
say? And if there was a war it would be all the more reason for
coming to Ireland, which was unlikely to be involved, but she said,

firmly, "If there is war I shall stay in England," and her attitude, he felt, was not to be argued about.

He was duly appointed as master at Clongowes, and began work there with the autumn term, by which time, of course, the second world war had broken in Europe. When the bombs began to fall on England at the end of the following year Francis hoped that his mother would go north to Crag House for the duration, and wrote urging her to do so. She replied by return begging no less earnestly that he would not press this course upon her. *I am an old woman* [she wrote] *and I have lived to see my dearest dream richly fulfilled. I am quite ready to finish with this life, and I am not afraid to die. When the bombs fall near by I say my prayers, and not for myself alone, and you must believe that I am not indulging in heroics when I insist that I am not afraid. You do not need me to remind you of the importance Father Sullivan attached to prayer, therefore you will understand when I tell you that I feel quite safe—and a great deal happier sharing the common danger than I should feel in running away. If I had come to Ireland, as was still possible at the beginning of the year, I should almost certainly have come back when the raids began; I could not have sat there uselessly. There is not much I can do here, but still there is a little in a small unobtrusive way. You will picture me making cups of tea and filling hot-water bottles, of course, rather than stamping round in a tin-hat and trousers in a self-conscious glory of 'war-work'.*

He smiled when he read that. He certainly couldn't picture her uniformed and militantly patriotic; whatever she did, he knew, would be quiet and personal and unobtrusive, and in the sincerity of her belief in the Christian ethic she would, given the opportunity, do as much for the enemy, since she was not of those professing Christians who translated 'love your enemies' by supporting their destruction. . . .

Steven and Honor [the letter continued] *have begged me to go to them, and I cannot make them understand that I prefer to remain; but I trust to your understanding. I am not being heroic, but I am 'all right'.*

She was all right. It was what she had said when he had first gone away to join the Society. It was what she had said when they had parted for another two years and he had gone to Stony-hurst. It was what Cathryn used to say in the difficult places on mountains. From a rock or ice foothold above her you could shout down to her, "You all right?" and her thin clear voice would come back to you, "I'm all right." "Tired?" you could inquire of her, and always the answer was the same, "I'm all right." The people who won one's gratitude because they made no fusses; the blessedly self-contained people who made no emotional demands; the people who were proudly and independently all right. Lotte resolutely smiling and insisting on that cold winter's night in Vienna that Chekhov or no it was a good ending. Lotte walking briskly away with her head high; she would be all right, God keep her; she belonged to that blessed order of people who would always be all right, because they carried reserves within themselves. Johann in the midst of his tragic bereavement could still believe in the compassion of the Sacred Heart of Jesus; he, too, would always be all right. It was people like Johnny and Sue who were not all right, because for happiness they depended upon their emotional relationships with other people, and when they failed them they had nothing and no one to turn to, since they denied God. Johnny relied on something he called his rationalism; Sue sought refuge in work; but Johnny's rationalism hadn't stood the test and he had taken a jump from a bridge at midnight—and Sue's restless discontent could find expression but no relief in work.

Very well, then, with the bombs falling round her his mother would be all right; she would say her prayers and be unafraid, and that was something that Steven and Honor—and Johnny and Sue—would not understand, because for Steven and Honor God was no more than a convention, and for Johnny and Sue He did not exist.

Nevertheless it was not easy to sit in Ireland those six years, teaching boys Latin and History and Greek, coaching them for Matriculation, taking them for walks, correcting 'Prep', hearing their confessions, living in an oasis of peace in the howling wilderness of horror that the rest of Europe had become. It was not that he wanted to see Ireland involved; he prayed night and day, on the contrary, that she be spared that; it was not undue anxiety about his mother, but the feeling of helplessness in the face of suffering, the feeling of impotence in the presence of tragedy. He prayed night and day, not for Allied victory but for peace; he could not feel that it was his Catholic duty to pray for anything but that; he was living and working in a neutral country. He was an Englishman, but over and above that he was a Catholic, and aware of the millions of German and Italian Catholics fighting and suffering and dying on the other side.

He had come up against this issue during the Spanish war during his time at Milltown Park. He found it impossible to take sides. On the one hand there was his feeling for the Church, and the fact that the Republicans, and the Left elements associated with them, were its avowed enemies; and on the other his feeling for the principles of democracy, which the Franco militarist *coup* had violated. The Republican attack on the Church was abominable, but so was the fratricide forced upon the country by those with Christianity on their lips. Either you accepted democratic principles or you didn't; he accepted them. His dilemma was that if you supported the democrats you also supported godlessness. Russian intervention underlined the Communist element in the struggle, and Francis did not need to be a Catholic to abhor Communism; he abhorred it as he did Fascism, seeing it as merely another form of dictatorship, and in its suppression of freedom, of the right to opposition, of the principles of democracy, and in its regimentation of the people and the glorification of the State, nothing to choose between it and Fascism; why choose between the Gestapo and the Ogpu? If you were a democrat Franco and Stalin were equally undesirable, despite Franco's vaunted Christianity. Then he began to be aware that there was another element in Spain which agreed that Franco and Stalin were equally bad things; there were sets of initials representing anarchists and anarcho-syndicalists and independent Marxists, all allied against Franco, but also at odds with the Republicans and Communists; they had a private war called The Revolution; you could take sides with them against the Falangists and Communists, and then you found they were anti-Catholic. . . . There was nothing you could do as a sincere Catholic but pray that Spaniards might stop murdering each other for sets of initials all supposed to be saving Spain from the Spaniards. Marx or Bakunin, or the gospel according to this new person, Adolf Hitler—in practice it was all equally bloody. And un-Christian. You did not love your fellow-man by dropping bombs on him or slinging hand-grenades at him or machine-gunning him, whether in the name of Marx or Lenin or Trotsky or Bakunin or Christianity, or Stalin or Franco or Hitler or Mussolini, or anyone else. So you prayed for peace . . . and good Irish Catholics went off to fight for Christianity in the name of Generals O'Duffy and Franco, and no less good Irish Catholics went off to fight on the Republican side—and if reports were true the Spanish war began on the boats going over. . . .

You prayed for peace; and you prayed for peace in the second world war, because there were Catholics on both sides, and the Church was universal, and as a Christian you could not subscribe to mass-murder as a means of settling international disputes. The destruction of Monte Cassino filled you with horror, but if it was true that the Germans were using it as a fortress they were no less guilty than the Allied airmen who bombed it. You reflected that it probably was true, for there was no morality in total war. You could only pray for both sides, 'Father, forgive them for they know not what they do.'

And all the time whilst the horror of murder and destruction went on you taught boys Greek and Latin and classics—and history that was nothing compared with the history in the making. And you wondered what had become of the Amanshausers and the Meisels . . . and your heart ached; and you read about the bombs dropped on Vienna, and you could not bear it. But you had to bear it, because you were an impotent part of this doomed and damned civilisation. You were witnessing the decay and collapse of a civilisation given over to materialism; men had turned from God, to their own damnation. You prayed, and tried to give the young people who passed through your hands those spiritual values which kept the flame of a living Christianity alight in a nation. Ireland, it seemed, was the last stronghold of a living Christianity; it was a country which knew right from wrong; it was the oasis of sanity and decency in the howling wilderness of madness and amorality. He had this deep devotion to Ireland, and to its rising generation, and could never be sufficiently thankful to Father Connor for sending him to Ireland in the first instance, because 'it might have something for you'. What it had for him was Father Halloran and Croagh Patrick and the weather-beaten rosary, and the conviction that his destiny lay in this Christian country. But behind Father Connor was Johann Amanshauser,

and behind Johann was Cathryn . . . who as far back as their Montparnasse days had countered his material values with her spiritual
ones. Cathryn who had had to die that he might live. Cathryn
whose painting of St. Francis of Assisi bore the face of Francis
Sable. . . . He could still remember that only with a deep sense of
humility. The picture could be taken as prophetic in that the
Franciscans had played their part in his spiritual education, but
he seemed to himself still so very far off from sanctity that he
always recalled the picture with sadness, and even embarrassment.
He would accept it as no more than that she had seen some
potential good in him. What the Quakers called 'that of God in
every man'.

At the school he was popular with the boys, as he had been
popular with his fellow-novices and scholastics, but he did not
feel drawn to any boy as he had felt drawn to Gustav Meisel, or
feel as close to any man as he had felt to Father Halloran. He
had a general diffused affection for the boys he taught; here and
there one of the older boys stood out for a time for some special
quality of character or intelligence, but term after term, year in
and year out, there were always boys coming to his room out of
lesson times with their personal problems and worries, or from
simple eager friendship with the good-natured master, and he had
no favourites among them. But suddenly, early in 1945, just
before he left the school to return to Tullabeg for his year's
tertianship, there was a boy who stepped out of the procession and
stayed out.

3

He was a fifteen-year-old boy called Maurice Hennessy, and if
Father Sable could be said to have had a favourite pupil at that
time it was this boy. He was of merely average intelligence, but
what he lacked in outstanding gifts or ability he made up for with
an immense personal charm. He was physically attractive—tall,
with a lithe athletic figure, fair hair, and a peculiarly winning
smile. He was high-spirited and good-natured, and was immensely popular. He was a keen footballer and cross-country
runner, and was, generally, the extraverted type always more

effective on the playing-fields than in the class-room. He had a great affection for Father Sable, and between that and the boy's natural charm it was difficult for Francis not to capitulate. He reflected that if charm was indeed a form of genius, as Voltaire declared, this boy had genius, despite his deficiencies in the class-room. He had to admit to a special affection for Maurice Hennessy. It was not the deep feeling he had had for young Gustav, but it was, nevertheless, something more personal than he felt for the general run of the boys; though he was careful not to betray the fact, since he had a strong dislike of any manifestation of favouritism.

Young Hennessy was captain of the school football team that year, and whenever the school was to play an important match he would lead the team in a cross-country run by way of training. There was a sunny afternoon in March when the captain and his team set out on such a run, in charge of Father Joseph, a junior master.

In the middle of the afternoon there was a telephone call—Father Joseph speaking from a hospital. Maurice had gone leaping like a hare ahead of the rest of the party and had sprung across a cross-roads and under the front wheel of a motor-cycle driven by a young man with as reckless a disregard for cross-roads as Maurice himself. Both the driver and Maurice had been taken to hospital unconscious. The driver appeared to be suffering only from a broken arm and concussion. Maurice's injuries appeared to be extensive.

The rest of the team came back alone like sheep without a shepherd; they were silent and awed. Father Joseph returned later in a very distressed state, feeling himself responsible. He had shouted to Maurice as he headed for the cross-roads, he said, and Maurice had looked back over his shoulder and laughed. If he hadn't looked back he might have seen the motor-cycle speeding along the other lane. Various people attempted to assure Father Joseph that he could not hold himself responsible; it was right that he should have called out a warning to the boy; it was not his fault that instead of slowing down the boy had merely glanced over his shoulder, laughed and rushed on.

Francis watched the young man with a contraction of his own heart. That terrible sense of responsibility that no amount of reasoning could dissolve; that agonised *mea culpa, mea culpa,* turning and turning inside oneself . . . who should understand it better than himself? He saw the torment in the young Father's eyes, the locking and unlocking of his fingers as he offered the explanations and excuses that satisfactorily explained and completely exonerated him in the eyes of everyone except himself. And he knew that nothing he could say could help him, and that if Maurice died . . . but Maurice must not die. Not merely because he was young and lovable, and the thought of death in connection with him incongruous, but because Father Joseph must not be allowed to carry all his life the burden of remorse, the unquenchable sense of guilt, which Francis Sable carried.

He laid a hand on Father Joseph's arm.

"We will pray for him," he said. He added, "You know what Father Sullivan used to say—that prayer is the greatest power on earth."

"But if it should be God's will—I mean they said at the hospital——"

"Never mind what they said at the hospital. We will pray."

They prayed. The whole school prayed. Every day Father Joseph went to the hospital and Maurice was still unconscious. The motor-cyclist had regained consciousness within a few hours and was progressing. But day after day went by and Maurice remained unconscious, and at the end of a fortnight the hospital surgeon feared that he was weakening and would not regain consciousness. At the request of the distraught parents Francis went to the hospital and administered Extreme Unction. Mrs. Hennessy asked specially for Father Sable, knowing of Maurice's affection for him.

It was Francis's first visit to the hospital. Whilst the boy remained unconscious there had seemed no point in going. It had seemed more useful to stay at the school and take over Father Joseph's duties in his absence. Before he set out Father Joseph besought him, "Pray as you have never prayed before!"

Francis pressed the young priest's arm. He felt there was nothing he could say. If it was expedient for the boy's salvation he would recover. But Father Joseph knew this as well as he did.

At the hospital, behind the screen round the boy's bed, he

found the parents, and a table set out for the administration of the Sacrament. Beside the candles Mrs. Hennessy had placed a little vase of flowers in the Irish fashion—some snowdrops and early violets. When Francis arrived Mr. Hennessy was sitting gazing with a stricken look at the still figure on the bed. He was a handsome, heavily built man, prosperous in the export trade, and his manner was usually brisk, energetic, very much the successful businessman. Now he seemed to have sagged; his heavy jowl had sagged, his shoulders, even his big-businessman's paunch. He sat staring, pouches under his eyes, his hands palm downwards on the knees of his striped trousers. Mrs. Hennessy was a pretty little woman of about forty; there was sweetness in her face, and not much else. Maurice had inherited her smile and her easy-going good-nature—her facile charm. She was the ultra-feminine type of woman, given to veils and flowers, and furs hunched up to frame her face. To Maurice she had always seemed everything that was delicately feminine and lovely; she might be forty, but she could never be dowdily middle-aged like other fellows' mothers. He had always been proud of her when she came to the school on parents' days. In the summer she wore big hats and flowery dresses; in the winter furs of the kind that other women talk about. "Father Sable, this is my mother!" Looking at her now, with the tears resting in the hollows under her eyes, Francis could hear the ring in the boy's voice. Now there was something pathetic about the thousand-guinea mink coat, something ludicrous about the jaunty fashionable little hat. Now, it came to him, she was no more than any ageing shawled countrywoman summoning the parish priest to her dying son. She sat with her eyes closed, her lips moving in prayer, passing a pearl and gold rosary through elaborately ringed fingers.

Mr. Hennessy rose and his face brightened when Francis came round the screen.

"Father——" he said, eagerly, and turned to his wife.

"Father Sable is here, Eileen," he said gently.

She opened her eyes and tried to smile.

"Father, it was good of you to come."

It came to Francis that even in extremis people had to say the meaningless conventional thing.

"Let us pray," he said simply, and they knelt beside the bed.

Francis stood a moment looking down at the boy, the dead-white face, the closed eyes, the dried, partly open lips, the head swathed in bandages. Then methodically proceeded with the Sacrament, using not the crucifix laid in readiness on the table but the ivory one which he carried with him everywhere. After the blessing and anointing he knelt beside the bed and was lost in the intensity of prayer. It was as though he had gone out of his corporeal self, reached the level of pure spirit, wherein is the communion of saints. He had gone out of his sensible being and into that infinity which is eternity, illimitable, immeasurable, time-less. So profoundly absorbed in prayer every physical sensibility was quenched, so that when at last the tremendous concentration of the spirit was spent, no longer to be sustained, he had a sense of returning to his body, of coming back from far, far away, and with this a feeling of physical exhaustion.

He stood up, and the two at the other side of the bed also rose from their knees. He blessed the boy again and was on the point of departure, when Maurice opened his eyes and gave a little sigh, as though he too had come back from a long distance.

There was a gasp and a little whimpering cry from Mrs. Hennessy. She clutched her husband's arm. Francis took a step forward and touched the boy's unbandaged hand lying on the coverlet.

"Hullo, Maurice," he said, gently.

"Father Sable," Maurice murmured. And then, drowsily, "What time is it?"

Francis turned to Mrs. Hennessy. "You have a watch," he said.

He went out, to speak to the ward sister, and to telephone Father Joseph.

4

It was not uncommon for a patient to recover after the adminis-tration of Extreme Unction, and to Francis Maurice Hennessy's recovery proved nothing except what he had long devoutly believed—that prayer, as Father Sullivan had said, was the greatest power on earth. It did not occur to him that he had any special gift, and when Maurice's parents waylaid him after Mass in the

People's Church a few days later to thank him for the 'cure' he was at first confused and then embarrassed.

"But why do you thank me? We have all prayed for your son."

"It wasn't until he had your blessing and prayer that he began to recover, Father," Mr. Hennessy said. He stood erect again, four-square, confident.

"Thank God, not me," Francis insisted.

"You have the gift of healing, Father." Mrs. Hennessy smiled her sweet smile. Francis was vaguely aware of her perfume, and automatically his mind registered *Numero Cinq*.

"Nonsense," he said, sharply, almost angrily. "I have belief in prayer, that's all."

"All the same, God bless you, Father, from our hearts," Mrs. Hennessy almost pleaded.

"Thank you. Thank you." It was with relief he turned aside to speak with someone else who plucked his sleeve.

But nothing could stop the story that Father Sable had 'cured' young Hennessy. It ran through the hospital; the nurses got hold of it, and the patients, and he was besieged with requests to pray for the sick, to say Mass for them, to come and visit them.

He was profoundly troubled and felt himself desperately in need of guidance. That he should pray for the sick, and in special cases say Mass for an individual sick person, and where it was expedient administer the last sacraments, was natural to him, a proper part of his priestly duties. But if he accepted, individually, all the cases brought to him for special prayer, then, it seemed to him, he was following up this 'cure' story, setting himself up as someone with a special power of intercession, and such an idea he found completely unacceptable. It was not uncommon through the grace of prayer for a sick person's physical recuperative powers to be stimulated; it was part of God's grace, with nothing miraculous about it. Let who so benefited physically through Extreme Unction give thanks to God, and credit to none other. Charity to the sick, prayer for the sick, yes, yes, but to accept this rôle which was being thrust upon him as a second Father Sullivan was too much; his humility would not permit of it. Did not Father Sullivan himself always insist that it was to God that thanks were due, and at times demand of people why they came to him when they could pray as well at home? Then who was he, Francis Sable, who had not a particle of Father Sullivan's virtue, to accept such a rôle? On the other hand how could he refuse the comfort of prayer to those who came to him? Was not everything in the intention?

He wrote to Father Halloran on this problem of conscience. The old priest replied, *Father Sullivan did not ask himself what will people think, what will they say; he did what he could to comfort the sick; very often his prayers were answered; sometimes they were not. You attach too much importance to what people may say or think; what is important is that you shall give such comfort, physical and spiritual, as lies within your power. When favours are received thank God in all humility. The extent of your power of intercession is something which only the Church can decide.*

After that Francis did what he could, devoting such time as could be spared from his school duties to visiting hospitals and infirmaries, and sick people in their homes. Not every dying person for whom he prayed recovered, but a number did, and there were some striking examples of recoveries in cases pronounced by doctors incurable. Where recoveries were not effected there was sometimes granted relief from pain, and in every case great spiritual comfort. He never referred to these recoveries as cures, and continued to be embarrassed when he was thanked. He disliked intensely any manifestation of reverence shown towards himself—a shy touching of his garments, as though some special virtue attached to them. His dislike of these marks of awe and respect made him develop a brusque manner towards those who came to him. He imposed mortifications and prayers on them, that they did not lightly value such favours as he was able to secure for them from God. He demanded that they join him in prayer, that they too might do their part, and no special credit attach to him for favours received. He demanded invocation of saints, and that thanks be rendered to them. But he could not kill the legend gradually being created around himself.

5

At the end of that term he went, without any intermediate rest, to Tullabeg for his year's tertianship. He was desperately tired; more tired than he knew. For thirteen years now he had been straining his physical resources to their utmost in the service of the spirit. He had subsisted on the barest minimum of food, and had trained himself to keep going with the minimum of sleep. He had had six years of teaching, with most of his little spare time taken up with visiting the sick and in the kind of praying which consumed like a flame. His holidays had been taken mostly in the form of retreats, with no cessation from fasting, vigils devoted to prayer, and always, endlessly, his ministry among the sick. Had his Superiors any idea of the extent to which he was burning away his life he would have been restrained, but he was careful that they should not know. There was always the pretence that he needed little food, that he had never required much sleep, that he actually disliked warmth. That he was intensely devout they were all aware, but the extent of his mortification of the flesh he managed to keep secret, along with the numbers of hours he devoted to prayer. He came to believe that he had been endowed with the grace of a special gift of intercession for the sick, and that this work was of even greater importance than that of teaching the young. He did not consider that he had any special gift as a teacher; boys liked him and he found that he could often help them in personal difficulties, but he was perhaps too easy-going for any particular success in coaching boys through examinations, and a number of the subjects he was required to teach, such as the elements of political economy, so little interested him that he could not make them interesting to his pupils.

He was glad to be going back to Tullabeg, to settle in for the Long Retreat, at the end of the spring term at Clongowes. Thirty days devoted to prayer and spiritual exercises; an entire year devoted to things of the spirit, seemed to him mental relaxation, peace and blessedness, after six years of boys passing in endless procession; for the duration of the retreat, too, there would be rest from the sick.

He looked more like a man of sixty than a man of forty-six when he returned to Tullabeg. Certainly to the novices he seemed an old man. He was always referred to as 'the old fellow', though he was a long way from being the oldest of the Tertian Fathers. But his hair was now completely grey, and his face was deeply furrowed as a result of the years of abstinence and spiritual struggle. Every winter, too, for the last few years, he had had bouts of influenza and bronchitis, to which he had refused to give in, insisting that he merely had a bad cold, and the same intensity of will-power, which in the old days had kept him going at exhaustion point on mountains, kept him going through his illnesses; he held on, hardly knowing how he did it, as he had held on to almost holdless rock-faces. He had at such times very similar sensations to those he had known in the difficult places on mountains; somehow you kept going, you put one foot before the other . . . because the alternative was to lie down and die, and a kind of flame burned in you which resisted the idea of dying just yet. So you kept going, and there were, as on mountains, light-headed moments when your body seemed to melt away and you were just a thin streak of flame moving forward, poised somewhere in space. If the flame went out it would be the end of you, but it was all the more persistent for being a small thin flame.

In the outside world, because over a great area the guns stopped firing and no more bombs fell, they called it peace. Whole populations, starving, homeless, destitute, despairing, milled around like the ants of an overturned ant-hill, but the mass-killing and the wholesale destruction were over, and the victors hung out flags and bunting and their governments decreed general rejoicing, and people were glad the fighting was over, only somehow it all seemed unreal; for the victors things seemed curiously unchanged, and for the defeated they seemed worse, for now there were new horrors, and no hope to give courage for endurance. Then in the summer of that victory-year, as it was called, the ultimate horror was released upon the world, and the atomic age was inaugurated. That historic day the evening papers carried as headline the single word 'Obliteration'. After Hiroshima, Nagasaki, described by the press as 'the lost city', and then the mass-killing really was officially over, and everywhere there was the profound sense of shock, with the realisation that the face of the world was changed for ever. . . .

But after a little the shock died down, and the world's statesmen went on jockeying for position as though nothing had happened, and within a few months World War III was being discussed as a foregone conclusion, and the potential enemy named. You could only work and pray for a change of heart in

human beings, since now if they did not accept the Christian
ethic and learn to love one another they must perish from the
face of the earth. Now the need for the peace of Christ in the
Kingdom of Christ was urgent as it had never been before in the
history of humanity. Now humanity was confronted with the
choice between life and death, good and evil; between St.
Augustine's 'city of God' and the city of the world; now if
humanity did not accept the beatitude of peace, the Christian
ethic of loving its neighbour and forgiving its enemies, it automatically gave itself over to destruction.

In the monastic seclusion of Tullabeg, Francis Sable prayed
that the heart of humanity be changed, and that he might faithfully play his part in the work of this conversion. In the spring of
1946 he returned to Clongowes and took his final vows, as Father
Sullivan had taken them, in the Boys' Chapel. He regarded the
whole fourteen years as a novitiate; now, it seemed to him, his
apostolate could begin. He would have said that he was spiritually
strengthened and refreshed by his year's tertianship, but he was
in fact far more exhausted in every way than a year ago. The
horrors of the peace had put a far greater strain on him than the
war itself; whilst the war was being fought there was always the
hope that somehow humanity might be purged by suffering and
something good emerge; it was possible at least to hope. But the
peace had produced only the atomic bomb, hopelessness, and
acceptance of the inevitability of a third world war. It became
necessary to fight the hopelessness in your own soul. Peace was
supposed to have brought back the lights to the world, but it
seemed only to have put out the last one. . . . But you turned to
St. Augustine for help, for a light in the darkness, and unfailingly
he supplied it, for he too lived and worked and prayed when a
civilisation was crumbling. 'Evils abound', he wrote, in one of his
sermons, 'and God willed that evils should abound. Would that
evil men did not abound, and the evils would not abound. Bad
times, troublesome times, this is what men say. Let us live a good
life, and the times are good. We are the times; such as we are so
are the times. But what are we to do? We cannot, it may be,
convert the mass of mankind to a good life. But let the few who
do give ear live a good life; let the few who live a good life endure
the many who live ill.'

Augustine of Hippo, in the fourth century, speaking to his times, his generation, and speaking into the centuries ahead—the tragic twentieth century that had known two world wars and was preparing for a third. . . .

Augustine went on to inquire, 'But what is this evil world? For the sky and the earth and the waters and the things that are in them, the fishes and the birds and the trees are not evil. All these are good; it is evil men who make this evil world.'

And in another sermon, the same theme, so applicable to the atomic age—'And you say, the times are troublesome, the times are burdensome, the times are miserable. Live rightly and by living rightly you change the times; you change the times, and you have not whereat to grumble. For what are the times, my brethren? The periods and cycles of the ages. The sun is risen; after twelve hours are accomplished it sets onto another part of the world; rising in the morning on another day, it again sets. Count how many times this happens. These are the times. Whom has the rising of the sun hurt? Therefore the time has hurt nobody. Those who are hurt are men; those by whom they are hurt are men. What an affliction! Men are hurt, men are despoiled, men are oppressed, and by whom? Not by lions, not by serpents, not by scorpions, but by men.' O wisdom, so ancient and so new! And how at all times St. Augustine could speak to one's condition, and not least to the mood of hopelessness—'I have done everything; whatever powers I had I have expended and have drained. I see that I have prevailed nothing. All my labour hath been spent; sorrow hath remained. . . . The revilings of men I cannot bear . . . to do good to them I am unable, O that I might rest somewhere, separated from them in body, not in love, lest love itself should be confounded in me. With my words and my struggling I can do no good to them; by praying for them I shall perchance do good. . . .'

All the answers, it seemed to Francis, were to be found in the pronouncements of St. Augustine; all the answers and all that was necessary to the reaffirmation of faith. Triumphantly you found St. Augustine asserting, answering his own moment of despair, 'We need not despair of any man, so long as he lives.' Always this return to the wisdom of St. Augustine, always this reaffirmation of the belief in prayer. His thoughts flowed out to Johann, but he had no desire to write. He wanted only to remain enclosed in the world he had chosen, as though in an enclosed order, going out to those he had cared for in the outside world only through prayer, his mother the single exception. In his first year at Milltown he had heard from his mother, through Johann, that Gustav Meisel had been received into the Capuchin Order. A little later he heard from Johann himself that Lotte was happily married to a young Viennese businessman and that she wanted Francis to know. *Tell him* [she had written] *that my husband is all the things we said he should be in our last conversation at the Westbahnhof, including* galant. *And give him my love, and tell him that I still wear his ring.*

Francis wrote to Johann that he was glad for her and wished her every happiness and lovely children. He remembered the conversation on the station very well, and he remembered her always in his prayers. When Johann showed Lotte this letter she smiled, but her eyes filled with tears, and when she was alone she shut herself in her room and cried a little. . . .

Francis was very happy for Lotte. He remembered that he had hoped, out of his love for her and the pain of his renunciation, that she might marry a man who adored her, and she had laughingly added that he should be rich and handsome, and he that he should be witty and gay, and, *cela va sans dire*, a good Catholic. During the war he wondered very often about them all, and was glad of the news, early in 1946, that they had all survived. Lotte's husband had been taken prisoner by the Americans and was now released. Johann had been badly wounded early on and was discharged. He was not likely to ski or climb again, he wrote, but, philosophically, *Perhaps I was getting too old for much more in any case. Now I walk with a stick all the time, dragging a foot. I think there is an English expression you have for it—'dot-and-carry'. But I am alive, and back among my books, and our beautiful Salzburg has been spared. There is even music again here . . .*

It was difficult to picture the robust, athletic Johann limping about with a stick, looking up at the snow-slopes down which he would never ski again, at the peaks he would never climb. That was what the *Anschluss* had meant for him, the good Austrian Catholic, who had never aspired to being more than that; and he was only one of many. His brother had been killed.

Francis had not known Franz Amanshauser, but he was saddened by the news of his death, for they had been such an united family, and he recalled how at that Christmas, in other worlds long ago, Herr and Frau Amanshauser had declared that he and Cathryn should take the place of their beloved Franz and Heide, who could not get home for Christmas like the unmarried Johann and Lotte. Now neither he nor Franz would ever be under that hospitable Tyrolean roof again . . . nor Cathryn. He wrote to Johann asking him to convey his deep sympathies to Herr and Frau Amanshauser in their loss, and to tell them how he still held in his heart the Christmas he and Cathryn had spent with them. *Now both Franz and Cathryn are gone from us, may they rest in peace, and may your beloved Franz come as close to you in the spirit as from time to time my beloved sister comes close to me. It is hard for us to lose those we love, but we can pray for them, and renew our own prayers that not our will, but God's be done, and in this way strength comes to us to bear what has to be borne.*

He was not at all well that spring, unable to shake off his usual winter cold. There were times during that summer term when it took all of his mountaineer's capacity for endurance to carry on, and his Superior insisted that this year he take part in the community summer holiday. When he learned that they were going to Ballyroon, and that Father Halloran was giving a Retreat at the Franciscan monastery there was no need to insist on his going. His happiness was complete when he obtained permission to stay at the monastery. His mother had proposed to come out to Dublin to visit him during the school-holidays, but when he wrote her that he was going for part of the time to Ballyroon she replied that she would postpone her visit till he got back. It was not that she was not prepared to face the long journey to the West, but that she felt that there would be more peace and rest for him if she did not intrude upon him there. She knew that he had a very special feeling for the monastery, and that with his beloved Father Halloran there he needed no one else. This was true, and he was grateful to her for her understanding. He would value her visit all the more when he got back, mentally and spiritually refreshed, he wrote her; at present he felt more exhausted in every way than he had ever felt before; he was confident that Ballyroon and Father Halloran were what he needed,

It seemed strange going out from Galway by 'bus, but the little train had gone years ago, the grass grown over the track, and at Ballyroon donkeys and cattle grazed on the station platform and on the sleepers. It afforded him a sentimental pleasure that now that there was no train to go and meet, people went to meet the 'bus.

He walked up from the 'bus alone, through a fine soft rain. The hills were merely pale blue shadows against a grey sky. The hedges were crimson with fuchsia, and there was the strong clean sweetness of meadowsweet from rushy meadows. The rain had brought out the blue in the limewash on the cottage walls—he had forgotten that that happened, and the sudden sight of it gave him a curious feeling of having come home. An empty turf-cart, painted orange, clattered past him, driven by a young man standing, flourishing a whip, as though driving a chariot. Three old women, black-shawled, red-petticoated, passed him sitting side-saddle on donkeys, and it came to him that it was Saturday, and therefore market-day. Now that he was back it seemed impossible that it was more than fifteen years since he was here. Nothing was changed; they were surely the same old women, the same donkeys, the same small black cattle grazing between the boulders. Even, it seemed to him, the same crimson fuchsia tassels dripped in the same rain. And there was that plaintive cry he had not heard for so long—the cry of curlews along the lake.

Then there were the monastery gates, still needing painting, the rust coming through their crosses. He turned in at the side-entrance and at the end of the rough drive saw a brown-robed figure stacking turf. But the face that turned to him as he approached was not that of Brother Anselm, but the face of a young man.

The young brother smiled, pleasantly.

"You're Father Sable, aren't you?"

"Yes. For a moment, from a distance, I thought you were Brother Anselm—stacking turf was always his job. We did it together sometimes."

"I am Brother Michael. Brother Anselm died in 1943, God give him rest."

"Amen to that," Francis murmured. "I didn't know."

"He was nearly sixty years in religion," the young brother told him. "You'll find his grave beside Our Lady's grotto."

"And Father Halloran, how is he?"

"Not too well. In fact they were wondering ,whether you would take the retreat——"

"Of course I will. But what's wrong with him? Have they had the doctor to him?"

"He won't see a doctor. He says it's nothing. Just a pain in his side he gets sometimes."

"His right side?"

Brother Michael thought a moment, then said "Yes."

"Does he vomit?"

"He does. 'Tis most of the trouble."

"Take me to him," Francis commanded.

The familiar whitewashed walls, stone floors, brown-robed figures. The Superior clasping him by the hand with both of his.

"Little did we think we'd have you back among us as a Jesuit priest, Father! God give you long life in His service!"

Francis thanked the old man, confusedly; he could think only of Father Halloran, and asked after him, anxiously.

"He's sick all right," the Superior told him. " 'Tis an old appendix trouble he suffers from. It passes, he says, but he's an old man now, Father Sable, and frail, and we were wondering— if it wasn't asking too much, and you on holiday—but as a fellow-Jesuit——"

Francis said impatiently, "Yes, yes, of course I'll take the retreat, but take me to him now—and if we could have a few moments alone——?"

"Of course. Of course."

Father Halloran lay on a high narrow iron bedstead in a whitewashed room like a prison cell. Above the bed was a wooden crucifix; twisted round a brass knob of the bedstead was a cheap wooden rosary such as Francis had picked up on Croagh Patrick. Francis's first impression was that the old man, always thin and drawn and frail, had shrunk almost beyond recognition. But at the sight of Francis he smiled, and it was the same smile, with its strange sweetness and charm.

"Welcome back, my son!" he said.

Francis went over to him. "You're in pain, Father?"

"Ah, 'tis nothing. An old trouble. They want to make a sick-bed case of me, but I tell them I'll be saying Mass in the morning."

Francis turned to the Superior who stood at the door.

"If you would send a brother with some holy water," he suggested.

Whilst he was fetching it Francis stroked the old man's forehead, which was wet with sweat.

"You have a healing touch, my son."

"It was you who taught me to pray, Father, in this house."

"I remember. So long ago now. You said you didn't know how to pray. Now you pray people back from the edge of the grave!"

There was a twinkle in the faded blue eyes as he said it.

Francis returned his smile. "Only sometimes, Father—by the grace of God."

The Superior came with the holy water, in a tin mug used for measuring milk. Francis smiled, remembering that Father Sullivan carried holy water around with him in an old lemonade bottle when he visited the sick. He sprinkled the holy water, and Father Halloran folded his thin veined hands and composed himself for prayer.

"We will pray for the intention of your recovery," Francis said. "We will begin with the Our Father, because that was how you taught me to pray."

They prayed together for an hour, saying Our Fathers and Hail Marys, and then for an hour or more Francis knelt beside the bed and prayed alone, lost to everything external in the intensity of concentration. When the effort of will was no longer to be sustained, and there was that sense of his spirit returning to his body, he opened his eyes and saw that the old man was sleeping peacefully. He blessed him and tiptoed away. Not until he was alone in his room did he realise the extent of his own exhaustion.

Father Halloran said Mass in the monastery chapel in the morning, and after that there was no question of his not being able to conduct the retreat. Francis, to his embarrassment, found himself credited with another 'cure'. . . .

6

He was besieged after that as he had been after the Maurice
Hennessy cure. Not a day passed but people came to the monastery
asking would Father Sable say a Mass for someone, would he
come to the house and pray for someone, would he come and
administer the last sacraments. Old women in shawls came
asking for him, and barefoot children, and sometimes people
in cars. He would borrow a bicycle from one of the brothers
and cycle for miles in all weathers in response to these requests.
He had so many successes that wild wet summer in the West
that the word 'miracle' was freely used, and he could not
prevent it.

When he was not cycling out along the dusty roads to
some sick person he walked along the narrow path between the
monastery grounds and the lake, or paced the tiny graveyard at
the end of the path, a small walled garden where the brothers
lay side by side, each with a small stone cross stating his name,
the date of his death, and his number of years in religion.
Planted on each grave was box clipped to the shape of a cross,
and there were small childlike crosses of shells from the foreshore of the lake; each brother had his stone cross, his cross
of clipped box, his little cross of sea-shells. At the end of the
path between the two rows of graves was a little grotto of
canterbury bells and geraniums and grasses, and a blue-robed
figure of Our Lady standing against a stone wall on which
B.V.M. had been lettered in sea-shells. By this grotto was the
latest mound and cross where Brother Anselm lay. This little
'garden of rest' lay with the lake beyond one wall and the
monastery kitchen garden beyond the other. It was entered
through an iron gate at the end of the lakeside path. There was
a sycamore tree arching over, and in summer a sweetness from
a smother of honeysuckle beside the gate.

When he had been at the monastery in 1930 Francis had no
more than inspected the graveyard; he had always taken his
walks along the lakeside path, or on the foreshore of the lake
itself. This time he found himself drawn to the place where the
good brothers rested at the end of their earthly service. The fact

that Brother Anselm now rested there gave him a new interest in the place; in an odd sort of way he felt that to have stayed away now would have seemed a churlish neglecting of the old man. There was that, and something else. Something that had to do with the fact that it was a place of rest and he was himself so deeply tired. One ought not to be so tired at forty-seven. Ought not? He smiled at the thought. That was like his father. Sir John was always asserting that people ought not to feel this, that and the other. That they 'ought to want', and 'ought to like'. But the fact remained that people went on feeling what they ought not to feel, and wanting what they ought not to want, and not wanting what they ought to want. The fact always remained. The fact of the nonconformity of human nature. And the fact remained that Francis Sable at forty-seven was as tired as though he had struggled with earthly existence for one hundred years. The last sixteen years, devoted to prayer and fasting and vigil and spiritual struggle, had left him drained. Perhaps he would be given strength to go on again. Perhaps. But every time he prayed intensely for some such person's recovery he had the feeling of something going out of him that was not replaced. And there was the exhaustion of those recurrent bouts of bronchitis. The fact remained, he thought, wrily, he had burnt himself out, one way and another, in the last sixteen years of intense spiritual experience. He had a weak feeling now that he would like to lie down beside Brother Anselm and sleep through all eternity. . . . But it wasn't as simple as all that, not even when you were dead, and anyhow, tired or not, his ministry on earth was not finished yet; there were sick people still to be prayed over, last sacraments to administer, Masses to say, confessions to hear, and the endless uneven procession of boys struggling with Latin and Greek, History, Mathematics, the Elements of Political Economy—and their restless young souls. This weak feeling of not wanting to pray for strength to go on must be overcome. When you were on a difficult pitch on a mountain you struggled on; you didn't just lie down in the snow and die. . . .

Yet there persisted with him, in those weeks of sun and shower between shadowy mountains and blue water, the feeling that in thirty odd years of adult living he had had all the experience intended for him; the sum of this experience added up to a life—the life of Francis Sable. It had been a wide experience. There had been the experience of Oxford—with the radicalism rooted in his youthful worship of Shelley-as-revolutionary; there had been the experience of the First World War, which had touched him only in passing. There had been the physical experiences of sex, and travel, and mountaineering, each with their excitements, their interests, their ecstasies even. There had been, also, spiritual adventures, aesthetic excitements—Bach, El Greco, Francis Thompson. There had been Rimini, Assisi, San Geminano; there had been Venice; and Rome. There had been the experience of worldly success as a distinguished author. There had been the experience of tragedy, of the heart torn up by the roots, and the-dark-night-of-the-soul. There had been the light on the mountain, the dayspring from on high, and the discovery of Saint Augustine. There had been the fourteen years of profound spiritual experience which culminated in taking the final vows in the Society of Jesus. And, finally, the experience of the gift of healing through prayer. Undergraduate, *rentier*, *bon vivant*, successful author; mountaineer, traveller; lover, celibate; bookseller's packer; novice, scholastic, ordained priest, schoolmaster . . . father-confessor and penitent. And now at forty-seven this feeling of nothing more to come but repetition, of being at the end of the road, and of having had enough. Of wanting now only a long sabbath of the heart. And this sense of the world failing, of the world growing old, and a weariness of it, and of the flesh that bound one to it, and a longing to have done with it and be reborn spiritually in eternity.

Father Halloran, to whom he spoke of this weariness, these spiritual longings to be free of the flesh, as of an encumbrance, and of the world as a prison, reminded him that Father Sullivan had said it was natural to be homesick for heaven, since it was our home. . . . But homesickness, he added, smiling, was never an excuse for not doing good work, whether as schoolboy, novice, schoolmaster, priest, or anything else. God, in His own good time, would decide when we had had enough, done enough—lived enough. . . .

Francis accepted the rebuke, did penance for his weakness by further mortifying the flesh with vigils and fastings, prayed for the strength to continue with his instruction and guidance of the youth, both as schoolmaster and as spiritual father, and his ministry with the sick.

There was a pouring wet evening when a youngish red-haired man, ragged, unshaven, nervously twisting a weather-beaten cap in his rough fingers, came to the monastery asking for Father Sable. Brother Michael who answered the door to him said that Father Sable was having his supper; he had been out all day in the rain visiting one person and another, and might he not have his supper in peace?

The man leaned wearily against the lintel of the door.

" 'Tis my wife," he said. "Dr. Sullivan was in seeing her this evening. 'You'd best send for a priest,' says he. She would need a priest anyhow, but if 'twas Father Sable——"

"I'll fetch him," said Brother Michael, and went along the corridor to the refectory.

A few minutes later, with the holy water in a milk-can hung over the handlebars, Father Sable was cycling through the downpour with the red-haired man. He learned, on the way, that the man's wife had had a child—her seventh—two days ago, and had gone down with what sounded to him like puerperal fever. The eldest child was eleven, the father said, and added, "If she's taken God knows what is to become of them!"

Francis said, confidently, head bent against the driving rain, "She won't be taken."

He could not have said why he was so sure of it. He was not always sure; sometimes he was even quite certain that it was useless to pray, except for the relief of suffering, and he would know this before he had seen the sufferer. He did not know how he knew; he would have, simply, this deep conviction, a kind of inner vision. When he told Patrick Byrne that his wife would recover he did not mean that she would in any case recover, but that that favour would be received through his intercession.

The cottage to which he was taken six miles away was like so many he had visited—dark, stone-floored, comfortless. There was the usual big dresser occupying the whole of the wall opposite the fireplace and piled with the usual miscellany of chipped and cracked crockery—plates, jugs, teapots, dishes—a bare table down the middle of the room, and a few nondescript kitchen chairs drawn up to it. There was no other furniture. A large kettle hung on a chain above a turf fire. There was a coloured replica of the Sacred Heart above the door, and on the wall by the window a crude colour print of the Virgin in a shabby frame. There were great brown patches of damp on the limewashed walls, and in places the plaster was crumbling. A bedroom opened off each side of the kitchen in the usual fashion. And there were what he had come to think of as the usual swarm of tousled-headed, barefoot children. They stood huddled together staring with wondering, frightened eyes. The rain beat against the windows and blew in under the doors, and the wind was blowing the smoke back down the wide chimney.

The children huddled closer as their father entered with the priest. Something was going on which they only dimly comprehended, and they were afraid. First the doctor, then the table set out beside their mother's bed, with a clean white cloth, candles, a crucifix; then their father going for the priest. And the new baby kept crying, crying, refusing to take milk from the bottle, and Mary, aged eleven, was tired alternately rocking him in his cradle and pressing him to her thin chest, the way he might be believing it was his mother and be comforted, but nothing seemed to comfort him; he went on 'roarin'. . . .

The plaintive wail was still going on when Francis came into the kitchen, but it came muffled from beyond the closed door of an inner room.

"Have that child quieted when I get back with his reverence," the father had commanded Mary. She hadn't been able to quiet him, but she had done her best; she had carried him in his cradle into the other room.

Her father said angrily, as she had feared he would, when he came in with the priest, "Didn't I tell ye to have that child quieted?"

She answered a little defiantly, because there was nothing more she could do, "He won't stop, then. He's hungry. He won't suck from the bottle. He wants our mother."

Francis was aware of the tears not far off, behind her self-protective defiance.

He smiled at her. "It's all right," he said, gently. "Your mother will soon be well now, then you can take the baby to her."

"Get some tea wetted for his reverence," the father said, roughly.

"Presently," Francis said. "When I am going will be time enough." He looked at a half open door that showed a V of light. "Is she in here?" he inquired.

"She is." Byrne pushed open the door and went in.

Francis followed him into a candle-lit room which seemed to be filled with a big black iron bedstead, shadows, and a smell of sickness. The woman on the bed was young, with a tangle of curling brown hair matted on the pillow, but she had the look of death in her sunken eyes and drawn cheeks, yet still Francis was confident that she would live.

"Father!" she whispered, and there seemed to him a hunger in her dark, fevered eyes; a hunger for life.

"Ye'll be all right now," her husband said, with forced heartiness. He glanced uncertainly at the priest, then at a motion from him went out, closing the door behind him . . . but it was impossible to shut out the persistent wail from the room at the other side of the kitchen, pitiful in its persistence, like the weak bleating of a new-born lamb. . . .

It was over an hour before Francis came back into the kitchen, in which a single burner lamp with a tin reflector behind the globe had now been lit and placed in the middle of the table. Paddy Byrne sat alone by the fire; the children had been given slices of bread and sent off to bed in the other room. The baby had stopped crying.

Paddy got up as Francis came in.

"Your wife is asleep," Francis told him. "The crisis is passed. She'll be all right now."

"God be praised!"

"God be praised indeed," Francis echoed.

"I'll wet the tea now, Father," the man said, eagerly. "If you'd draw up to the fire, now——" He tilted the kettle over a battered enamel teapot.

Francis drew a chair up to the fire and sat down, and his wet clothes began to steam. He shivered, suddenly, in spite of the strong heat from the fire.

The tea, served in a chipped enamel mug, was strong and sweet, and normally Francis disliked strong sweet tea, but now he was glad of it . . . as glad as he had been of the same kind of tea brewed on Primus stoves in tents pitched at high altitudes on mountains. He felt as chilled to the bone, and as mentally and physically exhausted, as though he had just come in from a long and difficult climb under bad weather conditions. . . . This rough kitchen with the fire on the hearth could quite easily be a mountain hut. If you opened the door, across a narrow terrace of snow you would find a precipice dropping thousands of feet into space. . . . He jerked his mind back to the present. You were not on a mountain; you were in a very poor cabin in the West of Ireland; you were wet to the skin, and you had a six-mile ride through the wind and rain back to the monastery. But at least you were so wet that you could not get any wetter. . . . You had been given the grace to draw a woman back from the edge of the grave, restoring her to her husband, her children, her new-born child; to do it you had made a long and exhausting journey into the timeless world of space and eternity, a journey that demanded more of you than any mountain. You had known an overwhelming sense of immeasurable immensity, of winds that swept not the world only, but whole firmaments, the sense of life everlasting, as it was in the beginning and shall be to the end, and in this immensity, this eternity, you had known a communion of saints. . . . Now you were back in the material world, and virtue had gone out of you; spiritually you were a spent force, and physically you were wet and cold, and there was the grateful trickle of hot sweet tea into your thin chilled body, and the rain beating against the window and blowing in under the door.

When he got up to go he suddenly noticed by the door a small framed reproduction of Botticelli's 'Madonna with Child'. He turned to the man with his hand on the latch of the door and smiled.

"That's nice," he said. "Where'd you find it?"

"Herself brought it from Dublin when we were first married. The lady she worked for gave it her." He reached out and took it from its nail, rubbing the glass of the frame with the sleeve of his coat.

"Have it, Father. Herself would be very glad, I'm sure."

For a moment Francis hesitated; he had no desire to possess the little picture; he had merely been startled at seeing it there—

an old friend in an unexpected place. But there was such an eagerness in Byrne's manner; in his poor home he had something the
priest admired. . . . There was both humility and pride in his
offering. Francis took the little picture from him.

"Thank you," he said. "It's kind of you. I shall treasure
it."

"You're welcome, Father. More than welcome."

Then, as he wheeled his bicycle away from under the dripping
thatch, "God bless you, Father."

That was the last of Father Sable's services to the sick from
this side of the grave. He went shivering to his bed that night,
and by morning was running a high temperature. Even so he got
up to say his customary early Mass. The floor of the corridor to
the chapel seemed to come up to meet him, and he collapsed at
the door of the chapel. He was taken back to his room by Father
Halloran and one of the brothers and put to bed. He strongly
resisted the idea of a doctor. It was just his usual annual bout of
influenza, he insisted; he had it every winter these last few years.
It had come early this year owing to the bad weather and getting
wet so often; a day or two in bed and he would be out and about
again before the end of the week.

His condition, however, very obviously worsened, and on
the third day the Superior sent for Dr. Sullivan, who diagnosed
pneumonia, as the Superior had expected he would. Father Sable
was very seriously ill. "But we'll pull him through," the doctor
declared. "We don't lose pneumonia cases like we used to.
Wonderful stuff, penicillin."

Father Halloran asked, "Wouldn't a lot depend, doctor,
on the extent to which the patient's constitution had been
undermined by his mode of life, and, too, on his will to
live?"

"Certainly, Father, but Father Sable must have a remarkable constitution to have lived the rigorous life he has lived,
by all accounts, these last few years. You would hardly deny
his tremendous vitality? I understand he was a mountaineer before he entered religion? I should hardly question his will
to live."

"Sometimes," Father Halloran said, "a man feels he has got
to the end of the road—that his earthly ministry is finished. I

don't think penicillin is going to be stronger than Father Sable's homesickness for heaven, doctor!"

Doctor Sullivan was a good Catholic, but just a little he was nettled. His professional pride was challenged. He smiled, but there was a slight edge to his voice as he answered, "Well, we shall see, Father. We must hope for the best."

The smile the old priest gave him in return was enigmatic. "Yes, doctor, we must hope for the best."

When it became evident that in spite of the penicillin Father Sable was unlikely to recover, the Superior was much exercised about notifying the sick man's relatives. He consulted Father Halloran, who agreed with him that if Father Sable were asked he would almost certainly protest that it was unnecessary—that he would be about again in a few days. Father Halloran suggested wiring Father Connor, who would know where to find the dowager Lady Sable, and this the Superior did.

Father Connor received the telegram in the morning, and Dorothea was able to get the afternoon train to Liverpool and the night-boat to Dublin, and in the evening she arrived at Ballyroon. She had left it to Father Connor to send the telegram to the Superior to expect her; he did so, and Father Halloran met the Galway 'bus. He had no more idea how he would recognise her than had Johann Amanshauser when he had gone to meet her on that tragic occasion at Drindel, but, as with Johann, he had faith that somehow they would be made known to each other.

Actually it was she who made herself known to him. She saw the priest waiting with the crowd who had gone to meet the 'bus and went up to him, asking him if by any chance he was from the Franciscan monastery.

He gripped her hand. "You're Lady Sable. I've got an old car here—it was all we could get in the town, but it'll get us there in a few minutes."

He led her across the road to where the car and driver waited.

As the car started up she asked, quietly, unemotionally almost, "How is he?"

"He was able to receive Viaticum from me just before I left to meet you. And he has received final Absolution."

"It's the end, then?"

"Yes. Be glad for him. He is ready to go."

She leaned back in the jolting car and covered her face with her gloved hands for a moment, then made the sign of the cross. Then she asked, "Does he know I am coming?"

"Yes. I told him I was going to meet you off the 'bus. He said he would hold on till then. He used that expression. . . ."

7

Hold on . . . on the almost holdless rock-face. You gripped with your fingernails and the toes of your boots; you held on by sheer force of will, and the friction of your clothes. And the great winds went over trying to tear you from your hold; the great winds of eternity. Presently you would be able to hold on no longer; you would drop off into space, into eternity, become one with the infinite. But for the time being you held on despite the forces that were trying to tear you away, because there was something you had to do. Between the great winds that tried to tear you from your hold, and the tremendous effort of will fighting your failing physical strength, it was difficult to remember. . . .

His fingers gripping on the rock-face of his delirium tightened on the cold ivory of the crucifix and brought him momentarily back to reality, so that he opened his eyes and looked up into the grave face of the brown-robed figure beside his bed.

He smiled. "Brother Michael!" His voice was very faint, little more than a whisper.

"In a few minutes now your mother will be here, Father."

Ah yes, of course, that was it; that was what you were waiting for, holding on for. She against whom you had so greatly sinned. The terrible wrong you had spent the rest of your earthly years attempting to expiate. But you had been given the grace of conversion, the grace to become a priest. Someone had said that only God's greatest friends were given that special grace. You could not think of your sinful self in such terms, but you could in all humility accept that grace as a sign of the compassionate forgiveness of the Sacred Heart. You had been given this special gift of healing through the power of prayer, you, Francis Sable, who had known the-dark-night-of-the-soul, made-the-journey-to-the-end-of-the-night, known the night-between-nights, the man-abyss and the night-of-the-heart . . . and emerged to see the light on the mountain, know the dayspring from on high . . . you, Francis Sable, because of whose cruelty a boy had sought to end his life, because of whose selfishness a mother, your own mother, was robbed of a daughter for the Church, even you, vouchsafed this forgiveness, this grace . . . O Jesus Christ, my God and my Redeemer! I trust in Thee, in Thy Heart, in all, for all, in spite of all, and for ever. . . .

His fingers groped on the coverlet, and Brother Michael lifted the wooden rosary from the knob of the bed and gave it into his hands. Francis smiled as he felt the wooden beads between his fingers . . . a dead girl's ivory crucifix, the humble weather-beaten rosary picked up on Croagh Patrick, the little reproduction of Botticelli's Madonna, a poor man's present, the last material gift he would receive—these were his worldly treasures. When you had possessions you had bequests. Try now to concentrate . . . but it was hard to hold on; you felt yourself slipping. . . .

There was a sound; there were voices; that must be the rescue-party . . . just in time.

"Your mother is here, Father."

You got a fresh grip on the rock-face . . . on the crucifix, and looked up, and there she was on the ledge above you, smiling. . . .

"You beat me to it, Cathryn!"

There was a cool hand on your forehead.

"It's your mother, Francis."

You opened your eyes and smiled up into hers. With a tremendous effort of will-power you held on, said what had to be said.

"It's good-bye indefinitely this time, mother."

"I know, my son."

"You'll be all right, though, won't you?"

"Yes, dear, I'll be all right."

"I want . . ." he broke off, moving his head, restlessly, seeking air. When he went on it was in a whisper. "Some bequests. If you'd let Johann have Cathryn's crucifix, and Lotte the rosary, and Sue—the little picture . . . My worldly goods." He made the final effort and opened his eyes and smiled.

His mother smiled back, resolutely. He made a movement to take her hand. She took his left hand; he held the crucifix in his right; his fingers gripped hers for a moment then loosened, fell away, as he gave a deep sigh and slipped into unconsciousness as into a longed-for sleep.

He died that night without regaining consciousness.

8

The news of his death spread quickly, as the news of his illness had spread, and there was a procession of people to the monastery chapel right up to the time of his burial, coming to look their last on the face of the man who had brought them or their loved ones back from the edge of the grave, or eased their sufferings, or given them spiritual comfort and help. They came in from the country-side in all directions, from miles around. They came on bicycles, they came in pony-traps and gigs, they came in donkey-carts, or riding donkeys; they came on foot; old women in black shawls, men with caps that had known all weathers, neatly dressed young women with bright scarves on their heads in the prevailing fashion, barefoot children, people in cars, people of all ages and all classes; poor people who scraped up a living on a small-holding, with two or three cows; comfortably off farmers; cattle-breeders; shop and hotel-keepers; visitors; sisters from the convent, student-priests from a holiday-home . . . and the members of the Clongowes community with whom Father Sable had worked for so many years. An endless procession filing into the monastery chapel to pay their last respects and touch the coffin with rosaries, crucifixes, prayer-books. Patrick Byrne came begging a lock of the reverend father's hair to take to his wife, for though she was recovered she was not yet well enough to leave her bed. He brought a few rain-drenched crimson dahlias, apologising to Brother Michael who was on duty beside the coffin that they were not up to much, but 'twas terrible hard to get flowers to grow out there by the edge of the sea, he explained, and with all this rain of late . . .

Father Joseph knelt all night before the coffin the night before the funeral. His heart seemed to him a physical ache in his body.

He found it difficult to imagine Clongowes without Father Sable.

Father Halloran, who had given Francis the Apostolic Blessing for the hour of death, and his final Absolution, said Mass for him in the monastery chapel on the day of the funeral. He was buried in the Ballyroon graveyard laved by the heathery, bouldery 'mountain' above the estuary, where the lake flows out to the Atlantic. The Celtic crosses that mark the graves look out across the water and the wide sweep of bog to the mountains clear or shadowy in the distance. On the day that Francis was buried they stood out boldly and darkly blue, for it was one of the few brilliantly sunny days of that wet summer. The water was lapis-lazuli, and the 'mountain' was splashed with gorse that was burnished gold in the strong clear sunlight, and patches of heather that were luminously purple. It was a gay day, with a wind whipping up the water and flecking it with white, and gulls wheeling brilliantly white between blue sky and blue water, and a mountainy exhilaration on the rain-washed air.

As well as those who followed the bier, in cars or on foot, people in their neat best clothes came in all directions along the white roads, their crimson bunting of fuchsia gleaming in the sunshine, along the little narrow boreens with their stone walls, and cars, bicycles, donkeys, donkey-carts, traps, gigs, were lined up in the lane leading to the graveyard for about a mile. Without trampling on the graves there was not room for everyone in the graveyard, and many people stood looking over the ivy-covered low wall outside and filed in past the grave later, as the others began to file out. The Bishop presided, and said prayers at the graveside. By the graveside, in addition to the dowager Lady Sable, there stood Sir Steven and Lady Sable, and 'Miss Susan Lester, the well-known artist', as she was afterwards described in the local press. Outside of the local press there was no interest in the funeral, for the man being buried was not Francis Sable, the well-known author, but a Jesuit priest not known outside of Ireland. The national press carried small notices but these were more interested in the deceased's association with the famous Jesuit college than with the who's-who of his English family and friends. The English press was naturally not interested in the funeral of an Irish priest—for to all intents and purposes despite his English nationality he was that. Francis Sable had died twenty years too late for his death to be of any interest to his fellow countrymen; the older generation had forgotten him long ago, and the younger one had barely or never heard of him. The death of Father Sable, S.J., was purely of Irish interest.

It was Steven Sable's first visit to Ireland, and his first insight into what had been his brother's life for the last sixteen years; and he was bewildered. He was bewildered by the quality of strangeness in the wild lost beauty of the land; he was bewildered by the people for whom, quite clearly, God was, in their own idiom, 'nearer the door', and for whom the Church was a living part of their daily lives. He observed to Honor soon after they arrived in the West, "They all seem to talk about the Virgin Mary as though she were their next-door neighbour!" He was half amused, half impressed.

"But they call her Our Lady," Honor said, thoughtfully. "You feel that they know her as well as their next-door neighbour but that she's a great lady, a kind of queen, whom they love and respect. They say it with a kind of loving respect, if you notice."

She, too, was puzzled.

A great many people, both clergy and laity, made a point of speaking with Father Sable's relatives after the funeral. They wanted them to know how much he had been loved everywhere he had been—at the school, and in the neighbourhood all round, out here in the West, and in convents and monasteries where he had given retreats. He was the friend of the poor, they told him, comforter and healer of the sick; he had such a power of prayer in him that even those who were dying would be restored to health and strength. They pointed out a tall fair lad called Maurice Hennessy who had been unconscious for weeks they said, and after Father Sable had administered the last sacraments he had opened his eyes and smiled. That red-haired man over there, Paddy Byrne, him with the barefoot chislers round him, his wife had been dying of some fever after the birth of her last child, and she was Father Sable's last cure. . . . Then the Hennessys introduced themselves, and pretty little Mrs. Hennessy was clasping Dorothea's hands and the tears were streaming down her face.

"Your son was a saint, Lady Sable," she said.

"He was another Father Sullivan," Mr. Hennessy insisted.

Steven and Honor had no idea who Father Sullivan was. Dorothea told them, adding, "He may be canonised. It is thought that he will be."

Steven stared at her. He had never really thought of the saints as real people; certainly not that there were such beings nowadays. . . .

"Are you suggesting that when Francis prayed for people and they got better it was a miracle?" he demanded.

"That wouldn't be for the ordinary person to decide. Father Halloran tells me that, like Father Sullivan, Francis would not use the word miracle, and very seldom referred to his cures. He would say only that prayer was a great power, and that thanks must be to God, that all he had done was intercede. I think he acknowledged towards the end that he had a special grace in the matter of intercession."

"Of course," Steven said, uneasily, "you Catholics use a language quite foreign to us Protestants. All this business of grace and intercession——" It embarrassed him even to say the words.

Mrs. Hennessy smiled her sweet smile. "Perhaps one day you will be given the grace to understand, like your brother, Sir Steven." She turned to her husband. "We ought to be going, Michael."

The Hennessys shook hands with the Sables and moved away. Sue made her escape from a woman she had known slightly in Paris years ago and who, it appeared, had a son at Clongowes—'and to think that we should meet again here!' She joined the Sables and they went out to the narrow lane and the long line of cars and traps.

Dorothea was quite composed; her pride in Francis took the pain out of the loss. Nearly eighty she was still straight and slim and graceful. Suffering as much as the years had deeply furrowed her face; she did not look younger than her years, but, on the contrary, much older. It was the face of a very old woman, very tired, and quite ready to finish with this life. She had given a son to the Church. His work was ended and the time had come for him to go. His apostolate had been brief, for God had so willed. In that brief apostolate he had done good work; saint-like work;

and he had died at peace with God. In this, she, his mother, was content. She sat silent in the car as they drove away from the graveyard, and she was glad that the sun shone, and that the end had come for Francis in this beautiful part of Ireland in which he had first found peace and spiritual direction.

Steven and Honor kept up a fitful conversation with Sue, about the weather, the scenery, the number of people who had turned out, the bad state of the roads. This elaborate matter-of-factness was supposed to demonstrate their composure, and offset what they felt was the strained atmosphere created by Dorothea's silence. Steven was terrified that his mother was going to weep. At Cathryn's graveside she had collapsed. He had a horror of emotionalism and scenes. He had watched his mother anxiously all through the service in the church, and at the graveside, and she had not shed a tear; all that remained now was to get back to the hotel without her breaking down, and then he could relax. He was grateful to Honor for helping him maintain the conversation; he was sure that she felt the strain no less than he did. Sue Lester's presence helped, he thought; she had poise, and, thank goodness, she wasn't a Catholic. . . .

Both he and Honor were feeling bewildered, and it was a great deal more than the strangeness of the Catholic ritual. There was the impact of a quite new approach to life; it was as though they had arrived in a country whose language they did not speak, and whose whole way of living was different—the whole conception of life. And in a sense it was true. They came from a world whose values were materialist, and they found themselves in a world intensely alive to spiritual values; a world in which the Church was not a convention and Christianity a mere matter of lip-service to a formula, but a living force controlling and directing human life; a world in which prayer was no mere vain repetition but a power that could move mountains; a world peopled by men and women on intimate terms with God and the Mother of God, and for whom the communion of saints was a reality. It took, they agreed, some getting used to. It was a little embarrassing, and, in a curious way, moving. Before he left the country Steven went so far as to acknowledge that 'there's no getting away from it—these people have "got something", as we say nowadays! Something we haven't got.' He had none of his

brother's gift for expression and he could not define that something. It was Honor who, a little diffidently—because of that
Protestant English embarrassment—suggested that it was 'something to do with moral values'. She rejected the word 'spiritual'
as 'shy-making'. One didn't, really, talk about these things at all.
There was that horror of sounding and being thought 'religious'.
Yet if anyone had suggested to her that the English were, in the
main, 'irreligious', she would have been shocked and offended.
She admitted that it was true that these Irish Catholics had, as
Steven said, 'got something', but it was not, she felt, anything on
the whole suitable for export. After all, what had they had the
Reformation *for*? The inconsistency of her recognition of the
moral values on the one hand and her reluctance to have them
exported on the other quite simply did not occur to her. She had
never known Francis well enough to have any personal feeling
about his death—and Steven, she knew, had disapproved of
Francis ever since their Oxford days, and could not be expected to
mourn him now—and when she got back to England, away from
what she could then think of as the 'sentimentality' of the Irish
scene, her chief feeling about her brother-in-law's death was one
of relief that he had faded out as a writer long enough ago for
most people to have forgotten that he ever was one. It would
have been embarrassing to have had a lot of press publicity about
him 'going Catholic' and becoming a Jesuit; as it was his death
fortunately had no English news value and could pass unnoticed.
Awful to have all that Lourdes miracle-working stuff tacked on
to the family name! But when she said this to Steven he frowned.

"The fact remains that dying people he prayed for got well,"
he said, a little sharply.

"They would probably have got well in any case!"

"Doctors know whether their patients are dying or not.
Certainly it's not for people like ourselves to judge. It's easy
enough to dismiss the things we don't understand, but that doesn't
account for them. It's not as simple as all that. At Oxford Francis
was an atheist. He discovered that that was no answer to what
used to be called the riddle of the universe. I have an idea he
found the answer. He was a kind of saint, really. It was how
Cathryn painted him, if you remember."

"Because she idolised him!"

"It could be that. Or wishful thinking. Or it could be something more—some inner vision. . . ."

Sue, on the way back from the funeral, was thinking along similar lines. The carefully sustained chatter of Steven and his wife jarred on her. She longed to be alone, and replied absent-mindedly to Steven's unimportant questions and comments. She was suffering not from bewilderment but from an almost overwhelming sense of understanding. She filled with shame at the recollection of her wilful lack of understanding in the past. That last time when she and Francis had met in Paris, when she had set her will stubbornly against understanding him, and let him go from her without a single word of affection and friendship, telling herself that he had become 'a religious maniac', that he needed psycho-analysis, trying to explain everything away through the mumbo-jumbo and clap-trap of her own materialist and degenerate world. . . . She felt herself as far off from acceptance of his ideas as ever, but no longer hostile to them. To call oneself an atheist was to presume too much; at most one dared call oneself an agnostic and say 'I do not know', which, if those on the side of the angels were right, was a matter for pity rather than condemnation. It must be great grace to know, to be magnificently sure, as Francis had been. As all the people who attended his funeral were. As millions were all over the world. To be able to assert triumphantly, 'I know that my Redeemer liveth', and, at the last, in one's flesh to see God. . . . That was grace indeed. To deny God was easy enough; a materialist world did it all the time; it had its scientific explanations for everything—even for the perfume of a rose, even for where the flame went when you snuffed out a candle; and still it was not as simple as all that. You were still left with your inability to conceive of nothingness. You still had, as it were, eternity on your hands. You could explain the stars, but you could not account for them. Science could explain everything except life—the reason-why of the force that animated all things living. Science gave a name to that force—protoplasm— but it could not account for its existence. Science could provide chemical and biological analyses of the life-force, but the source remained a mystery. The rationalisations of the rationalists came to a dead end in the dissecting room and the laboratory. Was this what you discovered, Francis, at the end of your journey-to-the-end-of-the-night? Was it this you meant when you said, 'There's something called revelation'?

Alone in her room at the hotel she picked up the shabby little picture Dorothea had said he wanted her to have. The rosary for Lotte, and the crucifix that had been Cathryn's for Johann, and the picture for Sue. It had been given him, Dorothea had explained, by the husband of the woman who had been his last 'cure'. He had shown it to them all when he got back to the monastery that night, Father Halloran had told Dorothea. He had seemed very touched by the gift. "My sister was a great admirer of Botticelli," he had told them. It was the first time he had ever spoken of her.

On the back of the picture he had written, faintly, in pencil, "Which of us has his desire, or having it is satisfied?" She turned the picture over now and read the words again. They must have been the last he ever wrote. When did he write them—when he came in out of the wind and rain that night he had prayed a woman back to life? Or when he knew he was dying? Did he remember them when he had said, 'And the picture for Sue'? And what had he in mind when he wrote them—the futility and emptiness of the dreams men set their hearts upon? Or some more personal application? For the mourners the tragedy of death is that it leaves all the questions unanswered.

She replaced the picture on the table beside her bed and went out of the room and down the stairs in search of Dorothea. Honor called to her from a small dark bar across the hall. Steven was with her. He looked tired, Sue thought, and rather miserable—but it was the dejection of a man uncomfortable in his surroundings rather than suffering from any deep unhappiness. With his greying fair hair he had a look of Francis about him—a coarser edition of Francis. She had disliked him on the few occasions when they had met previously; he had always seemed to her arrogant, overbearing, complacent. Now he seemed a little pathetic. He didn't 'belong' in his present environment, and he gave an impression of being aware of it, and vaguely apologetic for being there. Honor was as self-possessed as always. She looked what she was, Sue thought, an English 'lady', and she would remain such in any setting, in all circumstances; the lines of her immaculate tailor-made suit, the correctness of hat and gloves and shoes and handbag, even the set of the waves in her hair, all insisted on the fact. She was tall and slim and dark— good-looking in a bright, bird-like sort of way . . . you could paint her, Sue thought, in good tweeds or in riding-kit, as Portrait of a Lady. . . .

"Come and have a drink, Miss Lester," she called. "I think we all need it."

Sue joined her and Steven at the bar.

"I was looking for Dorothea," she said.

"She went off with Father Halloran somewhere—up to the church, I believe," Steven told her. "What will you drink? They've no Scotch, but there's Irish, if you can take it. You get used to it, I find."

"I won't have anything, thanks. I don't feel like it just now. I'll go and find your mother."

"A drink will buck you up if you were feeling down," Steven urged.

"You were very fond of Francis, I believe?" Honor put in quickly, determined that Sue should not get away. She looked shrewdly at her, curious about her—'intrigued' was the word she herself would have used.

But '*touchez*' was a game Sue was not in the mood to play. She, too, was of the world worldly. She met the quizzical gaze with a look of complete candour.

"I was in love with him," she said, simply.

"Really? What a pity you didn't marry him and prevent him wasting his life as he did."

"He didn't ask me to marry him. But I wouldn't say he wasted his life." She turned to Steven. "Would you, Sir Steven?"

He looked away from her, confusedly. "Don't ask me. I wouldn't know. He seems to have done a lot of good——"

Sue smiled. "It makes you wonder, doesn't it?"

"Wonder what?" Honor demanded, impatiently.

"Just wonder," Sue said, and, still smiling, left them.

In the middle of the road outside the hotel a cow stood bellowing, confused by the movement of people and cars and bicycles, and the clatter of donkey-carts and pony-traps, in return-procession from the cemetery.

A black-shawled old woman stopped beside Sue under the porch of the hotel and stood watching.

"You'd think it was a fair-day," she remarked, and added, "Thank God the weather kept up!"

"Were you at the funeral yourself?" Sue asked.

"Oh indeed I was. I didn't stay to go up to the grave, there being such a great crowd. I'll go there tomorrow, please God, and take a few flowers."

"You knew him, I suppose?"

"Indeed I did, Miss. Wouldn't I be dead and buried a month ago but for himself? 'You're too late, Father,' says I, when he comes to see me, 'I've received the last sacraments and I'm finished with this life.' Dr. Sullivan was there at the time. Then didn't Father Sable turn to the doctor and say with that kind of twinkle he had in his eye sometimes, 'I'm sorry to contradict you, doctor,' says he, 'but your patient will be at Mass next Sunday!' And sure enough I was! Ah, he was a great hand at praying, sure enough! God give him rest now!"

The old woman wrapped her shawl closer round her and moved off down the wide street. The stream of vehicles was thinning now, but people in their best clothes stood about in twos and threes discussing the funeral and exchanging anecdotes of the man whose name had become a legend among them. Shopkeepers who had closed their shops for the funeral began taking down the shutters, and the little groups of people began to break up. It was all over now, save his memory in their hearts, and there he would live forever.